Praise for *Woke Up Lonely*

"The talented Maazel has plenty of imagination."　　*—USA Today*

"A fun farce."　　*—Cosmopolitan*

"Dynamic and wildly imaginative."　　*—The Oregonian*

"There's nothing better than a really good cult novel—especially a wonderfully written, brutally satiric one."
　　—Flavorwire, "10 New Must-Reads for April"

"Fiona Maazel possesses a formidable imagination and considerable linguistic virtuosity."　　*—Chicago Tribune*

"*Woke Up Lonely* easily refutes the idea that the novel is a staid, obsolete form of writing. The stakes in Maazel's book are at least as real as any work of nonfiction, and it's a good deal more fun to read than any manifesto."　　*—The Daily Beast*

"Maazel is a witty and accomplished wordsmith, filling each sentence to the brim with an apt and unusual metaphorical lode. This antic novel with its sober underbelly is testament to Maazel's inventive and fertile imagination."　　*—Star Tribune* (Minneapolis)

"Considering (among other things) solitude in the digital era, Maazel's rhythmic prose carries the twisty tale with confidence."
　　—Time Out New York

"Maazel takes a cue from Kurt Vonnegut by creating a novel that blends the plot of a dramatic thriller with wacky humor and bits of science fiction."　　*—BUST Magazine*

"Fizzy and intoxicating."　　*—Kansas City Star*

"One of the best pieces of fiction and social satire of the year. . . . I lost myself in Maazel's gorgeous, dryly comic prose." —*The Millions*

"One of the best books I've read this year." —*Vol. 1 Brooklyn*

"[Maazel] plumbs her subject by combining surgical prose and cavalier plot twists. And humor. Curious, dark humor." —*BookPage*

"[A] rollicking ride of a novel. . . . Successful at every level." —*Kirkus Reviews*

"At turns satiric and heartfelt, Maazel's novel brims with energy and life." —*Publishers Weekly* "Signature Review"

"Wildly imaginative. . . . This ambitious, wide-ranging novel should appeal to those who enjoy complex, edgy, and ironic literary fiction." —*Library Journal*

"Maazel is a prodigious talent and a true original. . . . As thrilling, dynamic, and unique a novel as I've encountered in some years. It's a brain rearranger and goddamn funny too." —*BOMB*

"Compelling, contemplative and laugh-out-loud funny." —*Cincinnati City Beat*

"Fiona Maazel has crafted a novel that baldly reveals our national obsessions. . . . Read it now, at your summer leisure, before the inevitable screen adaptation into a Wes Anderson movie." —*Santa Fe New Mexican*

"A madcap, darkly comic tale that twists through Pyongyang, New Paltz, NY, a fantastical, horrifying secret city underneath Cincinnati and a House committee meeting. . . . [Maazel's] America is surreal, but not incapable of redemption." —*The New York Observer*

"Sweeping, achingly honest. . . . Both a mirror and magic looking glass, reflecting who we are and who we have the potential to become." —*Los Angeles Review of Books*

"Dark twisty satire with a healthy dose of heart thrown in for good measure. Come for the wacky hijinks, stay for the sad sweet moments of humanity."   —*Book Riot*

"A wild read teeming with emotion."   —*ZYZZYVA*

"Seethes with sex and intrigue. . . . [Maazel's] rich prose is veined with wit and wisdom. Though diabolically entertaining, she's a writer with something to say."   —*San Diego City Beat*

"*Woke Up Lonely* is a vibrant, engaging, and endlessly inventive exploration of loneliness, and is easily one of the year's finest novels."
—*Largehearted Boy*

"Quirky and original. . . . Part thriller and part love story, this ambitious novel explores longing and the burdens of society on a global and individual level."   —*Brooklyn Exposed*

"[Maazel's] study of loneliness becomes boisterous and surprising, broad on one page and incisive on the next, funny and repulsive in equal measure. . . . There is a desperate, bloody heart pumping life through *Woke Up Lonely*."   —*The Outlet: The Blog of Electric Literature*

"Maazel's imaginative sense of the absurd is well-balanced by her sensitivity to the real isolation that characterizes so many in 21st-century America. Social media's got nothing on an ambitious novel like this."
—*Shelf Awareness for Readers*

"With moments of humor and suspense, *Woke Up Lonely* investigates what it means to feel alone in contemporary America."
—*Brooklyn Daily Eagle*

"Maazel is a master sentence-maker and has a black sense of humor that makes for an addictive reading experience."   —*The Rumpus*

"Maazel is a great novelist, and this is a great novel. Great, major, important—say it however you like. This is a book you need."
—Darin Strauss, author of *Half a Life*

"It grabbed me from page one and didn't let me come up for air until the last page; I really think I may have bruised my ribs from laughing."
—Karen Russell, author of *Swamplandia!*
and *Vampires in the Lemon Grove*

"*Woke Up Lonely* is the novel equivalent of a sonic boom—it builds, it explodes, it leaves your ears, mind, and soul ringing for days. Who else writes sentences like this, who else writes sound art prose that transports a heart-killing story of human frailty, susceptibility, loyalty, and isolation? No one."   —Heidi Julavits, author of *The Vanishers*

"No one does loneliness, self-abasement, and dread like Fiona Maazel. And maybe no one other than George Saunders illuminates with as much sadness and comic brio the grotesqueness of the extent to which we fall short of who we imagine ourselves to be."
—Jim Shepard, author of *You Think That's Bad*

"Fiona Maazel's imagination is so wild—wild being an under-observed variety of honesty—that you feel like you've woken up into one of those rare novels as real as life. Hooray for such a talent!"
—Rivka Galchen, author of *Atmospheric Disturbances*

"Ignore Fiona Maazel at your peril. *Woke Up Lonely* is hilarious, whimsical, and brilliant."
—Wesley Stace, author of *Charles Jessold,
Considered as a Murderer*

Woke Up Lonely

WOKE UP LONELY

A Novel

Fiona Maazel

GRAYWOLF PRESS

This publication is made possible, in part, by the voters of Minnesota through a Minnesota State Arts Board Operating Support grant, thanks to a legislative appropriation from the arts and cultural heritage fund, and through grants from the National Endowment for the Arts and the Wells Fargo Foundation Minnesota. Significant support has also been provided by Target, the McKnight Foundation, Amazon.com, and other generous contributions from foundations, corporations, and individuals. To these organizations and individuals we offer our heartfelt thanks.

Published by Graywolf Press
250 Third Avenue North, Suite 600
Minneapolis, Minnesota 55401

www.graywolfpress.org

Published in the United States of America

ISBN 978-1-55597-638-5 (cloth)
ISBN 978-1-55597-672-9 (paper)

2 4 6 8 9 7 5 3 1
First Graywolf Paperback, 2014

Library of Congress Control Number: 2013946928

Cover design: Kimberly Glyder Design

Cover art: iStock (crowd); CSA Images / B&W Engrave Ink Collection / Vetta / Getty Images (man)

FOR CALYPSO

AND IN LOVING MEMORY OF
MY STEPDAD, PAUL

Woke Up Lonely

I. In which a cult leader does his thing. A bad idea gets its start. A sighting, a fat suit, the blues. In which no one is happy but everyone tries.

THEY WERE TOGETHER. In their way. Dad on a bus, gaping out the window at a little girl and her mom. The pair not five feet away. He swiped the glass with his palm. Stop the bus, he said, though no one heard him. Stop the bus. His wife and daughter tromped through the snow. His wife? His ex-wife, bundled in down, soldiering on. His daughter, whom he had not seen in nine of her ten years. She jumped a puddle of slush. Wore a hat with braided tassels. He told himself to get up. Get up, Thurlow. But he couldn't. He was stuck being someone else. A man to whom life had become a matter of seconds, to whom a bus was the universe, and the instinct to watch, all that there was to being in love.

Ida yanked her tassels like she was tolling the bells. Esme kept eyes on her footing. The bus stalled in traffic. Thurlow willed his wife—his ex-wife—to turn his way. If she could just see his face. He squinted and winced as if to enlist those muscles in the recruitment of her attention. She said something to their daughter and then, *poof*—she looked right at him. At her ex-husband. Thurlow had many epithets of notoriety, but this was his least known. Ex-husband. How about: Cult leader. Fanatic. Terrorist. On a bus in D.C., staring her down with those eyes. Not the pellucid blue of men who compel for being unreachable, but the crepuscular blue of day into night, a transition as reliable as it is fleeting and, for these twin qualities, emblematic of the thing you'd love all your life. She was rooted to the ice like he'd staked her there. Her heart was like corn in the popper.

He put up his hand to wave and then to knock on the glass and then to pound on the glass, when she grabbed their daughter's arm and began to run away.

No, no, don't do that. Don't run. Why are you running? He'd seen what he had seen. Esme's face registering its thoughts up front, as if she'd forgotten all her training, forgotten how to lie and conceal. Forgotten, even, how to vanish successfully. A few years ago, he'd gotten word they were living in the U.S., but with no way to track them— God knew which government agency was protecting Esme now—he'd accepted the news like a guy at the peep show, minus the part where you get to look. After that, he heard they were in Tucson. Portland. Detroit. Every year a new city. But now: a sighting. And not just a sighting but a reason to live. Because what he'd seen in her face? It wasn't *all* dread and loathing, which were vestigial, anyway, but rather a vacancy where some other feeling could bed down.

At last, the bus came to its stop. Thurlow pushed his way out and climbed a bench. It was just past eight in the morning. The sidewalk was packed; Esme must have been taking Ida to school. Think, think. How many elementary schools could there be around here? He was about to ask someone for directions when he remembered himself. He'd left his hotel on foot. Broken about four other rules that were especially paramount now: never take public transportation, never carry ID, always use the driver, never be alone. He bought a baseball cap and sunglasses from a gift store. Stopped the first person he saw, who said, "Sorry, not today, pal," because the cap was pink and sequined and the glasses were opaque, as for a blind man. Someone else said there wasn't any school within twenty blocks.

Thurlow spun around. The good news was, he had narrowed the terrain of his loss to one city, when before it had encompassed them all. The bad news? Just because you know *where* your arm is broken doesn't mean you know how to fix it. Even if he found them, what would he say? Character is fate, my name is Legion, but love me, anyway? He'd been running his organization for ten years, and it was huge. The Helix, a therapeutic community he'd banked to stardom. Scientology in America claimed eighty thousand; the Helix would double that by year's end. But who actually appreciated his work? He tossed his sunglasses in the trash and headed for a Laundromat across the street. A good place to think and summon faith in the possibility of a better future for himself.

In the Laundromat, where the redolence of spring—of flowers and grass, in essence, of renewal—was central, he felt his pulse slow down. D.C. wasn't that big, was it? He walked the colonnade of washers and dryers and settled in at a table piled with rainbow gunnysacks.

Suds tided up the glass of a machine nearby. The Laundromat owner asked him twice if he needed anything. Perhaps just to wash the clothes he was in? Thurlow's hair was up and out like thistle. He'd slept in his sweater, which felt like a blanket because he had gotten so thin. He sat there for an hour. He was just looking at a sock discarded in a basket and thinking, moodily, about its better half—Where are you, better half?—when he saw a parting of dress shirts hung on the line and Esme coming at him like a guest on tonight's show.

He sprang from his chair. Over the years, he'd spent hours fashioning sentences and gestures to launch if ever they met again, but no matter: his gear malfunctioned. The words wouldn't come. But Esme—the world rested lightly on her skin. Under a tube light that glowed in spurts, her eyes were green droplets flecked with gold. Still, her look was the kind that made you take cover. They had lived together once; he knew the signs. She was about to yell at him.

She said, "Lo, just what in the hell are you doing?"

"What do you think?" he said. "Of course I'm going to come after you."

"That's not what I mean."

He looked around the room and saw it with new eyes. "How did you even know I was here?"—though the question wasn't half out before he wanted to take it back. Esme didn't work for the feds, or not *just* the feds. She worked for them all and always seemed to know things no one else could. "Okay, forget that," he said. "Thank you for coming. Ida's gotten so big. That was her, right? Were you bringing her to school? You look beautiful, you know. Same as always."

She was wearing a wool cloche with its brim upturned, and a lemon scarf that dangled from her neck. "I'm going to start over," she said, and she twined the ends of the scarf around each wrist like shackles.

He waited. Looked down at his pants, which were pleated at the waist. He'd actually left the hotel looking like this, in a squash-colored jersey and pants that creased at the waist.

"Let me ask you a question," she said. "Have you really become a fanatic, or do you just think there's something to be gained in pretending?"

"I'm on a mission," he said.

She tilted her head back and released a dry and protracted groan.

"I was doing this when we met. You didn't seem to mind back then. I'd say you even liked it."

"You do realize that people are rallying across the country in your name? That there's talk of real violence and uprising in your name? Have you lost it completely? Whatever 'back then' was, it didn't involve this."

He shrugged. He didn't know what to say and knew if he said something incriminating it'd be all the worse when she listened again later, because probably every washer in this place was bugged, not to mention her earrings and brooch, which were, unbelievably, of a set he'd bought her so many years ago. He put one fist atop the other. She looked so pretty. He asked if she was well. He hoped she was well because he loved her, but because he loved her, he also hoped she was miserable.

She parted her lips, though she wasn't smiling. Her front teeth were buckled. A capillary small as thread tacked across her forehead.

"Lo, I am just trying to protect you. If you carry on like this, it's not going to end well."

He nodded.

"Am I getting through to you?" she said. "If you don't stop, they will throw you in jail. Or worse. You're trying to make friends with the wrong people."

He said he understood but that he knew what he was doing.

"You are crazy making," she said. "Can't you just listen to me? People I *know* are all over this cult of yours. I want you to stop." By now, she was leaning so far over the table, the edge looked to be severing her in two. Her fingers were braced like a runner at the line. "I'm worried about you," she said. "Happy now?"

He was. He told her he worried about her, too, her and Ida, which gave him huge pleasure and relief. It was the best thing, really, to be able to speak your heart where it landed.

"Ida is not your concern," she said. "But thank you just the same."

"I can't believe you're here," he said. "That you *live* here. You do, right?"

"Oh, Lo," she said. "It doesn't mean anything, us talking like this. I came out of a decent regard for you and our past together, but that's all." She folded her arms across her chest and then muttered something about him not bothering to find out more, never mind that he'd been trying since the moment she left him nine years ago. Back then, she had given him a PO box address, which he'd been using to communicate with her ever since. Forget tracing the box or putting eyes on the box—it was in Minnesota, and seemed to forward nowhere—but he hoped she got his letters. Four hundred and eighty-two, so far.

He stood up and reached for her. "How is she, Ez—is she okay? Does she know about me? Does she even ask?"

And he thought: Please. Just bring me traces of my daughter. News of her heartbeat. And with it a small blooming inside, all colors and stars, so I can know something more of fatherhood before my time is up.

She stepped back. "Amazing. For you, it's like these last few years never happened. It's like we're still in our twenties."

"You were closer to thirty."

"And should have known better. But, Lo, it's been forever. Don't you think you need to move on?"

"I don't see a ring on your finger, either."

"There are other ways to move on. You don't know anything about me."

He shook his head. He had no tolerance for this kind of talk. He got to the point. "Doesn't it mean anything to you that I've loved you all this time? That you and Ida are my *family?*"

She looked away. "Sure, me and all the people you slept with while loving me. So much love, Thurlow. So much. You really are perfect for the job you have."

It was his turn to look away, but only to conceal the joy overrunning his face. Esme was bitter! And this bitterness was sourced in anger, and anger at someone you once loved can only mean you *still* love.

"Just so you know," he said, "the Helix is not a cult. We are a *thera-peutic movement*. We just meet and *talk*. And it's not me people are getting behind but the group."

She rolled her eyes. "Yes, I know. Share and confess. Want to share something now? Tell me why your therapeutic movement is armed and talking to North Korea. Because that doesn't sound so harmless to me."

Ugh, North Korea. He nearly threw up his arms in disgust. For all of their time together, it had always been about North Korea. At least for Esme. At least until Thurlow had decided to go there himself. A month ago on a visa extended to a group of Japanese tourists, which was supposed to indemnify the North Koreans against charges he'd been coerced and to conceal from the Americans news of his trip. One ambition had panned out; the other obviously had not. He had felt the scrutiny of his life and doings intensify the minute he got home. The feds had been on him for years, but this was worse. North Korea had made everything worse. And it had accomplished nothing.

"There are extremists in every movement," he said. "Doesn't mean they represent that movement."

"You're really going to pretend you're not responsible for those people? Because last I checked, *you're* the one who went to North Korea."

"We're not armed. We are a peaceful, *therapeutic community.*"

"For now. But what do you think North Korea expects you to do with their investment? Host a social in Pyongyang?"

"Maybe."

"Oh, Lo. Not even you can believe that. Unless you really have gone mad."

"Has it even occurred to you," he said, "that maybe I had a *good* reason to go there? That maybe I was trying to do something good?"

She took a seat across from him. She looked stricken and tired. "Maybe no one cares, Lo. I shouldn't even be here, but can't you listen? You're in over your head. And I'm not sure how much longer you have. Things aren't good on the Hill, you know that. They don't like what you're doing."

And this was true. It was a dicey time: January 2005. In December, a tsunami had overrun Sumatra, which mobilized a big relief effort that forefronted just how discrepant was the government's will to aid victims abroad and those at home. The White House had just been returned to the incumbent, in large part because his opposition was a drip. It was the highest voter turnout since 1968; the electorate was engaged and angry, and finally disappointed. The two-party system was offering up leaders no one wanted to champion. The Helix filled a niche, its membership had spiked a thousand percent, and now North Korea wanted in. To fund what it presumed was a dissident movement poised on revolt.

Not that Thurlow had given them this idea. And yet they had it. Perhaps because he *was* attracted to the North Korean principle of *juche*—independence of thought and self-reliance alongside an intermingling of people united behind a common cause, which was to be together. That, or because Thurlow had actually accepted their money in the name of friendship. Sure, North Korea was broke, but only insofar as it refused to fund anything but the military, which is to say that it was not broke but discretionary, and that diverting funds into the Helix coffer from a sale of missiles to Syria was not out of the question.

But that did not make him a militant, never mind what the North Koreans thought. Never mind what half his followers thought. There were the members, steeped in apprehensions of the forlorn, who just wanted to belong. And there were the fringies, who wanted to blow up Capitol Hill.

Dissidence and despair. Should he confess this was not the miscegenation of feelings that had birthed the Helix? That this movement's origin had, instead, everything to do with her?

He'd been back in the States for three weeks, but his sleep schedule was still a wreck. That, plus regular insomnia, and he could lose track of his thoughts for whole minutes at a time.

"Stop staring at me like that," she said. "I'm serious," she said. "Stop it."

"Did you get my letters, at least?"

"Have you been listening to me? You haven't changed at all. Always in your head. Always thinking about yourself. What am I even doing here?" And she stared at her palms as if they had an answer.

His mouth opened. His heart frothed. "No, no—" he said, but she cut him off. She had to go. Fine, he said, but would she come to his hotel later? She could yell at him all she wanted at his hotel. He said he was sorry. For everything. Just please come. He had a Helix event this morning, but how about later? Any time this week? He'd cancel Seattle and Eugene and Santa Cruz.

"I'll do anything," he said. "Just ask."

And then he commanded all the readiness and solicitude in his heart to show in his eyes, so she would know he was in earnest. After all, he had gone to North Korea for her and botched it entirely. And now North Korea wanted something in return for its investment that he was not willing or even equipped to give. What was he supposed to do? The Helix was not the Confederate Army. It was single dads, divorcées and widows, lawyers and dermatologists. It was average Americans. People with migraines and high blood pressure. People who watched a lot of TV. Who tested poorly on the UCLA Loneliness Scale and, if asked, would sooner trade the invisible companionship of God for someone to share with in this life until such time as they had to meet God on the other side.

"I might come," she said, but she frowned saying it.

He felt a trembling down his legs but hid it as best he could.

"But listen," she said. "Whatever you're thinking about North Korea, it's not too late to change your mind. To think if it's worth it." And she reached over and touched his sleeve. Then she zipped up her coat in a hurry.

Thurlow didn't say a word. He was faint with hope and fear, which countenanced each other, but warily. She was up and walking out the door.

"Don't leave," he said, and he grabbed her arm.

"I have to. Unlike some people, I actually have a job."

"Don't leave! You can't imagine the strain I'm under."

"Whose fault is that? Just think about what I said. And if that doesn't work, then okay, think about Ida."

He squeezed her arm even tighter. "I think about her all day long. Promise you'll come over later. Just to talk."

She freed herself. He tried to follow her out, but the Laundromat owner, who'd been leaning against a dryer and watching them the whole time, put out his hand, saying, "Hello, I recognize you. My name is Max Chen. I haven't paid my taxes in three years. I have a wife who doesn't love me and a girlfriend who doesn't love me, either, now that I stopped paying for her English classes." Thurlow nodded and called out for Esme, except a woman folding Incredible Hulk Underoos said, "Oh my God, Thurlow Dan in a Laundromat? You really *are* like the rest of us. Hey, see how big these Underoos are, my boy's going on thirteen but he's still got some issues since his father died and God knows I'm scared to raise a boy on my own and it's not like I have anyone to confide in about it." Again, he watched Esme trudge through the snow, away from him, only this time, he thought there was a chance she'd be back.

"That's good," he said to the woman. "I feel like I'm closer to you already. No wait, I *am* closer to you"—and he smiled because sometimes for preaching the same thing over and over you forget you also believe what you're preaching. He patted her shoulder. "There's an event later, not far from here."

"Oh, I know," she said, and pointed at the double helix tattoo inched across her wrist.

By now the Laundromat was clotted with people. Taking photos, sharing their stories. He told them all to come to the event; he was headed there himself. At last, his SUV pulled up outside, and in came the driver with such purpose of stride, everyone got out of his way without being asked. He took Thurlow by the elbow and led him out.

Dean was waiting for him in the backseat, with a coat across his knees. "Did something go wrong this morning?" he said, and sent the driver an angry look, which meant he'd chewed him out already.

"Do you really have to carry that thing around?" Thurlow said, and he nodded at what appeared to be a rifle nosed out from under Dean's coat. "It's stuff like that that's giving people the wrong idea about us."

"Sorry," Dean said. "I can put it away, just stick with the Glock," and he felt for the holster strapped under his arm. He unzipped a gear bag in the trunk and, from the sound of it, stashed the rifle among several of its kind.

Dean was head of security. Part bodyguard, part bureaucrat, and, as of late, part freedom fighter. He'd come into the Helix after his wife died, and had ascended the ranks with the hooks of his faith. But now, in his fourth year, he'd gotten overzealous in the prosecution of his work. Sometimes, in a panic, Thurlow imagined him and the thousands like him just miles away from the Helix House in Cincinnati, closing in like zombies but still under his command.

He gripped his forehead. He was sweating. He'd had a Twix for dinner last night and nothing since.

Dean leaned over to retrieve a hunting knife strapped to his calf. He cut an apple in four slices and put the plate on the seat between them. The soft sell: sometimes it worked.

"Any news?" Thurlow asked.

"We're frisking the staff every day now. No cell phones, nothing. Chances of infiltration are nil."

"Good. But I want you to do it twice a day. Morning and night."

"Check," and Dean jotted it down in a spiral notebook. He seemed glad for the orders. He scratched his neck, which was collared in green from a double helix bijou at the end of a gold chain.

They were headed to a warehouse by the airport. "We're expecting five thousand," Dean said. "Give or take. The whole country will be Helix in no time."

"Nice work," Thurlow said. "But get me a new driver."

Dean nodded.

"And buy me a new suit. And have some flowers delivered to the hotel. Roses. And get to a toy store. No, a clothing store. Ask them what all the girls are wearing these days and buy every color."

Dean wrote it all down.

"Make that two dozen roses," Thurlow said. "Red and white"—because he wanted a bouquet for Ida, too. In the vestry of his dreams was always one in which he reunited with his child, bearing roses.

He looked out the window and tried, for the rest of the drive, to reinstate the paralysis that had overtaken him on the bus. A terrifying moment—to be so helpless—but also transcendent, because how often does love overrun your experience of life so thoroughly that it lays waste to everything else?

They arrived at the warehouse, which could probably fit five thousand, but, just in case: a Jumbotron outside for spillage and stragglers. It was twenty degrees out, but no one would care.

Thurlow sat in a small office. His nerves were like the third rail, like if he thought too much about what had just happened with Esme, he'd electrocute himself. He took a few deep breaths and focused on his speech instead. He thought of the audience, which calmed him down. Five thousand people who'd come to plead their needs. Bodies packed like spices in the rack. Faces upturned, hope ascendant. Tell us something great, Thurlow. Charge the heart of solitude and get us the hell out.

He stayed in the back for half an hour, then marched onstage. In the room: eyes pooled with light, skins pale as soap. He leaned into the mic and began.

"Here is something you should know: we are living in an age of pandemic. Of pandemic and paradox. To be more interconnected than ever and yet lonelier than ever. To be almost immortal with what science is doing for us and yet plagued with feelings that are actually revising how we operate on a biological level. Want to know what that means?"

Decor in the warehouse was bare-bones. Just a couple of spotlights trained on him and the dais, and a screen that lit up just then with a double helix. The sound from the speakers wasn't reverbed, but it was gritty. The upshot was to make this gathering lowbrow and intimate, despite how many people were there.

"It means," he said, "that loneliness is changing our DNA. Wrecking our hormones and making us ill. Mentally, physically, spiritually. When I was a young man, I felt like if I didn't connect with another human being in the next three seconds, I would die. Or that I was already dead and my body just didn't know it. Sound extreme? I bet not. I was lonely by myself; I was lonely in a group. So let me ask you: how many of you feel disassociated from the people you love and who love you most?"

He heard, from the audience, nodding, grunts, snuffles. Applause from a group cozied in the rafters. And a woman who began to cry. To wail with her head flung back, so that her arms seemed to lift of their own accord. She began to talk to her neighbors. She'd been married thirty-five years. Could you really be this alone after thirty-five years? Her husband worked for the Department of the Interior. He was about to turn sixty, was a good and kind man. And yet here she was. Someone passed her a microphone; she shared her story with the room. Sometimes, she said, she'd wake up in the night, stare at the stranger next to her, and say: Olgo, I like cheese sticks and corn in the can, and when no one's looking I wet my finger and dip it in the rainbow sprinkles at the back of the cupboard, and you love these things about me, you know me, so why can't I be reached? And then she cried some more.

Two Helix came up on each side of her. They held her hands. They said: We know.

The woman blotted her eyes with the cuff of her sweatshirt. She would join, no doubt. She might as well. It cost only ten dollars a head to be here, but the reward was priceless. The idea, thus: Come in with your best friends, whose lives are as alien to you as yours is to them, come in steeped in the tide of loneliness and despair that grows out of precisely these moments when you're *supposed* to feel a part of things, because, after all, you're hanging out with your best friends. Come in a wreck, leave happy. How? Start from the beginning. Start over, start fresh. Tell me something real. At issue was not just isolation born of actual, literal solitude, but the solitude of consciousness. The very thing that lets you apprehend feelings for other people also tends to keep you severed from them.

There was a Pack for her not two hours away. As soon as membership cleared five thousand in any one area, a Pack was born. The Helix was seventeen Packs in seventeen states. Fifty-two million website hits a month. Bonds nationwide.

Thurlow drank from a water bottle. He said, "Now, I know what people say. They say that extreme detachment usually means mental illness, but that the pioneering spirit of individuality just means you're *American*. Freethinking and unencumbered. But what we have today? When so many of us are destitute of intimacy with other people—intimacy of any kind—that's American, too. And it's not right. Now, believe me, because I know. I know firsthand. From my life and also from polling and statistical modeling procedures that corroborate a decline in frequency of every single form of social, civic, religious, and professional engagement since 1950. These stats are the God of tedium. But I've read them. The Roper Social and Political Trends survey, the General Social Survey, the DDB Needham Life Style studies, Gallup opinion polls, Mason-Dixon reports, and Zogby files. The bottom line? We are cocooned in all things, at all times, and it's only getting worse. Today we debrief with our pets and bed down with Internet porn. So what can we do?" He paused here while the crowd said, "Tell me something real!"

"That's right," he said. "Tell me something real. Talk to each other. Get back to basics. And start feeling better."

As he spoke, he managed to contact the audience with his eyes, to see people one by one, and in this way to blinker and laser his attention.

When he was done, he thanked everyone for coming. He said they'd made his day.

Cheers, applause, exeunt.

There was a new suit waiting for him at his hotel. Twenty-four roses and puffer vests in red, blue, green, purple, yellow. He had it all sent to his penthouse, then headed there himself. He pressed his head against the elevator door and nearly fell out when it opened to his room. He was so tired. The event had taken hours—they all took hours—so he had time enough only to shower and shave. Perk up. Esme was coming. She might even be on her way. He had forgotten, though, about Vicki, who was standing tall at the foot of his bed with legs apart. PVC boots zipped up her thighs. A latex corset and thong.

He tossed his coat on the duvet. "Get dressed," he said, and he took off his shoes. "Not today." He made for the window, peered out the blinds. The White House facade was soft-lit, soft yellow.

Vicki looked herself over and shed her leather gloves. Her arms were marbled with self-tanner. She slapped the floor with a crop. "Slave!" she yelled, but she gave it up fast. "Oh, come on, Thurlow. Even a hooker has feelings. I've been waiting here forever."

He plopped on the bed, faceup. Two minutes of rest, and then he'd shower. "Traveling Companion," he said. "Please."

She folded her gloves. "Sorry," she said. "But what's wrong? Are you okay?"

"Just tired," he said. "Not to worry. Now get dressed—you have to go."

Instead, she lay down next to him. She'd just had her hair cut and dyed. It was brick red and shorn so close, he could see a birthmark the shape of Vermont traverse her skull. He reached for the side table and handed her a gift certificate to a cosmetics store. "Here," he said. "Spend it however you want."

"Wicked," she said. "I love presents."

He went back to the window. Vicki sat up on her knees and jutted her lower lip. Pushed her head into his ribs. She wore silver studs in both cheeks, which she'd gotten after a Helix rally in North Hampton to celebrate the start of her new life. She had been coming to Thurlow twice a week for two months and traveling with him as he went. Everywhere except North Korea, about which she was peeved but smart enough not to say so.

"I need to shower," he said. "If anyone knocks, take the back door out."

The concierge rang to say he had a message, and could he send someone to deliver it? Vicki put on a robe and brought the envelope to Thurlow, who turned it over in his hand.

"Aren't you going to open it?" she said.

"No." He tossed it on the table.

"Can I?" When he didn't answer, she opened it herself. "*Do-si-do in Pyongyang? Think*. That last part's underlined," she said. "What does it mean?"

He closed his eyes. "It means my ideas are stupid and my life is worthless."

She came up next to him. "Oh, honey," she said. "You are so not fine," and she swiped a tear come down his face with her thumb.

He pointed at the roses boxed on the dresser. "You want those?"

"If they're from you. So how did it go today? I bet you did great."

He perked up a little. "Five thousand floes. I think we got them all."

"Amazing," she said. "All those people whose lives you're improving."

"I'm glad you think so."

"Don't you?"

He nodded. He knew he was helping people but often lamented that, for his efforts, he hadn't been more helped himself.

She put her hands on his chest, and when he did not push her away, she got on her knees and unzipped his pants.

He touched her cheek. Traced the flume at the base of her neck and rested the pad of his thumb there. It was always the same with his Traveling Companions, them trying and failing to rout the grief that tyrannized his inner life. And yet for Thurlow, this was the essence of a fetish—maybe, even, of all his doings: their incapacity to resolve a need alongside their aptitude for coming just close enough to sustain hope.

After a minute, she said, "Is it that you don't want me anymore? Is that what's happening?"

"Vicki," and he tried to raise her to her feet, though she would not budge. "I want to say something to you. If what we have here ever comes to an end, if the Helix comes to an end, you should know that you have the right to a lawyer. And that you don't have to say anything to anyone without one. Because it's possible—the way things are headed—it's possible this could all end badly. And soon. I've put us in danger."

She laughed and burrowed deeper between his legs. She worked her lips and jaw and the studs gleamed and his heart cracked because whatever optimism he'd marshaled under the banner of finding his wife in D.C. had starved in the poverty of his chances.

"I'm serious," he said. "I think you should go home. It's not safe with me anymore."

She paused—"Uh-huh"—and then carried on. After a minute more, "This isn't working, is it?"

He helped her to her feet.

"Can I try again later?" she said.

He shook his head. "Go home, Vick."

"I *am* home. Remember? You're scaring me, Thurlow. Can't I just sit here with you? Talk for a little, like you say all the time?"

It was dark outside, but he turned off the lights and led her to bed. She got on her side to face him. It was true, she *was* home. And in this he could take comfort. He could say his TCs had benefited from their association with him. Vicki, and before her Lois, Charlotte, Isolde, Ruth. A girl like Ruth would never have seen Santa Cruz or the Rockies if she hadn't joined up. When he found her, she was anemic and homeless, trading blow jobs for blow under the BQE in New York. Had her life gotten worse? Or what about Isolde, whose name marked the extent to which she knew anything beyond the one-mile radius around her shack on the banks of the Cache River in Arkansas? He'd taken her to South Korea. He'd taken her to North Korea, where she'd doled out mints to children who'd spent the morning exercising outside the Study House of the People.

Vicki pressed her body up against his and said, "So, you know how my parents are sick and everything?"

"Yes, but tell me again. Tell me everything."

And she did. She'd been a griddle chef at a diner off I-95 while also teaching adult literacy at the corrections facility in town. Working eighty hours a week to pay off interest on debts acquired from her parents, who had been in a house fire and lived in hospice because neither could breathe on his own.

"But you know what?" she said. "I couldn't even bring myself to visit them. It was too hard. Isn't that horrible? That's my dark secret."

He looked at the clock. He said that one time, when he was a kid, the Christmas tree had caught fire, and for the seconds he should have been calling for help or getting a bucket, he just watched the flames lash the wall and craze the windows—the bubbles were mesmerizing—but when the firemen showed, he pretended to have been asleep.

"Oh, I get that," she said. "That's a fear of responsibility. I fantasize about my parents dying at the same time because, as bad off as they are, it'll be worse if they don't have each other, and worse for me, too. Which is even more horrible. I mean, I love them, but still."

And when he didn't respond, she said, "Is this helping? Do you feel better? You always say that being always happens in a social context. Is this a social context?"

He took her hand in the dark and held it to his chest.

She kept talking until the winter dawn grayed up the walls and bedspread. And so, for Thurlow, another sleepless night. Alone, but not. Ever thus.

ooooo

ESME RUSHED OUT OF THE METRO. Or walked as fast as possible, given the rubber gams distending her legs, and her chest vest, which weighed a ton. A C-cup bosom that swung low, and a furl of belly fat that D-curved around her waist, not to mention the load of vulcanized ass piled on her rear. Christ, this fat suit. Christ, this life.

Times like these, she wished she and Jim had a more convenient rendezvous point. The Air and Space Museum was in the middle of nowhere. She spotted him at the entrance. She pinched his arm, and when he gave her a confused look, she laughed and said, "Hey, it's me."

"My God," he said. "You are terrifying."

"Nice to see you, too," and she pecked him on the cheek.

"Totally unrecognizable. I don't think I've ever seen your face all worked up."

"That's one way of putting it," she said, and she glanced at her reflection in a window. Today's prosthetic: a nose brinked on caricature that appeared to have been launched from the putty of her face like a dart. Today's chin: prognathous. She wore a wig. Sawdust blond, washed out, limp. Bowl cut—a vase, really—that came in at her chin.

"Terrifying," he said. "And what, like, fifty pounds heavier? You seem shorter, too."

"I think the word you're looking for is *matronly*. I call this look the Lynne Five-Oh. Effective, right?"

He took her arm as they made for the space hangar. Rocket boosters hung from the ceiling like Christmas ornaments. Jim said, "So how's our boy?"

"Back in Cincinnati in a few days."

"And you?"

"Fine."

"Good, because after what happened in North Korea, you're lucky to be getting another chance."

"For what? Everything's status quo, everything's fine over there."

He stopped walking. "Are we even talking about the same guy anymore? Do you need a leave of absence?"

"What? No. I'm just saying I don't know why now is the time to try again. Nothing *happened* in North Korea. Thurlow never met anyone. He just drove around. I was on him the whole time. I was even in a *car* with him, face-to-face. Didn't recognize me at all."

"In this getup?"

"No. Something even better."

"Wow."

"So what more do you want? Should I have made something up?"

He gave her a nasty look and pinched his earlobe, which he did when stressed. He'd been working on this assignment nonstop—his file was huge—but the bureaucracy was worse. Under whose purview did a man like Thurlow Dan even fall? A domestic cult leader with foreign ties sounded like simple Joint Terrorism Task Force fare—the FBI doing its worst—but then the National Counterproliferation Center was not likely to hands-off a guy in chat with North Korea. Of course, it wasn't like the center actually talked to the JTTF, which was probably for the best, since the JTTF took its lead from the NJTTF, which was just sixty guys stumped even by having to order lunch. Jim was at the Pentagon with Homeland Security—who knew how the job of dismantling the Helix had fallen to him. No one understood how business was run at that level.

What's the latest, Jim? Don't screw this up, Jim. You got *nothing* from North Korea, Jim? The pressure was intense. And he was losing patience. How could Esme have screwed up North Korea? And how many chances was she supposed to get? He'd been told she was the best. And when she did that Kegel thing, he *knew* she was the best. Also, to her credit, she did produce a lot of information. And she always knew where Thurlow was. So he would be patient. All they needed was a smoking gun.

Esme paused to admire a Corona film return capsule and to read news of its magic: a film bucket dropped from outer space, bearing snaps of the Soviet Union. And then she remembered why she liked this place so much. The early Explorer satellites—Explorer 1, which launched in '58—marked the start of modern espionage, at which she was expert.

Jim leaned over the case.

"Unmanned surveillance," he said. "Take the human factor out of things, and nine times out of ten, it goes better."

"Your confidence in me is overwhelming," she said. "I am touched."

She leaned over the case, too, and pressed her fingers onto the glass. He left smudge prints; she did not. She never would, and in this was a reminder that you are often born perfect for the life you get. When she was eleven weeks fetal, thanks to the genetic perversion dermatopathia pigmentosa reticularis, the cells in the upper layers of her skin were marked for death. Six months later, she was born with no fingerprints. Luckily, other symptoms attached to the disorder did not present. Her hair was thick, her teeth were intact, and the rawhide that should have been her hands and feet was but your average volar padding. No, it was better than average. Smooth and soft. She had no friction ridges on the parts of her most likely to extend themselves in love, which was depressing, since in the transmission of love one hopes for (a) friction and (b) cells buoyant and irrepressible. She left no trace of herself wherever she went.

Jim moved down the aisle. His shoes slapped the concrete. "Esme, this is the deal: You need to send people down to Cincinnati again. I want round-the-clock surveillance on the house. He bites his toenails, I want it on camera. You so much as see a toy sword, and I'll have ATF shut him down. This time, you have to produce. We can't go in there cold."

Did Jim have a warrant? Of course not, though she knew better than to ask.

"If that's what you want," she said, trying to imply that surveillance would not produce anything, but without faulting herself for it. "No problem."

"Put whatever team in place you choose, except this time, I want them to report to me."

She rolled her eyes, but more to roll back the panic that would show in them any second. "You know I don't work like that," she said. "Either I'm running things or I'm not."

He frowned. "I gotta go see my wife in a few days. Wife, lawyers, divorce. My life is a shit storm. Don't make it worse."

Esme nodded. She wanted to get out of there. So much to do. "You should take me with you sometime. For backup."

"Then I have to go pick up my daughter, which means seeing my in-laws. You know what's the last thing I want to be thinking about when dealing with those people? Your psychotic fuck of an ex-husband."

She linked her arm in his and tried, despite her ogre face, to remind him of their intimacy. He was Jim Bach. Her Department of Defense liaison and paramour of use. A henchman. Also a facilitator of plans brewed by men who were part of the furtive and freakishly right-wing Council for National Policy, though if asked, it was, No, no, never heard of those people, no way, no how.

They had been working together for a year. Before him, there were others, though all with the same bugbear, the Helix, and, in turn, Thurlow Dan. No one knew exactly when Dan had become such a threat, just that in 1995 he was that annoying socialist whose rhetoric offended people powerful enough to have him watched, but by 2005 he was doyen of a movement with reach. So Esme's orders were more urgent than ever: produce enough intel on Thurlow to make the case and shut him down.

They walked past the space shuttle *Enterprise,* where a little boy was saying, "It's too heavy to fly, Daddy, it's *too heavy,*" and throwing himself on the floor as he did so. At the door, Jim stopped and faced Esme his way. Pinched both her arms and squeezed—the squeeze hostile and sexual in equal doses—and said, "Esme. *Lynne.* I've never told you how to do your job before, only now I have one piece of advice."

She freed herself of his grip. "What's that?"

"Don't fuck it up."

All the way home, she tried to feel nothing. But it was no good. For her, anxiety was like many people talking at once: no clue what anyone was saying, just that no one was happy about it. And so, if you can't beat 'em, etc.: she tried to pull from the rabble some thoughts of use. For instance: I am alone; I self-sustain; these ideas are ballast for who I am. Bywords she'd relied on for years but that were of no help now. She was afraid. She'd been on Thurlow before they were married and every day since, but really, how long could this go on? How long could she protect him? Her job had been to produce a reason to throw him in jail, and she'd managed not to with remarkable skill. When the Helix didn't pay taxes. When the Helix had a brothel. One or two or twenty. Whatever the members did in a Bond, Esme made sure no one knew. Or covered the bases when the Helix didn't. Think Dean actually had permits for all those guns? It hadn't been easy, but it had been doable. Only now Thurlow was getting reckless.

And it wasn't like confronting him was easy. You couldn't talk to a man like that. And you certainly couldn't have him in your life. He was who he was: monstrous in his disregard for anyone but himself, and if Esme could barely handle it, her daughter couldn't handle it at all. She shouldn't even have to; she was just a child.

So, fine, she'd stay away, as always. And do her best. And in the meantime, she'd put together another team. Four people who would have no business being sent on a reconnaissance mission. Who'd come back with snapshots of the Helix House that were out of focus. The house in the snow, and maybe some hooker in the window. Esme would identify the hooker for Jim and then say that was it, nothing else of note to report. Nothing at all, and that would end it until the next time. And the time after that.

She got to her bathroom and sat at a vanity with mirror and bubble lights. "Martin!" she yelled. "Get this thing off me. The face, too. I'm done for the day. The Lynne Five-Oh is great."

She leaned in close to the mirror, trying to find herself exposed in the silicone vamped to her skin. But she couldn't. Martin was a genius. He had managed her looks for a decade. Together they had fooled everyone she knew. Even her lovers. Even her parents, though here was cause for regret, because it was hard enough getting your parents to know you in plain face—witness her own child, whom she barely knew at all.

Martin used a butter knife to peel a flap glued to her cheekbone. "Ow," she said. "Easy."

"Sorry," he said, and he knelt to take off her calf plates.

She put her elbows on the vanity. She fit her index under the elastic headband of her wig and pulled. The wig sailed overhead and landed on a couch. Her real hair was tamped under a swim cap seamed to her head with mortician's wax, which Martin dissolved with acetone. She removed the cap as per the wig and plunged her fingers into her hair to rouse its inclination to chaos. It was dark blond with copper veins, shoulder length and undulate.

"Where's the case?" she said. She had forty-three different pairs of contact lenses. The blues with the pupil cast in a flax corona were her favorite. Tonight, she wore the hazel taupe. They radiated an unease that itself radiated sorrow. She looked at them in the mirror and wondered if they telegraphed feeling better than her own eyes, which were white grape.

"So it all went okay?" he said. "Anything feel loose?"

"No, just fat. I look like a fifty-year-old hag. Lynne the hag."

"Anything else I can do?"

"No."

"Okay," he said, which was as far as the conversation would go. Martin was not a confidant. Not even a colleague. Their first project, he'd had to regender her face and age it ten years. As he'd applied spirit gum to a hollow in her cheek, he'd asked about the job. Why a man? Why the years? She'd said, "You know how people like to joke around—if I told you I'd have to kill you—you know that joke?" He did. "It's no joke." And that was that.

It's true she wasn't a case officer. Or even a spook. In the official parlance of human intelligence, the acronym was NOC. Nonofficial cover. Go out into the world, and if you screwed up, no one would bail you out, no one would reel you in, no one would say you were alive. Only difference was that a real NOC was affiliated with a parent organization that had an interest in getting her out despite the blowback. Esme did not have this luxury. Her burden was to go unacknowledged but also untethered. In the unofficial parlance, she was a freelancer. Hired by the government, case by case. Some more harrowing than others.

During her tenure, she had done many of the absurd things that an officer does but that don't seem absurd when the plans you've come to wrest from a sham curl of dog shit are for India's fast breeder test reactor. But mostly this was adjunct work. Assignments to divert her self-regard from evidence that she'd devoted her career to the study and pursuit of Thurlow Dan. Had they really been married once? It seemed like another lifetime.

Martin fit her wig over a Styrofoam head and combed out a snag.

"The morgue called," he said.

"What'd you tell them?"

"Same as always. You'll call them back."

"They say anything new?"

"Your parents are fine."

She smiled despite herself. Her parents were dead. How else would they be?

He checked his BlackBerry. "When will you be needing me again?"

She'd put on a terry cloth robe and slippers, which she kicked off from bed. "Not until tomorrow," she said glumly, before pilling what makeup and glue were left hewn to her chin with her fingertips.

"And now?"

"Reading files. Go on, have fun."

Sometimes Martin forgot who he was—butler or F/X man—so he backed out of the room and bowed at the waist. Other times, he did not forget, and bowed just the same. Esme Haas was one scary woman.

She watched him go. Sad. Martin had a life outside the one he experienced in her charge. She wished she had that life, too. But no. Her house was sized for God; it was cold and quiet and quarantining of intimacies that inhered between people.

On a console of TVs set into her wall: footage from every room in the house. Her daughter was asleep. Everyone else was out. If she killed the radio, it would be deadly. On the topic of isolation, she liked to blame her work: This isn't my fault. Only it was her fault. Her character. Type A shy: gregarious, lively, protected. Prized qualities in a sleuthing mercenary, less so for the woman inside. But never mind— she was her job 95 percent of the time.

And so: manila envelopes on the table. She opened them one by one. Looked at photos, résumés, stats. It wasn't like she was unprepared to do Jim's bidding. She was always plugging people into the system she might need later. People she paid for small jobs here and there. People who were willing to do something odd for reasons she would divine first and exploit later. For this gig, she chose four who seemed perfect: Ned Hammerstein, Anne-Janet Tabetha Riggs, Olgo Panjabi,

Bruce Bollinger. She'd wooed them to the Department of the Interior a few weeks ago, them and fifty like them, because who kept track of what went on at the Department of the Interior? Most everyone there was astonishingly without job description. She'd once caught a guy arranging the envelopes in the mail room by size, and when she returned three hours later, he was still doing it.

At the bottom of her files was a letter she didn't want to see, which was why it was on the bottom. A note from her daughter's boarding school, a report card plus blurb from each teacher re: the emotional stylings of Ida Haas midway through fourth grade. She was, they said, good with the other kids. Played nice. Appeared to compensate for surplus rage with martyring gestures that won her many friends, though perhaps this way of things would not go over as well in the real world, be advised.

Esme skimmed the rest. She did not enjoy having to get news of who her child was, though it was probably better to have something to go on next time Ida showed, which was now. She could feel it, her daughter's gaze scalding the back of her neck. She did not even have to turn around.

"What's the matter, tulip? I thought you were asleep."

"Ma and Pop let me stay up till whenever."

Esme considered all the other ways her parents might have let her child grow up unbridled and decided this was okay. Besides, who was she to have an opinion? She didn't know if she'd done wrong *today,* but no matter: yesterday's guilt imported fine.

Ida was leaning against the wall, one bare foot flamingoed to her calf, working a Twizzler across her lips.

"Then stay up. You want to play a game?"

"No."

"Want me to come read to you?"

"Ha," Ida said, and she threw herself on the couch. She was wearing cotton pajamas—green with white stripes—that had banded cuffs at the wrists and ankles. It was hard to reconcile the scorn in her voice with the dress of her choosing, but so be it. Esme thought this conversation ranked among their finest in days.

"I've got work, honey bun. But you can stay. Tomorrow I'll take you to dance class."

Ida nose-dived for the files. Flipped one open. Stared at Ned. "Nope," she said. "Too young." She rolled on her back, legs in the air.

"For what?"

"For Dad. *Duh*," and she grabbed at the next file, which Esme had in hand and wouldn't let go.

"Mohhm. Give it."

"Okay, this is not playtime, and we're not looking for your dad."

"Are, too," Ida said. And, as though buffeted by the fury of it all, she lifted herself from the couch and sailed out of the room.

Esme shook her head. She had not done the easy thing of telling Ida that Thurlow was dead, just that he had vanished when she was a baby. And because she had never elaborated or furnished the story with verisimilitude—what he did for a living, what he looked like, where he was last—Ida must have known she was lying. But who was to say what went on in the mind of a nine-year-old? She was so much like her father, the passions accreting with each year. Sometimes Esme looked at her and thought, How do you even have the room?

She put her files away. Tried to relax. The years without Thurlow were cairned in her heart for the life they never had, but just because she'd grown used to the weight did not mean that it wasn't heavy or that sometimes she could not bear it.

And to think it was her job that had brought them together. They'd known each other since they were kids, but their first real encounter came after she'd been assigned to him. And he never knew. He still didn't. And now, a decade later, she was still following him around. Five minutes at a Laundromat. A few hours in North Korea.

Under her bed was a queen-size strongbox instead of a box spring. It was designed to conceal thirty-five rifles and seventy handguns, though she used it for DVDs and letters. Four hundred eighty-two letters from Thurlow. A thousand DVDs. She grabbed one from last year, marked *11/04*, right after the election. She had filmed that night herself; the weather had been awful—a storm, a flood—but everyone still came.

She popped the DVD into her computer and closed her eyes. Thurlow's voice was enough for her; she knew the rest by heart. He'd been wearing jeans and a long-sleeved polyester crew that hung off his shoulders. His hair was mopped across his face because he'd just showered and that was what conditioner did to it. His skin was pale and freckled, which gave him an injured, boyish look that made the traumas issuing from his lips seem all the more unjust. He had put his hands on the lectern, and she could make out the swollen knuckle that had never healed from when he fell off his bike at age twelve. He thanked everyone for coming. Three hundred in the audience? Four? A drop in the bucket.

"Now, listen," he said. "A lot of people think solitude comes from a deep need attached in our social history to the dread of convention. Or even just the dread of belonging. How can I belong? I live in darker registers of inquiry and feeling than anyone else on earth. Does that sound familiar?"

Esme was mouthing the speech with him. She'd heard it and the others a thousand times. She remembered that this one went on for hours. And that somewhere in the middle, the rain stopped, and the wind died. And that by the time Thurlow was done, the sky was fledgling blue.

She turned off her computer. It wasn't that she didn't agree with Thurlow. Loneliness *was* a pandemic, and she had only to look at herself to see the proof. She had spent more time alone than anyone she knew, despite her daughter, whom she loved but whose presence was not companionship. Ida was just a child. Sometimes she was even an affront. So, the premise—Thurlow had that right. It was the rest Esme couldn't get behind. Fellowship among strangers as antidote to a life's worth of estrangement? As if when the romantic or familial valence of your secret self falls short, you can just entrust that secret self to the Helix and feel better?

She grabbed tweezers from her bedside table and stripped her cuticles. Examined her fingers, as she did almost every night. So strange not to have fingerprints. Growing up, she had let the condition ask of her questions most people spend their lives trying never to ask, among them: What the fuck is wrong with me? And: Do the affectations of my body—and doesn't everyone have something? that dreadful mole? a sunspot?—proceed from a darker and more dire malady clutched to my heart? Phrenology and palm reading may have been fatuous, but they still derived from a basic impulse to solipsism and self-hatred: everything in the world is but evidence of my failure.

Esme had her problems: an ex-husband she still loved and a child who might not love her. She popped a finger in her mouth. The blood about her nail had gathered like pectin.

There was nothing to do but what she could. Assemble a team: Ned, Anne-Janet, Olgo, Bruce. Execute reconnaissance on Thurlow and the Helix House. Listen up, look hard, and if, in the crosshairs between hurt and sorrow, she felt the tremor of longing—Where are you? and, I miss you—then, yes, some part of her continued to do the right thing, despite all.

II. In which the Lynne Five-0 creeps her team out. In which stories begin to assert themselves like pebbles thrown up from the sea. Cloud seeding, speed dating, clogs. The language of back then. A joust.

**Alone with her problems: Anne-Janet Tabetha Riggs.
DOB 3.4.75 SS# 145-08-633**

Anne-Janet tarried. Outside her mother's hospital room, gelling her hands clean. Next up, the mantras: Forty-five minutes are all I need to stay. Forty-five minutes look like love. Multiple attempts to visit the patient look like love. I will be kind. If not for her, then for the propitiation of God, in whose caprice illness comes and goes.

So far the news was bad. Her mother had a stent and a clogged lumen in her calf. Immobility can do that, they said, can increase the threat of embolism. So they'd plunged a tube in Marie's leg. Her charge? Stay put or bleed out. For Anne-Janet, the sight had been dreadful, her mother's lips collapsed for lack of teeth, the skin of her face pleated and wan. It was one thing to regard her own face and note the loss of its selling points—when was the last her eyes had spangled with the greens of mint and holly for which she was known?—but quite another to confront decay in her mother, who was timeless.

"You're up," Anne-Janet said. "How are you feeling?"

"You don't want to be here," Marie said. "Hospitals are where people come to get even sicker than they were before. You have a depressed immune system. I can tell you want to go home."

"You're up!" Anne-Janet said, and she sat in a chair next to the bed. "Sleep well?"

"Ech. I am on so many drugs. And I'm thirsty. You wouldn't want to go get me some juice, would you?"

"I'll have to ask the nurse. Be right back."

She stood and made for the station. It was awful having to bother a nurse about kid stuff like juice. But then what if Marie was on blood thinners that turned evil with sugar? What if her liquids were being restricted for a reason? Anne-Janet would corner a nurse, who would refer her to another nurse, who would not be pleased—not at all—to answer Anne-Janet's questions. Next would come anxiety about having pissed off the nurse, in whose disposition hung the balance of a good or bad stay at the hospital. Ring the bell at 3 a.m. and get help, or just lie there in your own vomit. Sometimes you had to enlist a roommate to get attention because the roommate was still on good terms with the staff, in which case the roommate did not always want to imperil those terms by helping you. Every patient in a hospital needed an advocate to raise hell on her behalf. Anne-Janet beelined for a woman pushing a cart of towels down the hall.

"I'm sorry to bother you, but my mom, in room thirty-four—"

"Marie, sure. And you must be Anne-Janet. She talks about you all the time."

"She does? Well. We're wondering if she can have some juice. Also, while I have you, do you know when the doctors are coming by? Or when they're going to remove the stent? Is the stent permanent? Why haven't they scheduled her surgery yet? She's just getting the plate, right? Not a whole new hip or anything?"

The nurse said, "I'm Lynne. I don't really know the answer to any of your questions, but you're free to walk with me while I distribute these towels. I've sat with your mother a fair amount today. She's a great lady."

Anne-Janet stopped walking. People didn't say these things about her mom. She looked the nurse over. Maybe if Lynne just stood up straight—but then maybe she couldn't. Maybe that hunch was permanent. Or maybe it was just her uniform, which was oversized, even for her. Could be, though, it was just her face that gave Anne-Janet the heebie-jeebies. Imagine high school with a nose like that.

"Thanks," Anne-Janet said. "But I'd better go."

"Okeysmokey."

The hallway spooled around reception, as it did on every floor. If Anne-Janet closed her eyes, she could be in oncology, awaiting results from one scan or another. After five years with metastasized colon cancer, you stopped caring about the names of the tests or what they were for. Your tumors have grown, they have shrunk—these were the words that mattered. For now, they were shrunk. All but gone. Anne-Janet was on a cancer furlough and wanted to make the best of it. She wanted, even, to date. To date with minimal exposure to men, which explained her plans for the night. A Helix event. Speed dating. Since she was twenty-five, cancer had given her ample excuses not to date, among them feeling too ill, too ugly, too pointless. But finally, this was not the inhibition that needed surmounting. She was, simply, afraid to be touched. Her memories of touch were steeped in terror. It was the thing she talked about most, not in its fraught detail but in general. She would not hide it; it was always there. And seemed to come up whenever she made a new acquaintance, people being unable to call her by her full name and wanting, immediately, to call her AJ instead. *Could* they call her AJ? Well, her father used to call her AJ and her father had touched her inappropriately. So no, they could not. Not unless they wanted to rouse in her memories so vile, she had not had intercourse since age eight.

She looked at her mom. Probably it had been worse for her. Not to know what evils were transacted in her own home.

"No juice?" Marie said. "Did you check every floor?"

"I'll get it in a bit. Have some ice chips."

"So how was work yesterday? Like the new job?"

"It's where God has landed me, I guess." She said this wistfully because she did, in fact, marvel at change. Yes, she was surprised to have landed anywhere—to be alive, really—but mostly she was surprised to have landed at the Department of the Interior when two weeks ago she was still hawking celebrity mouth guards on eBay.

"But what's your title?" Marie said. "What do you do?"

"Are you asking so you can tell your girlfriends? Because if so, you can tell them I am head of Research and Development."

"But is that true?"

"No. Hey, I met a strange-looking nurse just now. Says she's been hanging out with you. I think her name is Lynne."

"There are so many, I can't keep track."

"She's got weird posture."

"The one with the nose?"

"You got it."

"She's new. She showed up out of nowhere. Listen, my angel, you wouldn't want to get me that apple juice now, would you?"

"I think you're on a restricted diet. Because of the surgery."

Marie sat up. "I'm having surgery? No one said I was having surgery. What? Oh my God."

And with that, she tried to swing her legs over the edge of the bed, never mind the stent or that her hip was fractured in two places.

Anne-Janet dove at her mother. Yelled at her. "*Get back in bed.* You want to die? You could die. Just get back in bed."

She rang for the nurse while struggling with Marie, afraid the struggle would make things worse and eyeing the heart monitor as if she knew what all the numbers meant but certain a spike in any direction was bad.

"Let go of me!" Marie yelled. "I can't stay here. You can't put me under!"

"Mom, don't be like this." But her mother pushed her away with a strength she'd obviously had on reserve. "Mom, you are scaring me. I can't help you if you are doing this."

"Get off me, AJ!"

"Don't call me that!"

And they struggled still. Anne-Janet depressed the emergency button. She could hear it ringing down the hall. But no one came. She looked to the roommate, who'd been shot in the gut by a bullet strayed from gang violence, but she just shook her head. No one had come to visit her, she had no advocates on the outside, she had to protect her standing in this hospital no matter what. Would she ring for the nurse? No.

Finally, Lynne of the jumbo duds stormed in with a syringe poised above her head. It was one of the scariest things Anne-Janet had ever seen, this stout little woman who wore her hair like a baseball mitt, coming at her mother like a slasher—practiced but lusty. She stabbed Marie in the thigh.

Marie went slack with the sense of being outnumbered. "You are psychotic," she mumbled, and she let herself be helped back into bed.

Anne-Janet glanced at the heart monitor. The numbers were blinking. She looked at Lynne.

"Don't ask her," said Marie. "She is the stupidest nurse ever." And then, turning to Lynne, "It is strange, the way you know nothing."

She settled into the mattress. The numbers stopped blinking. "I'm going to sleep now," she said. "You look like you want to go home anyway."

Lynne said she had other places to be but that she'd come back later. Anne-Janet wet a towel in the bathroom. Wet and wrung and tried to return her thoughts to something safe, though instead they alighted on the whys of her being here in the hospital alone, the whys of having to shoulder her mother alone, the mistakes she'd made, the chances she'd never even had.

She passed the towel across her mother's face and hands. "There," she said. "Good as new. You're going to feel much better in a second." She swiped the cloth behind her ears and along the folds of her neck, and the room said: Washing your mother when she is incapacitated looks like love.

As soon as Marie fell asleep, Anne-Janet slunk out. The sedative would probably give her a few hours' reprieve. Time enough to go speed dating without thought of her mother calling out her name in vain.

She headed for the bar, just a couple of Metro stops away. Options to drink in this neighborhood were limited to the New Wave—an all-night karaoke bar for British punk—or Nixon's, whose three rooms could accommodate multiple events at the same time. A favorite among government staff, who came for the beer as much as the decor: renderings of the presidents no one cared about or even recalled. Zachary Taylor, who died of fruit and never brushed his teeth. Chester Arthur, of the morbid kidneys and rowdy facial hair. Warren Harding, whose reputation would have fared better if his wife really had poisoned him, and, next to him, a vacancy where once was the sober likeness of Rutherford Hayes, whose contentious election was, these days, just too much grist for argument. In point: good-bye, Hayes; hello, Reagan of the unifying landslide, whose triptych depicted the president with dog, horse, and gun, respectively.

The bar was packed. Half the place was given over to a birthday party, the other half consigned to the Helix, whose logo was postered all over the walls and spiraled from the ceiling in rainbow pipe cleaners.

Anne-Janet looked around. Speed dating had already begun, which gave her full view of the roulette being played among these single men and women with nothing happier to do. Was it too late to leave? This night was going to be a bust, she knew it. She searched for the coat-check ticket in her purse, the plan to about-face, go home, and do nothing.

Eh, enough; stay focused. She'd heard the testimonials, same as everyone else. Helix Heads. Members who'd directed their goals, resources, and beliefs to practice empathy, no matter how hard. Members who were happier for it. They were together, she was not, so just shut up, Anne-Janet, and date.

Besides, she wouldn't go home. She'd go back to the hospital and watch the State of the Union with her mother, which was worse. *Our generation has been blessed.* The speech bawled from speakers in the next room and careened off the windows and wood floor of cappuccino tint.

She signed in and collected her date cards. At orientation for the Department of the Interior, she'd been told that new hires who wanted to thrive did well to go to Nixon's, and so she was not surprised to see Ned Hammerstein in a corner with a woman fifty times prettier than she—the woman sporting a red baize spencer and suede skirt with edelweiss buttons. Throwback Bavarian, repressed but hot.

Anne-Janet hadn't actually met Ned at work, but she'd been eyeing him from day one. She chose a table across the room from his. And started her night. On your marks, get set, talk.

"Hi," she said, and looked at her date. His stats were: Gandhi glasses; facial hair goateed but unkempt; skin pallid, eyes pallid.

"Hi," he said.

"Hi back."

A minute spent. There were prompts on the list; she chose one. "My worst high school moment? This girl Dawn on my gymnastics team tried to switch the talc in my bucket with boric acid because my Yurchenko double-twist vault was better than hers, except a rat got in the bucket and died, and Dawn went to juvie, but the rest of the team blamed me. So, yeah, that was it for friendships meant to last forever."

"You know," he said, "you have an asymmetric mouth. I find that very attractive. I think we as humans like symmetry but that we also like to see a pattern, and then to see some slight variation. Music is a great example of that. Establish a pattern and then throw in variations. I guess what I'm saying is, your face is like a song. Like 'Take Five.'"

Speaking of which: *ding.*

Ned stared at his drink. There were cherries in his highball glass; he stabbed one with a cocktail pick. Tried to stab for emphasis. Get it? I hate that my life has brought me to this.

His date scanned a list of questions. "You got any hobbies?"

"I do," he said. And he looked her over. Her smile was big, and he could see that her front teeth were canted in the direction of her throat and that her lips were tight against her gums, all things moving one way, which boded well if you were a guy with a libido, which Ned was and was not. Not for weeks, but here trying.

"I study the weather. Weather as warfare. Technically, there isn't much use for the skill because of the UN's 1977 Convention on the Prohibition of Military or Any Other Hostile Use of Environmental Modification Techniques. But the fact is, no one cares. I mean, really: if you can roll in a float of clouds just when the enemy needs a sight line, you're saving lives."

"Are you a lifesaver?"

"No."

"Is this your first time doing this?"

"Yes," he said, but quietly, as though the word, quartered among pride, defeat, disgust, and hope, were not able to assert itself.

"How about we talk about you," he said.

"No problem," and she told him she'd just finished six months of psychiatric analysis. That her husband's helicopter went down in Afghanistan during a training exercise. That the army, finding in six months' psychiatric surveillance more than enough penance for having murdered her husband, stopped paying for it. "So here I am," she said. "Trying to make new friends."

"Jesus," he said. And he nodded, with the helper literature in mind. It said the only way to assault estrangement and isolation was to pursue ego diminishment. How? By living the life of your contemporaries. So he nodded and frowned and let himself be visibly moved because this woman's story was awful.

Two down, seven more to go. *Ding.*

Anne-Janet had worked her way to Ned's table at last. She asked if he was having a nice time. Her eyelids fluttered as she spoke, and he couldn't tell whether she meant to keep them open or closed, which impulse she meant to heel.

She didn't wait for an answer. Asked, instead, about his life.

"Adopted," he said. "Just found out, actually. Not even six weeks ago."

"That come as good or bad news?"

"Both." And he thought, You are what you are until you are not. Not the genetic progeny of Larissa and Max T. Hammerstein. Not an only child. Yes, a child with a twin, who, for being a girl, was not palatable to Larissa and Max T., who remanded her to foster care on the day she was born, thirty-three years ago.

"Sounds bad," she said. "But great Prereq." And she rubbed her eye with the fat of her palm, which jutted from a sweater sleeve that was too long. "You know, like whatever in your life sucks enough to count as prerequisite for wanting to join the Helix."

Ned smiled. Thinking, This woman's all right. She hates her wrists.

"Me, I don't normally do this kind of thing," she said. "Mostly I set up other people, even if I like the guy, because I figure the other person could make him happier than me. So it's like doing service."

"Wow. Sounds like you have good Prereq, too."

"I know. You got a rash?"

He'd been farming for a spot, several spots, on his back. Anxiety Itch. So many women, so much to tell. Sweat began to front along his hairline and rill down his face.

"No," he said. "I mean, yes. I get nervous around people."

"You read the helper lit?"

He shrugged.

"Me too," she said, and she tugged at her hat—a beanie, really—which saved her at least one confession: I've got a crew cut, and whatever the reason, it's not good.

She reached in her bag for the brochure. It was glossy, picture heavy. Smiling people who didn't look brainwashed so much as happy, and, of course, a snap of Helix honcho, Thurlow Dan.

They looked over the material, which seemed to fortify the whys of their finding themselves here. What else was there to say? From the lounge came news of the birthday. *Happy birthday, Olgo Panjabi, happy birthday to you.* The voices sang at length, they sang with joy. The hodgepodging of ethnicities in this man's name was all very beautiful—very consolidating—and people wanted to think about that, especially now.

"That was nice," she said.

"You're nice."

"We should hang out at work," she said, though he just stared at her blankly.

Ding, and the MC's voice: "We are taking a break. Mingle."

There was birthday cake in the lounge. There was Bruce Bollinger, whose lips were kissed with ganache. There was Olgo Panjabi, source of it all. Olgo, who was now sixty and in whose face was a foreboding about his new year of life, tempered by this impromptu swell of affection for him. There was, also, Anne-Janet and Ned. Interior claimed fifty-eight thousand employees; here were four. They had just met.

From the TV: *"Each age is a dream that is dying or one that is coming to birth."* The president quoting FDR, who himself quoted an Irish poet.

From the TV: *We have seen the threads of purpose that unite us.* Two terms with this guy. That nasal voice. Those platitudes.

The bartender snorted. He was fluent in drinks that made you sick. Tonight was $5 Trips to Hell, a multi-schnapped, Red Bull, Jägermeister shot he mixed for six at the counter, saying, "The Helix probably pulled in ten thousand people tonight, events all over the country, and this jerk-off is saying we've seen the threads that hold us together? Unless he's Helix, too, he hasn't seen a thread in years."

There was laughter. And secret looks. Half the bar was Helix already. Out to recruit, then back to the Bond. The Helix had bought personal data from ten Internet dating sites, which meant it had the emails and psychological vitae of more than fifty million people who had already contributed to the effort of finding each other, and, as such, were reasonably disposed to attend these events. Rest of Your Life Socials. And when the RYLS didn't produce—when, in fact, they depressed everyone—a Helix Head would swoop in to suggest an alternate means of camaraderie. Weekly meetings. Daily meetings. A lovely house not five miles from here.

Ding.

"So this is my theory," Ned said. "There is no more famous prototype for twins asunder than Luke and Leia. You know, from *Star Wars.*"

"Uh-huh."

"And a twin rent from its other will always feel the loss."

"Sounds reasonable. Only wasn't there something hanky-panky about Luke and Leia?"

"No," he said, appalled. "Luke is an ascetic."

"Do you have a job?" she said, though her voice was so slouched in boredom, she sounded like a teller at the DMV.

"I guess. But it's weird. I was reading a lot about weather-modification offices in China, silver iodide and cloud seeding. You know, how to make rain and stuff. It's big in Texas."

"And?"

"I got a call."

"Saying what?"

But Ned did not want to say. It was too personal, even for this. He was obsessed with the Vonnegut brothers—one a scientist who discovered the prowess of silver iodide, the other a novelist whose ice-nine plunged the world into the next Frost—and it was Ned's idea to be like a hybrid of the two. So when he got a call, the decision was easy. Did Ned want to do something for the Department of the Interior that had something to do with changing the weather, which itself had everything to do with snubbing his powerlessness in the world? Why yes, yes he did. Ned had been with Interior for three weeks. But no one had asked him about the weather or anything else.

"It's boring," he said. "Tell me about you."

"I'm anorexic—what more's there to say?"

"Do you want help?"

"Oh, hell no."

They laughed until the bell.

Anne-Janet pressed her napkin into a tear blooming at the corner of her eye. You were not supposed to sit with the same person twice, but there are glitches, there is fate.

She looked at Ned and said, "My mom broke her hip yesterday morning. I got home at about six and found her on the floor. Know what that means?"

"God, that's awful. Is that why you're crying?"

"Seven hours on the floor. Just lying there. She's asleep now. I hate hospitals."

"I'm sorry."

"Being here isn't so bad, though. You think you're gonna join up?" she said. "The Helix?"

He shrugged. "I'm kind of a member already. But just for stuff like this. I've got this twin sister now and have never felt lonelier in my life. So I'm not in it for the politics or whatever. I think that part's bullshit, anyway."

"Which part?"

"The armed-and-dangerous part. You hear rumors, but I don't believe them."

"Oh, that," she said. "Probably right, only I have a couple friends who joined a Bond and now no one knows what's up with them because they won't talk to anyone but each other."

"A Bond?"

"Like a commune. People living together in some house or building. They're all over the country. But I gotta say, I actually think it sounds nice."

"I bet the Branch Davidians thought their gig was nice, too."

"No, but they were bonkers. And anyway, how do you know? Maybe they knew they were in a cult and just liked it that way." She cast her arm like it was the line and she was fishing.

Ned tilted his head, gave her a look. "Wait a minute," he said. "Do I know you from someplace else?"

Her face said it all. "I work four doors down from you, Ned. I see you every day."

"Oh, jeez. How embarrassing."

"That's okay. I'm not all that stand-out."

Ding.

Ned thumbed through his date cards. Five dates, one match. *Anne-Janet 358.* He returned to the lounge for a last drink and a closing look at her because he was determined to remember her face. He found her with Bruce. Bruce and Olgo.

Ned said, "Happy birthday, Olgo Panjabi."

Bruce said, "So what is that, anyway? Italian-Indian?"

Olgo wanted another drink. He was feeling vibrant. Sixty years old. Sixty today! Sixty at a time when sixty was the new forty, or so his wife liked to say after orgasm, which she still had, with decent frequency and élan, so that even as he thought about it now, he felt a gathering of love for her ramp up his chest and blossom across his face.

"Okay, one more," said Bruce, as he assessed the détente in his gut—would it keep until home? He had a bad stomach.

When asked, Bruce said he once did consulting. And Olgo? "Arbitration. I used to envoy proposals between people who hate each other. I wrest accord from the teeth of hostility."

"Wow."

"My wife put that on a business card for me once. Just for fun. *Olgo Panjabi: Wresting accord from the teeth of hostility since 1945.* Year I was born."

Bruce said, "I used to work in TV. *Trial by Liar*—my baby."

Anne-Janet laughed. "And now we all work for Interior, and none of us knows why."

A man tapped Ned on the shoulder. He was the organizer of the night. He was saying: Nine minutes, nine women. When you do eight, or *four,* you leave a woman in the lurch. There is a woman in the lurch, and she is demanding satisfaction.

Good grief. Ned was directed to a private room, which was empty barring a single woman at a table and, weirdly, a security detail in the nooks. These guys were so conspicuous. So maybe this woman was a higher-up. Maybe she had powers. Not that powers were such an asset if they meant having to take your security team on a speed date. This woman had a stoop—he could tell even though she was sitting. And though there was supposed to be an age limit here, the woman's neck said fifty. Drapes of neck. Cascade of neck.

"Ned Four Four Four," she said. "Sit."

There are men, it's true, who like to be bossed around. Men who want to be called *bitch* and *slave* and *whore.* Typically these are men in power who just want to give it a rest. Ned knew such men. His father—his *faux* father—was such a man, though no one had known. At least not until two months ago, when he had confessed, in his sleep, to having affinities at odds with his wife's temperament in bed, so much so that he was pleading for things of which she had never heard. What, for instance, was a hog tie?

His mother might well have let it go—a dream is but a dream—but she didn't. Instead, she flew into such a rage that she intimated gratitude for Ned's lineage unknown—thank God he could not inherit this sickness, this depravity!—at which point, she realized, the game was up. The truth will out: he was adopted. Ned left home with a folder of documents and letters, and a sense that the wasteland he'd come to regard as his inner life owed its provenance to strangers.

He sat. The woman produced a clipboard. "Drugs?" she said.

"No."

"Illnesses?"

"None. My dad has hypertension, but then I guess that means nothing for me anymore since he's not really my dad."

She checked things off as she spoke.

"This is efficient," he said. "Do you multitask at home? I've got it so I can piss, shave, and brush my teeth at the same time. Assuming you're man enough to sit on the toilet, it's no problem."

"You're very talented," she said, and she seemed to lean forward, though perhaps it was just the illusion produced by her nose and jaw, as though these features wanted off her face and were just waiting for the chance.

He checked his watch. Seven minutes to go. He said, "What's your name?" and looked at his date card. Because, in a way, this bossy little woman was hot. Twenty years older than him, but hot. Go figure.

"My name is Lynne."

He leaned forward, wanting to whisper something about the security detail, only as he moved in, so did they. One got his forearm between Ned and Lynne so fast it came down like a tollgate. The arm appeared to say: Sit back. Good thing Ned had powers of deduction, since the man also appeared incapable of speech. He was so much brick, there were probably bricks all up and down his throat.

The woman waved him off—"Martin, enough"—and the Brick went back to his corner.

Ned retracted. Pulled out his chair. "This is getting uncomfortable," he said. "I don't think I'm the guy for you."

But Lynne kept to the script. Fears? Phobias? Allergies?

"I don't handle eggplant all that well."

"Anything you can tell me that your basic spy wouldn't catch within a week of surveillance?"

He had to think. He scratched his back with kitchen utensils, wore

Star Wars costumes to relax, and sometimes talked to Kurt Vonnegut in the bathroom because the man's photo—from a magazine—was taped to the mirror.

"No," he said. "Probably not. Though if you had someone spying on me, it'd be for a reason, which would make me way more interesting than I am. So it's sort of an unfair question."

"Okay, let me ask you this: Do you ever feel like you want to do something great? Something that will make you king of the world?"

He sat back. Studied her face. Did he know this woman, too? He didn't want to risk asking.

"I guess," he said. "That's why I study weather modification. I mean, if you can turn water to ice, you are powerful. You are *all*-powerful. So who knows? Defy Nature in a small way and maybe you can do it in a big way."

"And that appeals to you?"

"I'd like to be in charge of my own life, yes."

She seemed to approve. "So you just found out you're adopted, is that right?"

"How could you know that?" he said. "Okay, please tell me you are just really into me and did some research."

"Is that what you'd prefer?"

"Don't write that down! Am I safe in assuming we've long since ended our date? I'm going to try to be smart about this and venture you are from Interior and are, uh, interviewing me for one reason or another."

"Don't be silly. I just overheard what you said earlier. And anyway, here comes the bell."

"You are weird," he said. "That was weird."

"Nine-minute dating is weird. Get over it."

He watched her leave the room, security on either flank.

In the lounge were the bartender and backs. A few guys watching golf highlights. A woman saying it might be nice to watch the minority response to the State of the Union, and another saying: Bohhhring.

Ned grabbed his coat from the stand. He felt for his gloves and was reassured to find them there. Outside the window, he caught sight of one of his dates getting in a car with the security guy of brick. One date and then another, and Lynne bringing up the rear. Well, how do you like that? The silent brick thing was not supposed to work. The Helix said so. Equity theory said so—only people in receipt of a self-disclosure will respond by sharing about themselves at a companionable level of intimacy, which was code for putting out, and yet there was the Brick with half the bar in his pants. Ah, the world was a mystifying place. And being in it was not so much an exercise in humility as disjuncture.

Ned checked his watch. It was only nine. Guess he'd go home and pelt the TV with wasabi peas. Or have a drink like his boss, the Secretary, who would inherit the earth if the Capitol blew up on this night of all others. Somewhere in a safe house mandated by the doomsday caveat to the Succession Act of '47, the Secretary was sipping Bénédictine and napping through the State of the Union like everyone else. Probably, though, Ned would go home and study the weather. Rawinsonde data from balloons one hundred thousand feet in the air; thunderstorm identification, tracking, analysis, and nowcasting info; Stüve diagrams and the CAPEs of every cloud deck within ten miles. An hour's worth of study that would help him counter dread of the unknown with his command of the fates. He needed all the help he could get for that moment when he'd find his sister and disclose their kin. He had, after all, seen *Star Wars* a thousand times.

LUKE: I'm Luke Skywalker. I'm here to rescue you.
LEIA: You're *who?*

He spotted Anne-Janet on her way out and ran to catch up with her. "Hey," he said, "if you're not doing anything right now, maybe we could have a beer or something?" Because, romance or not, it'd be nice to have a friend at work. Share your boredom, and next you know, you're streaking the Pentagon for kicks.

"I can't," she said. "I have to get back to the hospital. Mother calls."

He nodded and felt like he didn't need the Helix to get this one right. He understood perfectly. We are put on this earth to rue the family that comes apart. Look after you and yours.

Anne-Janet took the long way back, and when she found out her mom was still asleep, she went to the lounge. Most unhappy place ever, the hospital lounge, except maybe the playground after a miscarriage. It was empty but for a coffee station and snack machine with offerings strangely antagonistic to health. Not just candy bars and chips, but the really caloric foods, like Marshmallow Fluff shortbread and maple honey buns. Honey buns in a bag. Anne-Janet bought water and a pack of gum. She sat on a couch frayed at the arms and pecked with holes. Nails burrowed into the fabric while people waited for death.

She retrieved her Helix membership card from her back pocket. She should laminate the thing and yoke it to a string around her neck, just to advertise her need. That or rip it up because, really, those people were lame, the socials were lame, and just because the energies of the lonely tended to mobilize in vigilant and constant pursuit of an end to loneliness, that did not make their aggregate any less lame.

Even so: Nine men, one match. Ned Hammerstein. She'd spent most of her first weeks at Interior trying to find out more about him. But the results were minimal. So either he was this wonderful enigma or the most boring man ever. It didn't matter which, only that Anne-Janet liked to know in advance what she was getting into. She hated surprises. As a girl, just knowing when her father was coming took the edge off the assault. In time, she hardly cared what he did because she was prepared. On the other hand, nights he showed unexpectedly, she sobbed into the dishrag he thrust in her mouth.

She put the card away and crossed her ankles. Was about to go to her mom's room when Nurse Lynne plunked down on the couch and said, "There you are. Been looking all over." She seemed out of breath. And looked as if she'd applied her eyeliner in an earthquake. What kind of nurse had a hand that unsteady?

"Why? How's my mom?"

"Down for the count. I gave her a sedative."

"Another one?" And because Anne-Janet was a little afraid of her, she looked at Lynne's shoes. Not the rubber clogs made famous by that fat Italian chef, but black suede pumps. "I've never seen a nurse wear those," she said.

Lynne outstretched her foot. "Shift's over. I'm on my way out. Just stopped to check on you."

"Oh. Well, that's nice."

She noticed that Lynne's calves were tremendous. Water balloons. Amazing.

Lynne scratched one with the tip of her pump. She said, "Your mom tells me you work for the Department of the Interior. What's that like? It sounds grand."

"You're kidding, right?"

"No, I mean it. I'm a nurse, what do I do all day? A man came in this morning, he weighs five hundred pounds. We had to get him from the gurney to a bed. Exciting, right? But you work for the government. You're doing something that matters."

Anne-Janet blushed. She had never thought of herself as a woman who did work that mattered. "Well," she said, "I guess it's *sort of* grand. I don't know how up you are on the divvying of responsibilities in government, but my department pretty much runs the show. I mean, the fundamentals. Land, water, energy."

"Wow. And what's your part?"

"Research."

"Yeah? Do you go out into the field or whatever?"

Anne-Janet sat up with zero regard for the crossroads before a giant lie and said, "Yes. I am out there all the time. Oil production, gas lines, reservoirs, coal mines—you wouldn't believe what would happen to these things if we didn't step in. People need guidance. They need oversight."

"It's great they have you," said Lynne.

Anne-Janet smiled. She plumed and bluffed and grinned.

"But I've been thinking," said Lynne—and here her face lost that admiring ingenue quality Anne-Janet had quickly come to love—"I've been wondering: is it hard working for the government these days? Because of what's happening?"

"What do you mean?" Though the fact was, even World War III would have registered but faintly on Anne-Janet's screen. Such was the colonizing tyranny of cancer; you hardly noticed anything else.

"Oh," Lynne said. She looked disappointed. "So you're not involved with how to deal with the Helix? The movement's so big, there are rumors of an Indian land-claim thing going on. Like they want to be self-sufficient. Carve up the states. I hear Thurlow Dan is a *secessionist*."

"Uh, yeah," Anne-Janet said, feeling the need to recoup Lynne's respect tussle with the need to defend or conceal her patronage of the Helix—she wasn't sure which. "We're on top of that," she said. But also: Carve up the states? What? There were rumors, yes, but they were stupid conservative rumors. The Helix wasn't militant. It was about reconciliation, and, in Anne-Janet's exercise of the fundamental option of faith, it was about consigning the pitch of your heart to God and letting him restore what being human fractures to bits every day. So, in fact, the Helix was about the opposite of secession. And Thurlow Dan? He *started* the thing. Had devoted his life to bringing unity where there was strife. Who knew what this nurse was on about. She was an idiot.

"Aha," Lynne said. "So you're not interested?" She inched forward with a disregard for personal space that gave Anne-Janet the creeps. Already Anne-Janet had retreated to the edge of the last cushion; any farther and she'd fall off.

"No, I am. I'm interested."

Lynne was squared before her; their knees touched. "What do you really know about the Helix?"

Anne-Janet frowned. "Is there any chance you're talking DNA because we're in a hospital and my mother broke her hip and maybe I am next because osteoporosis is genetic?"

"No."

"Okay then. As far as I know, the Helix has a pretty comprehensive website. Lots of info. Events, literature, stuff like that. In its name, people get together to talk and share about their lives. Make new friends. You know."

"Yes, fine, but I mean—oh, never mind. Why am I even asking you." Lynne pulled back a good two feet.

Anne-Janet took offense. It was bad being crowded in but worse to repel the crowd once it had started. She thought hard. *Did* she know anything about the Helix that departed from what anyone else knew? Some nights the only info she got on just what Interior did was from collecting strips of paper from the shredder bins on the Hill and recreating the original sheets. Her mother would say, "Oh, honey, go out, get a boyfriend," and she'd say, "I am dating the shredder." Last week, she'd pieced together a memo, which she'd forgotten about until now, that did say something about Dan and his people in Cincinnati. Was this what Lynne was talking about? Her mother's nurse, Lynne?

She said, "I'll let you in on a little secret. There *is* something afoot with the Helix. I think it's at the Defense Department, but I can't talk to you about that. I don't even know how you'd get that kind of information. I guess people talk. Loose lips. No respect for confidentiality."

She said this and felt indignant and then bolstered, equally by the idea of herself risen above the leaking crowd as by Lynne's face, which had reinterested itself in her life.

"*Do* they talk?" Lynne said, sitting up. "Like, everyone, or just a few people?" Her tone was a little aggressive. Again she leaned.

"I might have overstated it. There's talk, sure, but probably there's talk everywhere. I haven't made too many friends yet—I mean, because I'm rarely at my desk—but the people I know seem moderately interested at best."

"But you're *in* the Helix, right?"

"I'm not sure that's any of your business."

"How well's it working out for you? Have you found *true love?*"

Anne-Janet frowned. There was venom here, but who had the energy to care? "Not *yet*," she said. "But if you must know, I was just out with some department friends, and, since you mention it, I did meet someone. A colleague. It was a Helix event, jam-packed."

"I see," Lynne said. "So, basically, if I'm getting this right, you don't give a hoot about anarchists or revolutionaries so long as you're avoiding your mother and scouting for love."

Anne-Janet's mouth opened. Her front teeth were overlaid, of which she was conscious to the point of never opening her mouth except to yawn, talk, eat—certainly not to express surprise or, in this case, alarm, because this Lynne of the close quarters was the most repellent nurse ever.

"I have to go now," she said.

Mental notes: Lynne Somebody, midfifties, Reed Memorial Hospital, short in stature, face arranged like an open cash register. Wears surgical gloves at all times; might be wigged. Further research: look up Jewish Orthodoxy or female hair loss. At least Anne-Janet would have something to do at work.

She returned to her mother, who was, in fact, still asleep. No, she was feigning sleep to avoid chat with her roommate, who had grown vocal about how stuff happens for a reason, like maybe a shot to the gut was going to open doors for her. Maybe her son might come to see in her scrambled intestine a reason to stay out of the gangs. Maybe her boyfriend would come to find in the accident purchase for his self-esteem: he could take care of her, be a man. That neither son nor boyfriend had come did not so much rock her theories as grow them to include the virtue of patience.

Anne-Janet sat on the edge of her mother's bed. "Now, Mom, listen to me. You're just getting a plate and some screws in your hip. Not a big deal. You will piss off everyone at the airport, but that's about it. Recovered in a few weeks."

Marie opened one eye. "I understand I can stay in a rehabilitation center until I am well enough to be self-sufficient. That way I won't be a burden on you."

"Mom, you are not a burden."

"But you can't handle my needs at your place, can you? It's too much. I don't want to be a burden."

Anne-Janet looked away, settled her eyes on the rise and fall of the roommate's chest. It was so tedious, this runaround, her mother never saying what she meant but always getting her wants across.

The roommate said, "You ought to talk to each other—don't just sit there in silence. When my son comes, you can bet we won't just be sitting here in silence. Unless I'm slapping 'im up the head or something. Ow, don't make me laugh. Ow, ow."

Anne-Janet turned to her. "It's fine to sit in silence. This is a hospital. Silence is *fine*."

"No, that's not right. People want to feel like they got people."

"Feel whatever you like," Marie said. "But the bottom line is the same. You're born alone, you die alone"—and she closed her eyes with the thought.

"Mom, you are not alone," Anne-Janet said. But it's not like she didn't know what her sick parent was talking about.

Ned Hammerstein: In my heart, I knew it was true.
DOB 1.18.72 SS# 615-47-2165

Esme couldn't get her clothes off alone, so she used scissors. She cut through the foam tubed around her arms as well. Probably Martin had doubles in the basement. Doubles and triples. Same for her face—he had all the molds—so she pulled it off in haste. She never went to the basement, but it was like an almanac of all the lives she'd taken on as a means of escaping her own. And Martin was her curator. In this way, her only friend. He knew her better than anyone. He'd lifecast her body a hundred times. He had, over the years, captured its bow to time. He could even tame the outpouring of her moods—acne, sweat, tears. They'd had their glory days, though none so glorious as their stint in North Korea. Even Esme was shocked by what they'd managed to pull off there. Shocked and elated and dismantled in ways she hadn't thought possible for anyone, certainly not herself.

She put on a nightie and sleep socks, which came up well above her knees. She looked at her console of TVs. At her daughter's room, where a stuffed platypus was bedfellowed among several sheep and a brindled whale, while Ida kept quarters under the box frame. On a scalloped foam pad. Why choose the underbed instead of the bed itself? Esme couldn't say, but she imagined it was because down there, Ida felt both denied and protected—safe under the crossbeams but also in self-sacrifice, as if martyring her comfort would keep her mother home.

It was too early for Esme to sleep, and so, instead: surveillance, what she did best. She could do this all night; it would be company enough. Ned, Anne-Janet, one feed per channel. She'd had their places bugged and wired. She took out a pen and paper and sat back to record what she saw.

Ned Hammerstein, 2221 hrs: At his desk, typing. Wearing a *Star Wars* X-wing pilot's costume procured via new friends in the 501st Legion's Old Line Garrison. The 501st was mostly a Stormtrooper outfit, but it had connections. Compassion, too. When a man discovered he had a secret twin, and his response was to brandish affinity with the ur-twin, the 501st understood. The costume was pumpkin romper, chest box, black utility belt, leg straps, and, on the floor, a Rotocast vinyl helmet, which Ned would don for video conferencing. For now, though, he was just in a chat room.

> **Girlfriend in a dumpster:** But if Luke & Leia were supposed to be twins in Lucas's grand scheme, why were the actors so dissimilar in appearance, and why all the flirting?

> **Curious Yellow:** Yeah, I still remember my reaction when I heard, "Leia. Leia is my sister!" I was like, huh? Totally UNLIKE my reaction to, "Luke. I am your father." In my heart, I knew it was true!

> **Thomas Merton:** You know, I'm just going to say it. Incest is a taboo because it produces defective children. But if the twins live in a galaxy-spanning Empire, surely they can get gene therapy, or produce their children in a lab so there'll be no defects. And if that's the case, there's NO REASON for them not to get together if they want to.

Ned leaned back in his chair. He liked where this chat was going. He wondered what his sister's name was. And whether she knew about him. His father's company had a PI on retainer, whose job now was to find her. So far, he'd found nothing. But give it time.

The day Ned got back from L.A. with his adoption papers, he changed his voice mail greeting. It still had all the perfunctories—You've reached Ned—but with a new variation: No matter who you are, please leave a message. So far, the upshot had been to encourage his mother to leave several messages when she might otherwise have been cowed, the scene in L.A. still fresh in her mind. Ned answered one call for her every six. She was so sorry. She had never meant for it to come out like this; it was just that his father's antics had her crazy. Neddy, say something. Say something or I will turn on the car in the garage and close all the doors.

Monday was only two days away. What a horror. Was it too soon to call Anne-Janet? He could always find her at work, which might make it that much less of a horror. But it would do nothing for him now.

The phone was ringing. Caller ID said it was his mom. His fake mom. He did not want to answer, but one day she would be dead, and then wouldn't he be sorry.

As it turned out, she was calling not to apologize but to ask about a rumor she'd just heard at a buffet cocktail fund-raiser for the Los Angeles Philharmonic.

"What rumor, Mom?" He said this with a groan.

"Well," she said.

He walked to the fridge, in which was a yogurt and a jar of peanut butter. The choice was obvious. He grabbed a plastic spoon and a paper towel and forked a clump of peanut butter into his mouth. He would not be able to talk for three minutes.

"Am I on speakerphone?" she said. "I hate speakerphone. Oh, go on, don't talk with your mouth full. Okay, so this *rumor*. Wait, you need some background. Ned, honestly, do *not* talk with your mouth full."

He spun in his chair. Nicest thing in the apartment by far. It had wheels and adjustable features like height and angle of recline. He loved this chair, even as it did not love him. He had not been able to wrest it from its current posture in three years.

"So," she said. "You know there are a lot of bigwigs at these functions. People who put a lot of money into politics and expect to be kept in the loop. I was at the oyster bar and looking at your father because he was just sitting by himself. I understand we are having a situation at home—"

"You know, Mom, this sounds like girl talk, and you know who likes girl talk? Girls. *Daughters*. Hey, I heard you had a daughter once. Good thing she's not here for you now." He sounded angry, but really he was depressed. His sister! Maybe she had twists of hair that pecked her neck and shoulders as she walked. Maybe the naves of her eyes were where you went to pray for happiness and got it.

Larissa's voice went dead. "Do you want to hear the rumor or not?"

He posted to the forum. *The thing about Luke is that he's able to do what no other Jedi has so far: he can feel love without turning evil.*

"What, Mom, what? What is your rumor?"

"That the Helix is *weaponized* and that the FBI or CIA or whatever is about to launch some sort of campaign to stop it."

Ned snorted. "I wouldn't know about that, ma'am, I just till the land. Department of the Interior, yeehaw." Like he was going to tell his mother about his speed dates, the RYLS, or anything suckered to the baileys of his heart and climbing over.

"Neddy, I get that you are upset, and that I'm supposed to be patient with whatever you say to me, but at some point, my patience will run out."

"I'm sorry," he said, and then he stopped to consider whether this was true. He tended to apologize by default and figure it out later. But yes, he was sorry. He didn't want to be an asshole, no matter that his whole life was a lie and it was this woman's fault. He yanked at the crotch of his suit; it had been riding up his legs. Maybe this was what he should tell his mother, that he was dressed like Luke Skywalker and, let's face it, would take his privates in hand the moment they hung up. He stared at the strap mullioned down his chest and between his legs.

"Nice rumor," he said.

"Do you think it's crazy?"

"Probably. The Helix is dangerous? Far as I know, they're just trying to help."

Then again, it was possible. Anything was possible now that so many people had thrown in their lot with a weirdo cult whose galvanizing and inexhaustible resource was loneliness in America.

There was a pause on the line. He could hear her thinking. She was worried; he'd have liked her to worry more. Finally, she came out with it. "Do *you* need help, Neddy? Because I know some people in D.C., and if your insurance won't cover it, your father and I have, you know, the funds for it."

He laughed. "You want to palm me off on a shrink?" He laughed again until he noticed a slick of peanut oil on his X-wing fighter jumpsuit.

"No," she said wearily. "I think it'd be better if you just kept it all inside."

"The Helix is harmless," he said. "But even if it weren't, that stuff never goes down well. What are they going to do? Storm the castle?"

"There's a castle?"

"Compound. Whatever."

"They have a compound? How do you know?"

"Mom, stop. I don't know. I'm just saying."

"It's amazing," she said. "The passion is there. Everyone seems so excited about the Helix."

"Are you seriously wondering why?"

He knew she was staring at the family photos ordered atop the piano—her, Max, Ned, year after year—because when she said, "No, not really," it was plangent for all the ways those photos betokened what had been lost to them as a family.

"I gotta go, Mom," he said. And even though she had not said bye, he hung up.

Esme turned off the TV. She was peeling a clementine. The rind was clotted under her nails and tinting them orange. She was not surprised news of ARDOR had gotten out. Security leaks were a D.C. special, ever since that megalomaniac sprung the Pentagon Papers. These days you couldn't piss on a toilet seat without someone telling the *Washington Post*. Still, it pained her to imagine the project name on someone else's lips and contextualized poorly. It wasn't even her idea, this name, just some guy at the Joint Chiefs tapping the JANAP 299 for a suitable word, the irony being that these words traditionally hewed to projects that did not bear out their meaning (Manhattan Project, anyone?). And yet there it was, ARDOR, which classified Jim Bach's stint to dismantle the Helix and its guru.

Esme heard a phone ring, but since it was not her phone—cell, in-house, or the secure line—she looked up at screen two just as Anne-Janet considered the name on her caller ID—Do I answer? Do I have the stamina? Can I alchemize my mood from depressed to effervescent?—and then listened to the dial tone on the machine. Ned had hung up. Damn. Double damn, since now she couldn't call him back. If she called him back, he'd know she was screening. What sort of a woman screens? A reclusive, awkward woman who doesn't know how to wear makeup or to feather the underside of a man's penis with her tongue.

Anne-Janet pressed her feet into Lyndon/Lady Bird slippers. They looked like cots wrapped in the American flag, and at the head of each, on a pillow, a rubber face that couldn't sleep; the future of the country was on their minds.

She plunked on the couch and flipped on the TV, except that the TV was broken, what the fuck? She was big on visualization and tried, immediately, to picture herself at the bottom of the ocean among fish and kelp. It was placid there, and all was well. All was well except for the part where her TV was broken, and OH MY GOD, her TV was broken! Maybe the RCA cable had gotten loose. It was not loose. She checked her Internet connection and this, too, was out. So the cable was out in the building. Fixed tomorrow. Or the day after. An inconvenience for some; a fiasco for Anne-Janet. She did not even have a radio. So the question posed by this cable outage was: How will I ever fall asleep tonight and, more alarming, if I cannot sleep, how will I bear the solitude? Anne-Janet could not stand solitude. If left to her own thoughts, she would think of her dad, at which point she'd retreat so far into herself, no one would be able to get her out. And how can you expect to be loved when you can't even be reached? Five nights out of six she slept on the couch so as to be with the TV. Other nights she listened to podcasts on her computer. The more boring the show, the better. She had taken to listening to a man share negotiating tips—how to haggle a raise—which knocked her out in eight to nine minutes. If the speaker was British, she would not last five. Academic men who touted God were her favorite—three minutes—followed closely by men who tracked wildlife in Africa. The whispering was key: *Here we are looking at an African aoudad nursing her young.*

Anne-Janet looked for a cassette player, a CD player, an iPod, knowing she did not own these conveniences. She picked up the phone. Maybe she could call a disconnected number and put the response on speakerphone. If you'd like to make a call, please hang up and dial again. Would that put her to sleep? She began to panic.

Esme logged the scene. She knew how to condense. *2315 hrs: Anne-Janet Tabetha Riggs bursts into tears for fear of silent night.*

After, she got in bed and thought it over. Ned would be happy to go to Cincinnati—plenty of cloud cover in the Midwest. And Anne-Janet, she'd be cake, too, Esme's logic being that people who were dead inside would do most anything. This was true of Esme, and while there was a degree of faulty generalization in her estimate of the world, she'd never been wrong yet.

Two recruits down, two to go: Olgo and Bruce. Both men were planked across the ruin of their private lives—how hard could it be to entice them elsewhere?

She called Martin to schedule his magic. First thing tomorrow, 6 a.m.

Olgo Panjabi: Wresting accord from the teeth of hostility.
DOB 2.2.45 SS# 035-33-4932

Sunday! Day of rest for some, for others a carnival at a high school gym, where couples were wrecking and rebuilding each other's lives with every toss of the bean.

Olgo was by the launch site. "I still wish you'd been there," he said.

His wife dropped her mallet. She'd launched fifty frogs, though none at the pad of her aiming. "We celebrated before," she said. "Who needs two birthday parties?"

"The Helix was there, which was interesting, I guess."

"Really? Why didn't you tell me?"

"You would have come for the Helix and not me?"

"Don't be silly. Did you see Thurlow Dan?"

He sighed. Scanned the gym for his granddaughter, who was just making her way back to them. Tennessee Panjabi Bach. She could stay at this carnival for hours; Olgo might not last another minute.

"The lunatic? No, I imagine he was at home, voodooing the president."

She frowned. "Like you'd understand. That man is giving us purpose. Now stand back," she said. "Here we go."

She shimmied her rear and made to spit on her palms before gripping the mallet.

Tennessee laughed. Olgo turned away. Thurlow Dan was giving them purpose? He hated talk like that. Talk like that nicked the shared ethos of his marriage, which had been his pride to consolidate every day.

"Where's my mom?" Tennessee said. "When's she coming?"

He took her hand. They had been through this nine times. "She's with your father. She'll be here soon. Now, watch this." He asked for a drumroll. Quiet, please. Kay uprose the mallet and whacked. She whacked and missed.

"I wanna try," said Tennessee.

"In a sec," Kay said. She hoisted the mallet and whacked. This time the resulting *thwump* meant contact between the mallet and her shin.

"Crap!" she said, and she covered her mouth.

"I wanna try!"

Kay's T-shirt was gamy with sweat from the day's play—bean toss, spill-the-milk, Skee-ball, down-a-clown—but still wearable so long as Tenn *let go*. And then, "In a sec. One more try for Grandma. One or two. Frog hop is my specialty."

Whack. Whack, whack, whack, whack, whack, whack, whack.

Kay dropped the mallet and bent forward, hand to knee, panting. "I'm done," she said, and she stood upright. Her lips were dry and notably chapped, given the dew that overspread her face. Ventilation here was poor. And the smell of laps and burpies rose up from the floorboards, no matter the Lysol charged to suppress it.

Olgo looked for the exits. As part of the school's talent for child endangerment, it had blocked one door with a basketball net. The other door was near the bleachers. He tried to take Kay's hand. In recent weeks, she had been cranky in ways too minor to dwell on but that, in sum, had come to seem alarming, and maybe indicative of bad health. He'd heard people could get testy apropos bad health. Like if her eyesight were shot and she couldn't see the frog, wouldn't she pound on it in denial? Or if her ears were wrecked and she couldn't hear the phone? Last week it had rung twenty times before she picked up, Olgo calling from work to say he missed her—they still did this kind of thing—and Kay saying, "Well, maybe if you bought a better phone I could *hear* it; this phone is pitched for bats," followed by a slamming of the phone into its cradle and the cradle into the fridge. Apparently, his wife had something she needed to work out.

Kay gave Tennessee the mallet and leaned against the wall, which was padded in blue mats. "*Basta,*" she said, "Grandma's moving on."

Only the child had other ideas. She ran to where the frog had landed, east of the bull's-eye, tossed it in the air, and swung. Frog baseball.

Olgo looked away. Last week, he'd tried to call Kay back. No answer. After that, he'd scanned his office, because you somehow expect the upheaval of your life to attract notice and are often disappointed to find otherwise. He was caboosed with problems he needed to unload. There was anxiety about his new job because he thought the Department of the Interior had hired him to mediate the Indian land claims, except no one had told him anything about them since. There was anxiety about his age—maybe sixty was not the new forty—and a sense that his daughter's divorce imbroglio would bleed his pension dry. And finally, a growing fear that no one wanted to drink from the fount of wisdom that was, in the town square of his mind, its centerpiece.

He could not discuss these things with Kay—she was his wife, not his therapist—but he thought it best to talk to someone. So he'd cruised his office building, looking to offload. Except just having to walk the hallways, which were girthed for a bus, maybe two, and traverse the floors— caramelized rock, cream and liver diamonds—to pass eyes across the framed photos on every wall (nature is beautiful!) and the pastorals of farmers harvesting the land: this safari through Interior was to trade the humdrum of nine-to-five for a venture in self-pity.

"So were there lots of Helix there?" Kay said.

"I don't know. I only have eyes for you," and he kissed her on the cheek.

She swatted him away but smiled.

"And another thing," he said. "I *am* doing something at work. I'm setting a big meeting up now. With the Cayuga Nation. We need to bring everyone back to the table, else one of these days there are actually going to be mini sovereign states all over the country. Wouldn't that be insane? And wouldn't that mean something if I could help?"

"I guess," she said. "Though you've been saying that about the home front, too."

"Hey, I *offered*. I told Erin she didn't need a lawyer."

And with this he stood up tall. Lawyers were adversarial by design— they did not know how to compromise—and so what his daughter's divorce needed was the smooth handling of a man with skill.

"Must be some lawyer, though," Kay said. "They're meeting on a Sunday. Maybe Jim's having an affair with her, too."

"Kay!" He spit a little by accident. "I hope this mess doesn't affect Tenn badly. Divorce is awful. Just look at her." Though he was still looking at Kay, pleased to have fired a killer word of his own— *divorce*—which no happily married woman could hear without it reaffirming her vows in silence.

They looked. Tennessee was whaling on the frog and attracting other kids to the game.

Kay said, "I wish Erin weren't coming with Jim. That guy is such a creep. All those Defense Department guys are creeps."

"He's not coming to socialize. I guess he has Tennessee for the rest of the weekend."

"He's a creep."

"You liked him when they got married."

"I liked *you* when we got married. What's your point?"

Olgo blinked.

"I'm kidding," she said. "But don't look now—here they come."

He turned. His daughter's hair was cantaloupe and often gathered in a high ponytail, so that in a crowd you tended to spot it well before she spotted you. This had its benefits—for instance, the chance to wrest Tennessee from the execution of Mr. Parker (she'd given the frog a name because, she explained, every frog has a *name*) and to present her in fine form, shaped by an hour's exposure to her grandparents, their bonhomie and warmth.

Erin kissed him on the cheek.

"How did it go?" Kay said.

Olgo surveilled his wife's face. Was she thinking about the lawyer bills, too? Because they were funding this thing until the judge took from Jim everything he owned.

"It might have gone fine," Erin said, "if Jim hadn't shown up with his new sugar-mommy girlfriend. At least, she'd better be a sugar mommy, because otherwise he's lost it. You ought to see this woman. She's older than him, and she looks like someone beat her face in from both sides."

Olgo looked down at his shoe. Female jealousy, awful. Probably Jim's girlfriend was Brigitte Bardot.

Kay said, "It's okay, honey. So she's a troll. You get what you deserve. What did the lawyers say?"

"Standard stuff. They couldn't agree on anything. We're going to court."

"What do you know," Olgo said.

Erin closed her eyes. "Like you could have done better? I get the bed, he gets the sheets?"

"See," he said, "that off-the-cuff thing you do, that's exactly why you need a mediator. A *compassionate, trained* mediator."

"Dad, try to think of something *besides* how useful you are to the world. I'm getting a divorce, remember?"

Kay said, "So where is Prince Charming?"

Erin pointed. Good God. Jim and lady friend were in a clearing of children by feed-the-monkey, the children giving berth to the lady because, while she was only slightly taller than the tallest, she was clearly not of their kind.

"Wow," said Olgo.

"Wasn't kidding, was I? Sugar mommy."

"Let's be cordial," said Olgo.

"No way," Kay said.

"I disagree. We should set an example for Tenn. Divorce is not the end of family."

He said this and shuddered, while Kay made for Jim and Sugar Mommy.

Olgo regarded his daughter, who looked tired. At work, on his corkboard, among the push pins, list of log-in names and passwords, phone numbers and extensions, was a photo of Erin with Tennessee. And next to it, a JFK quote—*Let us never negotiate out of fear, but let us never fear to negotiate*—because it was smart and also a tribute to the syntactical conceit known as the polyptoton, a redeploying of the same word in different form, *fear* as noun and verb. It was JFK's genius to use the polyptoton as much as possible, and Olgo had tried to use it to rear his child as she grew from adolescent to teenager to woman. They'd be sitting at breakfast over Cheerios. She might have gotten a bad grade in algebra. He'd say: Erin, when you're upset, it upsets everything you do. And she'd say: What are you talking about? They'd be on the porch swing. She might have broken up with Jake, high school lothario. He'd say: You don't need to love a love like that. And she'd say: Oh, Dad, enough.

He touched her sleeve. "Are you sure you don't want to give me a chance?"

"Yes, Dad. This isn't your fight. Jim's been cheating on me with that troll. And he's at work the rest of the time, anyway. Thing is, I know he's up to no good at the department. I should just use that shit against him."

"What are you talking about?"

"The Helix? Earth to Dad? Jim's up to something. And you know what? Toasters will fly before it's legal."

"You shouldn't get involved."

"I *am* involved. God. I gotta say, this head-in-the-sand attitude of yours isn't doing you any favors."

"Just because I don't care about the Helix means I don't live in the world? Five seconds ago you were railing at me for being *too* involved."

"I think you missed the point on that one."

"I always do, right?"

She snorted. "It's just so perfect you work for the Department of the *Interior*."

"Did you really just make that joke? What has happened to all the women in this family?"

"Just be glad you're not related to *her*"—which made Olgo smile despite it all. Jim's new girlfriend—she could probably pop balloons with that dagger of a face.

Enough. He walked over to Jim. Inroads would be made.

"Jim!" he said. "So nice to see you. Lost a little weight, I see. No one to cook for ya, huh? Har har."

Jim was in jeans that were cinched below the waist and bunched favorably at the groin; a V-neck cashmere sweater; crisp white T; and leather boots. His affect was self-conscious casual, which typified the way he belittled Erin—the offhand remark hatched in his head hours or years before.

A nod, not hostile but distanced. "This is Lynne," Jim said, and he motioned to his woman, who produced a hand gloved in tweed. The shake took longer than Olgo intended, and throughout, she gazed on him with an ill will whose aura was unwholesome. Smutty, even. He withdrew his hand.

Jim went off with Kay, which left Olgo alone with Lynne.

"Well then," he said. "Nice carnival. Have you ever been here before? This is my first time."

"Of course," she said. "I have a daughter," and she retrieved from her purse a dusting cloth, which she passed across the face of her personal digital assistant. Olgo took this as a good sign. She was going to show him pictures of her daughter. In the literature of negotiating theory, this move harked back to the now-famous and seminal gesture of solicitude in which Jimmy Carter personalized photos for Begin's eight grandkids at Camp David. Meirav, Michal, Avital, Naama, Avina,

Avinadav, Jonathan, Ayellet. Whole thing might have collapsed if he hadn't done that. What a winner.

Olgo waited as she fussed with the device, except when she was done, she just put it away.

"So," she said, and nearly yawned. "Jim tells me you work for the Department of the Interior."

She took three steps for his every one; he had trouble keeping pace. How odd that Jim mentioned him.

"It's a new appointment for me, but I'm working a few of the Indian land claims. Interesting stuff."

"Really? Jim made it sound dull as bones."

Ah, so he mentioned it for the purpose of trashing the appointment. Typical Jim.

"Not all of us get to big-shot around the Defense Department, that is true. But it's still fascinating work. We're keeping things together."

"Together," Lynne said. "You're sixty?"

He nodded. "Just the other day, in fact."

"I see. Happy birthday, Olgo Panjabi."

"You see what?"

"Nothing. Just—nothing."

"What?"

"Oh, just that it must be hard, getting to your age and knowing you never quite made it past the first rung. That probably they'll force you to retire with no fanfare. I guess that's just the way, though. I mean, what does any federal employee do with his time? Wander around the building looking for someone to talk to? Fight with his wife? Read the Indian Reorganization Act and prod it for holes?"

"Are you always this rude?" he said. "Because I think it'd take some real effort always to be this rude."

He looked away and tried to compose himself. She had, after all, struck a nerve. Ever since he was a young man, he'd felt like he was hurtling through life without a plan. Other people had talent; what did he have? Ambition. To be great, to be famous, to hallow the immigrant story of his father's life. Problem was, the pressure of having to succeed had left him without anything he wanted to succeed at. His parents thought he was just dreamy and clung to the idea that their boy was a work in progress whose afflatus would yield something great in time. It never had, though maybe his time was now. The Indian land claims were a mess, but there was real opportunity in this strife to abate solipsism and ill will.

"Maybe we should just join the others," he said.

"Not yet. I think your wife and Jim have a lot to talk about."

"I doubt that," he said.

"No, really. The Helix brings people together. Which should interest you, no? Because of your work?"

"Right, the Helix. My wife's not a member. Since when is Jim?"

She laughed. "He's not. No chance of that. And yet just look at them go."

He watched them by the water fountain. Kay and Jim were, it was true, talking animatedly.

"I gather your wife's found a new passion."

He turned Lynne's way but was stopped by the hatred that seemed to cement in his blood; he suddenly hated this woman beyond reason.

He looked again at his wife. When was the last she had spoken to him with such presence? Weeks? Years? He could probably trawl their history together and come up short.

They would be married for thirty-five years next month. The first thing he'd noticed about her when they started dating was the ferocity of her independence. He had wanted to open doors; she refused. He'd try to walk nearest to the road; she'd balk. She did not want to be taken care of. And yet she'd flirted with him desperately. So forget what she said; she needed him. Or someone. Her mother had left her family without warning—what does that do to a girl? He had an idea. And the idea saved his life. A girl whose mother splits looks for a man whose best accomplishment is loving her.

Lynne said, "Thirty-five years is a long time, Olgo. Way to keep the love alive."

He stopped their progress to the booth. These barbs Lynne was tossing his way—enough! "Do you have something to say to me?" he said. "I can't for the life of me understand what your problem is, but I'm willing to have a go at solving it. I don't know what Jim told you about us, but the way you're acting, my guess is that it was pretty bad."

"On the contrary, Jim said you were all very nice. Kind and decent people."

His eyes popped. He didn't know how to handle this woman. If he'd met her at the negotiating table, he'd have wept.

Luckily, Kay returned with Jim in tow.

"Nice chat?" Olgo said.

"Very. Look, the line for the pedestal joust is the shortest it's been all day."

"You want to do that?"

"What, are you too old for the joust? Come on, Gramps," and Kay took his sleeve, pulling him through the crowd. The arena was inflated—like a giant kiddie pool—and home to sponge blocks on which the players tried to maintain balance while fighting. He thought she just wanted to squirrel him away for debriefing post-Jim. But no, she actually wanted to joust. They got in line.

"So what happened?" he said.

"We didn't really talk about the divorce."

"Let me guess: The Helix? Thurlow Dan? Kay, am I missing out on something here? I feel like I'm being left out. "

Kay seemed about to tell him what was on her mind, but then reared as if the wind had blown her back from the edge and she'd never come that close again.

"We're up," she said.

A student gave him the required helmet, and when he couldn't fit it over his head, the student yelled to a classmate behind the arena, "Get the stretch machine, we got a big one."

"This is humiliating," Olgo said. "I don't want to do this. Why is my head so much bigger than yours? Than anyone here's?"

"Ego," she said.

He flushed. "Are you mad at me? Did I do something?"

She squeezed his shoulder. "Here, watch. Jim and I will have a go." She gave him her purse to hold. He was tempted to upturn its contents and discover a clue—a report from the lab: prognosis dire; an arrest warrant; IRS audit—anything to explain this hostility.

Kay and Jim mounted the pedestals. They wore hockey gloves and visors. Kay held her jousting pole like a spear, like she might just hurl it at Jim and hope for the best. Jim stood with pole upright. He was waiting for her to make the first move. She squared the pole and swiped at his bread box.

"What's this?" Erin said. She had Tennessee in hand.

"I have no idea," Olgo said. "But, sweetheart?"—and here he took a deep breath. "Have you noticed anything different about your mother? Anything at all?"

He did not look at Erin as he asked. He was almost trembling. You did not invite your child into the travails of your marriage.

"She's dyeing her hair. I noticed that first thing."

Olgo looked in Kay's direction, but she was, of course, wearing a helmet.

"A new color?" he said.

Erin cocked her head. "Maybe it's you we should be worried about. No, not a new color. Just to strip the gray."

The joust was over. Neither fighter had lost touch with the pedestal, which left a panel of three kids to decide the bout based on number of swats landed and which adult they liked best.

Kay wrestled with her headgear. Easier to get on than off. She looked like one of those domestic animals caught with its snout in a paper bag. Finally the helmet popped off, and her hair came down in rowdy strips. Bark, cocoa, black cherry—the flaunting of colors was hard to miss, only since Kay wore her hair pinned up, even to bed, how was Olgo to know?

She won the decision. Two to one.

Erin said, "Tough break, Jim."

Kay drank from a water bottle, letting the excess dribble down her chin. She'd yet to corral her hair and was flush with victory. She lapped the group with arms high, saying: "Kay Denny-Panjabi takes the gold! What an upset! Anything is possible for her now!"

Olgo shook his head. He didn't need to use the bathroom, but he went anyway. He was so confused. Tears were likely. Lynne, Erin, Kay—it was as though they were teamed up to kill the motor that kept him going. He pushed his way through the crowd, slowing down once he got clear of the others. An arm linked up with his.

"Cheer up, Olgo Panjabi. It's not so bad." Lynne smiled up at him. "Tomorrow is a new day. Things could get interesting for you, and maybe that's just what you need. There're other fences to mend besides the Indians'."

"Who the hell *are* you?" he said. "And what do you want with me?"

"Tomorrow is a new day, Olgo. You heard it here first."

He kept walking. Stopped at the door to the bathroom, afraid she would follow him in. But she was gone. So was Jim. Erin and Tennessee. He scanned the room for Kay, fearing she had left, too. But no. She was at the *zeppole* stand, licking powdered sugar from the tip of a finger cleaved to a hand cleaved to an arm, a torso, a body, and finally to a man—a *stranger*—whose life was not consecrated to Kay's happiness, her needs and care, but to something else altogether, chiefly to the ruin of her marriage to Olgo Panjabi.

He retreated to the bathroom. Looked at himself in the mirror. Said: "There are other fences to mend. Tomorrow is a new day. I did not see what I just saw."

Bruce Bollinger: Whose features do not impress on their own but which, in the aggregate, give the impression of a man who's verged on disillusion with everything that matters; he's calling it quits any day. Henceforth: *Verge Face.*
DOB 9.4.62 SS# 202-64-1592

Bruce picked at a gristle of cheese welded to an oven mitt. He thought: Okay, Crystal, where are you? It's Sunday, and I want to leave this house. I cannot babysit my wife. I love my wife, but today I can't do it. How long before she starts crying? Has there ever been a wife who cries more than mine? If Crystal ever gets here, there will be no crying.

He put his ear to the bedroom door. Rita was crying. And calling his name. He tiptoed to the kitchen and crouched behind the fridge. She called again. In doing so, she dwelled on the *ew* of Bruce so that his name toured the house until it found him. During their early court-ship, this had been hot, the melody of the call a G–E progression that generally meant Come here, lover boy. Now, the progression reversed, it meant simply Come here, shithead.

Why? Because she was pregnant and it was not going well. Her uterus was loose, the upshot being four months in bed. One hundred twenty days. She'd only just started, and it was torture. As much for him as her. Just now, she'd dropped the TV remote. What did bed rest mean, exactly? Would she actually lose the baby from picking the re-mote off the floor? The baby would *fall out?* Why was it okay to walk to the bathroom? Here was an idea: maybe she could grab the remote on her way.

"Bruce!"

He checked his watch. He'd never taken interest in Rita's friends until now. Now they marched in one after the other, bearing casse-roles and pie. He and Rita were putting on weight at the same pace. Only Rita was not experiencing the same gastrointestinal distress. He wondered at her resilience. A hormonal thing? To mention it seemed ill advised, but since Bruce frequently departed from his better sense, he let it be known he envied her. To which: You *envy* me? Get out. And close the door behind you.

He'd been sleeping on the couch. Pregnancy can strain a marriage. A bad pregnancy can test your vows. Crystal was the day's rescue. She was half an hour late.

He turned on the video camera and stormed the bedroom.

"Turn that thing off," Rita said. "You know I hate that thing. I look awful."

"You'll be glad for it later. Trust me."

She pulled the covers over her head. He deposited the camera on the floor. He'd been filming her pregnancy in snatches—when she wasn't looking, as she slept—because his son's ratcheting to life was too precious to ignore. Also, the tedium and stress of her venture were moving. Humane. An easy pregnancy would have been great, preferable to be sure, but without emotional content. At least not the kind Bruce was always wanting to capture on film. Normal people drafting their lives, and getting it wrong each time. Reality TV moved him to tears.

He picked up the remote and got in bed. Hand on her belly, he imagined the life inside. A little boy, ready to stretch and grow and case the joint.

She blew at her bangs. He loved that she still wore bangs. Blond and wispy.

"Just look at my fingers," she said, and she began to cry.

They were swollen. At this rate, her wedding ring would have to be cut off. No way was it sliding over her knuckle. Look at that knuckle!

"It's okay, baby. You get skinny fingers from changing diapers. I read that somewhere."

She thwumped him in the chest with a felt sack of herbs, because she had opinions about karma, chief among them that good karma could be bought for the price of a sack of herbs.

"That stuff reeks," he said. "Junior's probably getting high and loving it. No, no, wait, I was just kidding, don't cry again. I was just kidding! I'm sure the herbs and candles and quilt and rock fountain are all doing their job. Come on, honey, let's see what's on TV."

"I'm trying to read," she said. "You took so long for the remote, I decided to read instead. It relaxes me."

He laughed. In the last few months, his wife had taken an interest in political philosophy. She was, perhaps, having an identity crisis hastened by the onslaught of progeny who tend to ask questions like: Do I have a penis? Does God exist? What is a libertarian? Rita did not know her leanings because she did not know what any of the parties stood for.

Today's text was Carl Oglesby and his speech at the March on Washington in '65.

"This is relaxing?" Bruce said. He skimmed the flap copy to see who the hell Carl Oglesby was.

"It's edifying," she said. "I want to know things for when the baby comes."

"I hardly think he'll be asking you about Carl Oglesby. At least not before age two."

She closed the book. He tried to free the remote from her hand, but she resisted. This was her kingdom, the bedroom TV; no way was she ceding control to him. She began with channel 2 and went from there.

"Seen it," he said of the vampire drama in syndication on three channels.

"How do you know? It's a commercial."

"I've seen them all."

"Where do you find the time?"

"Such is the burden of the unemployed. What do you think I did all day while you were at work?"

"I don't know, look for a job?"

This was not a pleasant topic. He was on thin ice. Before the Department of the Interior, he'd been unemployed for six months. The only career he wanted was one, if his track record was any kind of litmus, he had zero chance of getting. Errol Morris. Ken Burns. Michael Moore. They *sucked*. You know who didn't suck? Or who might not suck if given the chance? Or who, if he sucked, would kill himself? Bruce. Bruce Bollinger, who sounded just imperious enough on the phone to get through to some producer who would shut him down immediately. Something like: Oh, Bruce Bollinger who wants production money, funding, yes, yes, a very important film, life changing, I see, sounds great. No.

Bruce kept a notebook in his bag at all times. In it were sayings of spiritual value. *A documentarian walks among the living, though he himself is dead.*

He used to refer to that one a lot; it helped with his day jobs. Working on set for TV shows imported from abroad and dubbed to fit. His last: chess-playing families who enacted their moves on a battlefield. His job? *Cue the rooks!*

After that, he seemed to catch sight, wherever he went, of a new television show on which contestants ate worms for money. Worms, millipedes, ants. In general, he tried to restrict his TV intake to offerings that did not question God's wisdom in peopling the world with such as us, but sometimes stuff happens. The show had been on at the gym, on a screen right above the only elliptical trainer left. It was on at Best Buy, where he'd gone to peruse gadgets he could not afford. So there he was, eyeing the cameras, just him and the bug show that grossed millions. Where was the human side of this show? The intrigue? Every competition needed intrigue.

Thus: an idea. A show in which there were, okay, trials of fortitude, though these would hardly be the point. Say the show was called *Trial by Liar*. Say you had one person who knew what the trial was but could lie about it, and another person who had to guess. Lying or not? The show would be about people having to figure each other out. They might live together for a week to this end. It could be moving. It could be a documentary series in the guise of something just stupid enough to sell. The Helix was out there doing basically the same thing, so why not Bruce?

He spent three days drafting the proposal and first few episodes. Meetings were set. He flew to L.A. the next day. Chop, chop, Bruce. And when Rita said: What's the rush? he went: Chop, chop, Rita. He had five minutes before the networks lost interest or stole the project.

She said, "But you've been down this road before. Fly out there like a slave, get feted for a day, and then six months later no one has gotten back to you, yea or nay."

He was throwing socks in a duffel. "You need faith, Rita. This business is not for quitters."

She rolled her eyes. "Okay, but don't cry on my shoulder when it falls to pieces."

He stood with boxers in hand. Said, "And the Oscar for best supporting wife goes to . . ."

"I just don't want you to be disappointed."

He got to L.A., had his meetings, and it was exactly as Rita had said. Two months waiting by the phone and then an email from his agent: Sorry, but no.

A documentarian drinks to excess.

Bruce managed to keep the information to himself for two days before Rita broke him down. To her credit, she did not say I told you so, just held his hand and said there would be other opportunities.

A month later, watching a movie about boarding-school kids and their nasty parents, he heard tell of the carpe diem spirit, which he took to mean: for the sake of *Trial by Liar,* you should collateral your house and take out a loan. He'd already promised Rita that, no matter what, he would not gamble to finance his projects. She thought he had a gambling problem, which he didn't, though if he did, she got the idea from that one time at Atlantic City. On their honeymoon. She'd gone from slot to slot, betting nickels and dimes. He had nibbled her ear. They had pulled the handles together. He had just started prep on a film about people who fake their own deaths to escape the law. She'd thought it was a great idea. He'd needed to raise about $30 K. He had 2. They'd talked and laughed and she'd leaned over his shoulder at blackjack and it was romantic and it was fun. Fun until it wasn't. By night's end, he was out nine thousand dollars, and she was online, ordering books that promised to attenuate addiction. It was impossible to pair these words—*attenuate, addiction*—but the books said otherwise. They said his problem, though he did not have a problem, was surmountable. But what did they know? His problem, if you could call it that, was that he just wasn't very lucky. He never gambled without a project that needed funding in mind. That he always had a project was beside the point.

Was a loan gambling? Only if you weren't 100 percent sure you'd pay it back on time. So, no: not gambling. *Trial by Liar* was going to make it. He went to the bank, and the rest was easy: a deal with a cable station that broadcast only to the East Coast but was seen in a million homes. As for Rita, she was on a need-to-know basis; that was what a good marriage was about. He'd make the money back and use the profits to buy her peridot earrings.

The show attracted notice. It was raw and depressing. Some of the people were crazy. Others were violent. There were fights and tears. And for Bruce: vindication. He was not making money, not *yet,* but he was pleased. There was room in the canon of documentary filmmaking for work such as this. Unhappy people engaged in the venture of character assessment, which is a venture of love.

In the meantime, though, he was running out of capital. The major networks had not called. Pepsi had not called. The interest rate on his loan was awesome, and his wife wanted a baby.

Many nights over dinner he'd say the finances were prohibitive, to which she'd say: Oh come on, and woo him to bed. Which was, in the end, just fine. Those times together ranked as some of the best of their marriage, Rita being of the idea that the more explosive his orgasm, the smarter his sperm would be. She tried hard. She tried everything.

Bruce, for his part, enjoyed what he could and sabotaged the rest. He'd been working with a laptop poised hotly on his groin. He'd started wearing briefs a size too small. And with each passing month, he began to think his efforts were paying off. That, or there was something amiss on her end. Never mind. Their sex was great, she was not getting pregnant, he was safe.

But not for long, because Rita decided to do what most women her age do: make appointments, get tests.

The show got canceled. Bruce was paid to give a few talks about underground programming and used the fees to bankroll an online gambling bender that cost him one of two savings bonds, the other of which he used to shred his debt, which, it turned out, was impossible. There would be no money for a college fund or life insurance. There'd be no money for a crib. But still he said nothing. He spent his days in the park and came home to his wife stabbing herself in the gut with hormones. She braved the drugs and procedures and shots, and so there was just no telling her what he had done.

The day she got pregnant was etched in his mind as the most confusing of his life. The panic was incredible. The joy unbridled. The effort it took to hide the panic almost life threatening. The ease with which he took her in his arms and squeezed: wonderful. They were having a baby! He threw up in the bathroom. He had sworn never to tell her about the gambling and the loan, and then he told her everything. This meant the day she got pregnant became the most confusing of her life, too. Could she still trust her husband? Did she still love her husband? She was so angry, she threw up in the bathroom. He would have to get a job. Any job in any field. She'd take on extra work until maternity leave. They'd fire the cleaning lady and cut out the luxuries. It all seemed reasonable, and he swore to do exactly as told. But a job in any field? Was he supposed to janitor just because he was creative and creativity did not pay? Was he being punished for wanting more than the next guy? No, he was being punished for ruining their life. He promised to look for work the next day.

He cruised the job sites online. He uploaded his résumé and met the relevant parties and tried to be agreeable, though it never occurred to him actually to work in these places. A job in HR at a pharmaceutical company? A super for Curtis Building Management? Come on, he was a show runner! In most cases, he was not offered work, anyway, which was fine. He could say he tried and spend another day watching the vampire slayer on TV.

The weeks passed. Rita would spot blood and cramp and spot some more. Spotting, gushing. Something was wrong. On the day she went to the hospital for surgery and was prescribed bed rest, Bruce was offered a position with the phone company, customer service. Only such was his rush to refuse the job, he'd forgotten to wipe the answering machine before Rita got home. They spoke for a while on the couch. She wasn't feeling well. And she was worried. They'd consolidated their debt and cut way back, but to minimal effect. They weren't saving money. And the baby was due in less than five months. She'd had her head on his shoulder when she noticed the 1 on the answering machine and went for it. Bruce did nothing. It was like watching a bottle of wine roll off the table. Not enough wherewithal to stop it but full knowledge that here was a disaster.

They fought. She hemorrhaged. Two weeks later, the phone rang. "This is the Department of the Interior," said some strange woman who seemed to know a lot about him, followed by a job offer and signing bonus. To do what, exactly? Footage consultant. Had he applied for a job there? He couldn't remember. Never mind, there was no arguing at dinner, no discussion. Bruce simply accepted the job and started work.

"Can I have the remote now?" he said.

"No."

They'd been watching *Les Misérables* on pay per view. She said,

"You know, most of the radicals in this country are fixated on their commitment to revolution way more than on the revolution itself. They don't want to succeed. Because if they did, they couldn't be radicals anymore, and a radical is most interested in his sense of being a radical."

He shifted to his side. "See, this is why you need to stop with all that reading. It's making you sound like a crank. Where do you get these ideas?"

"Just look around."

"I am. And what I see is a middle-class couple watching *Les Mis* on a Sleep Number bed."

"Crystal could probably put what I said better, anyway."

"Oh, so this is Crystal talking. I'd like to meet this fount of conservatism."

"She's not conservative. She's Helix. A level-headed reformist."

"Aha."

"Get me that brush while you're up?" she said.

It was on her nightstand. He tossed it her way. "Anything else?"

"It's snowing out. I bet Crystal's not going to make it."

His heart sank. Crystal, do not do this to me! The doorbell rang. And rang again, because he was so busy lamenting the afternoon ahead, he didn't hear it.

"Want to get that?" Rita said.

He made for the door. A young woman with a canvas bike bag and a box of chocolate peppermint bark. Eighteen years old. Twenty, tops. "Yes?" he said.

"I'm here for Rita. You must be Bruce."

She wore a hat with a yarn pom-pom dusted in snow. The cuffs of her jeans were soggy.

"You're Crystal?"

"The very one."

She took off her boots in the doorway. They were shag Inuit boots with tassels and incongruous rubber soles. She took off her gloves, coat, scarf, and sweater, and piled them on the radiator. She'd looked much bigger a second ago.

"My wife's in the bedroom," he said. "Follow me."

"I know the way."

She trotted down the hall: guess she'd been here before.

He decided to make nice. Brew some tea, make a tray of chocolate and whatever else was in the fridge.

Crystal had pulled up an armchair and rested her feet on the mattress. Awfully chummy, these two. Her socks were penguins on the beach. Rita had put on her glasses, which she never did in company. They were giant. Brown and plastic, and hitched to a chain around her neck. She was reading out loud. Bruce leaned against the door frame and waited.

Crystal put up her hand as if to say: Not in front of the husband. But Rita shrugged it off. "He's fine," she said, and she kept going:

> As the seizure, four years back, of the presidency from the will of the people has perverted the Constitution.
> As liberal Americans have a common stake in the enterprise of justice and must be common sufferers of its dispatch.
> As the government's hostility to principles of democracy mandates a reluctant but immediate exercise of protest.

Rita looked over her glasses at Crystal, who said, "So what do you think? We're passing them out at the meeting today."

"I think it's good. It's got moral authority."

Bruce cleared his throat, wanting to jump in.

"You think?" Crystal said. "Because we haven't gotten input from HQ. Not yet, anyway. Thurlow's a busy man."

Rita nodded. She'd read every speech Thurlow Dan had given, and none had actually mentioned interest in the travesty helming the government or that he thought the political strife of 2000 had turned into a bald divide no country could sustain, so revolt. But still, the message was there. Implicitly. Loud and implicit. Revolt!

"We were going for a certain tone," Crystal said. "Like, you sort of want to call up the language of back then but not the substance."

"Exactly," Rita said. "Because if anything, the Confederates have all the power now. Total role reversal."

Bruce cleared his throat again. And when they continued to ignore him, he said, "Uh, there are no Confederates anymore."

Crystal returned her feet to the floor so she could one-eighty and regard the idiot by the door. Rita gazed at him from above the rim of her glasses. Their faces were the essence of pity.

"What?" he said. "Don't look at me like that."

Crystal said, "Okay, but surely you've got a problem with what's happening. Everyone with a brain has a problem with it. This government represents only half, *half*, of Americans. And the wrong half at that. You call that a union? It's time we found each other. Started something new."

As she spoke, her hair began to take on an unruly look. Static, perhaps. Or sympathetic arousal. Maybe her skin was on fire. She was so young.

"I thought the Helix was more of a therapy thing," he said.

Crystal sighed as though to say: Who has time for this.

"Well," he went on. "I'm apolitical, anyway. I choose not to get involved. Do I have opinions? Of course. Do they matter? No."

"Gross," Crystal said, and she looked at Rita, like, How was Rita married to this oaf?

"You have to know that pamphlet sounds like some ridiculous secession manifesto," he said. "Are you in a club or something? High school play?"

"Don't be absurd," said Rita. "Crystal is my new assistant. I *told* you."

She told him? Really? "Oh, right," he said. "When did you start?"

"Couple weeks. But I feel at home already. Lucky to have been assigned to Rita. We get along famously."

She turned to Rita. "So, you ready? Meeting starts in about an hour. I got a car outside. And there's plenty of couches, so you can lie down the whole time."

"You bet," said Rita. And, to Bruce, "Honey, get me my coat?"

"Whoa, whoa," he said. "You can't go out. What are you doing? You won't even pick a sock off the floor, and you're going to some silly model congress with lounge furniture?"

"Since Rita's vouching for you, you're welcome to come," Crystal said. "The more the merrier. Strength in numbers."

She bent over to pick up her bag, brimming with propaganda. On the small of her back was a tattoo. A blue double helix.

"Rita," he said. "This really isn't a good idea. You don't even know these people."

"Oh, come on. You heard Crystal: There's couches. Now help me up. *Slowly*. God."

He put on his coat. Grabbed his video camera. He was not going to let Crystal the levelheaded reformist take off with his wife of no sense.

They made it down the hall and into the mudroom, Rita availing herself of techniques used to prevent a pee, should one have to pee en route to a place where peeing is welcome. She was also cupping her vulva, but this was a different matter.

Outside, Crystal's vehicle came to life. It was a Hummer, with side wheels mounted on the curb.

"Mind if I drive?" Bruce said.

"Normally, no. But it's my godmom's car. Don't worry."

It was a box. Pewter and black. Silliest vehicle ever. On the plus side, it had reclining seats and a DVD player, which meant Bruce could live in this Hummer without complaint.

"So where are we going?" he said.

"My godmother's. She's got a huge basement with a separate entrance. She thinks I have parties down there."

"Is she sympathetic?" Rita said. "To the cause?"

Bruce, who was sitting in the back, popped his head between the front seats. "Let me get this straight: we have a cause?" He was clutching their headrests and pulling.

Crystal turned to Rita. "You sure he's okay? I don't mean for this to be rude—he's your husband—but there's a lot of us who can't include our significant others. It's not even about priorities, putting the Helix above your husband; it's just about keeping everyone safe."

Bruce said, "Just to play along here for a second, your saying all that *in front of me* sort of undoes the point of excluding me."

But Crystal just looked at Rita, who said, "I promise he's fine. I just haven't had a chance to fill him in."

"Because you've been so busy," he said.

He sat back in his seat. The windows were tinted; the world was grim. Crystal caught his eye in the rearview, smiled, and seemed to say with her smile, We could fuck but it wouldn't be worth it.

They drove down to D.C. and through a residential neighborhood. Eventually, they turned off and down an inlet that meandered for several miles before pooling in a cul-de-sac. Crystal parked and said, "Voilà." She jumped out of the truck—it was so high off the ground, you actually had to jump—and opened the rear door.

"Give me a hand, Bruce?"

He went around back. "I don't even know where we are."

The land was barren. Plaqued with ice. The only disturbance to the snow was a set of tracks that wandered off into a copse several hundred feet away. He thought he could make out a hedge, but it was too far to tell for sure.

"What's this for?" he said, and he helped Crystal with a plastic sled. It was shaped like a bathtub, though it was half as deep.

"Rita, of course. How else we gonna get her there?"

He thought she was kidding and laughed.

"Clever," said Rita, eyeing the sled. "You do think of everything."

She lowered herself into the well. Crystal gave her a Burberry throw and said, "Okay, Bruce, we're going to walk in single file. We'll make like sled dogs—you've seen them on TV. Oh, and try to keep to the footprints that are already here."

"Why?"

"It helps to make it look like there aren't so many of us."

He looked at the prints. "You're saying more than one person has come through here?"

She squinted, did some math. "About fifty, I'm guessing. Let's go."

He took hold of one of the ropes and secured it over his shoulder. He looked back at Rita, who had pulled the blanket up to her chin. With her hat brought low, her bangs pressed into her forehead and eyes.

"Ready?" Crystal said.

"Hang on." He ran back and tucked Rita's hair behind each ear. She was adorable, his wife. All snug and pregnant in a sled.

They started off. It was slow going, having to stick to the prints. The steps were spaced so tight, he tangled in his own pants.

"Mush!" cried Rita. She untied her scarf and lashed his back. "Mush!" She was laughing. He fell down.

Crystal stopped. "Okay, guys, this is all very nice, love in the snow and all, but I've got a meeting to run. Can we pick up the pace a little?"

Bruce said, "Where the hell are we going? There's nothing out here."

"Course there is. Just up ahead."

He realized they were making straight for the hedges, which were twenty feet tall, at least. You didn't see hedges like these in D.C. These hedges were pledged in the defense of hearth and home. Like Beverly Hills or Bel Air.

Bruce whistled. "Holy cow, look at the size of this place."

They had passed through a gap in the bushes and were on a path flanked by stone walls on which yew and juniper sat in pots three feet high. It was an arcade, almost. You couldn't see the sky.

The lane egressed into a patio framed with garden chairs stacked by the dozen. The patio had just been shoveled and gave the impression that there were such festivities here as to accommodate hundreds without inconvenience. Beyond the patio was a porch in balustrade—all limestone, very old—and behind that a manor home the size of the Capitol. Twenty thousand square feet, at least.

Crystal said, "Wait here," and she ran around the side of the house.

Bruce squatted. He took Rita's two hands in his and blew.

"Crystal *lives* here?" he said.

"Her godmother."

"Her godmother is God?"

"I guess so."

"And Crystal's working for you why, exactly? I bet whatever's in there sells for more than we make a year. Combined."

"You steal anything and we are through."

"I'll keep that in mind."

Crystal reappeared with six men in tow. Men in bomber jackets and bomber hats. Matching Timberlands. They looked like a boy-band militia.

Crystal motioned to Rita and the sled. "Now, be careful. Three of you on each side."

They did as told and lifted. Like pallbearers. Rita went up five feet. "I don't like this!" she said, and she covered her face.

The men walked in step. Bruce felt in his pocket for his video camera. He wished he had brought a second battery. The crappy battery life on this camera was reprisal for his having read six reviews of the product in which crappy battery life was the main complaint, only Bruce had wanted the camera, *this* camera, because it was password protected. It was the only camera he knew of that could safeguard his work from the nosing of a certain wife, who had every right, at this point, to nose through whatever she liked.

The men whisked Rita through the side door, followed by Crystal, who stopped to say something to a security guard, himself secure behind a receiving desk in a booth. Bruce lingered by the entrance, marveling at the grounds. Twenty acres? Sixty? By the time he went inside, Crystal was gone. Rita too.

He asked the guard for directions.

"Driver's license, please. Arms out, please."

Bruce was getting frisked. "This is totally over the top, don't you think?" The frisking continued. And a search through his bag. "What the hell?" Bruce said. "You better have the president in there for me to be going through all this. Hey, if you all are so by the book, why wasn't my wife patted down? You think a pregnant woman in a sled can't blow up a house? Maybe she's got a bomb under the blanket—ever think of that?"

"She has security clearance."

"Security clearance," Bruce said. And thought: So maybe Crystal's godmom really is God.

The guard was unpacking his bag. Bruce always traveled with this bag, so it was complete with items unsuited to today's excursion but handy in a pinch. Tums. A hank of rope. Pajamas.

The guard said, "I might as well confiscate the whole thing until you leave. Unless you want to walk around with an empty bag."

"That's fine," Bruce said. He'd had the foresight, or luck, to have put his video camera in the inside pocket of his jacket—a great big poofy jacket—which had somehow escaped the security guard. He was going to count his blessings and move on. "But, just out of curiosity, what's the danger in pajamas?"

"Your receipt," said the guard. "And here is one for the camera. Electronics are logged separately."

Bruce dove into his pocket, but the camera was gone.

He stared into the booth. At the monitors along the wall. Each was split into quadrants and each quad appeared to broadcast from a different room. Five monitors, twenty rooms and scenes, among them an overhead view of an auditorium jammed with people, at least two hundred, and, in a clearing by the wall, his wife on a cerise banquette, sipping juice.

"Meeting's that way, sir," said the guard.

Bruce walked down the hall. It was paneled in wood, and underfoot were carpet runners in royal blue with sangria trim. He kept walking but found no meeting, just doors that were locked, except for one, which was ajar. He peered inside and listened. Listened hard, heard nothing. How could this building assimilate the noise of two hundred? It was all limestone and brick. In places like this, men were eviscerated on the rack, and their screams were heard for miles.

"Hello?" he said. And then louder, because in this parlor was a cup of tea, steaming; a half-eaten red velvet cupcake; and a cigarette butt smoldering in an ashtray. "Anyone here?"

He stepped inside and nearly upset a cart of desserts. Éclairs, profiteroles, soufflés. Poppy-seed cake and tiramisu. He eyed the spread and felt it narrated something of his future, like he'd snatch a dessert and indenture himself to the fabled witch of the house. He stepped away from the cart. Gingerly. Touch nothing. The cigarette smoke nested in his eyes. He put out the butt and spun around.

"Jesus," he said, and he brought his hand to his chest. "You scared me to death."

"My apologies, sir."

It was not the guard but a man in a tailcoat—a butler, it seemed—whose *sir* was of a different caliber altogether.

"Oh, well, that's okay. I'm probably not supposed to be here anyway."

"Mrs. Anderson will be in shortly. She asks that you make yourself at home and enjoy a pastry."

"That's very nice, but I'm just here for—"

He paused, recalling what Crystal had said about her godmother. How much she knew. Whatever they were doing, however ridiculous, he didn't want to blow it. Rita would get in trouble; Crystal would be mad; they'd all look at him funny in homeroom. He threw up his hands.

"For the party?" the butler said.

"Yes."

"Very well. I will tell Mrs. Anderson that you do not wish to see her."

"Wait, don't do that. I mean, who? Never mind. I'll just have this custard thing here. And a brandy, if you got any. I can wait for a bit."

He sat down in a chair that was probably a hundred years old. Victorian, maybe. Blue velveteen, cream frame, crimped seat and back. He bit into the pie. It was an individual serving, the size of his palm. He'd wanted to shove the thing in his mouth whole, but that was always when the lady of the house walked in. Wow, this custard was good. Smooth and light. He decided to sample the strawberry cheese-cake puff. And a few truffles, because they were exotic; it said so on the labels, scrawled in cursive. Like someone in the kitchen had taken the time to write in this elaborate hand the names of each truffle. *Mint julep. Pepper vodka. Ceylon.*

The butler returned with a brandy snifter and bottle. He was every-thing a butler should be. He was even bent at the waist. Ten years from now, he'd be an L.

"Care to join me?" Bruce said. "There's clearly enough for two."

A documentarian needs people.

The butler demurred.

"Some other time, then," Bruce said.

He crossed his legs. His fingers were sticky. He had slept but three hours the night before—the couch was a muddle of lump and trough—and the sugar was romping about his blood like it owned the place. He went: Okay, Bruce, let's think this out. Mrs. Anderson, lady of the house and Crystal's godmother, was partaking of afternoon tea and dessert when she heard you in the hall. She is a pale, recondite woman who consorts only with her godchild, the butler, and, perhaps, the ex-ecutor of her estate. Most of all, she does not appreciate a certain genre of man, call him stranger, a stranger documentarian who needs people.

The butler came in. Bruce asked for another brandy.

"Shall I just leave you the bottle?"

"That would be lovely."

"Mrs. Anderson," the butler announced.

Bruce stood. Crumbs tumbled down his thighs. She put out her hand. She was what—four foot nine? He tried not to stoop, but it was impossible.

"Sit," she said. "Please."

"Mrs. Anderson, it's an honor. You have a magnificent home."

"Call me Lynne. And thank you."

She settled under a lamp whose glow helped define the cut of her face. Very narrow. Unnaturally so. A face between cymbals after the clap.

"I see you've sampled some of our pastries. The head chef is a specialist."

"They were great, yeah. Look, I'm sorry if I chased you out before. I didn't mean to intrude. I think I got lost!"

"Don't be silly, Mr. Bollinger. More brandy?"

She was so small, the rest of the room began to stand up in contrast. Walls were cream, moldings were buff. No windows, much art. Giant amphora depicting the plight of Agamemnon.

"I'd love some, yes." He was drinking heavily now, except for the face-saving caveat that, unless you were Samuel Johnson, brandy was not drink. Brandy, Armagnac really, was just fancy after-dinner wine.

She poured with grace. Three-quarter sniff for him, half a smidge for her. She wore a red turtleneck and brown flats. The effect was to condense her frame in obvious defiance of what God had given her to work with. Think I'm small now? Think my calves are compressed and bloated in a way that's hardly possible in nature? Well, I can do worse. And frankly, what did she care. She lived in a mansion. She had minions. And if her goddaughter's appearance was any kind of bellwether, she had very attractive friends.

He held up his snifter and regarded the liquid inside. Such an odd vessel for drink.

She fussed with the string around her neck that attached to a stainless steel dog whistle. "Look over there," she said. As he did, a wall packed with framed impasto art broke in half like a curtain at showtime. The reveal was a console of monitors similar to that in the security guard's booth. Here, though, no expense had been spared for the quality of the picture. It was closed-circuit viewing in HD.

"Surprised?" she said.

He was not.

"Good. It gets lonely out here sometimes. Crystal has so many friends; I like to participate in some measure."

The whistle was in fact a laser pointer, which she trained on the first monitor: a man in a button-down with chest hair sprouting from the collar, sitting next to Rita on what had become for Bruce, in the past minute, a symbol of all things coveted but unattainable—the cerise banquette with claw-feet. Monitor two, of considerably less cause for distress: Crystal and the militia kids distributing literature. Three: a king-sized bed with canopy, rippled valance, and stuffed green platypus atop the duvet.

"Looks like a nice party," Bruce said, and he drained the last of his brandy. "I should probably get a move on. A move seems like a good idea."

His tongue felt swollen. Unwieldy too. Enunciation would fail him in about three minutes.

"I get sound, too," she said. "Want to hear?"

Bruce thinking: This Howard Hughes thing is weird, and I want to find Rita. Bruce saying: "Okay, and just another pinch before I go."

He returned his glass to a side table.

"Volume two," she said in a voice reserved for the commanding of equipment. "*Volume two,*" she said in a voice reserved for when your equipment does not work. "Martin!" she yelled.

The butler appeared with tray in hand. It occurred to Bruce that he had never seen a butler in person. "Fix the sound, would you?"

He nodded. Disappeared behind the console. Smacked the thing, which released Crystal's voice in stereo. Crystal haranguing a woman with a gold bone through her nose and spikes implanted in her skull. A metal headband.

Crystal was saying, "The helix goes on the small of your back, not your hip. The sacrum is a place of power. Whatever you put there is a guiding principle. If you tattoo it on your hip, it just means you want to get laid. Makes us look frivolous."

"Mute two," Lynne said, and the TV went quiet.

Bruce stood. "Mrs. Anderson, I really should be joining my wife. Thank you for your hospitality. If you'll just show me the way." He was listing, one arm braced on a chair back.

Lynne said, "She doesn't look too concerned," and she gestured at monitor one, in which Rita and her new Cro-Magnon hero were sharing a laugh. "Please, stay a bit longer. Some pastry, perhaps?"

He retook his seat. Accepted another brandy. He was drunk and glad for it. Now he could say what he wanted, which was this: "You know, Lynne, I figure since I had to leave my driver's license with security, that's how you know my name. But how do you know who my wife is? And what's with all the cameras? I'm a filmmaker myself, so I get wanting to look at people and their lives. But in this case, in this place, I don't approve of it so much. Not at all. Forgive me if this seems rude, but are you looking to take a lover? Is this *Sunset Boulevard?*"

Lynne laughed with her whole body, pitching back and forth and finally just forth, doubled at the waist, trying to breathe. When she regained herself, her eyes were bright and cold and the tears seemed to freeze on her cheeks.

"My, my," she said. "Aren't you to the point. But really now, what do you mean? Your wife is Crystal's employer. She told me."

He frowned. Waved his hand, waving it off, and said, "Right, of course. I am, you know, a jackass."

"What's more," Lynne said, "I know you like film because of Crystal, too. That's why I thought you'd like my setup here."

"A jackass! That's me. Bruce J. Bollinger. Lynne, you are a fascinating creature. You are the stuff of documentaries. You've seen a thing or two, literally and otherwise, so how is it you think they're having a party down there? No, I don't buy it. I got your number, Mrs. A. I do."

"Well," she said, and she smoothed down her skirt. "It's not my place to think too rigorously about what I hear. Now, tell me about yourself. Are you enjoying your new job?"

"No."

"No? That's too bad."

He pushed at the floor with his feet. His feet lost purchase—this rug was no place for purchase—so he nudged them under the crust and pushed again. Backing away from Lynne had become supremely important. He was not feeling well. The pastries and sissy drink had found kin in the malfunctioning of his intestines and were colluding to make him sick. He thought Agamemnon was dancing on the vase for the way he and the other figures moved about. He considered a lamp on the desk and decided four lightbulbs for one socket was a bit much. He thought, also, that Lynne's face was coming loose.

She moved her chair forward to reestablish proximity. "Maybe you just need to nurture your creative side."

He looked at her and smiled. So her face was melting before his eyes—so what? It was a spiritual condition. She was lonely. He was lost. Maybe they could help each other. "To tell you the truth," he said, "that's my whole problem right there. I don't even know what my job at the Department is, but I'm terrified it marks the end of a period in my life when I tried to do something that mattered. I don't know who I am anymore. I am estranged from myself. Isn't that ridiculous?"

She poured him more brandy. He'd gone through half the bottle and wanted something else. She offered him some Scotch. "Martin!" And then, to the console: "Volume one."

RITA: Oh, that's hilarious. The saddest part of any day is when you hear the vice president is still alive.

CRO-MAGNON: Want to take a tour of the house? It's pretty amazing, as you can see.

RITA: I'm sort of couchbound. And I'm waiting for my husband.

CM: Where is he?

RITA: Beats me. Probably trying to bleed money from the walls.

BRUCE: Oh no. No no nooooo, you did not just say that.

RITA: He makes (miming quote marks with fingers delicate and lovely) documentaries.

CM: An arty type, right. Those types are always looking for money. He's come to the right place. I hear Mrs. Anderson is a patron of the arts.

BRUCE (swiveling in his chair to gawk at Mrs. Anderson, to gawk and leer): Well!

RITA (puffing up, happy): No, we're done with all that. Bruce works for the Department of the Interior now.

BRUCE: I work for the Department of the Interior, and my wife is proud of me. How pathetic. You know, Lynne, this is some very nice Scotch you have here, but I am drunk. And no one is fun when they're drunk. My son is due in four months, and I work for the Department of the Interior. I am a man he will come to admire, not for what I did, but for what I *wanted* to do. I have to use the john.

LYNNE (standing): There's one down the hall.

BRUCE (sniveling): A documentarian cries. Okay? He cries. This is me crying.

"Mute one." And the room was silent but for the snuffles of the documentarian, who rallied and said, "How did you get so rich? How does it happen? Did you inherit? What do you do? What does your husband do? Is there something for me to learn here?"

She appeared to depress a button under the coffee table. The parted wall reunited. Not one of the paintings was askew for it.

She called for Martin and said, "Make Mr. Bollinger some tea and bring it to the green room, where he will be resting."

"I don't want to rest."

"Don't worry. And don't despair. Life sometimes offers up solutions when you least expect them."

Bruce could not control the slack of his lips, but some part of him smiled, and later, ensconced in a guest room that was all green, he crawled into a bed, thinking: A grant! This incredibly odd, rich woman is going to give me a grant. The hours passed; he slept through them all.

ooooo

ESME SAID, "Martin, just look at this."

He looked. And what he saw sacked his self-esteem for the year. It had taken him months to perfect the anchoring system of her face. So much trial and error, but in the end, it held. She'd worn it nine times. It had even survived exposure to wafts of sweat and BO in a gym carnival. So why today? Her left cheekbone had mutinied. It was actually falling away from her face. And her nose—my God. It was released from the bridge and tilting floorward.

"I can't believe it," he said. "I don't know what to say."

"Say: Esme, I am sorry. This will never happen again." She began to laugh. "Can you imagine what Bruce must have thought? Good thing he was drunk. Good thing, for me—" She looked at Martin with reproach. "Get him home, okay?"

"I'll do that now."

"You'll need the sleds. For them both, I think."

Martin nodded and left, but at the door, Esme said, "Be careful." It was cold out—the wind panned across the fields in great sheets—and Esme felt for Bruce and Rita. A couple expecting a child. She'd been part of such a couple once, and she remembered its pleasures. But also the ruination that came before and after and, in this arrangement of feeling: a reminder that nothing is ever as it seems.

On TV: the Great Hall. The meeting was long over, though the room was half-full. If she rewound tape of its highlights, she would have heard about weaponry and nation-states and living as one in a socialist community severed from the body elected. How was it Thurlow couldn't prune from his ranks people who believed in stuff like this?

On another TV: Ida reading under the covers with a flashlight. Esme considered paying her a visit. She wouldn't be home from school forever. Plus, no child should be up this late. Why was Ida still up? Esme frowned. Whatever the reason, it was, she feared, just the open eyes of anxiety atop a body of trauma nine years long.

She turned off the monitor. If she tried to comfort her daughter, she might end up exposing herself instead. Since Thurlow, she had not once turned on anyone with a look that might reveal the effluvia of her heart. Its overflow. The puffery of loss and guilt acquired in the span of her time on this earth. She worried now that for having waited so long she might turn that look on Ida, on her little child, and then what?

She just did not have a frame of reference for the happy stuff of intimacy, and it had been many years since she had tried. She'd been on her own since eighteen, though more properly thirteen, which was when her brother had an accident that left her emotionally abandoned and, in essence, without family. Though in the last couple of weeks, that phrase—*without family*—had succumbed her to variations of loss that shamed what she'd associated with the concept before.

Her brother had been a surfer, world-class, and had trained every day. Their parents drove them to the beach—mornings before school and on the weekends—because when there's manifest talent condensed in only one child, you spend all your time and money on that child and hope the other one knows you love her anyway. They were only one year apart.

His friends were surfers, too, a little older, and one day the eldest, who was fifteen, got fresh with Esme behind a shed of garbage cans, she gathering fish bones for a spell she wanted to try that night—Spirit of distaff and fertility, make my breasts grow now!—and he asking if she wanted to see something and maybe to touch something, and, wouldn't you know it, she kind of did. At first she was shy, but she cottoned to it pretty quick. So did he, since he ejaculated on her bathing suit in seconds. Next thing, she was back to the fish bones when her brother showed up, taking her by the wrist and saying, "Ez, don't be stupid, we are *assholes*," and her thinking he was jealous because his friend liked her more than him. Probably, she said as much. Probably, he was hurt.

An hour later, they were in the hospital. The kid who saw him go down said he didn't know, just that Chris seemed distracted. Took a bad part of the wave, but still, there was no way to know there was a sheet of fiberglass down there and that Chris would crack his head. Or that he'd stay under for the extra seconds that are the difference between relief, brain damage, and coma. The doctors did not bullshit around. Chris was indeed in a coma and, barring a miracle, would never come out.

In the twenty-four years he slept, Esme saw him six times, all in the first six months. Her parents? Maybe they saw him once. Was she to blame for what had happened to him? In a word: yes.

A tear dribbled down her cheek and settled at the base of her throat. People liked to say the greatest distance on earth was between your head and heart. And say it as if this distance were a problem. What problem? Esme would have been glad not to know anything of what went on down there. Because once in a while, a feeling would cover the distance, usually while she was on the job and stretched thin on emotional resources, so that when she got home: there it was, a feeling on her mind. Nine times out of ten, this feeling was about Ida, and the feeling said: You are ruining her life. And then she could not breathe. And the feeling, in triumph for having made it this far, would parade about her head, crush what forces she deployed against it, and lord over the place until another job came in. Which meant that, while she liked to think she was saving lives, it was really the job that saved her.

And so: Do not think; work. This was not work but rescue.

Olgo Panjabi, 2315 hrs: Nodding off in an armchair. Palm concealing his face because only old men nodded off in their chairs. He did not want Kay to come home to a drooling, narcoleptic husband. It was after eleven, and she was out. He did not know where. She had not returned his calls. She had not left a note. Still, he refused to worry. If he worried, he would call Erin, and that was a no-no. On the other hand, if he worried, it meant he still thought there was a chance Kay had been abducted, hurt, lost, instead of on a date. If that was what one called such a thing at her age. Could one still date after fifty? Of course. Every night with her had felt like a date, down to the weakness in his knees when she'd come out of the bathroom wearing a low-cut dress or black sheer stockings. He had always loved her legs. Lean and beautiful, and willing to part for him, always. They had had a wondrously sensual life together. He could not swear his experience had been a cut above the rest, but he guessed as much, given what people said about marriage over time.

He had stopped nodding off. Instead, he was pacing and producing reasons why a wife suddenly took up with another man. Suddenly? He felt tonight's ratatouille start to web in his stomach.

He heard a key in the lock and decided not to ask where she'd been. It was good to feign indifference and also to give space. He was not sure which tactic would help, but he was glad for one stone, two birds.

Only it wasn't Kay at the door, but Erin and Tennessee.

Olgo stood. "What are you doing here? Is everything okay?"

Erin said, "Where's Mom?" And she started to cry. Her high ponytail of yore was crestfallen, and the hair was ballooned in all directions. Tennessee, who had, from the looks of it, been crying for hours, crumpled to the floor to pound the linoleum with her fists. She did not *want* to sleep here. She *wanted* to go home.

Erin flopped into a second armchair. She was obviously forsaking her daughter to Olgo, who rushed to the kitchen to make hot chocolate with marshmallows. He set up Tennessee in the guest room with the TV on.

When he came back, Erin said, "Jim changed the locks on the apartment. We had a fight. He says it's his place, he pays for it, and we can't stay there. Says he's got too much work to deal with us right now."

"He threw you out? My God."

"He's an ass," she said. "And I bet his girlfriend's coming over. That trampy little hunchback." She looked around. "Where's Mom?"

"She went to the store."

"At midnight?"

"It's not midnight." But Olgo would not check his watch. If it was midnight, there was the distinct possibility Kay had passed into a mindset in which she did not intend to come home at all. Not until morning, in any case.

"Can we crash here for the night?" Erin said. She unlaced her boots. "Might be for a couple nights, actually."

Olgo returned to the kitchen to make tea. Erin followed.

He said, "Since when is the Defense Department God? Last I heard, you could work for the government and still have time for your wife." He said this with more heat than he would have liked, and quickly tended to the kettle.

They sat on either side of the counter, on bar stools.

"What's Mom getting at the store? What could be so important?"

"Women stuff," he said.

"Dad, what is going on? First you ask about Mom's hair, and now she's out past midnight on a Sunday. A *Monday*."

"Let's talk about Jim. We need to get him out of that house. You need to get a locksmith and do unto him and so on. So much for your mother's little tête-à-tête today. She said it went well!"

Erin hooked her toes over a rung of the stool. "You don't know where she is, do you."

Olgo slammed his mug on the counter. It was empty; there was no effect. "No, okay? No. I think she is out with friends."

"Friends?"

"Yes. Your mother has friends. And so do I. We do not have to do everything together. We *do* have separate lives. It's what makes a marriage work."

Erin was on her feet. "Are you saying I was too clingy with my husband? Are you saying this divorce is my fault? Because last I checked, he's always off doing some secret something or other. And you know what else? I didn't *ask* you."

"I'm talking about your mother and her friend. This has nothing to do with you."

"What friend?"

"*Friends*. She has many. I am speaking in general."

"No, I'm pretty sure you said *friend*. As in one."

"I'm going to check on Tennessee." But Erin stopped him.

"You know, Dad, people change sometimes. They need new things. They get involved with new things."

"Erin, really. It's late. We can talk about the birds and the bees tomorrow."

"Has it occurred to you," she said, "that Mom might be in trouble? Not out with her friend*s*, but in trouble?"

"Don't be silly. She's not in trouble."

"How do you know? You asked if I've noticed anything weird about her, and the truth is, I have."

"Your mother is a capable, intelligent woman. She's fine. Don't worry."

"*Dad*, I'm trying to tell you something."

He began to pay attention. His glasses had slipped down the bridge of his nose; the pads were greasy. "What sort of trouble?"

"Well, you know how Mom's gotten all therapy lately—"

"No, I don't know that."

"Yeah, okay, so you know how Mom's gotten all expressive lately? I think she's met some people. Or someone. And I think that someone has ideas about some things and that maybe those ideas are exciting for a person who's gotten all hippie a little late in life and missed out on all the sixties stuff. I mean, what, Mom was just a wife or whatever, hardly an exciting experience if you've got a passion for the hurt of people's lives."

"Since when do you talk like this?"

Erin poured herself more tea. "I might have been at a meeting or two with Mom."

"Please don't say it's the Helix. And how many is one or two?"

"Me, two. Her, twelve."

"*Twelve?* Erin, the Helix is for wackos!"

"Could be thirteen."

"Erin. What are you talking about? Your mother has never been interested in community work, *hippyism,* whatever you want to call it. And, okay, we haven't seen so much of each other since I started my new job, but I have not heard a peep out of her about it."

"I think she figured maybe you wouldn't have the patience."

"She got that right."

"Or maybe"—and here she began to pulp her words, which was what people did when they wanted you to hear but not hear what they were saying—"maybe it's just that you're part of the problem."

"I'm the thing she's going to the Helix to solve?"

"Dad, how much do you really know about the Helix?"

"Nothing." This was not true, but he was feeling so petulant and infantilized by this hint of how much bigger the world was than him that he'd reverted to the best juvenilia there was. No, no, no.

"Just keep your ears open, that's all I'm saying. Tomorrow I'll try to reach my lawyer and deal with the apartment. It's going be hard. Jim seems to have everyone in his pocket."

"What a shit," Olgo said. "And what do you mean *That's all I'm saying?* If you know something about your mother that I don't, you have to tell me."

"Don't raise your voice. I just think if no one knows where she is, maybe she's with this person she met and maybe they joined the Helix for real."

"What the hell does that mean? Is this a spiritual thing? A quest? Your mother is *soul searching?*" He did not have any idea what Erin was talking about, only that she'd conceded some kind of poverty in his marriage such that Kay had gone off to find her bounty elsewhere. "Never mind," he said. "I've heard enough. Really. So your mother's run off to join the circus. I'm going to bed. I expect she'll be back in the morning. You need anything? There's more blankets in the closet."

He headed for the bedroom and closed the door. Waited for Erin to join Tennessee and then said a short prayer. Please let her come home. He had gone to bed without his wife only once in thirty-five years, and then only because she had left on short notice to see her father. He stared at the closet and bureau. Pressed his elbows into the mattress because he was on his knees. Opened doors and drawers. All items belonging to Olgo? In place. All items belonging to Kay? Gone.

Esme closed his file. She had known Kay was about to split for the Helix but could not have known it would happen this fast. Perfect timing. She looked at a map of Helix communities and confirmed that Pack 7, Richmond, was the closest to his house. Kay was probably there by now. So, would Olgo go out to Cincinnati and do whatever it took to shut down the Helix? Absolutely. Would he bother questioning why him and not some Navy Seal trained for this purpose? Not at all.

It was after one in the morning, and Esme was spent. She nearly called it a day, because why bother with Bruce? He was proving the easiest of the four. Still, she got in bed and watched him from there.

She wrote: *All quiet on the surveillance front except for Bruce Bollinger,* who by 0149 hrs had vomited so many times, there was a crescent dented into his forehead from the toilet seat. He sat on the

tile, legs splayed, wearing pajama bottoms and a T-shirt. He said:
Benny, Jack, Lothar, Nick. They had not settled on a name for his son,
their son, though earlier today Rita had said, Che, how about Che? to
which Bruce had said, Yeah? How about Santa. It'll give him a leg up
come winter. And so another fight, more tears, and a foreboding sense
that already they were bad parents because probably the baby could
hear them, was being exposed early to this soundtrack of wrath, and
would, years later in therapy, hold these notes responsible for some of
his blues.

Bruce looked at his reflection in the toilet bowl. His throat burned;
his nose ran. He wrung a tube of Aquafresh, rubbed the paste on his
teeth, and made for the couch. As part of the downsizing of their lives
from comfortable to poor, they had disconnected their cable service.
This meant, in general, two things: One, in the hour it would take
Bruce to stream thirty seconds of porn using dial-up, the urge to touch
himself would have long since passed, so that he had not experienced
anything close to pleasure in this department for nearly five months.
Two: since what cable they did have was pirated, you never knew what
channels were going to come in, which taxied Bruce into new areas
of entertainment, among them, City Drive Live, which aired a traffic
feed from locations all over D.C. During the day: blah. But at night:
my God. A camera trained on the GW Parkway southbound, the footage gritty and dark, the cars speeding by, but staggered, because how
many cars sped down the GW at 2 a.m.? Watching this stuff was like
pawning the feel and hue and smell of your life for scenes of the forlorn. Bruce loved it.

From the bedroom, his wife was calling. He had his thoughts. Was an
alcoholic blackout advisable under the circumstances? You couldn't be
blamed for negligence if you were *blacked out*. He draped a blanket over
his shoulders. It was possible Rita had stopped paying the heating bill.

"What is it, honey?" He stood inside the doorway to their room. The
longer he slept on the couch, the more he felt the trespass of his return.

"Just thinking," she said. "Couldn't sleep."

He approached the bed slowly. Among the blankets and throw pillows, hers was still the most prominent stuffing there.

"You been sick?" she said.

He nodded, though she still faced the wall. This gave him the chance to step in further. Closer, one toe at a time. Could he really see his own breath? He shivered and looked at his wife, could almost feel her breasts and stomach, the pack of her thighs. Under those covers was a pound of flesh. And so, though the timing was awful, his blood began to jazz like seltzer. Neurons firing, he came to life.

He sidled along the wall undetected. The flap of his pajama bottoms turned him loose. He closed in on the edge of the bed but stepped on a comb that skidded across the carpet. He froze, heart stopped. She lifted her head, nose in the air. The draft in the apartment put him at a disadvantage, upwind. Desire has a whiff; if she caught on, forget it. She lowered her head. Snuggled.

He scanned the terrain of blankets for a point of entry and settled on a tiered approach, peeling back one layer of blanket at a time.

"Get me my lotion?" Rita said, and he all but reared as the nape of the duvet fell from his hand. Lotion? She said *lotion!* And like that, he was fifteen years old. Wanting to get over on his wife and wresting from language in one context arousal in another. Could he assist in the application of this slippery, thick, jerk-off *lotion?*

He watched her cream her palms and forearms, and he waited. She might say: I can't reach this spot, can you help? Or: I need some here and here. And if in the process he dragged the tip of his penis down her spine—an accident, he'd swear—it would be enough to get him off later, dial-up be damned.

He waited and watched, but still no orders, and so he was all but resigned when she said, "Baby, come here," followed by the unthinkable gesture of her turning over to look at him. He was backlit; there was no way she wouldn't see his condition, and yet he still tried to hide it. She patted the mattress. What were the odds? So, no, he would not be stupid about this. Would not mistake *come hither* for *meow,* would instead sit on the bed and regard the impudence of his erection with pity.

She touched his hand and said, "You're freezing!"

He got under the covers, actively trying to leach the excitement from his body. He knew Rita; she'd be appalled. She was pregnant and bedridden and no part of her was unfurling to accommodate his needs. Not tonight, not any night soon, not even for weeks or months after the baby was born. And anyone who thought otherwise was not just insensitive but sadistic, because this arousal did not affirm his wife's hotness blazed through the more immediate evidence that she'd lost her sex appeal so much as furnish her sense—her fear—that she'd married an asshole.

He stared at the rice-paper shade overhead and considered what disposable savings he and Rita would need to justify purchase of a replacement shade, something stained glass or Tiffany-like, and how they might never accede to this position of wealth, and where normally such thoughts deflated his courage to live, never mind a hard-on, tonight they roused him up the gallows. He was on his back with his arms fastened to his side. Entombed. Safe. Do. Not. Move.

"Honey," she said, and she scooted for him so that her kneecaps pressed into his upper thigh and her hand fell atop his chest. "Honey, I was thinking—"

Oh, to hell with it: he reverted to strategies that had groped at him through high school. He sat up to scratch his foot so that her hand rappelled down his chest and landed in the flesh well between his hip and navel. Maybe the landscaping of their bodies would give her ideas where before she had none.

She laughed. "Feels like a war in your belly," she said, and she pinched the mini-donuts tubed about his waist.

"Thanks," he said, but thought: A little to the left. Just a little!

"So, anyway, I was thinking," she said. "About the baby? What if we named him after someone I kind of admire?"

She was breathing on his shoulder, and the heat collected in his armpits. Her finger traced a halo around his belly button. "Someone he can be proud of his whole life."

Bruce tried not to move—his fists were tight—and yet there it was, his pelvis thrusting for her, gently and without commitment, but thrusting all the same while he watched in horror and waited for the tirade that was, instead, his wife vouchsafing her thighs, lathered in cream. He fit himself between them and smiled like an ape.

"Are you listening?" she said.

He was, he was! He was even going to climax with this name on her lips, their boy's name, Bruce Jr., because all his life, secretly, he'd wanted to have his own father's name—Henry—and felt this keenly and always in the presence of his younger brother, the doctor brother, the most renowned hematologist in the country brother, Dr. Henry

Bollinger II. And Rita knew this—in the courtship phase of releasing secrets you'd never told anyone else, he had told her—and now, suddenly, his beloved wife was making good on what she knew. Bruce Jr.! His baby boy. And this despite everything he had done. She was a marvel, he was a cad, and from this incoherence grew the tension that stormed out of his body and all over her legs, the sheets, and the duvet.

He was panting so loud, he didn't hear her at first. "The Helix," she said. "They're amazing. And the guy who started it?" She reached for a tissue and plucked the semen off her quad. "He's a genius. So that's what I want. They say he's nicknamed Lo. I think it's cute. So it's settled, okay?"

"What?" Bruce said, though he was laughing. "Are you kidding?" And he laughed harder. "The *Helix?*"

"Stop laughing!" she said.

"What? I can't hear you." He was laughing so hard, the piss romped through his pipes and the brandy lees down his colon, so that unless he got to the bathroom now, the rain of his ejaculate would be but prelude to something much worse. And so he got up not having said yea or nay, so that Rita began to holler after him: "Thurlow! I want to name the baby after THURLOW DAN!" at which point, Esme, who had fallen asleep on the job, woke up with a start, certain she'd been wandering the world in dream and calling his name. Thurlow, where are you? Thurlow, I miss you. Wait for me, I'm trying.

Team ARDOR: Ready, willing, able.

A municipal building two miles from the Capitol. A conference room with window, wall, and two-way mirror. Around a table, four Department of the Interior employees who'd been summoned from their place of work and given roast beef sandwiches with extra mayo. Standing up: some guy who seemed distantly familiar to Ned and Bruce, but not enough to distract from the oddity and thrill of what he was offering, which was, in the main: hope.

Ned stared out the window, looked up at the sky. In 1986, the USSR seeded the clouds above Chernobyl so that they would deposit their radioactive load on the peasants of Belarus instead of on the cognoscenti of Moscow. And it worked. The Soviets had engineered the weather to kill people. The Chinese, too, were obsessed with the weather. With rainmaking to forfend drought. But in all cases, for good or evil, these people were frosting the sky and changing the world. It was science at its most heretical. Do it right, and you could conjure a storm that was godlike in its rage, steeped in the punitive grammar of the Bible. Do it right, and you could show the heavens who was boss. And this mattered to Ned, since his fear of powerlessness had always aspirated whatever went sloshing about his heart, so that he couldn't date the same woman more than a few weeks, couldn't acquire any real friends, couldn't lock down a single feeling and make it last. But not for long. Cloud seeding and weather modification. It was why he'd been hired, or so he'd been told, and though studying cloud cover in Cincinnati seemed like a dubious application of his talent, it was still a chance to prove he could impose his will on the big things. Find his sister and be happy. Cincinnati, tallyho.

The guy in charge handed out envelopes. He said, "In each you'll find a key to one of four lockers at the Greyhound bus station. In those lockers, you'll find coveralls, badges, and clipboards. Anne-Janet, in your locker you will also find keys to the van, which will be parked on Court Street. Now, are you okay to drive the van, or do you want someone else to do it?"

Anne-Janet was startled. She'd been staring at Ned's shoes under the table. Brown lace-up gum shoes that were popular among the preppies at her school circa 1993. Did that mean he'd been a preppy and was hanging on to the glory days via his shoes? Or did he just shop secondhand?

One of the fluorescents overhead began to strobe. The effect was to slow time in the room and to repulse its occupants even further into themselves.

"I can drive," Olgo said, and he nearly stood up. Would have stood up, if not for his reflection in the mirror, which showed a man without purpose. Yes, he was working the Indian land claims, but no, he really wasn't. So maybe he'd started moping around the house. Maybe, for feeling so aimless, he'd stopped managing his looks, such as they were. For instance, his shirt, muddied with raspberry ganache from his birthday cake. But was that any reason to leave your husband? Not that Kay had left. She was just out to graze. Kay Panjabi was *grazing*. "I can drive us from here, if you want. Right now. Anyone object to leaving right now?"

"That won't be necessary," said the man. "But your enthusiasm is noted."

Bruce lifted his arm in the way kids do when they want to look like they've volunteered but don't want to be called on. Today was payday. If he did as told and allotted his income responsibly, he'd have enough money left to buy his wife and unborn a six-pack of Jell-O pudding snacks for dinner.

"You have a question, Bruce?"

"Yes. Can I keep whatever footage I shoot at the Helix House? Can I get the rights and use it for whatever I want?"

The man touched the hearing device lodged in his ear and said, "After it's been cleared."

"I'm ready to leave now," Olgo said. "Drive right to that man's door and blow the place up if I have to."

"What?" Ned said. "When are we going?"

"Whenever you're going," Anne-Janet said.

Esme stood. She'd been watching them through the two-way, but she'd seen enough. She patched in to Martin and told him to wrap it up.

She slung her purse over her shoulder but stopped at the door to answer her phone, and then not to answer, because it was Jim Bach. He'd want to know about her progress. He'd ask to meet the team. She let it go to voicemail, and when she listened two minutes later, it was as she suspected.

He said: Esme, the stakes have never been so high. Imperialist pretensions abroad are kid stuff in comparison. Are you sure you know what this means? She stopped listening there. Of course she was sure. And here was why: Some people hear voices and the voices are bad. They say: You're going to die alone. And: You suck. Sometimes, when these voices come to you via satellite because it is your job to listen, it is your career as a sleuthing mercenary, sometimes they say the last thing you want to hear: Thurlow Dan accepting money from North Korea. Thurlow Dan giving presents to a hooker. Thurlow Dan weeping into his pillow at five in the afternoon, knowing that if his muscles have failed to rouse him from bed, it is because they are instruments of depressing notice that he does not want to live. She had heard it all, and so when Jim asked, for the millionth time, if she understood what was at stake, the answer was easy: Yes, I understand, I understand better than you. Though if he asked for more, she wouldn't tell him. She could barely tell herself. Time heals all wounds? Ha, ha-ha, ha-ha, ha-ha.

III. In which a cult leader makes a tape. In which an ex-wife gets her chance. Like honeybees to the hive, Hostage Rescue to the Helix House.

THURLOW GOT THOUSANDS OF EMAILS A DAY, which Dean reduced to the few that seemed pressing or of interest. Among today's crop was one was from a girl petitioning him to visit her weekly meeting, it being the most popular in her district—hundreds aggregating to lament *the darkness of 2000; the squandered surplus; WMDs;* etc. He wrote: *Dear Crystal, I'm glad your meeting has attracted so many people, except I encourage you to reacquaint yourself with the Helix charter and core principles because they don't have too much to do with what you're talking about.* But then instead of sending it, he just shook his head. To another follower, who'd promised his mom the Helix would make him a better son, though he wasn't sure it had, Thurlow wrote: *The only promise that's been despoiled is the one I made you.* But then he deleted that, too. Turned off his computer and looked at the video camera aimed his way. There was one in every room of the house, programmed to record in his presence and to send this footage to his PC for compiling. He had modeled the system on Nixon's White House, only he never forgot it was on. Often, he'd look into the cameras and talk to himself. His work proceeded from the unhappiness of a deserted man—who else did he have to talk to? Plenty of people, it turned out. As of today, the whole world. Now that he was about to obliterate the trust so many had put in him, it was better to address them all in one go. He cleared his throat. And began.

00:58:12:12: Greetings from my home in Cincinnati. You all know my name, and by the time you see this tape, you will also know what I've done. So I want to use this as an opportunity to explain. But first, a few caveats, chiefly that I am not a crazy. The press will be calling me a crazy, but I'm not. Sun Myung Moon is crazy. Victor Paul Wierwille. Jim Jones and Chuck Dederich. But I am not them. What I am is heartbroken. Which will, yes, lead some men to do crazy things.

I think, too, that the press will want to sensationalize what's going on here, but I prefer the facts and a list of my doings: The seeding and growth of a therapeutic movement whose recruits are legion. A snatching from the Frenchies of philosophy the whys of bereavement and isolation. A crusade for the idea that if companionship makes you feel twice as lonely as you were before, it's because you're not doing it right. Disclosing, sharing. Principles! They're in the charter book, no need to labor them here.

Other behaviors that might warrant the *crazy* moniker if taken out of context: a blossomed rapport with North Korea; an intent taken up by some of my people to declare sovereign multiple counties nationwide; and, yesterday, the detaining of four federal employees, for which I bear full load.

And so this video, to be distributed in the event this doesn't work out as planned. Because there are other facts you can't know unless I tell you directly. For instance: Two weeks ago, I saw my wife and daughter for the first time in nearly ten years. After, I spoke to my wife for about ten minutes, during which conversation she promised or at least strongly implied she would be in touch. But she has not. Not in person, not at all. And I have not been able to locate her or my daughter since. Another problem? I cannot carry on this way without them. And so: I consider these desperate times. Why *wouldn't* they call for desperate measures?

The four people imprisoned in my den—I found them snooping across my lawn. In coveralls and work boots. They'd come in a repair truck, which idled by the curb. It bore the Cinergy logo and tag, The Power of Change, which claimed for the gas and electric company more esteem than it was due. I took down the license plate and had my head of security check it out. Then I waited. I sat on a couch, which felt like plywood.

I hate being here. This place is a clink. Three stories, fifteen rooms, stone facade, lintels. A Renaissance Revival in a corner of Ohio. See those windows? My head of security—his name is Dean—says they're bulletproof, UV resistant, and self-tinting. I think my Murphy bed is some kind of escape vehicle. And at night, when I'm scrubbing my teeth with the electric toothbrush he gave me last month, I think it checks my vitals.

This part of Cincinnati was his choice, too. A couple miles north of the four-block nexus called downtown, with its stadiums and street-name blandishments, Rosa Parks Street and Freeman Avenue. Since

1990, people have been fleeing this town in droves. Mine was the first new place to go up in years, which meant that every contractor in town wanted in. And yesterday, when we needed extra rebar—because what is a kidnapping without a cell?—the material was here ASAP. Not that rebar is the incarcerating metal of choice—the stuff bends, after all— but the point is verisimilitude.

Dean called back to say Cinergy didn't have any trucks with the plate number I gave him—no surprise there. And yet a little surprising. What sort of infiltration party was this?

I watched the four technicians clod through the snow. Their cover-alls were insulated and bulky, so that one guy looked like he walked on the moon, another like he had a pillow between his legs. They'd come under the pretense of wanting to dislodge a manhole cover. Who had the crowbar?

The third tech was Indian and held his clipboard upside down. The girl had trouble with her tool belt. One of the guys stared up at the sky like maybe my house had launched itself there. The tech with pillow pants had a video camera. He held it to his eye with his index finger on the zoom. I looked at his face; he looked almost happy.

Next they hopped the fence and were closing in as though they meant to ring the bell. I thought about going out there myself. Instead, I buzzed for Norman, COO of the Helix, who seemed to have anticipated the call and was here in three seconds. In a double-breasted blazer and chinos. A button-down that fought with the insurgency of his waist. A tie and kerchief.

"I saw them," he said. "Don't worry."

I could feel my Adam's apple ascend but not come down. "Taking pictures," I said. "We can't have that."

"It's not a problem. And there's nothing to see anyway. Just forget them. They'll leave eventually."

"And then what?"

Norman shrugged. He has a way of looking depressed no matter the context, as though his face were stuck in range of a vacuum hose hitched to his neck and always on. He is barely five-five, and alone with his color on this side of town. I've been told Cincinnati is the sixth-most segregated city in America, and to the extent that Norman is the only black man I've seen in months, I can only imagine what the first five are like.

"We go on with our work," he said. "There's an event with Pack 3, Colorado, in two days. You're expected."

"Our work," I said, and I moved away from the window. How much was I really caring about our work? I tried to picture my daughter. She'd been so well bundled on the street, I could barely see her face. God knows what she must think of me. If she even knows I am alive, it's possible she despises me in ways she feels without words but will put words to soon enough. She is almost ten, which is when your kid feelings petrify and cornerstone the prison that becomes your psychic life from then on.

I asked Norman if any of my people in D.C. had checked in. They had not. He wanted to know why, but I didn't tell him. There are just some things you cannot share. Even with your oldest friend. Poor Norman. He's been my wingman ever since we were kids. He has flirted with Centers for Change and Reevaluation Counseling, est and the Way, and lived in New York with Fred Newman's crew on the Upper West Side. By the time he came to the Helix he was already steeped in a version of Manichaean paranoia: from his toil could develop an end to grief but in his sloth would be the demise of man. Talk about pressure.

He asked if we could just get on with the day. He said we had a lot to do.

And I knew he was right. I should forget about the techs, the snoops, the surveillance, and get on with my life. What I'm trying to say is: It's not like I didn't understand what this situation would do to Norman and the Helix. I even scanned his face and tried to find in its expression qualities that *wouldn't* get trashed when this thing was over. I went: Hope, trust, loyalty, faith, and ticked off each one. But that didn't stop me. Because what kind of life am I having without my family?

I said: "Norman, this is what I want. I want you to bring those four people in. They are trespassing. We can't have it."

"I'm sorry?"

"I want you to bring them in and keep them here until further notice." And with that I turned my back on him, knowing that in some way, it'd be out of my hands from then on.

"But we don't even know who they are. And we certainly don't need that kind of attention. Florida just cleared five thousand. I'm going down there next week to make the Pack official."

"Great. All the more reason to protect ourselves. Now just do what I say."

His mouth opened, but he knew the discussion was over. He backed out of the room. His face seemed to drag across the floor.

On his way out, I told him to get them hoods. I didn't want to see their faces, didn't want to know their names.

Which brings me to the present. I now have four hostages I will gladly exchange for my wife and child. I will make a ransom tape and make my demands clear. But I don't know if it will work, and if it doesn't, then I would like to ask for something else, which is this: the chance to humanize this story so that among those for whom the expiry of my life will come as good news, there are two who might someday know of the sorrow wrought in my heart for them.

Thurlow put on his gym pants and a long-sleeved polyester crew and made for the sauna. Five pounds in five minutes, sweat therapy. He was what the professionals call TOFI: thin outside, fat inside. A skinny fat person, no muscle tone at all. His body fat percentage was 25, which he knew thanks to a medical resident, a dietician, who came once a fortnight to tell him how close he was to heart failure. She looked grim every time.

He opened the sauna door and found his crew waiting, as always, for the morning meeting. In attendance were Norman, Grant, Dean, in a sweat born of the excitement to which they were newly wed. That and the heat, 168 and rising. Norman wet the coals. The walls were Nordic spruce with burls that dilated in the grain if you stared at them too long. Thurlow sat on the top bench. His tennis socks were wet and printed the wood like flippers.

They'd had the hostages for twenty-four hours. Now it was time to deal.

Norman said, "I found a lighting crew in the area. And someone for hair and makeup. So how about we schedule filming for three o'clock—can we say three?" He swiped a finger across his brow and flicked what was there at the tile.

Dean's voice surged above the wheezing stones. "I was hoping to get you first. For gear and training. It's a brave new world. But we're ready."

Grant stared at his toes, which were bound in sandals and swelled with blood. He was the youngest there, twenty-nine and schooled in technologies that kept the Helix current. "We're gonna need more bandwidth, that's for shit sure. Our site's gonna pop."

"Totally ready," Dean said, with fists upraised. "Bring it on." He was dappled red in an allotment that seemed miserly in this context—it was 172 by now—but enviable the rest of the time. He never looked flustered; he was totally ready.

"A ransom tape," Grant said. "So excellent. It'll go viral in two minutes, so we have to be prepared."

"Exactly so," Norman said. "And with it, we will get our message out worldwide." He flung his arms as if to compass *worldwide* but stopped quick. "Which is the point, right?" And here he looked at Thurlow, whose eyes closed immediately. Norman's will to believe was profound. He had to believe; what else did he have? "We were stagnating," Norman said. "Of course. I can see that now. I slept on it, and now I can see it plain. So we'll use the tape to raise awareness. To let everyone know how dire the situation is out there by having these people *perform* what it feels like to be alone. To be severed from the world. So really, this isn't a kidnapping so much as social art. Is that right?"

"Correct," Thurlow said, though the word seemed to drop from his lips like a brick. "Now get going."

Meeting adjourned. But Thurlow didn't move. And when he checked in with his will to move, all evidence suggested this torpor would be ongoing. Brave new world? Gear and training? He'd had one night to indulge the romance of what he'd done before the logistics rained out the wedding.

The four hostages worked for the Department of the Interior, which was odd, to say the least. Who would send these people? They didn't seem to know themselves.

Thurlow got changed and went to the den. The hostages were sitting on the floor in burlap hoods, with hands cuffed behind their backs. One of them had been unable to coerce his gams into the lotus position, so he'd taken to flapping them like butterfly wings. Another was davening, less in prayer than distress, like one of the nuts you see in the ward or someone who needed a bathroom. The girl was unmoved, and the Indian—it was like his body hair was about to ignite for the tinder of being here and for the way he hated the Helix. Thurlow could feel this, though the man hadn't said a word. But it didn't matter. In a few hours, Thurlow would be in a director's chair. In the room: four hostages who had no burden except to hold up the day's newspaper and appear not dead. In his head: his wife and child and the bliss of their return, for which he'd ransom the four alongside the faith of every person who believed in him. Starting with Norman.

Thurlow adjusted his chair. Turned on the desk lamp. Turned it off. This was all wrong. The angle, the shot, the lighting. He felt like an anchorman for the nightly news. No affect for the relay of trauma, no stake in its outcome. This would not do for broadcast into every home in America. After all, it wasn't like he didn't know what happened to a cult leader's footage in the aftermath of a siege. Especially if people died. Especially if the cult leader died.

He looked at the camera again. He went: Roll tape, and said, "Now, look: I am not a crazy."

But it was impossible to maintain the pretense of dignity with his earpiece vibrating every two seconds. It had been vibrating for hours. It was vibrating now. The Helix was in the news, and everyone wanted to know, What the hell. What the hell, Thurlow? What have you done? He took every fifth call. This time it was Norman, bearing word: The hoods were a bust. They didn't breathe or wick, and one of the artists—he was calling them artists—the Indian, was getting a rash.

In the meantime, three calls had been forwarded to his voicemail. The messages were brief. They said: What the hell. Also: Close the blinds. It was hard to know what forces would mass out there against him, but he expected the usual: special ops, trained to kill.

But don't worry, Dean said. Message four. The house could take it.

He looked back at the camera. He felt a little sick.

01:41:11:09: What else should I say for starters? Nobody wants to hurt this much. Even people who court the hurt, who *need* the hurt by way of self-recrimination and penance—they do not want this much of it.

And not for this long. Because after this long, it's hard to acknowledge that hurt—*this* hurt—resolves into years of poor judgment.

On his computer: *If my wife comes here with Ida jubhjjjjjjjjjjjjjjjjjjjjjjjjjjjjj*. He lifted his head and felt where the keyboard had imprinted his cheek. He was in his study. Floor-to-ceiling bookshelves that receded into the wall. He had planned this room down to the grain of its boards, and yet its blessing was owed to chance. The lights were energy conscious and would turn off for lack of movement after five minutes. This meant that whenever he got to self-immolating about the past, the overheads would go dark and he would come round. Only this time, he'd fallen asleep.

Norman was at the door. He said, "Working on your speech? Great," and he marched in to have a look. Thurlow hid the screen.

"Sorry. It's just that the crew is here and we're ready to go. Everyone's waiting."

Thurlow clapped his PC shut. "Look, we only have one shot at this. And I want to get it right. You of all people should appreciate that."

"I do, of course, but I also—okay, just look at this"—and he waved a DVD in the air.

It was a video taken by a Helix Head who'd been emailing them views of Covington, on the Kentucky side of the river. It was a quaint spot, minus the National Guard, stationed in the farmers' market.

Norman rolled back on his heels. "So this is exactly as you planned, right? *International coverage.* Because, just to reconfirm, that is the point, right?"

"It's going to be fine, Norm. Don't worry."

Thurlow leaned in close to the computer screen, trying to count heads. Plus the Guard, there were probably one hundred special ops in the market, and more en route.

"In any case, the artists are ready to go," Norman said. "I assume, once the tape's out, we'll let them go, right? Send them off and, what, pay a fine or something?"

They paused in this exchange until Norman said, "Oh, you know what I mean. Half of D.C. is Helix. You've got friends. I predict you spend one night away from home, tops."

Thurlow sat back in his chair. Breathing in, letting out. But it was no good. His body had taken over the discharge of what Norman had roused in him, which was anxiety. Fibrillations of heart and eyelid, a throbbing wen on his forearm that had not been there minutes ago. Water coming down the ducts but stopping short of notice.

"Certainly no more than a week," Norman said. "And in the meantime! Anyone skeptical about what we're doing here is going to change his mind." Norman freed a sheet of notebook paper from his back pocket. "Not to be presumptuous, but I've been pushing some words around and wonder if maybe you'll consider including some of them in your address."

Thurlow pressed the wen with his fist. "What address?"

"On the ransom tape? Maybe something about how there's thirty million single people in the country. Or ninety million. How the system is designed to keep us apart. The class divide. The housing gap. Work ninety hours a week in a cubicle at a soul-sapping job whose chief enterprise is to proliferate dialogue about last night's TV fare, and what are the odds you find someone to hold your hand under the covers at night? Something like that, maybe?"

The wen seemed like it might erupt. Or migrate up his arm and into his brain.

"Norman, get out. I don't need your help."

"Okay, but just in case it wasn't clear, the United States government has sent the *army* for your artists."

"Hostages, Norm. They are hostages. But they aren't mine. I did this for the Helix."

"Right-o," he said, and he lifted his palms, which exposed his cuffs, his cuff *links,* and with them a suspicion Thurlow had been trying to repress since the moment Norman walked in. Cuff links? Really? Because even a conscientious, exemplary worker among men does not wear cuff links in the day-to-day. He told Norman to leave them on the table, which Norman did with vigor, so that they fell to the floor and to a hollow between the baseboard and parquet. Thurlow waited for Norman to leave and shut the door behind him before going after the links. The link-*microphones.* But they were gone. He took stock of the room. He'd always liked this room. But never mind. He would pack up his computer and papers of import and seal off his study forever.

But first: rest. He flopped into an easy chair and splayed all the limbs he had. He thought about the hostages. The troops in the market. His wife and daughter and the life they had together, pillaged by a lonely guy who screwed up every chance he got. The lights went out. A siren cried.

He buzzed for Vicki. At least Vicki would kiss him hello and put her arms around him and be happier for it. He buzzed for her again and got no answer.

The commissary: Impersonal and square. No weird angles to negotiate, no family photos to remove. Potted plants arranged around a director's chair. Dean wearing a boonie hat with chin strap and black aigrette pinned to the side, not fancy but more like he'd plucked a duck.

Thurlow watched him and the gaffer spar in one corner and Norman preside over the hostages in another. Their hoods were still on, though Norman had procured an emollient for the Indian's neck, which was aflame with rash.

Dean said, "Almost ready," and dragged a bouquet of assault rifles across the floor. They were arranged in a tin stand like umbrellas. He prodded a floodlight with the tip of his boot. "Except it's too dark in here," he said. "Too Goddamn dark. Hey, Edison," he said, and he frowned at the gaffer, who was hell-bent on chiaroscuro. "Watch it!" Dean said as the gaffer's ladder tipped and fell into the director's chair.

"Not the chair," Dean said. "We don't have another one here. Okay, let me think. I need an hour."

Norman, who had been standing by the cheese platter—his idea of craft services for the crew—smacked his head. "An hour? What makes you think we have an hour? Just use a different chair."

Thurlow stood. "And get rid of the rifles. Seriously. That's not what we're about."

Dean looked bereft, as if the seat of passion once vacated by his wife's death was now vacant all over again. He took Thurlow aside. He said, "You know it's my job to read everything that comes in here. So you know I've seen what the North Koreans have been saying. And I'm all for it. So are a lot of people. So you just say the word. Whenever you're ready."

"I appreciate that," Thurlow said, and was about to say more when a fist of disappointment and upset grabbed his voice and closed it off.

He made for the cheese platter. Nine kinds of curd, sliced thin. Those rounds with the red and yellow wax. Antipasto and toothpicks with tinsel finials half-mooned by a swath of wheaty biscuits.

Then he went back to his room and shut the door.

03:12:53:12: Some people know their destiny from the start. But not me. And even if I did, it's not like there's a manual for how to become what I've become. It's not like there's a school for brinksmanship or a ladder with rungs visible from the bottom up. There's not even a school for the presidency of the nation, and yet the road to that job is still clearer than mine. And so, a little about me, because I want people to understand how I got here. Plus, I think my time is running out.

My parents were part of the middling salariat that votes right but acts left. Men who tout family values while dropping a load at Tart's Bigbar. Women who abort their kids in secret. They were Reaganites who imposed an old-fashioned aesthetic on the scheduling of our lives, so that we seemed to meet only at dinners, which were opportunities to know each other that we never took. Our family congress was more like antecedent to purdah among friends, which is, not coincidentally, the experience and philosophy I have spent the Helix trying to retire.

As for my parents, for parents in general, there's the education they mean to give you and then what they actually give you; in a good family the two are discrepant because at least they tried to give you the best.

Our kitchen was meat and potatoes and squash, carrots in stock, brisket with pineapple Os, short ribs and stew. By age ten, I could out-girth a keg of beer. Or so I was told by my dad, who found in this razzing a way to be intimate that did not humiliate him. For many dads, the way is violence, so I consider myself lucky.

We were not excitably poor or evangelical, but we were striking for how little capacity any of us had to dream of a life outside the one we had. My mother collected Tweety Bird figurines. My dad was a facilities services manager for the convention center. We lived in a shingled bungalow-type residence in Anaheim.

In 1985, my mother was driving by the Larry Fricker Company when it caught fire, sousing the air with methyl bromide. Not long after she developed a cough, followed by a cancer from which she died two months later. I was fifteen.

It took time, but my dad acquired a second wife, which he still has. Mostly, though, he sits in a La-Z-Boy, wears a mouth guard, and watches TV, which pleasure is slain twice a week by epileptic spasms that have revoked his driver's license and aptitude for work. For the money I spend on his care—that's him grousing down the hall, by the way—I could have financed a cure for epilepsy, I'm sure. He and my stepmom have been living with me for years. They don't ask questions about my life, and I venture nothing. It seems to have worked so far.

I guess that's not the story I meant to tell. But my dad's calling, so I have to go. If I don't have time to edit this thing, try to be kind when you air it later.

"Thurlow! Answer me, son!" Wayne was seventy-nine, and since he couldn't be bothered to move, he'd just yell for people across the house. His wife had the same habit. It drove Thurlow nuts. They'd yell for each other and for him, and now Wayne was just deaf enough to go ballistic when he couldn't hear you, as though you were to blame. "Son!"

He was actually using the intercom, which Thurlow had asked him not to do. But he did it just the same, because the more he called, the more apparent it would be that Thurlow had not come, that Thurlow was neglecting him, the son grown too big and famous to tend his old man.

He headed for his father's quarters. He had installed a keypad just in case Wayne had a seizure and couldn't let him in, but mostly he endured the charade of being asked who was there and how could Wayne know for sure.

He found his dad eating a peanut-butter-and-banana sandwich. Most of the hair on his head had fallen off years ago, which made inexplicable the flocks spilling from his ears and nose. Today he wore a turtleneck and sweater-vest twenty years old, and jeans that were cropped at the ankle. His sneakers were white and of no recognizable brand. Who knew why older men always seemed to buy no-name sneakers, but it was a phenomenon common to his kind. He offered Thurlow some sandwich.

"Dad, what do you want? I'm having a busy day."

"Yes, yes, too busy for your old man, I heard that before."

Thurlow sat opposite his father and folded his hands on the table. They had never been the best of friends.

"Son, I saw something on TV just now that has me wondering what the hell is happening to the world. Something about a kidnapping. Four people who work for the government, and *poof!* they're snatched up by some fanatic who wants to change the world."

Thurlow sighed. His dad rarely took an interest in anything besides sports. He was so out of touch, he seemed to think Thurlow had acquired wealth from a well-placed investment portfolio. It also helped that he was half-blind without his glasses and kept the TV on mute. Still, Thurlow made a note to disable his cable box.

Wayne reached into his mouth to free a bit of peanut that had wedged under his denture plate.

Thurlow began to lose patience. "Dad, what do you want?"

Only Tyrone got in the way—Tyrone, who was his father's bird. "Silly bird," Wayne said, and he disappeared down the hall. It was times like these that Thurlow rued having made his dad's quarter of the house so big.

"Dad, I'm leaving." But instead he followed Wayne until brought up short by Deborah, who was standing in the doorway to their bedroom. She wore a thin pink nightgown. Her curly white hair, generally stiff, was wilting down her face. She'd been married to Wayne for fifteen years and seemed to be the worse for it every time Thurlow saw her.

"A visitor!" she said. "What's the occasion?"

Wayne reappeared with Tyrone on his shoulder.

Thurlow blenched. He didn't like animals, domestic or wild. He especially did not like this bird.

Apparently, the feeling was mutual, since Tyrone, whose wings had been clipped, took one look at Thurlow and thudded to the floor. Then went under the bed.

Wayne got on his knees. Thurlow looked at Deborah and asked for an umbrella. She looked at him, and the look was not nice.

Wayne said, "Come on, Ty, everyone loves you, just come out."

Deborah said, "Wayne, *please*, you are being ridiculous. All you care about is this stupid bird."

They carried on this way for some minutes. Thurlow didn't understand much about what was going on. It was true their repartee had always featured what rankled most, only this bravado felt new.

Deborah went to the bathroom to change clothes. Wayne enticed Tyrone back into his cage. Then everyone returned to the living room.

"Son," Wayne said, "the reason I was calling you is because Deborah and I, well, maybe it's obvious, but we're not getting along too well these days."

Aha.

"What your father means is that we are ready for counseling. You've given us a wonderful life here, but it's also a little strange and it's put a strain on things and we think we need to talk to an outsider."

Thurlow began to shake his head even as he tried to seem amenable. "Are you sure? Because I don't think counseling is a proven science."

Wayne snorted and stubbed his index finger on the table. He was about to slay Thurlow with evidence of how little he knew about marriage. "Maybe if you and what's-her-name had tried counseling—"

Deborah cut him off, but she looked pleased. She lit up a Virginia extra-slim cigarette and brought it within inches of her lips. She had quit smoking years ago, and this was how.

Thurlow swatted the air to clear a path. "Okay, okay," he said. "But leave it to me. I'll find Ohio's best," which meant he would hire from within and they would never know.

04:25:32:08: A marriage counselor? Now? The universe laughs at me, but I can't take a joke. Especially since my dad is right: I understand so little of love. Love and marriage. It's as though all my experience ramped up to these days has taught me nothing. My first billow of desire? Fifth grade, improper fractions with Mr. Coombs, and to my left one Esme Haas in striped tee, navy-blue short shorts with white piping, and Tretorns, which she'd had the foresight to wear years before they were a fad. She'd been assigned to buddy me through class. She was older and adept in the augmenting of her self-esteem via charity; I was stupid and courting a one-and-seven-fourths chance of failing fifth grade. We sat at adjacent desks. In the tradition of another famous love capsized on food, I had an apple in class the day she showed. Every time Mr. Coombs wrote on the board, we'd pass this apple be-

tween us, our fingers mating in the relay of this fruit. I took to offering
her an apple a day. But she stopped being interested. She had always
been good at tiring of a thing the moment I realized it pleased her. Also,
my grades were better; her work was done.

The years went by. We'd see each other in the halls. The sum-
mer before eighth grade, the rumor was that Esme had free passes to
Disneyland because her dad understudied for Pecos Bill in *The Golden
Horseshoe Revue*. She gave the passes out, and on my day, because
I got winded quick and was not much for walking, I headed for the
skyway funicular. There I found her on the floor, on a blanket, reading
Steinbeck. We spanned the park, then walked for a while, but still, I
never touched the ground.

Fast-forward to sophomore year of high school, Sunday in the market. Esme in a sleeveless denim vest and carmine mini. Bangles around
her wrists, ankles, neck. Hair in a high ponytail, strafed green. Me be-
holding the cereals the way some people look at art. I was sixteen, and
two years shy of a myocardial infarction because of my bad diet and
weak heart. I listened to soft rock, had never kissed a girl; I did not
know the president's name. I was, essentially, an archetypal American
boy growing up in the wealthiest, most enlightened country on earth,
staring at Esme Haas, who had stalled in front of the cereals, too.

I got within a couple feet of her when she turned my way. And it
was too late to be normal. I had no basket and no cart. I was backed up
against the gondola shelves; a bracket spiked my neck. My palms were
flat against the Special K. I looked like a jumper. I *felt* like a jumper.
The tumult of my feelings had struck me dumb. Esme with her box of
Kashi was leaving my aisle—Esme, whom I barely knew but who continued to rouse from me the urge to know her more.

She went to an East Coast university and then overseas, while I
tooled around Anaheim. I still thought about her, of course, but figured
she was lost to me and that in lieu of this fabled thing called happiness, I'd try something else. I started up a few meetings here and there.
The idea? Show up. *Talk*. Share something of yourself. Get to know
your neighbors. What I did not know then is that there are politics in
numbers, and that when you bring the isolates together, sometimes
they want to discuss the state of our union, to say that our lawmakers
are charlatans who should be deposed and that only a sundering of

this menace can return us to values touted in the Bill of Rights. And that sometimes, for saying this and joining up, they want sex. It's the strandeds' approach to intercourse: Let's rend ourselves from humanity so we can find ourselves in each other. Still, these people were here and there, hardly a notable constituency among those for whom the Helix—though we didn't have a name yet—was a way out of isolation.

The meetings got bigger. And more frequent. I began to think there was real purpose in this, which was when Esme reappeared. On my block. She was visiting her parents, driving a new car, and wanting to head into L.A. to a new restaurant she'd heard about, and did I know the way? I was twenty-four and enrolled at a local college but starting to be Helix full-time. I just happened to be home, looking for a Hamburger Helper Halloween costume I'd made with Norman many years before. In '83, when I was thirteen, the semiotics of the white glove were incandescent in the sequined accessory of one Michael Jackson, though for me, it was all about the four-fingered Helping Hand, with red cuff and smiley face. That Halloween, the last I'd ever celebrate, Norman and I sported the Hand's likeness through a gauntlet of evidence that said: Already, you are different.

So I'd come back for the glove, but really for providence, which explains itself post hoc, if ever.

I couldn't tell if Esme remembered me, but I decided our history was so dull, it would compromise our future if I brought it up. She was wearing a baby-blue cardigan buttoned to the neck, and sunglasses she took off when I gave her directions, botched the directions, and then insisted I didn't know the directions by name, only sight. She would simply have to take me along. I stood with my head braced against my arms, which were folded atop the driver's side door. She got out of the car. She was a foot shorter than me. I'd seen her kind of hair on a billboard for a revolutionary shampoo product—bright, blond, emulsive. Her fingernails were pastel. Creamy pink for the virgin bride. She wore white leather Keds bound tight. She was a fortress, a turret, and in those embrasure eyes were the guns of Navarone.

"Hop in," she said, and we were off.

A slop of Vaseline, the occasional sock, hole in the pillow—my victories in the ejaculate of love had been circumscribed by diffidence and, before the infarction and weight loss, the more apparent problem of repelling women in my age bracket because women under thirty do not yet realize they can't be this picky.

So you can imagine how it was with Esme. I was awkward in bed. Angles of penetration that were obtuse and painful. Slippage. The indiscriminate lapping of skin between her legs until she told me to stop, just stop it. She said good-bye with tenderness and relief. And in the instant that followed her leaving, it was clear: I would be with her again or kill myself.

That night I went to bed a wreck. The resolve of but a few hours ago had given way to anxieties about why I would never see her again. I turned off the light, keen on pursuing my thoughts. I needed to understand which failure had driven her away. I was a young man. I couldn't know then I'd be asking these questions for the rest of my life.

I mooned away the hours. I floundered at Cypress College. Esme had vanished. Her parents had vanished. I had no way to find her; it made me nuts. I started to lose even more weight. To think about food as the thing denied, the thing indulged, and to see in both a mortification of the body that I deserved. The closeness I had felt with Esme set my other relationships in relief. I would never be comfortable with my peers. I did not have any friends. I worked the Helix all the time.

Three months later, the phone rang. And just like that, she was at my place.

I made her some chocolate milk. We talked.

I said, "It's okay. We can handle this. I'm just so happy you called. That you're here."

"Handle? What's to handle? There will be no handling. None whatsoever. No way."

"What do you mean 'no way'?"

I wanted to crawl under the table, hasp my fingers around her waist, and stay there for the next six months.

"I can't believe you," she said. "You're supposed to flip out when I tell you, split the cost, and disappear."

I was appalled. "Disappear? What do you mean? We're a family now. We're in love."

"Good God," she said, and she stood up. Three months in, and it was terrible already. She had mistaken the spotting of early pregnancy for a normal, if light, cycle. She menstruated irregularly; how could she have known? But now that she did, it had to be done. Any longer and the procedure could get dangerous.

I tried to listen, but I was too happy. She had called. She was in distress, so she called. That would have been enough, but now this. A baby together. Surely we had to marry. Only we were not marrying. She was going to a motel.

I stammered. "But you called me. You came all the way to campus."

She reached over and put a hand on mine. I guess my incapacity to understand what was going on moved her.

"If you can just help me with the money, everything will be fine."

"Can you stay the night? Maybe if you stay the night, we can talk more about this tomorrow."

"No," she said. "You send me a check. You get on with your life. Do something useful. Forget the Helix."

I shook my head. If I couldn't have her, I obviously needed the Helix.

"I can't afford this on my own," she said. Her voice seemed to point itself at me. "You have to help."

"Then stay the night."

"On the couch."

"No. With me."

"But your roommates."

"It doesn't matter. I don't need them."

That night I crawled into bed with Esme. She wore one of my T-shirts. She did not want me to touch her, but I curled up behind her in spoon formation. She didn't resist. I put my hand on her stomach and tried to tell the baby I was there. We stayed like that for hours.

"I could babysit," I said.

She laughed. "You could darn socks."

"I could! What, you think I can't learn to knit? I could." I sat up and showed her my hands. "Look at these. They can do anything."

"*Shhh.* Your roommates. Let's go to sleep—I'm tired. Then I can go home and make an appointment."

I refit myself behind her and pressed my lips to a tendon at the base of her neck. She seemed interested in talk of my parenting skills. I would convince her yet.

"We're going to stay together," I said. And I believed this. Child or no child, we were bound.

She turned to face me. "Let me put this as best I can: I am not keeping this baby. Tomorrow I will go home, and you will not hear from me again. Ever. I know it sounds cruel. You're very sweet to understand. I have a life of my own. It doesn't include you."

She turned away and moved to the edge of the bed.

I blinked. Stunned. I could not lose her again. I could not return to my life without her. I tried to calm down and sync my breath with hers, and when I could not accomplish even this measure of intimacy, I went for the keys in my pocket. Locked her in my bedroom. Made for a spot under a desk in the common area, drew up my legs, and rocked myself to sleep.

The next morning, I ran to the store. Bagels, cream cheese, orange juice, raspberries, an egg-white omelet in case she was the type, a jelly donut in case she wasn't. Got home and prepared a tray. Coffee and tea, plus an origami flower, because I knew how to make exactly one origami gift, and it was this.

A breeze lilted across my room. I found Esme dressed and framed in the window, which was open. She bent the morning light. And as I watched her jump the sill and tear down the road, I was returned to the work that has been my life's thrill and challenge ever since.

Thurlow's cell phone rang; it was Norman. He'd been in touch with the FBI negotiator, who said it was now or never for the ransom tape. Seriously. Now or never. Dean had found a new chair that pleased him well enough, so they were all set.

"Any calls come in that weren't FBI?" Thurlow's ear sweat into the phone.

"The press."

"Anyone else?"

"No."

"I'll be there in a minute."

He went to the kitchen. Put a saucepan on the range. Added sugar, water, gelatin, lemon juice, grenadine, coconut. Heated it up, let it sit. Coated the result with silver luster dust, wrapped it in edible foil, and voilà: pink-lemonade coconut jellies for the playing of his last card.

It was almost four. He walked the central artery of the residence but was in no hurry. The house was quiet, though he bet the TV networks were in a tizzy. They awaited the ransom tape and were ready to preempt whatever was on air the second they got it, never mind that if you were watching *Oprah* at the very moment she disclosed the secret to painless and permanent weight loss, the last thing you cared about was some guy who just wanted everyone to get along.

He lumbered, dawdled, dragged ass. Heavy is the crown of self-disgust. It was true what Norman had said: Everyone would see the tape. And they would be appalled. To be sold out by the man in charge? Just so he could have a family of his own? Wasn't the Helix family enough? Wasn't it?

Outside the commissary door, he stood with an ear pressed to the wood. His plan was not to listen but to rest, only he heard what he heard, which added a new dread to the one already fixed in his mind. He swung the door open. No Dean, no film crew or even Norman. Just the four hostages on the floor—cuffed but unguarded and each staring up at him with the cow faces of kids in freshman comp, day one—and Vicki plus former TC Charlotte, screaming at each other.

The women verged on physical contact, so Thurlow took Charlotte by the arm.

She wanted to be on the ransom video. He said, Okay, just go get changed, because she was wearing boy shorts and a tank top. She debated whether it was wise to abandon the room, knowing he might lock her out. He swore up and down that he would not lock her out. She left, and he locked her out.

Meanwhile, Vicki was reapplying lip liner and Bare Escentuals foundation, which she had bought with the gift certificate he had given her. She was adamant he understand this was his gift, and began to tout the boons of mineral makeup and how well it looked on-screen.

He cleared his throat and said, "Vicki, you are not getting on TV, and you don't belong here, so get out."

She looked at him through the mirror. He had demoted TCs for less, and she knew it. He sat on the chair from which he would be making his demands, and stood her between his legs. He said, "Okay, Vick, tell me something: how did you even know we were filming today?"

She swiveled between his thighs. "Everyone knows."

"I see. And what is it you hope to accomplish by imposing yourself on proceedings that do not concern you?"

"Exposure." And then, because she had rehearsed this part, "So that everyone can see we're happy and that our way is good."

He didn't want to demote Vicki, but she was not leaving him much choice. She doffed her newsboy cap, which was black leather, and smiled, so that whatever was in her mouth reflected light from the overhead. It took him a second to register that it was not a filling or a crown and that she'd been slurring a little, lisping a little, because there were ears in her teeth. A little mic. That traitor.

He sprang off the chair and backed away. Reached for the blanket Dean had folded on a shelf—"Think fireside chat," he'd said—and threw it over his head.

"Spit it out!" he said, and he thrust his hand from under the blanket.

"What?" she said. "Spit what out?"

"Do it, Vicki. Hand it over."

"The jelly? You're mad because of the jelly? They were in the kitchen; I thought they were for everyone!"

"Get out, get out, GET OUT!" he said, and he used his wingspan—helped by the blanket—to corral her out the door, which he then barricaded with the desk. And the chair. And a five-gallon bottle of water he had to roll across the room on its side. Two five-gallon bottles. Three.

He was exhausted. But his labors were rewarded because neither Vicki nor Charlotte, nor both together, could force the door. He heard fists on the wood and a few body slams and then Vicki say, "This is some bullshit," and Charlotte say, "I left home for this?" though what was noticeable in their remarks was not an upswell of disillusion but the torpor with which it was expressed.

The blanket had fallen to the floor. In lieu of parquet, they had dusted the concrete with wood shavings, which cleaved to the wool. Never mind. Thurlow just wanted to sit and regroup. He took note of the hostages, who had watched the foregoing play out in silence.

These people had names. Their lives were sui generis.

Outside, it had started to snow, maybe to hail. The feds had just cut electricity to the house. It took a minute for the generator to kick on, and in this minute, Thurlow heard ice pelt the roof. Also a voice, one of the hostages, saying, "Mr. Dan? We're sorry to bother you, but is there any chance we can talk this over?"

He buzzed for Norman, and when he got Norman's voicemail—where *was* everyone?—he told him to reinstate the hoods and find a few dishrags, bandannas, whatever, because apparently the hostages had things they wanted to say. Also, he was afraid to leave the commissary without escort. Then again, he hated to be there with them. How bad was it when your only companionship was the four people you'd kidnapped? *Bride of Frankenstein* came to mind.

He left the commissary through a back door. Slipped through a walk-in closet and into a guest room with a trundle bed and tinted glass doors that overlooked a lawn tombed in snow. Dust congested in the monocle of a surveillance lens overhead. He swiped it with a Kleenex. Cleared his throat. Sat on the carpet, looked at the camera, and emptied his face of anything that was not love.

"Hi, little one," he said. "My little Ida. I guess it's time I should be addressing myself to no one else but you. So here is what I expect: Mistakes will be made. In the ferreting out of Helix staff, the wrong people will get hurt. Whoever is out there will scan the house for heat signatures and kill one another in the process. There will be hearings in D.C. and a passing of the buck, and I won't make it, and you'll never know."

It was probably five degrees outside. But with his dreams hanging off him like dead leaves and the winter of his unhappiness so cold it inured the body to minor pain but did nothing for the big stuff, he opened a window. And let the freeze rush in.

ooooo

THE SUN HAD BEEN UP FOR TWENTY MINUTES; the phone had been ringing nonstop. Esme was in the greenhouse: Jim Bach was calling. This early, he might be calling as her lover, DoD liaison, or both. She considered answering, considered not.

It had been many hours since her team last checked in from the Helix House. Too many for anyone to think all was well. She had their dossiers open on the table.

"What?" she said and yawned into the line.

"Crap," he said. "I gotta take this call. Hold on. *Don't hang up.*"

Her daughter's voice through the intercom—"Mohhhhhhhm!"—shrill and urgent, stout with need. Where are you, Mom? Are you here for me, Mom? What about tomorrow and the day after that? Ida was asking for the peanut butter. The kitchen staff had offered up a smooth and creamy variety that irked her preference for texture, and she was wondering why Esme had not come through for her in the execution of this simple task, the acquisition of a peanut spread to her liking, though what she was really asking was, Why didn't her mom know her? Esme addressed the intercom—"Check the cupboard above the fridge"—because, while it was true she didn't know what Ida liked, she did know there was hope in variety. One of Ida's classmates had seventy-two sweatshirts, and where once Esme looked down on parents who plied their kids with stuff, now she understood: if these parents knew their daughter's favorite color and bias for hoodies with a pink—not purple!—velvet band across the front—not the back!— they would have bought her just one sweatshirt, the most perfect one on earth. So maybe she had a more nuanced take on what it meant to be rich and buy your child's love.

"Natural?" Ida said. "Where's the natural kind?"

She would show up at the greenhouse in two minutes, which meant Esme had two minutes to put on her mom face. She hated to think it, but some part of her envied the stork. This bearer of child who got to skip town after. She had never asked for motherhood or the captivity of its dogma: no matter what, you will always be a mother. Your child dies, hates you, runs off—you are still a mother, stuck with this name, and hugged for life to the amazing little ID sprung from your own.

Jim back on the line. "You still there?" Esme was looking at the plants, how they soldiered on.

"I'm here," she said. "It's early."

She was about to finger the aspidistra but thought again. She had a killer's touch; this was not the time.

"Damn right it's early," Jim said. "So imagine me a couple hours ago getting a phone call. That early, I'm thinking it's you from downstairs in nothing but a teddy. Maybe Price Waterhouse calling with the good news. But no, it's the lovely and charming Erin Bach. Screaming. Any idea why my wife would be screaming at me at 6 a.m.?"

"Maybe because you're having an affair," she said, and she opened Olgo's file.

"Cute. Any other guesses? No? Then maybe I should enlighten you. At 6 a.m., my wife calls me up to say her dad's gone to Cincinnati on some strange work assignment that she thinks has something to do with the Helix, and what do I know about it? She says he hates the Helix, and what kind of monster am I to send him there?"

"Oh," Esme said. "That."

"So you know what I say? I say I know nothing. No clue what she's talking about."

"Good for you," Esme said. "You know nothing, check."

"Exactly," he said, and she could tell he was rethinking the anger. Sometimes his only job was to preserve maximum deniability. Other times, he was just too pissed off to care. "So, what the fuck, Esme? My father-in-law? Have you lost your mind?"

"I know what I'm doing," she said. If it came to it, she would tell Jim his father-in-law had an emotional rapport with the team's assignment that the others did not. She pressed the phone into the side of her face. "I gotta go," she said, and hung up.

Ten minutes later, Jim was at the door. He was in snow pants and sweater, like the ski lift had gone up without him. He walked so fast, it took Esme a second to hear the squall issuing from his boots, scraped across the flagstone. Like crampons were fanged to his soles.

"Sexy," he said, and he pointed at her slippers. One had a hole at the toe.

He held a cappuccino in a travel mug, which seemed like it would diminish the pleasure of this drink, except he uncapped the mug and routed the foam with a straw, which he used to point at the files on her table. "May I?"

She gathered them up in a stack on her lap.

"What do you want, Jim? Everything's fine."

He laughed. "Fine, huh?" And here his face started to clench in prelude to a release of venom she had seen before. The night his wife swore to win custody of their daughter and never let him see her again. The minute after his boss told him to nail Thurlow Dan this week or resign.

He leaned back in his chair. Eased the front legs off the ground. Gripped his chin. Appeared to be choosing his words, then gave up. "You fucking cunt," he said, sitting forward. "I find out this is some roundabout shit my wife hired you for, I'm going to kill you both. I ask for final intel on the Helix House, and you send in my father-in-law? Surely you know that if anything happens to him, I will not get custody of my daughter. That if he can connect me to this thing in any way, I won't get custody *of my daughter*."

He stood. Swiped at Ida's christmas cactus, knocked it to the floor.

"I want you to call them in right now," he said. "After that, you're done."

She looked at the broken pot and waited for him to catch up with her thoughts. What they had, after all, was mutually assured destruction. A plan to assault the private residence of a man who had committed no crime anyone could prove—a plan to observe this man, wiretap his phones, bug his house—was hardly the kind of activity divorce court smiled upon, let alone criminal court. Esme knew this much. Jim was screwed.

He caught up to her thinking and toed the plant. "Fuck," he said. He would buy her a new one.

"Just trust me." And she stood to square the neck of his sweater. They were still lovers. She slipped her hand around his waist and pressed into his hip.

"Mohhhhhhhhhhhhhm!" Now Ida was at the door, hands pressed against the frame like it might crush her otherwise. Esme said, "Tulip, let's talk," and pointed at the chaise longue next to hers. Ida padded the stone and left prints. Her feet were wet. Esme had promised they'd go ice-skating. Ida had been cleaning her guards in the tub.

"Hey, they fit great," Esme said, because she'd had Martin get Ida skorts in every hue. If her daughter wanted to icecapade, she was not going to flash everyone doing it. The skort was a magical thing. The hybrid was a magical thing. This child she had with Thurlow: pure magic. Her hair was straight and butter blond, parted at the side and slanted down her face, so that half the time, half her face was gone. Her skin was colored almond milk and freckled along the ridge of her cheekbones; she had acorn eyes—not just in color but size—and in all but height she looked just like her dad.

"They're okay," Ida said. "But I wanted black. They cost a little more, but whatever," and she swept her hand like a docent at work, here at Versailles, etc.

"If that's what you want, buttercup, just tell Martin."

Ida started to roll her eyes but stopped midway. What was the point? She was so accustomed to being palmed off, it was hard to muster the pique. "Can't you call me Ida?" she said. "Even Ma and Pop call me Ida."

Esme winced. These were not words she wanted to hear. *Ma and Pop.* Especially in the present tense.

"Okay, honey bun. *Ida.*"

"So when are we going?" Ida said, though she was not saying so much as whining. It was hard to know when the whine got telling of a developmental problem, but Esme was still pretty sure the distended vocals that sang her child's needs were age appropriate. "There'll be too many people if you take forever. Get dressed, Mom. Hurry *up.*"

Esme said, "Okay, okay. Should I wear a skort, too?"

"Don't try to be cute. Just get dressed."

And like that, and because her extracurriculars were no joke, Ida pivoted on the ball of her foot—she was all grace—and danced down the aisle. At the door, she said, "Can we call Ma and Pop after?"

And Esme, who had gotten no better at lying to her daughter in the three weeks since her parents had died, pretended not to have heard. For all Ida knew, they were still alive and missing her every day.

Esme shook her head. Tried not to see the big picture, though this was like squinting at the drive-in.

Olgo's phone. Ned's phone. Bruce's and Anne-Janet's. No one was answering, and still no update. From the wings of this mission, a creep of remorse. Surely they would resurface soon, report, and resume their lives at home. And for her trouble, Esme would have delivered a new day in a sequence that seemed to stretch without end back to that first day without her husband. She did not dwell on the years intervening. Or perhaps she just had the worst memory of anyone she knew. Episodes stood out, but mostly she moved forward as the great slab doors shut behind her. And maybe this was for the best. When people got married and trailed behind their car a mobile of cans whose clamor would follow them into their new life—what sort of metaphor was that? Sever the ties. Move on. Forget everything that had ever happened to you the second it was over.

She could not possibly go ice-skating with her daughter today. Too much work, other priorities. Crystal was the answer. Esme buzzed the garage attendant and told him to reroute her to the greenhouse. Poor Crystal. She was Helix, but on the fringe. Her and her thousand-plus friends. What absurdity that a movement for unity had a secessionist fringe. It was true the Helix had started well before the purloined election of 2000, but if ever people were going to feel disenfranchised and furious and wanting to sever from the body that had hitherto united them, it had been in this aftermath and dawn of a new century. And there he'd been, Thurlow Dan, plugging away. Why else would the North Koreans have taken an interest unless on the bent knee of the Helix demographic was a rocket of dissent? Only a man like Thurlow would see in their overture something peaceable and grand. She smiled with the thought, then moved on.

Esme had plucked Crystal out of foster care four years ago. Her thinking then: I am lonely without my own daughter but won't have to mind a teenager half as much. But then Esme ended up barely minding Crystal at all. And so, for having lived in the mansion and seen so little of Esme, Crystal must have realized that her foster mom—whom she called Godmom because it sounded less tragic—was less keen on her than on having acquired her.

In their time together, Esme had only twice seen Crystal pursue a goal with vigor, the first being multiple attempts to escape this house after she got here, and the other, seditious unrest. Now that she was eighteen, she also went to work. She worked for Bruce's wife, Rita— no coincidence there.

The attendant said Crystal wanted her car keys. That she would not come to the greenhouse; she was late already. Esme said, "Use the brain God gave you. Withhold the keys!" Crystal got on the intercom. She said, "Esme, I have to *go*. Some of us actually work for a living."

They sparred, Esme won, Crystal showed up in sweatpants and shirt. Sympathy clothes for Rita. She was chewing a straw; no drink.

"Your kid's pissed off," Crystal said. "I just saw her rip her skirt to shit."

"Skort."

"So you want to talk to her or something?"

"Actually, that's why I called you in here. And she has a name by the way. It's Ida."

"Oh boy," Crystal said, the straw flying into the larkspur and she settling into a chair. "Let me guess."

"Please," Esme said. "Something urgent has come up. It'll just be a couple hours at the rink."

"Have I mentioned she shredded her clothes?"

"How about I pay you?"

"Urgent like your nail broke, or like your colorist had to reschedule? Ugh, fine. For three hundred dollars, I will skate to Tibet and back."

"Sold. But try to be nice. You're her sister, you know."

"Oh, please. That didn't even work when I was fourteen."

"Just be nice, okay?"

"Whatever"—and she extended her palm, knowing Esme had a roll of cash in her bathrobe pocket. Esme was, to her, a woman of leisure whose conduct sustained a notion that rich women were weird, rich women had money on them, rich women spent their days in such boredom, no one thought to ask and so no one ever knew.

Laptop open. So many windows, so many views, but Esme knew where the action was at. Ida, in her bathroom, spread-legged, with the contents of her Spa Science kit arrayed on the tile. Scented oils, a couple of pipettes, sea salt, test tubes, glycerin bar. The walls were tickered with strips of fabric that had been the skorts. Just now, she had oats in the coffee grinder and a yogurt-honey blend she'd mix and apply to her face with a tongue depressor. Esme liked that she was interested in science, or girl stuff that masqueraded as science, because it meant something of Esme's father was alive in her, not to mention something of Esme, though she tried not to think about that part.

Crystal's head popped into the bathroom, and when it seemed she was not getting thrown out, she made for the lip of the tub, which was more sill than lip, and more seat than sill, this being a water closet of excess, 15 × 20 × 10, if ceiling height mattered, which it did, come time to feel yourself dwarfed by the expression of money your parents had lavished on you.

Esme muted the volume on her computer because what she imagined they were saying was probably worse than how it went, and this was the punishment she deserved. Funny Bruce had mentioned *Sunset Boulevard;* it's what came to mind now, Norma Desmond saying, "We didn't need dialogue; we had faces." It's what Thurlow used to say on days they spent staring at their newborn. Ida on that play mat with the arches overhead, groping for toys, gumming the fur, and them on either side, on their stomachs, watching the world dilate in her eyes. Esme did not get to see this reaction much anymore, though she couldn't know if it was because novelty no longer solicited at her child's door or because, when it did, she just wasn't there.

Ida retrieved rose petals from a dish of oil, and the only way Esme knew Crystal had broken the news Mom wasn't skating was from a pause in Ida's chemistry, just time enough for the love in her heart to freeze over.

Crystal appeared to laugh, and because this was not in the script, Esme upped the volume and heard her say, "I know, totally, and in those gross slippers, too. Just be glad you get to go with me instead," and Ida saying, "I dunno, I kinda like those slippers," so that Esme closed her computer, brought a hand across her mouth, and tasted the bile that had come up her throat because, despite all, her child continued to re-enlist in the collapse of her hopes. Her child still loved, still loved her mom. And this, it turned out, was worse than being unloved, because with love comes expectation.

Practice: Ida, honey, there are things you should know. Your grandparents are dead? The people who raised you, who are the only real family you've ever known, died in a car accident? I probably won't make any of your important events at school this year and might even miss your end-of-term play? Also, of some relevance, your father is wanted by the FBI for trucking in ideas that are anathema to the right wing's divide-and-conquer brand of governance? Not to mention for consorting with enemy nations? Esme's heart slammed against her rib

cage, and it was like the bones would snap and jut from her chest, because these thoughts were not apropos of nothing. They were apropos
of Jim, who was on the phone, yelling the news: "Fucking shit, Esme.
Thurlow took them hostage."

Breathe. Think. Relax. Permit dread of what you have done to para-
lyze you for ten minutes; then let this paralysis sell indulgences like the
Pope. Do not rue your choices. No one could have predicted they'd
amount to this. You are an eavesdropper, not a fortune-teller; you can
make sense only of what people say, and when did Thurlow say he was
going to do this? And how self-destructive can a person be? She felt so
defeated. All that effort to protect him in North Korea. The risks she'd
taken. And for what? He was in worse trouble now than before.

She held the phone tight. She said, "How long and what are his
demands?"

"I don't know. But I want you where I can see you. Be at the hotel in
ten. Fucking shit, Esme. Be here *in ten.*"

A siege in Cincinnati. This would not end well. No major standoff
since Fort Sumter could offer reassuring precedent. And Sumter hadn't
gone that well, either. The kids who had died at Beslan? The fatal
vapor that blew through the draw at Nord-Ost? At best, the siege gone
wrong provided empirical data. The stuff people were too stupid to
figure out in a controlled environment. From Waco and Ruby Ridge:
rubber bullets can kill; tear gas is flammable; when your rules of engagement permit deadly force, regardless of who's in danger, people
are going to die. Good lessons, but ones unlikely to preempt every fiasco brinked on a sniper's mood or the Special Agent in Charge's bow
to pressure to get this thing resolved yesterday. In the crosshairs of a
reticle, for a guy who had slept five hours in the last forty, and these in
a bivouac tent pummeled by the snows of Cincinnati—for this sniper,
whose thermal underwear was frozen with the drench of his labors,
Thurlow Dan was a stag trophy and his ticket home.

At last, a legitimate reason to go to Cincinnati. Get dressed, get dressed!
She had an emergency bag, of course. Jeans, sneakers, and BDU, which
covered most of the bases in a pinch except when you wanted to look

presentable, and God forbid a fractal pattern in olive should complement her skin tone. At least, she wanted to look better than her contact on the inside. She had never seen Vicki, but she certainly knew what this Vicki sounded like; she sounded like a donkeywhoreface in whore heels and thong. The microphone up her molars was highly sensitive. GSM technology, an itty-bitty mic plus logic board concealed in the same square of plastic a dentist uses for X-rays. Actually, it was smaller. She could keep it flush against her cheek, so that when it called Esme's phone—the apparatus was programmed to activate in the presence of what it thought were voices—it was often at a moment of climax, when this braying donkeywhoreface finished her work on Thurlow. Esme was supposed to compete with that? She could have, in her day.

She would need pants—a dress was absurd—maybe leather, but nothing standout. If she drove, she could be there in nine hours. She could jump on a plane, but there were only so many ways out of an airport, and she wanted to keep her options open. It was possible that too much info would leak before she got there, in which case she would be more white whale than white horse come time to figure out who could resolve this mess. If every U.S. marshal was after her, it was easier to get lost on the ground. Of course, there was always military transport, but then, those trips tended to make her sick. Commercial airliners got the quiet corridors, but for military flight, it was the vomit air from takeoff till landing. Her last trip in a C-17 was her and eight men in ghillie suits, which were, in terms of odor, bear shit in the mouth of summer, fungal feet, afterbirth. So, okay, no C-17, just Esme and the Hummer and fifty plates for fifty states.

Jim paced the room. He said, "Why hasn't the whore checked in, either?"

Esme did not know. Perhaps it was because Vicki was a whore with a whorehead for brains, though she kept this explanation to herself.

They were in their hotel; they had been here before.

Esme stared out the window. She could see, well in the distance, the Capitol Columns—their hats, anyway—which stood out among the gibbets of winter trees in the Arboretum.

Make a plan, revise a plan—this was a gauge of fluency under fire. Reassess for best outcome under amended conditions. She knew the drill, but Jim did not. "Fuck, fuck, fuck," he said. Palms braced on the window, head dribbling against the glass. She let the sequence loop, then said, "Look, just let me get to the house. I will talk him down, and everything will be fine. Don't you realize what's happened here? You've got a federal case dumped in your lap. Open and shut." She said this with brio, and for a second she saw Jim thrill to the prospect: Thurlow Dan, in jail, for life.

He flumped in an armchair upholstered in red-and-white gingham and kicked out his legs. He had on a suit, twilight blue, and a red silk tie.

"Don't you see?" she said, and got on her knees, between his legs. "I just did you a big favor. We couldn't *prove* North Korea. We haven't turned up anything on weaponry or funding for it. So probably I just saved your job."

Gears turning. "You must be kidding. You *planned* for this? You are insane. One, my father-in-law. Two, even if we do nail Dan for kidnapping, how are we supposed to explain having sent in these four morons to begin with? I don't think *sacrificial lamb* is going to make us any new friends."

"Just let me get to Cincinnati," she said. "Once they're free, no one will give a shit who they are or what they were doing there. Who even knows about ARDOR? Just call in some favors."

He flapped his legs, clamped them round her ribs. He said, "No one's heard from that asshole yet, just his fat-fuck number two."

"Thurlow hasn't *asked* for anything?"

"Nope. Maybe he's done us all a favor and shot his brains out."

Esme looked at the carpet. There was a limit to what equanimity she could impose on her features in the presence of talk like this.

He palmed her face like bookends. They were eye to eye. "This was all your doing," he said. "You got no encouragement from me. I came to you for counsel, given your history, but I never sanctioned this operation. You understand? If you do right on this, I know you've got a kid who's going to need some help down the road. I got a daughter, too, remember? I know how it is." His legs vised tight so that breath became a priority for her. But the message came through: if she betrayed him, the harm would go to Ida.

She ran her hands up his quads and at his groin. It didn't take a second; he unzipped and folded his arms behind his head.

"I understand," she said. "But I can talk Thurlow out. And you'll be a hero."

There was no action there, so she had to work hard. He said, "You won't even get close. Lockdown. Half the ops are probably in his bathtub already." But then his body perked up, and with it his mood. He laughed and said, "Jim Bach, national hero," which enlisted the perk for darker pleasures. He flanked her neck with his thumbs and dug in.

She had travel Kleenex in her hand already; the job was clean and then it was done. She expected to be in Cincinnati by the end of the day.

But Jim had other ideas. He picked up a glass cigar rest from the table and brought it down on her head. When it was clear she was still breathing, he dragged her to the bathroom and locked her in.

IV. In which fathers do what they think is best. Betrayal, betrayal. In which: My darling little girl.

05:50:21:03: MY DARLING LITTLE GIRL. My beloved Ida. This tape might be the last you see of your dad. I'm sorry about some of the other stuff on here. Maybe you'll understand when you're older. I'm sorry, too, if I can't finish the rest in time. But that's okay. I have some time now.

I want you to know that I started to chase your mother the second she fled my apartment and that I've never really stopped. I called every hotel in the area. I spoke to the people who had moved into her parents' house. Any clue where they went? No. Any forwarding address? No. In '94, the Internet was hardly the resource it is today, but still, I made use of what I could. I put ads in local papers across the country. The response was overwhelming, and at first, I tracked down every lead. Bus, train, hitch, hobo. I went to every state in the continental U.S. and probably through at least half its small towns.

Eventually I got word she was living in New Paltz, in New York State. At the time, I was in Miami, but decided I could be in New Paltz in two days if I hitched nonstop. I remember the ride into town. A college kid picked me up, then asked me to drive while he toked on air freshener. Butane high.

There wasn't a working stereo in the car, so this kid listened to his CD player. Sometimes, he'd slap the dash with his hands or sing along. But mostly he stared out the passenger window. I had driven long stretches of road before. I was accustomed to the populace of cars. The freeways. The solitude expressed by so many people en route together. But that day's ride seemed especially grim. I was going to find Esme, and yet I was grim. Probably this should have set off alarm bells, but who has that kind of foresight in the moment? I felt alone, even more alone than usual, so that I began to tremble all over, with tremors you could actually see ten feet away. A paroxysm of loss for missing Esme but also, maybe, because of the loss we're born into.

"I'm going to New Paltz to meet my girlfriend," I said. I said it once, then louder, and finally I punched the kid in the leg. "She's incredible." Because, really, this shudder from within was too much. Sometimes hurt just likes a stage.

The kid took off his headphones just long enough to say, "That's cool."

"She was my first, you know. You always keep them close."

"Look, I'm not much for talk," he said, and he turned up the volume on his CD player.

We made it into town. A town cloned from other college towns. Head shops, bookstore, deli. The kid said this was as far as he went. He gave me his number, and after I wandered around New Paltz for an hour, as if I'd run into Esme just for being there, I called him up.

There was a line outside his dorm room. Students with liquor and chips; one with a dog on a leash. I tried to get by. I tripped over a glass bong the length of my arm, but no one was letting me past.

The kid, whose name was Reese, poked his head out the door. He reached for me and clapped me on the back. "You get in free, my friend."

"Why's that?"

"I made some calls."

I'd been to a lot of campuses by now, and Reese had probably heard about some poorly attended events in which I insisted that a repeal of solitude was not only sufficient but ample grounds for a movement with only one requirement to join: a desire to join.

For half an hour, I wallflowered while a couple made out next to me. After that, a girl with a pink Mohawk took their place.

"Nice spot," she said. "One thing about me, I like to watch people. A place like this, you can really watch. All this space." She outstretched her arms.

"These your friends?"

"No"—and she sank to the floor.

"Come on," I said. "It can't be that bad," though I suspected it was. And I was right. She touched her belly. "Freshman with a bun in the oven. It *is* that bad."

"I'm sorry."

She returned to her feet. "Second wind, baby. Want to dance?"

I said no. I could not keep time. Even my heart beat erratically.

"Is it that you don't want to dance with *me?*" she said. Her eyes had tears.

"Oh, God, no. It's not that at all."

"You think I didn't want to be pretty? This isn't by choice," she said, pointing to her face. "How do you think I got knocked up, anyway? A girl like me, you get passed around."

It was nearly eleven. I dropped my beer. Three hours of sleep in two days. The dog lapped up the suds before they were lost to the carpet. I decided to make for the bathroom, where I planned to fold up in the tub.

"You know, I haven't told anyone about the bun," she said. "Weird that I just told you, right?"

I nodded and smiled because this was the Helix, right here. She asked if I wanted to have sex. I said no, but that I'd be happy to stimulate her clitoris if she thought it would do her any good. She said this was not the most enticing proposal, but sure, why not.

She took my arm. Only, when we got to the bathroom, I really did collapse in the tub. I was just so tired. She said there was a Korean doctor in town who was an OB but also a healer of some kind and maybe, from the look of things, what I needed was some healing. She had been to see him about the baby and in the waiting room she'd met another pregnant woman who told her about the healing. In fact, the other pregnant woman had recently come to town precisely to see this Korean doctor, who was, she swore, the best.

I almost passed out, though not from fatigue. What did the woman look like? She was lovely. How pregnant? Six months. A blanched star of skin on her earlobe? Could be, yeah.

I raced down the hall and turned on the lights. I was looking for Reese; I needed his car. A boy getting oral sex on the couch said, "Ignore it! Keep going!" Reese said, "Sure, man, but when you get back, we want to hear about the Helix."

The OB's name was Choi Soon Yul. I found his office in the phone book and sifted through a dumpster out back until I found an electric bill with what I took to be his home address. Two hours later, I was banging on Yul's screen door, smelling very much like the garbage I'd just been through. Porch lights went on, a dog went nuts, and I was sure someone would call the police, which would at least have given me a place to sleep. It was nearing 3 a.m. Instead, Yul came to the porch in slippers. Yes, yes, please would I come in and stop making that racket.

He was oddly self-possessed. He made us tea. I drank two cups and asked about Esme. He made a pretense of doctor-patient confidentiality but gave it up when it became clear I was not to be deterred and could, in fact, spend the rest of the night wailing on his doorstep. Finally he said yes, he had a patient who fit the description, but so what? Her file was in his office. I said we had to get it. He asked if I was threatening him. I was not. Only, was she okay, the patient? Was the baby okay? At last he seemed taken aback. And I was confused. Should I have been asking something else?

We agreed to visit his office the next day. In the meantime, he gave me a blanket.

I slept late into the afternoon and awoke to a flashlight pointed at my face and someone squirting me with water from a spray bottle. The room was dark; the shades were pulled. I felt massively hungover. I shaded my eyes and headed to the bathroom. My urine was a russet color I had never seen in nature. I was still feeling parched and groggy, so I went back to sleep on the couch. Next I knew, there was a voice saying, "Lift up your shirt," and a hand feeling for the softest part of my stomach and something sharp breaking the skin.

"B-twelve plus," she said, and again came the flashlight.

I swatted at the barrel until she turned it off. My Esme, six months pregnant, with hair parted down the middle and trussed in short pigtails. The look was not at all in keeping with the woman I knew, nor was her floral maternity blouse or canvas satchel. But it did not matter. She could have been in a chicken suit—my feelings were unchanged. I wanted to solder my body to hers, but it would not do to have Yul watching. He had served his purpose; now go away.

"B what?" I said.

"Twelve. Twelve plus. Will help with the grogginess. Yul said you drank two cups. One would have been enough."

I rubbed at my eyes and tried to think. But—what?

Esme sat next to me. "You'll be feeling better in a second," she said, and she touched my forehead with the back of her hand. I was starting to already. She took my pulse.

I'd had many feelings in the anticipation of this moment, though none was on hand to help me recruit Esme back into my life. I had intended to plead and, that failing, to use the adamance of my passion to win a chance. But my head was still gruel.

You will ask why I loved her, and the answer is, I do not know. Once we're past the qualities we all rejoice in our lovers—she is kind, she is funny, she is smart—there comes the X factor. Norman says that when you cite X factor, you are unburdening yourself of the onus to think. Imagine we chalked up all of our feelings to the X factor. Why do I kill? I dunno, it's just got that special something. Norman has a point, but it does not attend to the experience of meeting a person who makes you want to live forever.

Esme said, "In any other universe, a man coming for Yul at three a.m. is the RDEI. Only it's not the RDEI; it's Thurlow Dan come to find true love. Jesus."

"What's the RDEI?"

She slipped her fingers under her glasses and began to press and rub at her eyes. "You're going to cost me my job," she said. "Which is almost ironic, since you pretty much got me this assignment to begin with."

I didn't know what she was talking about, only that she was not saying what I most dreaded to hear. Go home, Thurlow. Leave me alone, Thurlow. I never want to see you again, Thurlow.

She leaned back into the couch and touched her stomach. "I'm going to be a tennis ball at a party tonight." She lifted her blouse, and there was the outline of a tennis ball in white paint. "A costume party at the high school gym. I'll probably be the only person without a date. Bare-balled and pregnant." She laughed grimly.

I did not ask whatever happened to not wanting the baby. I asked, instead, if she'd been feeling okay. She shook her head. There had been some bleeding early on, all-day nausea that sneered at the misnomer *morning sickness,* and a test for CF that boded poorly. I watched her relate these difficulties and was just beginning to marvel at the stoicism with which she'd met each one when the unexpected happened. She wept.

The effect was to make of the B12, in contrast, a shot of tar. I vaulted to her side and took her hand. She wiped at the tears with the hem of her shirt and said, "Listen to me very carefully. Yul is a North Korean defector. You don't know what I do for a living, but it's enough to say he's helping us. And so is this pregnancy. It keeps our cover. But, Thurlow"—and here she started to cry anew—"I'm scared. I'm going to have a baby. I've never held a newborn. I never even had a pet."

"You had lizards."

"They died."

We stayed like that for a while, her crying into my chest and me acclimating to the opportunities grown between us with every tear. When we'd both taken our thoughts as far as we could alone, we aired them out. She said I should leave; I said we should marry. She said, "Have you heard anything I've been saying?" I said, "Yes. Perfectly." We set a date for two weeks later.

I'm aware that for Esme, there was a degree of convenience to these nuptials. But that did not have to preclude feelings she might have had for me, or could grow to have in time. I saw the look on her face when she realized I was there to stay. There was incredulity and some pity—I would, after all, do anything for her—but also relief and gratitude. She would not be going through this alone.

In the weeks that followed, I heard more about Yul. He and his wife had escaped from North Korea through China. Crossed the Tumen River from Musan in the northeast territory using a flotation device for children. Traveled four thousand miles through the mountains down the coast, shirking border patrols, opium smugglers, and slave traders, any of whom would have sold his wife as a prostitute and returned him to North Korea, where he'd have been executed or jailed in a concentration camp, some of which are thirty miles long. Bigger than Auschwitz. Possibly more brutal in the day-to-day. They traveled at night, mostly by foot, passing into Vietnam and Laos, over the Mekong and into Thailand.

The Chois were not forthcoming with their experience; I got it all from Esme, in whose pillow talk were breaches of security that could have won Pulitzers for every journalist in America. Yul, though a trained OB, had worked as a propaganda writer when it became clear this was the only way to support his family. To live in Pyongyang and get rations that rivaled in bounty what the government allotted its prize citizens, among them four American soldiers who had crossed the DMZ in the early sixties and lived in Pyongyang ever since.

And here was where Esme fit in. And why, years later, I had good cause to go to North Korea myself. At some point, these four American GIs would get to be of growing interest to the White House, for two reasons. First, a Pentagon memo about the four would be leaked to the press. What an uproar! Were they defectors or prisoners? The Pentagon denied knowledge of any living POWs but did concede to having watched a North Korean movie, *Nameless Heroes,* in which, lo and behold, the four American soldiers had starring roles as Western agents of evil. For years, the army's theory on these men was that they were MIA. The North Korean theory was that they were promised body and soul to communist North Korea. Since neither seemed likely, the Americans figured maybe the thing was to get the three (by then one had died) to exercise influence from within. They were movie stars. And since Kim Jong-il was a movie buff with a library of twenty thousand films, and since he'd written volumes on the subject of the movie arts, the thinking was that he would not be able to withstand the allure of *four* movie stars, never mind the country of their birth or ended allegiance.

Second, one morning, a sub would wash up in the Sea of Japan, empty of its twenty-six North Korean commandos, who were apparently on the lam in South Korea, plotting God knows. The result? Sixty thousand South Korean troops on their tail for fifty-three days, and during this time, did the U.S. have any idea what was going on? Not really. Meantime, the North Koreans had flouted the Nuclear Non-Proliferation Treaty again and again. Did the U.S. have any clue what her intentions were? No on that, too. Wouldn't it be nice to have people on the inside? You bet. Enter Yul and Yul's contacts, some of whom were in the film business. Enter Esme, on a mission.

But I am getting ahead of myself. Before all this, Esme and I still had our nights together, when she'd read to me from Kim Jong-il's manifesto *On the Art of Cinema.* I had a hard time getting past the foreclosing austerity of the man's author bio—*Kim Jong-il is leader of North Korea. Kim Jong-il succeeded his father, Kim Il-sung, who had ruled North Korea since 1948*—though I did appreciate the singleness of purpose with which I imagined him recording his thoughts. The section titles were no joke. *Life Is Struggle and Struggle Is Life. Compose the Plot Correctly. The Best Possible Use Should Be Made of Music and Sound.* At no point did you ever get the sense that any of the tome's fluorescence was lost in translation. I can still picture Esme, whaled out on the bed, pointing a Cheeze Doodle to passages she liked. "Look at this," she'd say, and laugh so big I could see the snack-food paste around her molars. And so I'd look and read aloud: *"Once agreement has been reached in discussion, the director must act on it promptly, firmly basing the production on it and never deviating from it, no matter what happens. If the director vacillates, so will the whole collective, and if that happens, the production will fail."*

"Jesus," I'd say. "I would hate to be on that guy's set."

"Imagine he's directing your country."

Mostly, though, when it came to her work, I had no idea what she was talking about. DPRK, IAEA, DMZ, NPT—she'd rattle off this shorthand as though I were in the know, and such was my ignorance that I thought these were clandestine agencies entrusted to my discretion. The first time I heard mention of the IAEA in public, I thought it signaled the toppling of our secret service. But it was just news: the International Atomic Energy Agency, having exposed its inspectors as titular in Iraq, was going full tilt on its evaluation of North Korea's nuclear sites. As a result, negotiations were breaking down, and the North Koreans would likely not just defy the NPT but leave it altogether.

Esme would say, "If that nut job really does have a nuclear bomb, forget *five* bombs, we are in a world of shit." She'd be lying on her side with a pillow between her legs. I'd be lying on my side, too, and so there we were, belly to belly, while she foretold the end of the world and I touched her breasts because her breasts were so lovely that I always wanted an excuse to touch them, and I needed an excuse, since bald-faced admiration fell into a category of motives Esme could not stand. These included admiration without pretext, fear of the unknown, and indifference to situations just because you are unversed in them. I continued to touch her breasts and marvel at the summer palette of her skin—cream and sand, milk and flax—the gossamer above her lips, her sleepy breaths at night, and hair snarled across the pillow. And once she was asleep, I began to study the world in earnest.

For those last months of her pregnancy, our lives were routine. On the weekends, I'd meet with Reese and peerage to discuss *ideas*. It was a reading group. We assigned each other the usual suspects: Freud and Lacan. Schopenhauer, Hegel, Kant. Maybe Hume. William James. Mostly, though, I went there to lend credibility to what I'd been thinking about on my own. I was looking for quotes.

At issue was the predicament of being alone, which I thought about obsessively, because I was a little confused. I'd found Esme and married, and we were going to have a baby, and so the wasteland of my heart was to have been lush and gay and departed from the isolation whose fix was the Helix mandate. And yet something felt wrong. I still felt unmoored.

In the meantime, I needed a source of income. It turns out that having a child has pecuniary obligations you cannot quantify. It's not about allotting funds for diapers or food or even higher education, but about needing to afford whatever this baby needs, whatever this baby wants, may she have everything I can give her and all the things I can't.

Esme wanted to name the baby Roxanne. I demurred but did not press. She wanted to name the baby Ida. Ida Dan? Don't be absurd. Ida Haas.

I got a job filing cases for a law firm. They called me a paralegal, but all I did was file. It was a large practice. Corporate and, as far as I could tell, engaged to flout protections of the Hudson River. The office was a tic-tac-toe arrangement of cubicles and hallways. Most days, I came home feeling like mulch.

Still, I tried to retain this job because we had moved into a house that needed more renovation and repair than was apparent when we bought it. There were loans to pay down. A testy sump pump. Corroding pipes and backyard sludged with overflow from a septic tank twenty years old. The problems were menial, but of the sort I thought typified a young marriage.

In the meantime, Esme was spending more and more time with Yul, who had been unable to make contact with the Americans on the inside and who, frankly, did not want to. His desire to topple the system from which he had fled was nominal at best. He just wanted to deliver babies in the free world, maybe to have one of his own, and to move on. Esme was appalled and, for being appalled, spiked her blood pressure. The baby was due in two weeks.

Three days later, I was sitting at my desk, shooting rubber bands at the wall of my cubicle. I'd set up a bull's-eye of pushpins. I was league champion. Coworker Janice poked her head over the panel divide. She wore silver hoop earrings that slapped her neck.

I was in low spirits. That morning, I'd found a skein of Esme's hair atop the shower drain and been disgusted. The feeling passed in a flash, but there was no denying it. I'd been disgusted. By my own wife. The shock of it made me feel woozy, and I pressed my head to the wall tile. And then came a siege of misgiving. All the times I'd pressed my lips to her more delicate nature and *not enjoyed it*. The way she let her nail polish chip for weeks before reapplication. How, for no reason, she walked on tiptoe. And then, and *then,* her inability to wash cookware, so that, on mornings I wanted eggs, I'd find the skillet greased in fat. Her toes, which gripped each other during movie night on the couch— have I mentioned how much I didn't like her toes? And then perhaps the frequency with which she'd begun to say she loved me—perhaps I did not like that, either.

I'd stayed in the shower so long, my skin had crimped and the water gone cold. But this was nuts, right? That the dream—of marriage, love, togetherness—never accords with practice is a timeless bromide. Even so, I began to query the content of this dream because I had thought it was about Esme. About Esme's penetrating the horrible isolation that until her had struck me as simply the thing we are all born into. I am not certain what in her made me think love and family were an anti- dote, but I thought they were, at least until that moment in the shower, at which point I crouched on the mat, drew my knees to my chest, and promised with everything I had to suppress what I'd just come to doubt. I swore to be a good husband and a good father and petitioned God not to smite me for thinking ill of my pregnant wife. I didn't mean it; I was just scared and stupid and didn't know better.

Janice asked if I was going to Ed the custodian's funeral. He had collided with a tree on Putt Corners Road, the canard being that he'd had a heart attack, though everyone knew he'd done it on purpose. Everyone but Janice. I remember her saying he always seemed so happy and me saying, "Jesus, Janice, misery can be looking you straight in the face, and you'd never know it."

She said, "Work is just too boring today—let's play a game. It's a drinking game, but I guess we can adapt." It was called State of the Union. "You have to itemize everything that's good and bad in your life. You know, talking points. So, you want to play?"

This was the kind of thing we did at our Helix meetings. But I wasn't in the mood. "I have to call my wife."

"Call her after."

I slumped in my chair. "Okay. The good? I'm married to the woman of my dreams, and we're about to have a baby."

"Wow! That's amazing! But way to sound happy about it."

"The bad? I'm married to the woman of my dreams, and we're about to have a baby."

She frowned. "Is that like Nietzsche or something? Everything good is bad? You know Dale in HR? His brother goes to those meetings of yours at the university, so I know the stuff you guys read."

"It's your game," I said.

She returned to her side of the panel, so I stood and draped my chin over the ledge. "Okay, wait, maybe this will explain it. Don't laugh, but all my life, I've had this theory about loneliness, that it's congenital, fundamental, but that you could escape or defeat it. And I thought I had, only now I see I haven't even come close. And I'm worried it's not even possible. But forget that. I just have to work harder, redouble my efforts. I think that falls into the good category, right?"

She had been about to make a call, but now she replaced the phone in the cradle. "I just have no idea what you're talking about," she said. "But it doesn't sound good at all."

"No, no, it's good. I'm recommitting. I started those meetings a couple years ago, but now I'm going to make them huge. Nationwide."

I gave her my best smile. I'd wanted to try out my resolve, to see how it sounded aloud. To find in my speech a nostrum for anxieties fallen to me at that moment, among them my wife, the coming baby, and the fulcrum anxiety of knowing I might run out on them both.

But Janice was right: It sounded bad.

I went to the lounge and thought about Ed. If he was desolate inside, could the Helix have helped? Was suicide a more workable option than what I'd been trying to do?

Then I heard Janice yelling my name from across the floor and getting closer. And something in her voice—I knew what she'd come to say. I jumped behind the couch and got low. Dust bunnies clotted the air vent. I held my breath and waited for her to pass. Then I snuck back to my desk. Six messages on the machine, all from my frantic wife. She was in labor, hurry up.

That day, I was supposed to speak at an event on campus, and I felt the pull of this event so strongly that every turn I made toward the hospital had to be won from its clutch. The symposium was called "Iraq: Five Years Later." I was scheduled to speak last on the bill. I would say something about self-interest and question whether we'd have invaded Iraq to protect a place like Singapore, which has almost no natural resources. I would go on this way for a few minutes and then swell the discourse to include matters touching and dire and germane to the malcontent I knew these people were feeling, the organizer in particular. Her name was Marshall. She was well loved by well-meaning people, which meant that, besides feeling isolated and unreachable, she also felt guilty, because, come on, how much love does a person need to feel a part of? What was she doing wrong? Driving to the hospital, I could not have empathized with her more.

Ida, sweetheart, you were a breech baby. You nearly died from several problems, among them a dislodging of your mother's placenta and a noosed umbilical cord. There was a C-section. I'm told she stayed awake through the entire procedure, asking for me at intervals of one to two seconds. I'm told she cried and feared for my life, because only a terrible accident could have kept me from her. I was told this by a nurse while Esme slept. I did, after all, get to the hospital, at least to reception, where I counted black diamonds patterned across the floor and tried to will myself to her room.

The nurse told me you were in an incubator—you were having trouble breathing—but that Esme was awake and asking for me again.

I said I'd be right there. I had flowers delivered from the lobby florist with a note that said: *I'm on my way!* And then I did something awful. I left. I raced my car through every yellow in town and got back to campus.

Marshall gave me a kiss. And I was so relieved to be there with her. For months I'd been telling Marshall about the Helix. That I wanted to believe in this thing to save me from myself. Maybe to save a few other people, too. She said if I was going to be a leader, I'd have to shore up my pitch and make it coherent. Hone my ideas, communicate in story. She said I talked drivel and didn't have the charisma to hide it. I was, she said, more Koresh than Jim Jones, though we were agreed I was neither.

The plaza was full, which was insane for February. There were banners and balloons, torchlights and pizza. I started to panic. It would be hours before the horror of abandoning Esme tided over me so that I could not breathe, which meant the distress of the moment was caused by something else. And it was this: Those hundred people in the audience? Their lives could change for hearing me vaunt ideas I barely understood myself. Did I really think the predicament of being alone was soluble? I'd just left my wife and new baby to start their lives together without me for dread of us never being able reach each other, no matter what we said. So I don't know. I was afraid. Too afraid to test out the very ideas I was about to insist were a retort to loneliness and despair. And yet there I was. Because maybe one in those hundred applauding my name would be less scared than me.

They introduced me as a social psychologist who lectured nationwide and whose highly anticipated writ on the topic of loneliness would be issued by an eminent and heroic publishing juggernaut in the spring. I glanced at Marshall, who smiled big, and the smile said: In time, these lies will come true, so who cares?

From the dais, I did not recognize anyone. I found out later that my childhood friend Norman was in the aisle, three rows in, but that he didn't stay for the whole speech, just long enough to make eye contact with me. Or so he thought, because it wasn't faces I saw but the same face in every one, of my wife, anguished and alone. And so I started talking about her. I said I worried she was as unknown to me as a stranger in the park. I said that the negative space contoured by our absence in each other's lives gave shape to what was impossible to shape otherwise but which I could now see with a horror I could barely put into words. What does loneliness look like? So long as my wife was out there, this person I adored, clamoring for me and getting no response, I had a good idea.

I said, "But this isn't about me. It's about us all. Because everywhere and all the time, people are crying out for each other. Your name. Mine. And when you look back on your life, you'll see it's true: woke up lonely, and the missing were on your lips."

I blinked at the audience, which had been quiet for a while. As I spoke, the antiwar posters had come down like the flag post-death. I'd noticed a few balloons released and bound for paradise. I turned off the mic. The crowd dispersed. I'd say it was funereal except that no one goes into a funeral expecting to be stoked. This was more like the aftermath of a big loss for the home team.

Marshall gave me a hug. I told her that my baby was three hours old and that I had to go. She lifted the hem of her T-shirt, and there was a double helix tattooed on the small of her back.

I rushed to the hospital. This time, Esme had company. I found Norman sitting next to the bed and holding her hand. It was even possible he was trying to explain me. I was stunned but then not, because if Norman was his own season, he came every year.

I gave him the nod and took her other hand. Kissed her on the forehead and said I'd seen the baby, that she was a marvel. I had not seen the baby, but in my head, I knew I was right.

Esme's voice was quiet, and for a second, I thought all would be well. Then she said, "Where were you, Lo?"

I'd had hours to prepare an answer, but in my will to believe I was not shirking responsibility in the most horrible way, I had refused to accept this moment would come. I looked at Norman. I half expected a miracle to intercede on my behalf. Just give me a minute, let me think.

Her face was blanched; her hair was matted. I spliced my fingers with hers and thought I'd never loved her more.

Norman said, "Esme, it's like I said before: I'm so sorry. It's my fault. I talked Lo into leaving work early and taking a drive with me and the car broke down. We just got back. Lo was just paying the cab."

I nodded, restated, embellished, and finally I just wept. I pressed each of her knuckles to my lips and wept. I had escaped discovery—the relief was palpable—and so I wept for this. Norman had secured for me a chance to redress this terrible mistake, and so I wept for that, too. I wept because I knew I would not redress the mistake and, in fact, would do worse in the months to come. My wife loved me, my daughter would love me long before she knew what this meant, and for these travesties I wept most of all.

It pains me to have to say it, but I will: In the year after you were born, there were other women. Several. People I tried to connect with because I could not connect with you or your mother, though it turns out I couldn't really connect with them, either. Still, I tried. They all knew I was married. I told them everything. I talked and shared and it helped. At least in the short term. I'd come home less afraid. Less unknown. And, while I knew it was wrong, it also felt right. So I was confused. And depressed. And when it got so bad, and I stopped knowing what to do, Esme made the decision for us. She packed you up and split. She left me to the Helix.

After that? Magical thinking. I'd wake up with hope. Not hope legitimized by a real development for good, not hope born of faith in the world's benevolence, but hope that is your way of staying alive. I believed you were coming back. Some days, this was okay. Other days, I'd take myself down. What insanity! You're an idiot! They are not coming back; they are *never* coming back. The rest of the day might be given over to sobbing in a ball, only the next morning I was up and at 'em, sprightly as before.

It got so quiet in the house, I'd put a fork down the garbage disposal just so I could call a repairman. I clogged the bathtub drain with screws and dimes and a sock, and when the plumber took a break, I undid his good work. But these people never stayed more than an hour.

I quit my job and began skimming a salary from donations to the Helix. We headquartered on campus, but I went everywhere, and at every stop, I asked after my wife. I wanted a miracle. Esme worked for the government; if she wanted to vanish, she would.

I went to therapy all the time. The regret of what I had done was awful, but the permanence was worse. A shrink at SUNY told me I should believe in myself. And I did. I believed I was stupid and evil and without hope. I thought I would not make it. Only time intervened—it always does—and with it came the prize and mercy of endurance. In lieu of facts, I had possibility. Since you could be anywhere, I began to see you everywhere. My little girl, in saddle shoes and party dress.

Esme left most of your stuff behind, so I have your baby socks in a drawer by my bed. But these are just artifacts, and as the years go by, they have become less solace than rebuke. One time I had your baby photo age-progressed, then made the mistake of doing it again elsewhere, and when the results were girls who barely resembled each other, I postered my wall with their likenesses.

Do you have my blond hair? Is it thick like your mother's, does it lift and dip as you cruise the playground, do you have knock-knees and braces, are your eyes still bear brown?

For your last birthday, I sent you an unlimited gift certificate to the American Girl store in New York. It was returned. I sent you guest passes to the Oscars and afterparties and guaranteed a private interview with a teen heartthrob of your choosing. These were repulsed. I've sent letters begging for news. A photo. Something you made at school. And every day, every year: nothing.

What do you think this does to a man? I'll tell you. It sends a man to North Korea.

And so, at last, the story of why I am in this mess. The story of Pyongyang, City of the Dead.

To be fair, and for the record, it was the North Koreans who approached *me*. Under the aegis of wanting an improved image in the West. They knew the Helix had reach. Daily contributions were up; sales of the *Helix Monthly* were up. RYLS attendance had gotten so huge, we outsold the Spanish pop phenomenon Enrique Iglesias. In the meantime, Pyongyang's rapport with the United States was foundering badly. The U.S., which had promised to help them build two cold-water reactors, had called them a bad name. Others in receipt of the bad name were being bombed comprehensively. Pyongyang, nonplussed and ever sensitive to a patrimony of occupation, copped to having atomic weapons or, at the very least, the resources to make them, so back off. Another impasse that had already isolated the country to the point of starvation. Two million people dead of famine, which they blamed on cataclysmic phenomena in the soil. But which they also blamed on the American tyranny pledged to kill them all. Enter the Helix. They needed our help.

We were a good fit. For one, I sympathized with their anti-Americanism. I did. After all, what hubris on our part to have regarded Korea as war booty and divided it with the Soviets. The sundered families and affronted national esteem within five minutes of freedom from the Japanese. Kim Il-sung's aggression, though unwarranted, punished with a million dead. It was no small wonder they hated us.

Two: North Korea is the last black spot on the map. Solipsism, repression, and homogeneity are its standout qualities. So imagine what I could do for them. Improve their image? Fine. Use the Helix to forge ties—one person at a time—with the most isolated people on earth? Nobel Prize–winning. And in the meantime, because I knew to hedge my bets, I'd try to finagle contact with the American defectors Esme had been trying to recruit so many years before. I wanted to make her a hero. I wanted to make us both heroes so that she'd see in me something to love.

So I went to the North, to meet Kim Jong-il. To set up some Helix events, and to propose bringing many of my followers to participate. The plan wasn't just to thaw relations but to change the way we thought about each other. If this could be accomplished in North Korea, it could be accomplished anywhere.

I decided to take Isolde. She'd been a prostitute when we met, and so I thought her vocation would provide me with some comfort. Putage may not be unique to the free world, but it's still totem for the erotic and transactive possibilities therein, and I wanted these reminders of home to protect me in this forbidding and scary place.

We flew from Beijing on Air Koryo, one of only six flights making the descent into North Korea a week. I was sure the plane wouldn't make it. As soon as we sat down, the anachronistic hairstylings of the crew seemed to suggest other, more dire anachronisms—a gunpowder engine, for instance. We were the only Caucasians onboard, though the cabin was half-empty. Who wanted to visit North Korea? Who was *permitted* to visit North Korea? The occasion for the Japanese tourists we'd come with was the Mass Games, which meant the DPRK had relaxed its antipathy to foreigners to help internationalize the harmony of the socialist state manifest in eighty thousand gymnasts tossing a ball at the same time. The Japanese were excited. Isolde was excited. She had never seen an Asian or heard a foreign tongue, so consider the disarrangement of mind caused by so many doors flung open at once.

Our seats were upholstered in a tan fabric textured like denim. Our reading material comprised fictions sponsored by the North Korean government to the effect that the United States endorsed Satanism. We were a fount of colonialist doctrine currently or at one time expressed in the following: Mexico, China, Greece, the Philippines, Albania, Iran, Guatemala, Haiti, Panama, Vietnam, Cambodia, Zaire, Brazil, Cuba, Chile, Fiji, Turkey, Iceland, Taiwan, Lebanon, Nicaragua, Grenada, Haiti, Afghanistan. Where were the American imperialists most in evidence today? Iraq. What was the country most likely to stampede the third world on the flimsiest of pretexts? America.

I was hard pressed to argue with this agitprop, supplied in full by our stewardess. I felt bad for her. She had been chosen among a handful to consort with the alien ideology. Her ill will was patent.

The Pyongyang airport looks, from the tarmac, like a prison block.

It is a trellis of windows that together are lintel for a billboard of Kim Il-sung. We deplaned and passed through customs without fanfare. We'd had our marching orders. No cell phones, no laptops, no literature in which North Korea makes an appearance, no American flags or icons of patriotic zeal. Then we were relieved of our passports, which agreed with me but which Isolde didn't like. I'd forgotten to tell her that for the duration of our stay in the Forbidden City, we were captive to the Forbidden City. She wore stilettos that jabbed the floor until she snapped a heel in dudgeon. I promised to buy her flats. She hobbled to the bus.

We dined in our hotel, which was marooned on an island in the Taedong River, and were sent to our room at 8 p.m. I had the sense not to ask our minders when we might dispense with the charade that I was but another tourist, and spent the evening wandering about the hotel. As with most places in Pyongyang, it was large-scale and finessed to screen the essential poverty of the state. There was a bowling alley with lights and power that were turned on by request and shut down the instant you were done. Likewise with the casino, movie theater, nightclub, and bar. You might be looking at the largest movie screen in Asia, but with no electricity to run the projector.

That night the theater billed cinema verité, part one of the 1978 epic *Nameless Heroes*, which starred the four American soldiers who had defected. The movie is probably twenty-five hours long. Isolde and I got through twenty-five minutes. The theater was deserted, just us and a hotel guide who cautioned that to talk during the film was to discredit its organizing principle, which was the eminence of Kim Jong-il.

I told Isolde to keep quiet and that we would not stay long. She asked if there were any other movies playing, or maybe we could just watch TV? She wondered if *Friends* was syndicated abroad. I took her hand. She had frosted her lips pink and wore her hair, a sunny blond, fanned about her shoulders. Her Southern accent was not pronounced but was still noticeable—a swallowing of medial consonants and a tendency to diphthong her words so that they went on and on. Fire was ray-yed. Her favorite band was the Grateful Day-ed. You know what's not any fu-uhn? This movie lauding Kim Il-suh-ung.

Our guard told us to shut up. But Isolde just couldn't. She kept asking why the Americans in this film were killing everyone without cause and then remembering that killing people without cause is often just what we Americans do. And it wasn't like the North Koreans were ever going to forget that. God knows why I had thought otherwise. Where I saw in Pyongyang a desire to improve relations with the West and put the hatred aside, they saw in me distaste for my government and a stake in its downfall. Their thinking: What would happen if North Korea backed a heterodoxy opposed to the U.S. imperialist wolves and baby killers? A chance to destabilize the U.S. from within. Perhaps to lodge a spy or two among us. To get a foothold where before they had had none. How naive I am? Very, it seems.

And so, sitting there watching *Nameless Heroes*, I began to get a bad feeling. Perhaps I had not given North Korea its due as a repressor of men. The Pass of Tears to labor camp was but one misstep away. Sneak a Western soap opera—a favorite in the North—and you could be sent to the notorious prison compound Yodok. Consider this: It's midnight and all of a sudden, the People's Security Force kills the electricity before a house raid just so you can't eject your tapes smuggled in from the South. And for this: twenty years' hard labor.

If the Koreans were even showing us *Nameless Heroes*, it meant they knew to whom I'd been married and the nature of her work. It meant they knew she was after those soldiers. And so it began to seem possible they had actually invited me here to end my life at Yodok.

The only way off the island was by bridge. We had no transportation and no passports, and I hardly thought Isolde was dressed for the four-thousand-mile trek to freedom. There was nothing to be done.

They woke us up at 4 a.m. General Kim Jong-il, it seemed, had insomnia. It was unlikely Isolde was intended to join me, but when my five minutes to recoup sense and bathe were up, the escort was more than a little vexed to find her languishing in bed. One got the impression his livelihood—possibly his life—was riding on the timeliness of our arrival at the general's abode.

What sorts of men are granted audience with a quixotic, possibly insane but more likely astute megalomaniac? What sorts of men does this megalomaniac prefer? Men who drink. In the limousine were two in uniform and a third in civilian dress. The officers did not talk to us but decanted a malted beverage into four glasses. I don't much like the drink, so I gave mine to Isolde, at which juncture I was advised to take it back.

Traversing the city at night was not much different from during the day. In the day the roads were stippled with cars—a handful—and at night there were none. Lights were scarce, there were no traffic signals, and every road felt epic. These were not roads, they were runways. Tree lined. Swept clean. Flanked in the distance by the gray slab architecture we've come to associate with the Eastern Bloc. I looked out at the full moon and starscape and decided this must be the only capital city in the world with industry so depressed, you could see the starscape.

Isolde began to nod off. Both military men nudged my foot. I pinched her leg. She said, "All right, all right," and asked for a drink of her own.

Now, perhaps I am a Westerner who thinks all Asians look alike, in which case and insofar as I share this problem with millions, I should be forgiven the following observation: the civilian between the officers of rank looked a *whole lot* like Kim Jong-il. The multiple chins and pompadour. The tan leisure suit with elastic waist. The pudgy wrists and feminine eyeglasses that came halfway down his face. The way he regarded Isolde, whose Swedish coloring I'd been told the general preferred. Based on what I knew of him, there was no chance he was in our Benz, unacknowledged and without the pageantry imperious men like to grant a summit, but even so: the likeness was astonishing. But also discomfiting. Now and then, if a streetlamp happened to be on and illuminated his face, something about it seemed off. Skin grafts, maybe. Silicone implants. I'd heard he was vain like that. But still.

We drove through the city and out toward the coast. I knew Kim Jong-il had a beach residence and assumed this was our destination. By night's ebb, however, we were still driving. The guards never took their eyes off us, but the man in the leisure suit was charming. He tippled without pause, refilling my glass and his. We made small talk. I was fettered in my speech, assuming the car was bugged. A lovely city, Pyongyang. Most hospitable. Yes, yes, but how did I like the movie? I said it was testament to the creative genius embodied in the general's seminal tome on the subject of filmmaking. I said, and here was the biggest risk I'd ever taken in my life, "In particular, the Americans were great, a wonderful coup for Korean cinema."

He nodded and smiled and asked Isolde what she thought, and since

I'd told her that the Americans might be living in the Mangyongdae District, on the west side of town, I expected her to wile a tour of the area and a visit with at least one of the Americans for an autograph.

"What do *I* think?" she said. "I think that movie was crap."

From then on, I was sidelined. They talked about Elizabeth Taylor, Peckinpah, and the displacement film *Westworld,* set in a recreational frontier town of cyborgs. Isolde railed against cartoon movies and bristled when asked whether she agreed that *Friday the 13th* was the best horror movie ever. That honor she reserved for *Evil Dead II.*

The liquor was cognac, and I was starting to feel ill from thought of my caloric intake for the day, well in excess of what my diet allowed. I looked out the window and was certain we'd passed this bridge before. I despaired of this drive ever coming to an end.

I sat back. I was exhausted. The man in the leisure suit asked me about my family, and when I told him about my wife and child—how much I missed them—he finished the last of his drink and appeared to shut down. Stopped talking. Leaned back and stared at his hands with an expression so leached of feeling, it was as though you could source the country's bleakness to his face. Perhaps he was a paid look-alike, but no matter. I liked him and began to pity the fallout of having to live as we did, at the top of our field, commanding the people and forging ahead. I expected Kim Jong-il's personal life was no less dismantling than mine. He had four wives, seven offspring; I wondered how many of his wives couldn't stand him, either. I had the urge to pat him on the knee and say I understood. But the moment passed. And next I knew, we were back at our hotel. It was a Monday morning, 7 a.m., and the city, for its millions, was dead.

That afternoon, I met a low-level official who took notes on the Helix—our numbers and stats—and that was that. Homeward bound. Home to this, which is soon to be a eulogy. Can you hear what's happening outside? It's the madding crowd, come to hang the king.

There were choppers overhead. News crews just beyond a perimeter that berthed the house at fifty feet, and guys in bucket trucks who had already started to deforest the grounds. There was tension about when to aggress against the Helix House, and tension between SWAT, which would have welcomed the elevated vantage of a tree-house bower, and the National Guard, which wanted to tank through Cincinnati without stop.

Thurlow trolled the halls. Light from the clerestory windows had vanished behind clouds that had rolled in fast. Even the weather seemed to have been conscripted into the narrative of doom being written outside. People in Cincinnati always liked to talk about the tornado outbreak of '74 and its follow-up in '99. In '99, eight of the city's civil defense sirens malfunctioned or lost power, which betrayed the stupidity of relying a bad-weather siren on electricity when electricity tends to fall victim to bad weather. Most civil defense sirens made use of a minor third to sennet bad news. The sound was not the clamor of police or medical transport but a howl that seemed to exercise the grief of things unsaid; cf. the sob that issued from the Thunderbolt apparatus of downtown Cincinnati when a tornado was afoot. Thurlow had modeled the house alarm on it so that if the house were breached, the news would anguish for miles. But for now, all being inside, he was safe.

He checked his watch, seven o'clock, which meant he was expected online for his weekly appearance. Showing up today was probably not a good idea, though it might be fortifying to gauge the mood of his people. Maybe no one actually cared what was happening at the Helix House, in which case he could cut himself some slack.

On the back end of the website were chat rooms, among them one for the members wanting sex. Critics said that organizations like the Helix encouraged bacchanalia, and that as leader Thurlow must be an incorrigible roué, but it wasn't true. Or not entirely true. He'd made these rooms accessible by video because the I Seek You protocol rewarded disclosure at a clip, and faces could help. Or so he'd thought until the Play Room took hold. In there, what strides the video option had made toward facilitating intimacy were Pyrrhic.

Just last night he'd seen a man fellate himself with a Winnie the Pooh hand puppet, though what had Thurlow rapt was the affection and solicitude the man's free hand lavished on the bear, as if the only way to thank ourselves for love received was through displacement. This show, one among thousands. People registering disbelief and gratitude for what was being offered them. A longing for more. Please don't sign off until I am done. Don't leave, please. It was a peacocking of misery that reasserted the virtue of what Thurlow was trying to do with the Helix, and so depressing as to keep him riveted for hours.

Now he fixed on a live stream of Sophie18, who was a man in thong and thigh-highs, watching Lena04, who wore the same. They were doing for each other what could not be done otherwise. And so, for a second, Thurlow loved this chat room because it was a mercy killing of at least some of the self-hate grown in his heart for what he was soon to do to the people who supported him most.

Before he signed off, he scanned a thumbnail list of users and noticed someone new. A guy not looking for pleasure; he just wanted to talk. He asked if his camera was working. He didn't understand all this technology, but his wife had given it to him so that he might get out and make friends, he being incarcerated in his house and the Internet being the next best thing to bingo at the lodge. He was pecking at the keyboard with his index fingers. Thurlow wrote back immediately. He wrote:

> Dad, can you find some other chat room to be in? There's about ten million to choose from.

But Wayne wanted to talk about how his life was being dismantled from the inside out. How his marriage was on the skids. The torpor and routine. Mutual disinterest in all things relating to the home, money, or politics. Thurlow wrote back.

> But u don't care about these things, Deborah or not.

> Dont be smart ass.

> But codependency and trust and comfort are important. Marriage is a sum of parts, some good, some bad, but maybe the sum is still good.

Wayne smirked.

> Dad, sometimes u gotta take risks to get what u want.

> ??? Son wha ts the mater w/ y ou?

This was not the first time they'd had a conversation that veered in this direction, though its precedents were few.

"Dad, stop typing—you are driving me nuts. We can talk, you know. There's a microphone."

Wayne got up close to the screen and pressed his ear to the camera, which felt like the lewdest thing Thurlow had seen in this room to date.

"Dad, stop it, just sit in your chair." Only the volume was on high, and, since Thurlow was not whispering, Wayne recoiled from the speaker with shock and began to chowter, "Stupid machine. Who ever heard of this talking machine?" So Thurlow said, "Dad, I can *hear* you," and again with the shock, and because Thurlow was so strung out he couldn't remember who he was to whom anymore, he said, "Dad, don't make me demote you, too."

Finally Wayne sat back, which gave view to what Thurlow expected to be his room but was not his room at all.

"Dad, what are you doing in the commissary? You know you're not supposed to be there. What have I not given you such that today, of all days, you were moved to leave your place of dwelling and venture into mine?"

"I was looking for the marriage counselor. I heard you called one in. And why are you talking like some poofcake?"

"I have not called in a counselor. Where'd you hear that? And what made you think he'd be in the commissary?"

"Last I heard, it was called a pantry. Son, are you all right? These four people here have been telling me some things"—and he glanced the camera at the hostages, who were supposed to have been returned to the den gagged, hooded, cuffed. Wayne, who was suddenly adept with the zoom function on the camera, had zeroed in on Anne-Janet's nose, which was narrow up top but fanned at the base like maybe she'd spent her formative years face pressed to the window, waiting.

Thurlow said, "Dad, I don't want to see those people."

Wayne said, "You know, this one's a professional arbiter, which is almost like a marriage counselor, right?" He framed in close on Olgo.

"Dad, what? You've been talking about your marriage? To *them?* What else have you been saying?"

"Not too many options for chat around here."

"Dad." But he stopped there. He could not expect to rationalize with this man. This man was his father; he was intractable. "Dad, you need to stop talking to those people. They are full of lies. Just stay put until I get someone over there."

Wayne shrugged. "Where exactly would I go?"

"I'll call for Dean, and he'll escort you back to your quarters. There's pink jellies in the kitchen, by the way. Edible foil. FYI." He offered these as an olive branch because he didn't like to be stern with his dad. He did like to take precautions, though, and he made a note to disable Wayne's door opener and short the emergency override. Also: No more computer. And guards at his bed.

At last he got Dean on the phone. Dean, frantic, saying, Where the hell was he? Thurlow was so vexed Dean had left the hostages with his dad, he could barely contain himself. Only, Dean insisted Thurlow had called him not half an hour ago, demanding he meet him in the basement. Aha, so that mole Vicki had them played. Never mind. Just hurry up and get to Wayne. And reassemble the film crew. To hell with it—they had to make the ransom tape right now.

"Okay, Dad? You hear that? Dean's on his way, so just sit tight"— which was when he noticed Wayne's face derange and lock. Oh, crap. "Dad," he said. "Not now!" But of course Wayne had no choice. He lowed, he bellowed, his limbs clenched. And though Thurlow had seen this happen many times, it never got any less awful, and today it seemed worse. Perhaps because where the footage should have lagged for being streamed online, it seemed to mayhem twice as bad. The tonic phase of the seizure lasted for thirty seconds, which gave Thurlow no time to get there before the clonic phase, which was more dangerous, insofar as Wayne could fall and hit his head, which he did. Some epileptics flail and twitch, but for Wayne the movement was more like the string of an instrument, a cello bass, that had been plucked too hard. Luckily, he had pitched to his side, which meant he wouldn't inhale his own spit. Thurlow waited for Wayne's body to slow down and then made a run for it.

He had never sprinted across the house, so he was surprised how quickly he got there. Less surprising was that he was winded and likely to convulse himself if he did not sit down. The hostages were appalled, but what was he supposed to do? Wayne was on his side, unconscious. Thurlow propped his head on his leg and waited. The hem of his jeans had crawled up one calf. A vein thick and soft like pasta showed under his skin. Wayne's head weighed a ton. Thurlow had his back to the hostages, but he knew what they were thinking. He said, "It looks worse than it is, I swear."

Then he spoke to his dad, "Wake up, boss," which was the appellation Wayne preferred but never got. When he began to come round, Thurlow tried to diffuse wake-up panic with the facts: "You had a seizure, but you're fine." Only he wasn't having it. He said he'd broken his skull and needed to go to the hospital. Normally, it was hours before fluency with the language returned, and sometimes, for how long it took, Thurlow wondered if maybe Wayne didn't have a tumor lodged in his brain. But today, he was all rebound. "I could probably get a doctor to come," Thurlow said, but Wayne said no, it could not wait, his head was broken. The man tended to exaggerate—over the years he'd claimed six heart attacks and three strokes—but it wouldn't do to ignore him. Ignore him, and he'd just have another seizure from the upset. To be fair, he *was* slurring his words. And one of his pupils appeared larger than the other.

Thurlow said, "It's possible you are just experiencing a postseizure headache."

Wayne said, "Do I look like the sort of man who can't tell the difference between a headache and hematoma? Call an ambulance—I need to get out of here." He winced in pain and then seemed to pass out from it.

Dean arrived, breathless. He took in the scene and said, "Where's two through six?"

"How should I know?" Thurlow shook his head with disgust. So Dean had left guards on duty. But where were they now?

"He all right?" Dean said.

Thurlow nodded.

"Wayne's a tough old bastard."

"He wants to go to the hospital. Says he broke his skull."

Dean gripped his lower lip between thumb and index finger. A thinking man's pose. He had a set of formulas that helped him determine risk-to-benefit ratios so that when he spoke, it was never knee-jerk.

"Not good," he said. "Downright stupid. Chances of hematoma: slim."

Thurlow glanced at the hostages, hoping they agreed with Dean and would indicate as much in their bearing or demeanor. What he did not hope was that they would volunteer advice out loud, which Anne-Janet

did, saying, "Not to overstep, but you'd best let him out," the others nodding and maybe even weeping because, if nothing else, watching someone have an epileptic fit was terrifying.

Wayne looked peaceful, but his breath was short.

"Call an ambulance," Thurlow said. "And, I don't know, tell the
feds not to shoot anyone when they come out."

Then he kissed his father on the cheek. He probably would not see
him again, though he knew Wayne would be fine.

An hour later, a knock at the door. Norman.

"How is my father?" Thurlow said. "What's the news?"

Norman flipped through a notebook. "Dean handled it. Ask him."

"I'm asking you."

Norman palmed the back of his own neck like he might slam his
face into the desk. He said, "I thought I was the one dealing with the
negotiator. Dean let one out and got nothing in return. Good job."

"He's not *one,* he's my dad."

"Just trying to get with the lingo," Norman said. "Now that we're
all criminal."

"You weren't around, Norman."

"You could have called."

Was this really the time to be discussing his hurt feelings? Thurlow
said, "You should know and tell the others: Vicki is out. She was
bugged."

"I heard."

"She won't be the last, either."

"Naturally."

"So, can you find out about my father?"

His face blanked just long enough for Thurlow to realize he wasn't
listening. "Fine," Norman said. "I'll check it out. Sorry."

"You're sorry. Since when is 'I'm sorry' our panacea of choice?"

This time, Norman did not hesitate. He said, "'Self-indictment will
be considered adequate restitution for mistakes made in dereliction of
duty, so long as the derelict is earnest in apology.'"

Thurlow snorted. Norman said, "I'm *sorry.* I'll *look into it.*"

"Norm, look, I know this day hasn't produced yet, but let's make
it happen—right now, okay? Let's get this tape filmed. How hard can

it be just to hit Record? I'll talk about the Helix; we'll grow tenfold! Can't you round up the crew and get us going here?"

But no. Norman looked like candle wax come down the shaft. He was melting, drooping.

"Norm, come on, cheer up, things will change once the ransom tape is out—you said so yourself. When have I ever let you down?" But the look on his face stayed put, and it was as if the specter of their history together scared out all the breathable air in the room.

"We just got word from the money," he said, which was what he called Pyongyang. He pulled up a website, and there it was: a plaint from the North Koreans. Apparently, they appreciated how the Middle Eastern clubs communicated worldwide and, to similar effect, had usurped back-end control of websites unlikely to attract big notice. Today's effort had been dumped in noise on the Birdhouse Network.

The message said they were not happy. They were concerned about the safety of their investment. They wanted reassurance that the Helix had not been imperiled by this hostage situation, and they wanted this reassurance in the form of words Thurlow was to speak on the ransom tape. They had instructed him to pay tribute to the most beloved leader Kim Jong-il but to do so in a way that would not expose their relations. By way of subtlety, Pyongyang had suggested he say, "In the tradition of the most beloved leader Kim Jong-il, and though I cannot speak with half as much wisdom as he, and though the DPRK is the most blessed and enlightened nation on earth, the ascendancy of which I cannot even hope to broach with what feeble ambitions are mine and my people's, nonetheless, hello."

Norman read over his shoulder.

"These people have some nerve," Thurlow said.

"Maybe they just want what's been promised them."

"I promised to try to make them look good, that's all. Everyone's been promised something."

"Great," he said. "I'll be sure to pass that on."

Thurlow wanted to shoot him a look of such authority, it would crush the revolt in his heart. Except why bother? He noticed Norman's Helix boutonniere was brass, not silver, only they had never ordered brass, so it was all clear. Clear like Vicki—one by one, down they went. Norman followed his eye—"You must be kidding"—and he wrested

the pin from his lapel. He plunked it in Thurlow's hand with the inso-
lence of a kid surrendering his gum to the principal. Thurlow examined
it with a magnifying glass he kept in the desk, and when he was satisfied the silver was just tarnished, the button was a button, he squirreled
it away among other contraband, including a sunburst, a class ring, and
an ivory cameo heirloom his new TC had cried about for an hour.

"What do you want me to write back?" Norman said.

"Tell Pyongyang that everything is fine and not to worry."

"You should know a couple tanks just crossed the river. There's
kids giving the National Guard balloons and pie outside the stadium."

"So much for the stealth of night," Thurlow said.

"So much for everything," Norman said back. He tossed a crumpled sheet of printer paper on the desk, which he'd obviously snatched
from the garbage. It read:

If my wife comes here with Ida.

In exchange for the hostages, Ned, Bruce, Olgo, Anne-Janet, I
request. I demand. The Helix requires.

On behalf of the Helix, I demand that for the release of the four
detainees, Esme Haas and daughter Ida present themselves at my
door for cookies and milk. Tea and cookies. Hot chocolate and
pfeffernüsse, because what little girl can resist the spicy, chewy,
finger-lickin' euphoria of the German pepper cookie?

Christ fuck bring me my wife and daughter or I will kill myself.
Or them. Or someone.

Thurlow ironed the sheet with his palm. He summoned for calm—
Will the calm in me please stand up?—and said, "Norman, why are you
sifting through my trash?"

Norman shook his head. "It's one thing to do this to me, but what
about everyone else? They're *expecting* something. Something great."

"I wasn't going to say all that on the tape, Norm. I was just messing
around. You found it in the garbage, right? Where is your head?"

"Yeah? So what *are* you going to say?"

They gave each other the eye. When two people had been friends that
long, the eye was murder. Thurlow decided to murder first and thought
him the truth: Nobody wants to play the endgame of his life alone.

Norman leaned against the wall and murdered back: You are the collapse of all the hope I have ever had.

Thurlow said, "So you told the film crew to go home? No crew, no tape? Are we just supposed to walk out of here now, hands up?"

"There's worse ideas."

Thurlow didn't even have to tell him to get out; Norman turned his back on him unbidden.

His study was locked, and his bedroom was the least solacing place on earth. He could get to a meditation parlor via one of the tunnels, but, with the encampment outside and the rigors of what was left to him of this day, he settled on his stepmother. She was not parent enough to reap from his flaws motive to hug him, but she might not curse his name, either.

The halls were quiet as he went to her quarters. He had hoped to find guards outside his parents' door but was not surprised to find it unmanned. On the bright side, since there was nothing to keep Deborah from leaving, her being there was a gesture. She believed in him and wanted to help. That or, in her deafness and solipsism, she still had no idea what was going on. There were no windows on this side of the house, but there was still the noise of sirens and helicopters, and the special din of so many cameramen struggling for best sight line to the action. All part of what Thurlow imagined was a late stage in the day's ratcheting into chaos.

He found her at the computer.

"What news?" he said, and by this he meant, What was up with his dad? She was accustomed to Wayne's seizures, so he was not shocked to find her unruffled by his latest.

"I'm checking my Google," she said.

Because Deborah did not understand the principle of the Internet, she did not understand how a search engine works. He found this charming but for the part where he'd told Dean to disconnect their cable line. All he needed was for her to be getting word of the siege from some blog or, God knows, IMing with the feds. Did the feds IM? There was something weird about that idea, hard to say what.

"You want to tell me about Dad?" He tried to lure her gaze from the computer screen to the mien of the worried son.

She closed the laptop.

He put his hand on hers. "He's going to be all right, you know."

"Of course he is. He's in the bathroom. Tyrone's getting a shower."

Thurlow shook his head. He was beginning to despair of ever know-ing again what went on in this house. When did his father get back? How did his father get in? Why wasn't he told?

He found Wayne misting Tyrone with a bottle of Evian. He had stood the bird on the vanity and turned on the bubble show lights.

Thurlow sat on the lip of the tub and asked after Wayne's health. His head was wrapped in gauze.

"False alarm," he said. "Just a cut in the back. I had some stitches. The wrap is to prevent swelling."

It was tight and layers deep, and more like a turban than cladding swath. But since Thurlow had not sought medical care since the in-farction, perhaps the new science preferred a turban.

"You got out of the hospital pretty quick," he said, because if there was a new science, he hardly thought there was a new efficiency as well. "Did anyone talk to you?"

"Like who? I got in an ambulance. I went to the ER. They checked me out and sent me back. I figured you paid for the ride home."

"So you only spoke to the doctors? No one else was out there?"

He stopped with the Evian. "Like *who,* son? My paramedic had a hoop in her nose; she was leaning over me the whole time. Now, can I get on with this?"

He checked to see that Tyrone was wet throughout, then lathered his hands with baby shampoo.

Thurlow had the urge to cry. Sense was in exile from his life. His fa-ther was in the dusk of his power as a decently healthy and self-sufficient man, and here he was, lavishing what energies were left him on a bird. Not on his son, but a bird.

Wayne finished rinsing and said, "Hold this open," meaning a towel monogrammed with the Helix. "Don't just stand there," he said. "Wrap him up."

Thurlow enwombed Tyrone so that only his head was free, and thrust him at his father.

"Easy, son. You don't have to destroy everything at once."

"What are you talking about? I thought you said you didn't talk to anyone out there."

Wayne patted Tyrone down and inspected his breast and under-wings. "Son, I asked you for a marriage counselor, and you have not produced one. So if my marriage falls apart, I blame you."

"You asked me not three hours ago. I'm not a magician."

"Then let us talk to the arbiter. The Indian."

"Are you kidding? He's busy."

"He is not. But if you won't help, I'll find him myself."

Thurlow got between his dad and the door. "You will do no such thing. Just—just stop interfering."

He made for the door, only in the time he'd been here, Dean had carried out his order to disable the exit. Wonderful. There was no way out except a hatch in the walk-in closet, which his father and Deborah were not supposed to know about, but what choice did he have?

He closed himself in the closet and pulled back the carpet. Located the door in the floor, secured with a padlock and hasp. So far, the only blessing in this day was that he'd had the foresight to wear his key chain of universals.

He gripped the handle and tried to lift from the knees. He had passed on the compression-spring install, but finally the door opened. It had a holding arm that locked in place at ninety degrees. This was a welcome precaution against losing a finger but not ideal for closing the hatch after yourself. He left the hatch open and descended the ladder. The rungs were slippery with condensation from a heating pipe, but he managed just the same. For good measure, when he hit bottom, he turned the ladder on its side. Just in case his father decided to come after him.

The architect's best contribution to the house was actually the house inside the house. A warren: reticulate, waterproof, and climate controlled. Most of the tunnels were passable upright. Some of them led to underground and illicit facilities open to anyone privileged enough to get access, but this was not Thurlow's doing. Cincinnati was a strange town.

For his purposes, he'd had electrical lights arrayed throughout the network. Those failing, he'd had flashlights mounted on the wall every few feet. *Those* failing, he'd had secured to the floor photoluminescent strips. No foresight had been lacking in the preparation of this route to the basement, so why in God's name was it pitch-black? He was afraid of the dark. He had dermal crises in the dark. As a boy, he'd once woken up in the middle of a blackout and within five minutes was weeping fluid from sores erupted down his spine.

He threw out his arm and prayed to graze a flashlight along the way. He did, but the light had no batteries. He felt about the floor for the photoluminescent strips and found they had been painted over. He knew this because he could feel the impasto. He was going to kill Vicki. And Dean, because he had obviously been in on this. Who else had a universal? He wondered what the feds had promised him.

Thurlow had taken one yoga class in his life, so he knew what to call the position he was in, child's pose, which was part supplicant come to pray for his child's life and part child taking a nap. He had watched his daughter sleep this way, many years ago when she was not even a year old, on her belly, with upraised posterior and arms out like Superman. Most beautiful thing he had ever seen, before or since.

The tunnel floors were linoleum. Slick if there was moisture pearling on the walls and pipes, which there was. It smelled of boiler room. And wet fur. He told himself there was plenty of air in circulation and that, while he was afraid of the dark, he was not afraid of restricted space and, what was more, to manufacture anxieties post hoc did not suit a man of his stature. Never mind that a man of his stature should not be lumped on a tunnel floor, weeping in a pitch of love for his family that would not come.

He made it to the basement and felt along the wall for a light switch. With luck, his dietician would still be waiting for him by the cistern. They did this once a week, hydrostatic testing, which had him get inside the cistern, dispatch all the air from his lungs, and something about the water level and Brozek formula would tell him how fat he was inside. Today, though, the floor was wet—a couple of inches wet—and the cistern was overturned.

He was just about to investigate what toll spillage from the cistern had taken, when he got a bad idea about the how of its capsizing. It'd take at least two men to knock it over. Men with training, men with guns.

He heard a puling by the cistern, which turned out to be issuing *from* the cistern. It was the dietician, hiding. He said, "Marie, it's only me, you can come out."

She did not seem heartened.

"Marie, come on. It's not as bad as all that. Listen"—but as he said this he realized there was actually something to listen to, a voice in a bullhorn or speaker demanding they come out in pairs, unarmed and docile. No one had to get hurt. "You heard them—those people are not going to hurt you. Just come on, give me your hand."

But still she wouldn't budge.

"Do you have a flashlight in there?"

She did.

He told her to turn it on, and when he was satisfied with the conditions, he crawled through the mouth of the cistern and joined her. She was sitting upright with her back in the curve of the pot; there was plenty of room for two. Her lab coat was wet, and she was shivering. Poor Marie. She was a French exchange student who hobbied in nutrition and anti-American sentiment, cowering in a pot with a man whose days were numbered.

They faced each other. Their legs rafted atop the water pooled in the basin.

The helicopters circled overhead, closer than before, which had the welcome effect of drowning out the bullhorn.

He said, "Just tell me, did you see who tipped this thing over? Men in some kind of military uniform?"

She nodded.

So SWAT had already been in the basement. Good thing you needed pass codes to get into the house.

She had the flashlight in her lap, aimed up at their chins, so that they might have been telling ghost stories.

"Come on, we need to get you some dry clothes," and he made to leave the pot with her in tow. But she didn't come. He said, "What's wrong? Okay, let me rephrase. I understand there's a bit of a ruckus outside, but barring that, is there anything else I should know?"

"I'm afraid," she said, and she seemed to shrink just for having said it.

"Don't be silly," he said, and he put out his hand.

"I'm afraid of *you*," she said, and she whacked it with the flashlight before retreating into the gut of the pot. Whacked it so hard, he was sure she'd fractured a bone.

He leapt out of the cistern and wedged between his thighs what had instantly come to feel like the omnibus of every pain he had ever had.

So now he, too, was afraid. But also hurt. What had he ever done to Marie? He'd been putting her through school. What sort of thanks was this? His intentions were good. They had always been good! His knuckles looked like popcorn. He had to find ice.

It had been more than two days since the Helix had taken the hostages. Thurlow had not provided a ransom tape or issued any demands, so when he found Norman on the phone, hashing it out with the FBI negotiator, he could well imagine the impatience with which Norman's parries were met. The pain in his hand was blunt but durable. He could not move his fingers. Still, there was nothing like pain to make appreciable the rapport between crime and punishment. Suffering always feels punitive, even when it's not. Why should his hand be any different? And when ATF ignited the house and his skin took on the hue and texture of boiled toffee, why should that be any different, either?

Norman put the negotiator on speakerphone. Thurlow listened for a carrot-stick routine and got a version thereof, something like: Come out and get shot; stay in and be gassed. He looked at the fireplace. There was a Duraflame in the grate and a bellows on the hearth. A fire might be nice. The candent logs, crackle of wood. He was about to light up when Norman flipped closed his phone and swatted the matches out of his hand. Fire at a time like this? Need Norman mention the FBI wanted to *gas* them? That this gas was *pyrotechnic?*

Thurlow's phone rang, and for a second, his heart was conned—It's her! It's her!—only it wasn't Esme, just his father telling him to look outside.

He crawled over to the window on his stomach. He parted the blinds. He saw police cars and tanks, the Mount Carmel brigade, a few ambulances, a festival of lights, and several men in BDUs aiming firearms at the front of the property, likely the rear and sides also. And there, in the middle of this half-moon formation, was his father, sided with the enemy.

Thurlow's mouth fell open. He was not quick to anger, and when he did anger, he did it poorly. So, fine, he could not break things. What he could do was hurt people, so he left off from the window and ran to his father's quarters. His phone started ringing again, again and again, and he could hear Wayne yelling for help.

He punched for the elevator, and when it did not come fast enough, he headed for the stairs. At last, the house alarm went off in its minor key. And it was so sad, it wrung his heart of just enough rage that instead of taking the stairs three at a time, he took them by twos and allowed his father to beat him to his bird, Tyrone.

Wayne was barring access to the bathroom, though by now Thurlow didn't care. He didn't care about anything.

He could hear his father breathing hard; he was doing the same. He sat at the table. Flicked at the ashtray so that it skidded overboard. A cigarette butt rimmed with lipstick fell into his lap.

"So," he said, "father mine. Father dearest. How long? A month? A year?"

"Just today." His father unwrapped his turban bandage to disclose the smallest camera Thurlow had ever seen at the tip of a snake wire. "I'm sorry, son."

"Impressive," he said.

"Wireless broadcast. Good quality, too. Technology is a marvel."

Thurlow shook his head. "Jesus, Dad. How did they get to you? And what about the seizure?"

Wayne grinned. "Fake. You'd think for how many I've had, I'd have a clue what they looked like. But I had to study. Ask Deborah. She had to watch me flailing on the floor all morning."

"And your marriage?"

"Solid. The feds thought maybe they could get one of their own in here as a fake counselor or something. But, son, enough of all this craziness, okay?"

"Don't you care if I go to jail?"

Wayne had begun to pack up Tyrone's things. "Of course I care. But I'd rather you in jail than dead or carrying on like this. Now go tell those four people to come out. I swear. Sometimes I think you have totally lost your mind."

"I am not letting them go. They are all I have now to get Esme back. Her and Ida. Dad, she's ten years old next week!"

"*Ida? Esme?* Is that what this is about? You really have gone insane. All this for a woman? That witch. There is no more destructive thing on earth than a woman!" He pounded his fist on the table, upsetting an empty can of root beer.

"You weren't so sympathetic when it mattered," he said. "Too little, too late."

"Oh, for God's sake. If you tell the press your neglecting dad is to blame for this stupid thing you've done, I will kill you myself."

"Fine, Dad. If you can just wait five minutes, I want to give you a videotape I made for Ida. Then you and the bird can get out of here."

His father stopped his labors and came to sit opposite him. "Son, if you really want them back, how did you think this would help? Were you planning on ransoming—oh, good God. You were."

Thurlow frowned. "But I didn't. I was afraid they still wouldn't come, so I didn't."

"Right, and to hell with all the people who apparently believe in what you're doing." And when Thurlow seemed taken aback, Wayne said, "Do I look brain dead to you, son? The whole world knows about the Helix."

Thurlow put his forehead on the table and spoke into his lap. He said, "I have no hope of ever seeing my family again. I wish I were dead."

Wayne stood up. "But I don't. So let's go."

"Can't you wait a few minutes? Let me just give you this present for Ida. Just do this one thing."

Wayne said no and asked again if Thurlow would come. "Do you really want to change people's lives? You can. Every news station in town is here. Everyone is watching. I'm going to tell them that you are coming out and releasing the hostages and to hold their fire."

Thurlow put out his hand, and when Wayne shook it, Thurlow was surprised to feel the adamance of his father's grip and his own reluctance to let his father go.

Norman was dumped on a couch. The despair was coming off him in whorls.

Thurlow said, "How many of us are still here?"

Norman and him, the hostages, some midlevels.

"Deborah?"

No idea.

"Charlotte?"

"Split."

"The rest?"

"Split."

"This captain-goes-down-with-the-ship thing has its virtues."

Norman said, "Do you have to see everything as though it's not actually happening to you? There's a reality here. We need to deal with it and consider an exit strategy."

Thurlow held up his hand, which was red and thick like a beet. "The dietician," he said. "With her flashlight."

"That's absurd," Norman said, and began to laugh. "Of all the ways to get hurt on a day like this."

"Don't laugh."

Norman stopped, and the look on his face was awful.

Thurlow squinted and puckered the skin between his eyebrows, which he pinched until it hurt. "You know I didn't mean for it to get to this."

Norman knew.

Thurlow unwrapped his hand because he could not feel blood touring the digits.

Norman sat with his legs parted wide and flapped his knees. His lips began to quiver. He said, "I know how to get out of here, but where am I going to go?"

"You'll be all right. I have faith."

"When did things start to go wrong for us?"

"February 27, 1995. 5:43 p.m."

"Has it really been ten years? She must be a little lady by now."

Thurlow nodded. "I saw her, you know. Just by chance, on the street when I was in D.C. With Esme. She was wearing all green."

"Oh my God," Norman said, and so now he knew exactly what had gotten them to this moment.

"Norman, listen. I've been making this videotape for her. If you can just hang on for a little longer, I'll give it to you and then you can go."

But Norman was done hanging in. He wished Thurlow luck and turned his back on him for good.

11:58:11:29: And so, my little one, I guess that's it. I am all alone now, as I deserve. I hope, when you're older, you won't judge me too harshly. I've just been confused and hung up on the wrong questions. Do I think love is an answer to loneliness? Maybe. Sometimes. But I suspect there's more than one path leading away from estrangement, though for some people, there are no paths at all. But now I see the more important question is: What does it matter when you miss your wife and child? So what if I am the one for whom loneliness is insoluble—so what? I'd rather be lonely with you. I'd rather treat loneliness like the air I breathe, and breathe it with you. Why couldn't I have figured this out ten years ago? I know I have wrecked my life. I hope to God I have not wrecked yours. I hope, too, that you never have to struggle with this stuff and that you are among the lucky who, in their solitude, still understand themselves to be a part of the universe and beloved by others. Just remember this: There is no lonely course that doesn't still belong to the plexus of human experience being lived every day.

My darling girl, is there anything else I can tell you? Have I documented every stop along the plummet to this day? Should I buss your toddler socks and press them to my cheek? Will you think on me more kindly if I say I have the dried columbine of your mother's bridal bouquet in my safe?

I only had you for a year into life, but I still have memories that come upon me all day long. You in turtle pose, a month old, staring at the fuzzy dice I'd bought you myself. You swaddled in a ladybug blankie and wanting out. Your Mohawk hair and your arms thrown overhead as you slept. Your cactus pose. Your Jesus pose. Your seal and ostrich pose. The distended belly. Six rolls of fat per leg. The day it was five. You wobbling on all fours, going nowhere. Your callused little knees once you got going and never stopped.

I know you don't know me, and that you never did. You've grown so much. I was in D.C. a couple weeks ago, and I saw you. You were walking in green rubber boots with a frog face on each side. Soon you will need a new pair. I bet you look just like your mother. I hope you listen to her in all things, even though you are getting smarter all the time. If one day you ever wonder about your dad, please know that you are all he ever thought about from the moment you were born.

V. In which some women bat their eyes, others sit down and write. Guided by voices. The inconsolable child.

ESME WAS CONCUSSED AND LOCKED IN A HOTEL BATHROOM. There was dusk out the window, bullfrogs in one ear—no, both—and a bellows whumping through her brain at three-second intervals. She'd been passed out the entire afternoon, and, for the girth of the swell atop her skull, she guessed Jim had whacked her hard. The irony of getting knocked in the head while giving head was not lost on her, though it was also not top on her list of ignominies that needed undoing.

Jim had left her bag but no wallet or phone. No one was likely to come up to this room uninvited. The window was too small to get through, and even if she could, it was eight floors up. The lock had been jacked; she would be in this bathroom until Martin got a clue. Tick-tock.

She rinsed her face and showdowned with the loony in the mirror. By now, she knew, the siege was being broadcast worldwide. The thinking: We need to appear as though we're doing everything in our power to get our people released and to hold accountable the delinquent who sent them there. We. Ha. There was no *we*. There was just her and her madness and a break from the certainty that had floated her for years: that she would figure this out, hatch a plan, marshal the weaponry at her disposal against the anomie of love. The anomie of love! Who still pines for the same man nine years later?

One of her pupils was bigger than the other, as though to render the distribution of wherewithal that characterized her inner life. Much passion, no hope. Bold moves, no endgame, though the sequence of events that had gotten her here had been nothing if not a great match ranged across the board.

She sat on the floor. The tile was cool under skin. Even if she got to Cincinnati in time, what could she make happen? A guy who detains four federal employees has no intention of coming out alive. So for starters, her job would be to change intent. What she needed was a rhetoric of persuasion. How to spellbind in five minutes, because that was about all the patience the feds had left for this. Fred Lanceley, who tried to talk down Randy Weaver at Ruby Ridge, wrote out what he was going to say on index cards. So that's what she would do.

She found a pen in her bag. Checked her watch. She numbered her pages. She wrote:

1. Lo, if I'm reading this out loud, it's because you still haven't come out and time is not on your side. But I'm not sure what to say. You think you screwed up? Is that the problem? Let me tell you about screwing up. Maybe it will help.

2. I am an eavesdropper and a snoop. This you know. But what you don't know is how it all started for me. It started when I was a kid. My dad had been in the Arctic in '58, so I read everything about the International Geophysical Year and also a *Time* magazine article about a daring rescue—twenty scientists stuck on Drift Station Alpha as it broke apart, this mile-long ice floe, maybe 150 feet deep, that meandered around the North Pole while guys like my dad took notes on zooplankton and also on what the Russians were saying to each other from one submarine to the next. In '58, six years after the NSA came to life and eight years after its predecessor failed to predict the Korean War or the PRC's intervention, no one was messing around. SIGINT, COMINT, ELINT, were the order of the day, and so my dad spent months adrift in the Arctic Ocean, where there is no horizon, no color threshold between earth and sky, just the white-ice pageantry of one lonely day kissing its way into the next.

3. Some families have a swing set in their yard; we had an octoloop. A giant antenna, looked like a stop sign, three-quarter-inch copper pipe and telephone cable with gimbaled support beam through the middle, used to snatch VLF sound waves from the universe. Schumann resonances. Tweeks, whistlers, sferics—the low-frequency din life makes beneath our capacity to hear it. The physicist Schumann, who predicted the resonance of lightning emissions, was not related to the German composer of the same name, but I find it no small coincidence, the one a conjuror of some of the most arresting melodies on earth and the other sensitive to music of the earth's devising. My dad used to amplify what came through the loop—think fat in a hot skillet—and listen to it like opera while I did my homework on the carpet. Our soundtrack? The world's underbreath, one breath at a time.

From there it was easy to augment my fixation with voice. Voices in code, voices out loud, voices in whose timbre were hints of regret for everything the speaker hadn't done or said now that it was too late. Who wouldn't want to listen to that?

4. After the air force, my dad worked for Disneyland, which you probably remember. Back then, I was at the age when everything your parents do seems lame, but I didn't mind the *Horseshoe Revue* and even got to like it after I spied my dad with Slue Foot Sue, costar of the revue, with her breast poised above his mouth, and him on his knees, going for it like a circus seal.

I watched the scene play out. And realized, with some measure of shock, that I would not tell my mother or confront my father, but that I wouldn't suffer the isolation secrecy brings it its wake, either. Quite the opposite. I felt closer to my dad for knowing he was in pain. I also felt closer to knowing what I wanted to do with my life.

5. Maybe I'm not doing a good job of this. But how can I explain my choices without explaining it all? God knows I didn't tell you much when we were married. So, first my dad had an affair; then came my brother's surfing accident. About that part, my family's grief was private, even as its furnishings were hard to miss. We never spoke his name. I don't know how it happened, but from one day to the next, his name was taboo. His photos vanished from the fridge, his trophies and gear, and all were deposited in his room, whose door stayed locked. I figured my parents had fondled each item and packed it gently in a box while I was at school. But no, they had hired a moving company to shove it all in a few plastic crates and pile them in the boy's closet. That's what it said on the order form I saw tacked to the fridge—*The boy's closet*. After that, I figured they crept into his room at night, or maybe while I was at school, to go through his stuff and whisper his name. I tied a length of thread from the doorknob to the frame so that if it opened even an inch, the thread would break. Then I checked this thread, which never broke, every day for five years.

My mom took up with someone who worked at Disney's rival amusement venue, Knott's Berry Farm, while my dad kept on with Slue Foot. I bought books about satellites and radio waves. My dad lost his arm to a crossbeam in the theater where he worked; Disney paid him millions. My mom left Knott's, and then it was like a contaminant had settled in the house. Something dark and horrible that confined us to our own lives and made it impossible for us to talk to each other ever again.

6. Any idea how hard it is to get security clearance when you have no fingerprints? It took months, and in those months I could have gone to grad school, changed paths, started fresh. Instead, it was three years of Korean and a year's worth of NSA interviews, whose gist ranged from scenario to psych. A thousand questions. A thousand million. Your boyfriend threatens to break up with you unless you tell him what you did today; how do you respond? Do you think that family is more important than work, and if so, would you compromise your work to protect them? Already, these people seemed to know the grim stuff of my ambition.

7. My first job: Middle of nowhere, Australia. Eight hours a day listening to the North Koreans. Most tracking stations are remote, for the obvious reasons of privacy and uncluttered airspace, but what really matters is being within the footprint of a satellite's broadcast range. Hence: Nowhere, Australia, under Intelsat 2, stationed over the Pacific Ocean and handling the equivalent of 1,100,000 pages of text per second. It was grueling work, and peculiar for its mix of boredom and anxiety, both of which verged on the unbearable.

8. When you eavesdrop, you have to probe what you hear for nuance and sarcasm, doublespeak and lies. You have to wonder if they know you're listening. You don't have the pressure of an analyst, who has to slog through what you've translated and decide what's important, but you do have the problem of making sure you transcribe accurately the intent of what you hear. Old friends and colleagues share a language no one can fathom without initiation. It took me three years of listening to North Korea's vice foreign minister before I could diagnose the timbres of his voice, because the man never said what he meant, and I mean never.

9. There are so many ways to die, it boggles the mind. But the thing that's really going to get us, and what people don't talk much about since the end of the Cold War, is nuclear proliferation. I was sixteen when *The Day After* aired; it wrecked me for months. Me and everyone else, though apparently the movie's premise—that there would

actually *be* a day after nuclear holocaust—was supposed to gladden
our response to the prospect. It didn't. In 1983, the Non-Proliferation
Treaty was thirteen years old. Its gist: countries that have weapons
should not help countries that don't to acquire them, but if you do
help, not much harm will come to you, because the NPT has no teeth.
Join the NPT regime and you can leave anytime without consequence.
If it's in the interest of Consarc, Hewlett-Packard, and Honeywell to sell
"dual use" nuclear equipment to the highest bidder, go right ahead. The
International Atomic Energy Agency can inspect only nuclear facilities
that *declare* themselves, and need permission from the host country to
inspect anything else, and, on the crazy chance anyone gets upset about
the nine thousand ways you have violated the treaty, it doesn't matter,
because the UN will not vote to impose sanctions for fear of reprisal. In
short, Iran, Libya, Algeria, North Korea, Pakistan, India, South Africa,
Israel, and Iraq—not to mention all the states that tumbled out of the
Soviet Union—either had the bomb and weren't talking about it or
were getting there quick. There were some successes—Libya and South
Africa, for instance—but all it takes is one North Korean twink with
pompadour, and *wham:* the day after.

10. In 1994, things got hot in North Korea. That was the year they'd
defuel the core of their reactor at Yongbyon, unload enough plutonium
for about five nuclear bombs, and threaten war if the UN Security
Council imposed sanctions. It was looking very bad, very scary, and
all of us on the line were listening hard. And getting nervous.

11. Need some context for all this? I'll give it to you. Two years before,
things were on the up: North and South Korea were about to sign a
denuclearization agreement for the peninsula. The North had agreed
to the IAEA's safeguard protocols; the South had agreed to suspend
Team Spirit (which is, ridiculously, a series of war games between
the South and the U.S., designed to flaunt their ordnance). The U.S.
withdrew all nuclear weaponry from the region and had gotten past the
flirting stage and into the first high-level talks with the North in forty
years. An accord seemed likely.

But no. Delicate are the overtures between nations that hate each
other. Suddenly, the South wanted access to all of the North's nuclear
facilities. The North balked. The South threatened to reinstate Team

Spirit; the North balked. The IAEA insisted on special inspections of two undeclared sites; the North balked. Team Spirit went on as scheduled, the North announced plans to withdraw from the NPT, and everyone was screwed. What did North Korea want? Were they bluffing? Maybe the thing to do was to let them drop out of the NPT, because, though they had signed on in 1985, they didn't seem to have much regard for the international condemnation that ensues when you are found in flagrante. Also, they were making the NPT look weak and setting a bad precedent for other countries inclined to violate the regime on the sly. Possibly they were just stalling while they worked on their weapons program. Maybe they were just testing the lengths to which the U.S. would go to keep them in line.

Do we reward misconduct with high-level talks? Isn't that like negotiating with terrorists? Do we ask for help from the international community and watch it defang every resolution that comes out of the UN? What is the point of asking for things nicely? What is the point of making threats? If I were leading the free world, I would blow my brains out for indecision.

12. By early '94, forget accord—now it looked like war was imminent. A year's worth of talks down the drain. The South running hot and cold, the North swathed in the most useful ambiguity I have ever seen, and the U.S. quartered by the hawks and skeptics, the people who thought Pyongyang had the bomb and the people who didn't. Meantime, the IAEA's director general was making noise about more safeguards being broken and was told, essentially, to can it, because at this point, bad news was not helping. The director was nonplussed, but how do I know for sure? Because we eavesdropped on him, too. The *director general* of the IAEA, and we were listening. I guess every diplomat knows he is being spied on—that his privacy is not inviolate, no matter the Vienna Convention on Diplomatic Relations or the UN's Convention on Privileges and Immunities—but I was shocked. Was there anyone we weren't listening to? As a matter of fact, yes. No one was listening to me.

13. At the base, when you weren't prodding the sky for news of vital international importance, there was nothing to do but drink and fuck. Or so I'd been told, since I'd yet to see the salacious component of our

tenure. The guys on duty for the three-month siege at Waco? They drag-raced their tanks from sniper hive to home base at the end of each shift. It sounds appalling, but I get it. In boredom, you will turn to anything. Me, I just doubled down on my work.

One day, I spent hours listening to the DPRK's negotiator, who was scheduled to meet former president Carter for a last-chance dance. The man liked to talk to himself. He was ripped with stress and griev-ing the loss of his mistress, who had fled to South Korea. Mostly he was shocked. Did he really want to send in the goons to haul her back? Was he really so unappetizing that she'd crossed the border to escape? Bound up in this self-pity were plaints about the negotiations. He re-sented his new orders—if he'd been a better man and more expert in snatching advantage from the enemy, he would have never *gotten* the orders—only I couldn't tell what the orders were without listening sev-eral times over, the words coming out muffled and broken, possibly because he was speaking them into a pillow. I'd listened to him well into the evening. When my shift was over, I passed on what I knew to the next guy and called it quits.

14. I went to the pub. I took a stool at the bar and ordered a beer, but I couldn't stop thinking about the negotiator. What was he talking about? Why so down on the new orders? Why so emasculated? I decided to flush my mind with the night air and get ready to listen again. I would block out everything I'd translated already, home in on the rest, and find meaning in the carnage of this guy's self-esteem.

I went to the cave, which is what we called a mostly neglected lis-tening room in the basement. You went there primarily to do what I had in mind, which was to recue a tape and try again.

15. The door was unlocked, and inside were four cryptanalysts I'd seen around but never talked to. They were gathered at a work-station-turned-bar and were playing cards. I said I had some reviewing to do and not to mind me, though I was glad for the company. It's true I kept to myself and that I *liked* reclusion, but this did not militate against the loneliness of just breathing in and out and all the other fundamen-tals you do alone each day.

I sat with my back to the room, put on my headphones, and cued up. *Okay, now pay attention.* I listened once just to get back into the zone, twice to access my guy's headspace, and a third time to parse content from emotion. By the sixth listen, I had completely tuned out his whimpers and clamor of self-disgust, but I still could not make sense of the rest. I pressed my headphones into my ears and thought: Listen.

16. Meantime, the others were kissing. I'll just say it: they were kissing. Not that the card game had escalated into strip poker or spin-the-bottle, just that the four had tired of one pursuit and moved on to another. I went back to the tape. I knew that this was important and that if I missed something big, I'd get fired, and that I was running out of time. And so, wouldn't you know it, the tension that should have spurred me on to greater facility instead began to manifest in a libidinal stir whose accomplice was the knob of denim pressed against my vulva. Under the circumstances, orgasm didn't seem like the worst idea, albeit rough, given the knob of denim and on this occasion it being the cave at a tracking base in the middle of the desert, where—what do you know—two of the four, the two who were boys, had found their way to each other.

17. I'd seen this on TV, the phenomenon that is boys kissing, and felt then that my interest was anthropological. Here, too, minus the part where I could stare without offense. I was unclear if in the dawn of an orgy—because I was pretty sure that was what I was looking at—*staring* is ever met with offense, but what did I know? I tried to get back to work. I tried to listen to my Korean guy, in whose mewling hung the balance of war with the U.S., and to silence my screaming vulva, because the boys had moved on to the girl—her name was Morgan, and since when does a girl named Morgan let two boys touch her at once? And frankly, why was no one touching me? I was wearing a Disneyland sweatshirt with Tinker Bell in flight over the castle, jeans with an elastic waist, and clogs. Nothing says *I am a frozen bread loaf* better than clogs, but come on, was this a discerning orgy?

Well, fine. If I got orgied, I'd also get an STD, so lucky for me no one was noticing me panting across the cave. Why couldn't I understand what the negotiator was saying? Why couldn't I penetrate his wounded feelings? If I got fired and had to go home, I'd hang myself from the showerhead, never mind the war that would be my albatross for life. Where was the justice in that? I was just some girl from

Anaheim with a crush on her parents, a brother in a coma, and no talent for intimacy with anyone who mattered.

18. That night was a lesson learned: there's the erotics of a woman who feels so miserable and wrecked and anxious and sad that she will get on her knees and let four people have at her with varying degrees of rupture and bliss, and then there's everything else. I unplugged my headphones and let the tape feed through the wall speakers. None of them minded the Korean, and so it was as though his voice kept my head in quarantine while the rest of me went to town. Who took off my clothes? Had I ever kissed a girl? Were ministrations lavished with judicious regard for people's feelings and self-esteem? Are these the questions that spring to mind? We were five; it was exhausting. Labor intensive. You gave up what you got, were debased and exalted, and also profligate in the disport of your limbs so that they might land anywhere and on anything, and sometimes on the volume button of your listening console, so that just as one guy cums (and on your forehead, because you are not, after all, a porn star and can't even catch rain in a storm), you suddenly understand loud and clear what your Korean negotiator is saying: "I am not a man, my shame is paramount"—in short, the DPRK will bow its head and *freeze its nuclear program* in exchange for light water reactors.

19. A major concession. If the U.S. knew this ahead of time, they could call off Carter—Carter, who was making the administration look impotent and ridiculous, calling in an ex-president to negotiate for them. God, I felt good. *Alive.* And I was slick with the proof. My thighs were wet, my lips and hands, so that when I went for the tape, hit Eject, I don't know, my finger slipped and the tape jammed. Got caught halfway. Worse, I had done the horrible but corner-cutting thing of using the original tape—a dupe took days—which meant the only way to recoup the information was to keep hitting Eject until the button jammed as well. I knew that we shredded transcripts and that we had an entire building filled with tubs of acid to dissolve paper, but also that maybe we were not above dissolving the linguist who screwed up big-time.

20. Morgan was threading her legs through spandex, snatching her accoutrements—bra, earrings, pink panties—and bolting for the door.

The others almost clotted in the doorway for how fast they were trying to get out. I put on my clothes. Things in my body felt misplaced, but there was no time to get cleaned up. I went to my boss's quarters and briefed him on what I knew. Did I have the tape? Sort of. The cave reeked of jizz and sweat, the smell defying what meager perfumes I'd levied against it. My boss snapped the tape trying to get it out, and I was redeployed.

21. Back in the States, I knew a few CIA guys and went to them for help. The help was not forthcoming. They said I'd have to start from the bottom. Apply. Spend a year at *the farm*, which was a training center in Virginia, and after that, who knew, maybe I'd get assigned to a country of note, like South Korea or China, but just as easily I could end up translating again, and this time at Meade, in that horrible glass box south of Baltimore. So forget that. Communications intelligence had its limits; I wanted to be on the ground.

22. So: no work, though I did keep up with the news. The Agreed Framework brokered by the Carter meeting—which went off okay, I guess—would get signed soon enough, though the agreement would not last long, the North refusing to accept light water reactors from the South under the aegis of—who knows?—the bad karma of furnishing your house with the enemy's loveseat. Also, like anyone believed the North would actually abandon its nuclear pursuits. The upshot? Kim Il-sung almost dead, his pansy son ready to go, and me working in Anaheim at a Korean bar just to keep up with the vernacular. What kind of career trajectory was this? Sigint to dive bar?

23. I didn't take any money from my parents until years later when I had to care for Ida on my own. Instead, I just lived with them. It was not a good time. I had come back from Australia changed. Still secretive and cross, but training these qualities to serve new goals. Because, one thing I noticed at the bar? The white guys who came in for karaoke were actually coming in for me. To chat me up and take me home. The meaner I was to them, the more solicitous they got. And I liked it.

24. For six months, all I did was have sex. If a week went by without action, I'd find myself staring at people on the street, men *or* women,

and imagining them bent over or me just nuzzling my way up their thighs. I had no profession, no friends, and at twenty-seven, my greatest ambition was to wedge my body into places it had never been before. Every day, to work, the store, the *mall*, I wore crotchless thongs and shelf bras. Neither served a purpose—I had no breasts, and if I was manifesting arousal in the way some women do, *crotchless* panties were no kind of basin—and so these garments were all about alerting my skin to possibility. Know why I couldn't save enough money for a security deposit on an apartment? I blew it all on toys. And gear. Leather is expensive. A PVC slave harness costs $200, and this *without* the cuffs or chains. Take that, Vicki—I was raw in my day.

Still, I could abuse a guy for hours or get put in the stockade myself, but neither defined my needs. Femmes, doms, tops, bottoms, I wanted to be them all. But I was not confused. The psychology of my behavior was too glaring and trite for me to be confused. When you grow up neglected by the people you love most, it tramples your self-esteem, and when you are adult enough to stop blaming them, you end up blaming yourself, which means, *wamu!* even less self-esteem. And so, two models of conduct: (1) I lorded over men because I wanted to recover what self-regard was taken from me, and in this model, all men were the same man; (2) I wanted to be misused because this treatment squared with my self-regard, and sometimes it's just good to harmonize what you deserve with what you get. In the grammar of both models, low self-esteem ranked as subject and verb, and so I guess I knew exactly what I was: a woman with no self-esteem.

25. Hurt, hurt. When you sign up for hurt, hurt is what you get. I'd promise myself to stop. Every day, I'd promise. And then I'd go to work, watch the corn cheese resolve under my fingernails, and five hours later wake up with one guy down my throat and another up the rear. Roofies? Course not. Just a campaign of self-destruction, deaf, dumb, and blind.

We all do this, right? Blame ourselves for the wrong thing? My brother? The coma? Our fight not two minutes before he cracked his head on a fiberglass plate?

The bar got busy. More and more, guys started coming in from the poles. Guys with wedding bands. Guys with pregnant wives, first kid, second, third. Guys who worked for people who worked for other people who were not so keen on the consolidating ethic of a young man I used to know as a kid. According to these people, the country was given over to a liberal agenda that had colonized the White House for way too long. This young man from Anaheim was an affront. And considerably easier to take out. Need a job, Esme? Tired of your body's trade in extremities? Yes? Then go bring me something on this man. His name is Thurlow Dan.

26. It was not a chance encounter, a left turn when I should have gone right; it was exactly as planned, the guy I'd crushed on for five minutes in elementary school, sort of awkward and sad, biggest virgin I ever saw, Thurlow Dan, the pudgy kid, standing on the corner. Only you weren't so pudgy anymore—a study in alchemy if I ever saw one—but the memory was still there. A funicular over Disneyland. A camping trip in the Angeles National Forest. Glowworms in the leaf litter and a boy silhouetted against the sky, telling stories. Little moments nostalgia does not have to extol, because they were already nice to begin with.

27. I had a plan, and it was this: Do your job, do not have sex. For this plan, I wore a light blue sweater with white plastic buttons down the front, enough to make tedious any effort to undo them, and Keds. White leather Keds. I came to a stop sign. You were at the post. Svelte, almost gangly, and so awkward in your bearing, it was hard to take. In the movies, women like me pity the inexperienced and see in the vanilla putty of lust something to mold and color and fashion. But it's not really like that. Boys who paw all over you or wait to be told what to do, who cannot find your better parts or your any parts, they are ages twelve to twenty; they are sweet and certainly sweeter than the monsters they often become, but they are not for me. So I was certain that I would not have sex that day, and maybe, on one's day's abstinence, I could build another. And from there rebuild a life worth having.

28. We drove into town; I don't think you said anything the whole way. You sat in my car with hands clutched in your lap. I remember strings of hair playing across your face when I downed the windows. I remember you closing your eyes when the sun came in and squinting when it didn't.

At the restaurant, we sat outside on a patio under a sun umbrella. It had a wedge pattern, yellow and mint green, and the table wobbled for need of a matchbook you stuffed underfoot. Even now I have to ask why I remember these details—as though I already knew then that this dreamy boy would compass all the unhappy days of my life to come.

And that's how I still think of you. The boy who dreams.

29. I tried to play catch-up. What had you been doing all these years? You skipped the details, went right for the pitch. From the look of it, the way you were pulled out from the table and sitting with legs crossed at the knee, there was little chance you were addressing me. But I was rapt. The day was getting on, and it seemed that all around you was light, warm and flattering. You said you were so alone. That we all were. And, just listening to you, I was bowed down to the candor of people in pain. To people in solitude—imperious and urgent—and to your claim that we get so few chances to tender empathy as consolation for the trials of our epoch, but that you were looking for these chances every day.

30. I called for the waiter. We ordered gourmet pizzas—all white for you, shrimp and goat cheese for me—but as I ate, I felt my cheeks flush and wizen. My throat, too. Even my teeth started to parch. There was the water in my glass and yours, and three glasses after that, and still it was like trying to wet steel. You figured I was allergic to shellfish, and wanted to call an ambulance because people died from this allergy, it was worse than peanuts. And remember I said no, that I was fine? But the look on your face was tragic, and in your eyes was the desuetude of a life without me. I know it's strange, but already I could see the wasteland you saw for yourself, more comprehensive than anywhere I'd thought it possible for a man's loss to take hold.

I settled down. Went to the bathroom and doused my arms and legs with water supplied by the attendant. She was an older woman, from Mexico maybe, who probably issued naysaying prophecies to every girl who stumbled in drunk or high. Only it was daytime, so why was she eight-balling me? I pressed a damp paper towel to my forehead and the back of my neck and just tried to breathe, when this spooky woman spoke a pronouncement just vague enough to seem right on. "Eh, *guera*," she said. "You've got it bad."

31. I could not drive. I was exhausted and dizzy. But I wanted to see your place. I remember you lived with two other guys, but they were not there. I took mental notes. No posters or collegiate wall hangings. No incriminating pamphlets or volatile mix of paint thinner, alcohol, and toilet bowl cleaner. Just a couple books about healthy eating, and a navy blue duvet.

You were obviously nervous to have me there. "Want something to drink? Juice or soda? Water? Seltzer? I don't have any seltzer, but there's a bodega just down the street."

I decided to lie down. I slipped off my sneakers, and because I was still warm, and because it was disconcerting to watch you watch me with those giant, incredulous eyes, I did the simple thing of taking off my clothes. I undressed like a child getting ready for bed. And when you asked if I wanted a nap, who wouldn't have laughed? You were actually willing to turn off the light and let me sleep and probably to stand guard outside. I said, "Shut the door, but come sit here," and I tapped the mattress.

32. There was something platonic about the way you looked at me. Touched me. No one had ever cupped my elbow. My knees. And then the way you told me a little about your mom, who'd died. Your dad and stepmom. This wasn't seduction. It was intimate. And then you were back to the loneliness. And how maybe it was not so unassailable after all. And throughout, more and more, I just needed you to stop talking *like that*. I reached for you, and the rest was what I knew best.

I did not consider the chance I'd get pregnant. It never even crossed my mind. You, the young socialist, were my way back in. The ears of government awaited. I had many years to architect my life before a child would factor into the design, if ever.

33. Naturally, once I found out, I had the same thought every morning: Today I will make the appointment. And after I failed to get money for the procedure, I said: Today I will ask my parents for the money to make the appointment. And then the days went by. I had scruples about abortion unknown to me until then. Or maybe I didn't have scruples but just would not terminate this cell of a child that was ours. So you see, per usual, my body knew things that I did not. If it's any consolation, I swear I told my contacts you were clean. And I swear I thought

that would be the end of it. I moved to D.C. and kept news of the baby to myself. And when it was impossible to hide, my luck changed. I was pregnant; I spoke Korean. The CIA had just picked up word of an OB and his wife who were newly escaped from the North, settled in New Paltz, and wanting to work for the U.S. government, though they didn't know it yet. I was the most suitable candidate to recruit the pair.

34. I made contact. Yul and wife appeared willing, though mostly for fear of being returned to North Korea. I got bigger. And in my head, I accorded the growth of my body with the success of my labors. For those first few months, I just didn't seem to notice I was pregnant at all. I guess I was so terrorized, I couldn't let out my fear. Not in secret, not in guise. I went about my business, studied photos of the American GIs who'd defected to the North, and deaf-dumbed my way through Yul's prognoses: Only ten weeks to go, you're doing great!

35. What can I say about us? When you showed up in New Paltz, I didn't know what to do. I had no experience with feelings. All I knew was my job, so I called it in. The socialist returns. They said you were good cover and still a person of interest. Stay on him, they said. And I did.

But it was hard going.

You counted calories at every meal. I should have been annoyed. Instead, I found in displays of your self-hate compassion for my own.

You made love not as a man who wants to be hurt but as a man whose tenderness dredges the sex of whatever psychic drama I could bring to bear on the event. It was sweet and loving. It was safe.

You'd stretch your arms overhead and loop them round my waist on the way down so that I could not move, could not breathe in anything but you.

You'd complain about your heart but never go to the doctor. And then I'd worry about your heart.

You'd complain about my litany of gripes against you but never leave. We had a baby. You said, Let's not wreck this baby the way we have been wrecked, and then we went ahead and wrecked everything.

We had one year, twelve weeks, and three days together. The more you struggled to be a good man, the more I believed you were. And then, disastrously—gloriously—I loved you.

36. And so, yes, when I found out about the other women, I was shocked. Less that I had been betrayed, but that I had *chosen* this for myself. That somewhere along the way, I had decided to protect and love and believe in a person designed to betray me. What a horror. I shut down completely. As ironies go, when I did have a thought of even modest refinement, it was about how to absolve you. This crisis in my life had me groping for the person in whose betrayal this crisis was born. Who else did I have to talk to? I went to a professional. The professional said: You need to stop loving this person. You have to *want* to stop loving this person. I was thunderstruck. Why should I stop loving someone who is lovable? A dreamer, a sufferer, a guy who's all heart? Because he treated me badly? I hadn't treated him especially well, either, though he did not know it. I was confused. I had so many questions. Do we love people for how they treat us or for who they are? Is there a difference? I'd address these thoughts to the professional and she'd say: Enough with the horseshit. You need to stop loving this man and move out.

And I did. I could not do my job. I'd stopped providing information on you months before, and so, already, I was compromised. And now this. Also, some part of me understood that the next girl in line whose heart you were likely to assault was our daughter. I executed a maternal instinct, perhaps my last.

37. Lo, if I ever do find a way to tell Ida, and I will have to soon, what should I say? How am I to explain my part in this? And yours? Does she really need to know there are people out there who cannot help but destroy each other? Or that, for all my efforts to forget you, replace you, bury you, I have failed on all counts? I have been with many people since we split but have abandoned myself to none of them. Not even for a second. But I want our daughter to know different. I want her to think life is full of chances, not just one.

38. I have to stop writing now; it's time for me to go. I hear Martin at the door, at last.

It was time for Esme to go, and yet: more waiting. She had called her voicemail; there was a message from Ida: she and Crystal were ETA five minutes. Her child had been having fits all day, and now that Crystal was in the game, insofar as Esme's name had been pucked across every news channel in town, Crystal had refused to bide Ida while Esme raced to Cincinnati.

"I need another pen," she said.

Martin gave her two. He was her only ally left, though *ally* overstated the extent to which he would have her back if called to testify. No doubt a hearing was in the works.

"What?" she said, because he was looking at her.

"Nothing." And then: "You've got rosacea."

"It's called crying."

Martin said, "You don't have much time. The people downstairs can ID you if anyone asks."

"No one's going to ask until I'm long gone." She appraised herself in the mirror. "Did you bring your kit? I need work here and definitely here"—and she touched the skin girding her eyes. It was less swollen now but still pink and almost translucent.

Martin was at it in seconds.

"Just natural," she said. "Like me, but not ruined. Like a mom who's ecstatic to see her child and has no other care in the world but her."

"Right." He stepped away. These figments of joy were not anything he could heap on the expression she wore now and had, in fact, worn every minute since Thurlow Dan kidnapped her team and stopped responding to the lead negotiator. Also, science says people will recognize a happy face before a sad one, but only if the happy face is congruent with the emotional context these people have experienced to date. So if Ida was going to register the sparkle in her mother's look (beta lenses that pooled with light) or the bow tie of crow's feet at both eyes (to simulate motion of the orbicularis oculi muscle, which engages when you smile for real), if Ida was going to see in his work indices of happiness, she'd have to have known something of happiness, which she manifestly had not. She was nine years old with one foot in the grave.

Try and fail, try again. He crimped gelatin into wrinkle lines; Esme flocked her chin; and together, in haste, they produced a face that was, if not ebullient, not a billboard of despair, either.

He packed up his kit. Esme turned on the TV. Thurlow Dan had not been heard from in hours. There was rumor of a ransom tape— *Just tell us what you want!*—and, circling overhead, choppers with boys humping the skids and gunning for this cult leader of national import. The hostages had been identified, their families called. Jim's name had not come up, but already he had put the whole thing on Esme: Anonymous sources close to the White House say this has been a rogue intervention. It will be resolved amicably. The parties responsible will be brought to justice. Where are these parties? Hard to say.

"You want the Weather Channel?" Martin asked.

A blizzard was rolling in. Great time to hit the road. Visibility nil. Or at least the nil of snow pelting the windshield like rice when your ship clicks into hyperdrive. Nine hours to Cincinnati, going on 10, 15, 40. Reagan National had just closed.

"Animal Planet?"

She looked up and it was cops, and kittens who needed to eat. "No."

He continued to flip until his flipping got on her nerves, so she said, "Give it," only she was out of range, the remote didn't work, and where the hell were Crystal and Ida? Then, at last: a knock at the door that returned her to the state she was in.

"Should I go?" Martin said.

"No. You can stay." Though what this meant was, Please stay, because the reproach bound up in every word that would fall from Crystal's lips, mingled with Ida and her needs—the audacity and insistence of her needs—would undo what chance Esme had to disarm the blast of fate that said she was going to give up on everything; why not start now?

"Mom!" The voice a squall and the child barreling into the room, headed for her mother but stopped short by the sight of Martin, who made her blushy and knock-kneed. Here was a man of such intimacy with her mother, she might have begrudged him the time except that maybe, for this intimacy, he was also her dad.

"Hey, kiddo," Martin said, and tousled her hair, which was clipped on either side with ruby barrettes and not remotely inviting of a tousle, but what did Martin know? He had six brothers and an affenpinscher named Joe.

"Hi, muffin," Esme said, and she twirled her finger in the air to encourage Ida to show off the new coat Esme had left for her this morning. Snow leopard with hot-pink satin lining. "You like it?" she said. "You look ready for Hollywood."

Ida smiled but took off the coat and tossed it on the bed as though she'd caught whiff of a bribe. She was in blue leggings tucked into snow boots, and a cable-knit zip hoodie whose sleeves were too long and balled in either fist. Apparently, this was a stay against anxiety newly added to an arsenal of thumb sucking, teeth grinding, and rationing of her stuffed animals into family groups of three.

Esme tried to roll up her sleeves, but Ida demurred. Said, "This place is creepy. Why are we in a *hotel?*"

Esme looked to Martin, who was suddenly married to the reorganizing of his kit, and then to Crystal, still by the door, who smiled horribly and said, "I told Ida you'd explain everything when we got here."

But how much was left to explain? And what were the odds Ida still didn't know? CNN had been breaking revelations about the miscreant Esme Haas every five seconds. Ida was out of school, which meant Esme could not palm off the responsibility on some bratty kid calling her names and spilling the beans, because it was all the talk at breakfast and at dinner, too. In theory this should have come as a relief, but no. Esme didn't want to be the one to tell Ida. Tell her what? Your mother is going away for a *long time.*

"Yeah," Ida said. "There's news vans on our front lawn. It's kinda weird."

Esme took her by the wrist but got sweater sleeve instead. "Did you talk to anyone? Did anyone take your picture? This is important, Ida. Tell me. I won't be mad."

She let go of the sleeve. She worried the vibrato in her voice communicated panic.

"Just one," Ida said. "He was nice."

"A reporter, honey? What did he look like?"

But Ida had grown shy. She toed the carpet with her boot and said, "I dunno," shrugging and balling her sweater.

Esme asked if Crystal saw the guy. She had not. She was, she said, too busy patronizing the Helix coffers with her allowance to notice, not that Esme knew *anything about it.* Okay, so she was not just angry but hurt. And maybe even confused. The Helix was her first adult passion, and now it was being tested, and because in the nascence of any passion there was not supposed to be doubt, she felt cheated.

"Well," Esme said, and she gestured for Ida to come sit next to her on the bed. She needed to regroup and adopt a suitable interrogation technique. "What did you do today, turnip? After skating, I mean."

"Nothing."

"Nothing? Because I left you some DVDs for when you got home. They were on the kitchen table."

Ida paused to recall which movies and did the thing Esme was hoping for, which was to establish a baseline for truth telling from here on out: she looked right and snarled her upper lip, which was already too thin and blanched to rank as an asset. Esme smiled. Amazing how the second you objectify someone you love, she becomes at once less and more beautiful.

"They were boring," she said. "I've seen them. *Scooby-Doo* is for babies, anyway."

"There were some other movies, too," Esme said. "But I guess the reporters were more interesting." She added this last bit casually, even sighed a little, like: Oh well, this country's romance with the press has been in evidence for centuries untold, no harm done.

Ida perked up slightly. "Yeah, they were nice to me."

They. So before it was one; now it was many. The DoD had arms.

"So you talked to them through the gates, honey? That's a long walk from the house, and it's cold out!"

"Mo-om," Ida said, annoyed. "Don't you listen? They came up to the lawn. The back patio, too."

Crystal popped a candy in her mouth. She said, "I guess it won't surprise you to find out Rita fired me."

Esme shook her head. "I'm sorry."

"You got fired?" Ida said. She was gauging the mood of the room, trying to decide if this was funny or not. It was not.

"Yes. Because when your boss's husband gets *abducted,* sometimes your boss thinks it's your fault. She fired me from her bed. How humiliating."

"What's *abducted?*" Ida said.

"What, indeed," Crystal said. "Sometimes it means being stolen from your perfectly honest life in foster care and thrown in with people you don't know at all."

"Sometimes," Martin said, getting into the spirit of things, "it's like those alien movies, you've seen those, where people get invited to hang out on another planet for a while."

"Invited," Crystal said.

"Enough," Esme said. "Can we just talk about the reporters, please?"—forgetting she was trying to finesse her daughter and blowing the effort because Ida gave up on the adult discourse and retrieved an activity book from her knapsack. Esme could not help but notice that not a single animal was colored solid or even coherently. Why couldn't her daughter keep to the lines?

"Ida, you only just got here. Don't you want to pay me a little attention?" Esme was being weighed against the Little Mermaid and found wanting. "Just for a second?"

Ida rolled her eyes and said, "Ohhhkay," and then, without prelude, knocked her head against her mother's shoulder. Not hard, but insistent.

"Turtle, it's okay. It's your birthday soon, maybe we're going to take a vacation. Just us two. Maybe sooner, if you can tell me something about the reporter you talked to."

"Can we visit Ma and Pop?"

Esme nodded, and the words came out before she could stop them. "Sure, honey bun. Sure. Your grandparents miss you a lot."

She was glad to be pressing Ida's forehead to her neck, because in no way could she make eye contact with her. Already Crystal was remonstrating with jaw open and lids drawn so far back in disbelief they looked ready to dip behind her eyeballs. Even Martin shook his head.

What was worse than manipulating your daughter? Than lying in ways for which she would never forgive you? What was worse was your unstable DoD contact come to snatch your kid as collateral lest you cough up his name to the press. Jim had already left Esme unconscious on the bathroom floor. Who knew what he'd do next.

"So, the reporter," she said. "Was he fancy? Like, in a suit and tie? Did he know your name?"

But Crystal had had enough. She said, "No, okay? No. Just normal press guys."

"Okay, good." It was the answer Esme wanted, the tension chased from her body, the lights gone out, only Ida saw it wrong and so, pawing in the dark, she said, "Yeah, but you didn't see the one guy talking to *me*. You can't see everything I do!" followed by her storming the bathroom. *Slam* went the door, though it was broken already.

Esme stood. Tried to think. Were there any safe places left to send Ida? School was out; even the English-speaking lycée in Haiti was out, because that was where all the spook kids went. As for the few at the DoD who had been briefed on the Taskforce for the Infiltration and Dismantling of the Helix, they were smote with amnesia—Esme Haas? Never heard of her—and thus unavailing of protections in vogue among mafia turncoats and spies. So that was out. Only place she could think of was her parents' cabin in North Carolina, though Ida could hardly stay there alone.

Crystal said, "I'd better take her home," and motioned at the bathroom. They could all hear Ida crying. Esme shook her head; there was only one thing to do. "Why not let Martin take her to the mall first. Buy some new clothes. Toiletries, too. Pajamas are fun." Then, raising her voice, "That sound good, Ida? How about we take that trip right now."

The door opened a wedge, the child nodding, eyes floorward.

Esme squatted. "Now, listen," she said. "I know things seem a little weird, but everything's fine. Even if they don't seem fine, they are. Also, I have a surprise for you. Martin will tell you in the car." And as Ida looked warily at her mother and her mother at Martin and Martin at his phone, to make sure it was on for when Esme texted him instructions the second they left the hotel, an NPR commentator broadcast the news: the FBI had just issued Thurlow Dan an ultimatum. Come out or we're coming in. And, by way of subtext: If the hostages die, it's on you.

By now it was nighttime, which meant nothing would happen at the Helix House until dawn. Chances of a botched raid were high, higher still in the dark. The feds would wait.

When Esme saw Ida had fallen asleep, the release in her chest was awful. Had she really not been breathing? She was, quite obviously, afraid of her child. The child who was assiduous in the upgrading of her rage, so that by the time she got to Esme's age, she would have rarefied her temper into a bid for the sublime. Already, it was bracing. In sleep, though, people forget themselves, or come into the selves they've spent most of their lives trying to repress. Ida was fetal, with knees and forehead sewn to Esme's side. She had released the day's hatred and said with the array of her body what she'd been feeling in secret: Mom, I need you; Mom, don't leave. Her hair was in a twist, clutched in her palm. Esme checked her forehead, and, yes, she hoped it was warm, because whatever chance the world gave this mother to source her child's problems elsewhere, she would take it. Ida mumbled and flung her arm around her mother's waist. Esme felt Ida's nails dent her skin and thought that if she could just break Ida of need in sleep, it would do wonders for her awake. Also, she could not write like this. She freed her hand from her hip and slipped out of bed. For a second, Ida cast about the mattress; then she rediscovered her hair.

In every life, an unraveling. Esme's had started at her parents' just a few weeks ago. Surprise! She had dropped in for a visit. She had taken a bus and ended up calling from the road. Her dad answered. He was hard of hearing, so it was: Who? Leslie? About what? And then her mother, who said, Hello, Esmeralda, though this name was not even on her birth certificate; it was simply what Linda called her when she was angry. Esme didn't get a word in before she was hissing about Ida. Yes, of course they hadn't told her about her father, because, duh, instructions from the *butler—P.S. Don't tell Ida she is cognate with a cult leader*—were binding in every universe, except, Jesus, who taught Esme to parent like this? Because, as far as her mom knew, she'd done a good job with Esme, and her father had, too.

Their cabin was an hour afield of a sizable community in any direction. A two-bedroom in the woods. Esme understood wanting to live modestly despite their wealth, but she could never understand the privation of their lifestyle. Her dad drove an '88 Chevy pickup. The clutch was shot; the truck wouldn't go over forty or, who knew, might blow up if it did. When he got to the bus stop, it took him many tries just to get out of the cab. It had been months since her last visit, but he looked the same. When you are seventy-seven, what difference does the fluting of your skin make? She tried to give him a hug. One of his hands alit on the small of her back, while the other—and then she realized he wasn't wearing his arm.

She'd asked, "Where's the arm?"

He said, "I barely even need two arms nowadays."

She got in the truck, in the driver's seat, because technically her father was not supposed to get behind a wheel, with or without the prosthetic. Still, one had to wonder how he drove stick without it, maybe he used his shoulder to steer while he switched gears, and then she shuddered in fear for everyone else on the road.

Since she was always afraid to ask how were things at the house, she asked about his volunteer job. He was a docent at an astronomical research institute sited deep in the forest. A former NASA base—from there *One small step for mankind* was relayed to the world—that the DoD commandeered in '81 for "listening."

"Oh, they don't need me much. It gets pretty dull at times."

"What's the big question these days?"

He looked at her wanly. "What is dark matter."

Esme snorted. Five minutes together, and already they were negotiating the extent to which he was allowed to grouse now that his favorite pastime, the Internet, had been restricted by her mother. He'd been spending hours a day chatting with people online, and Linda didn't like it.

He coughed into his fist. The road went up the mountain in christie curves, the locals taking them fast and Esme wending along like Grandma. Her dad hammered the dash because no heat was coming up through the one vent aimed his way, and said, "That's some kid you've got," before whacking the dash again. She had no idea what this meant, though it probably meant nothing. For her dad, the world was middling. How's the weather? So-so. How's your grandkid? Fine.

If it was the truth Esme wanted, she needed to ask her mother. Or just stand within one hundred feet and Linda would tell her.

They got to the house. It had snowed, and because her parents never departed from the path to the road, the snow was untrammeled but for deer tracks and wild turkeys and, beautifully, a snow angel. Her daughter lived here. She thought she even saw her face peering out the window from behind a curtain, though the second they got out of the truck, the curtain stopped rustling and all was quiet.

The Helix had been making news for years, but by now it was making headlines. Rumors and gossip. Her parents didn't have a TV, but they read the papers, and there was always the Internet. And, while they had never met Thurlow, they knew who he was. Esme didn't think

it would be long before her mother took it upon herself to tell Ida everything. Her plan was to hope she didn't.

"Mom? Ida?" She walked through the house. It had two floors and
a porch that overlooked a valley and mountains in the distance. Half
the trees had lost their leaves; the view was a mixed treat. She went to
the kitchen and saw her dad by the fridge with an ice cream sandwich.
He had taken off his jacket, and, since his sweater made prominent the
empty sleeve hung by his side, she suddenly wondered if Ida was terrorized by the sight—if, despite the years she'd been living here, the arm
creeped her out.

In the mudroom were sneakers but no boots, the boots put to better use on Ida's feet as she and Linda played outside, the one making
a snowman and the other taking photos, a million per second, one for
each second Esme had missed seeing her child grow up. She had the
idea her mom was making her a scrapbook, though none such had ever
materialized.

She watched them through the window. Ida was wearing leggings
that looked like neoprene and a bubble jacket she did not recognize,
or recognized dimly; it was colored bark and had an HB Surf Series
badge sewn into the arm. And then it hit her: these were her brother's
clothes. His steamer wet suit. His travel jacket for that one surfing trip
off the coast of New Zealand when he was twelve. Esme was so floored
by the evidence her parents had kept his stuff and even brought it with
them to this place that it helped ease down the pill of her daughter ig-
noring her when she ran out of the cabin all smiles.

She hugged Ida anyway because the parent unloved is also undeterred. They had not seen each other in 3 months. Ida had been alive
for 117 months, of which most of her last $\frac{1}{39}$ Esme had been traveling.
There were other $\frac{1}{36}$s and $\frac{1}{27}$s and even $\frac{1}{18}$s for that half-year deploy-
ment to Diego Garcia, though maybe that was more like a $\frac{1}{12}$ expedi-
tion, since Ida was only six at the time, which meant not even math
could declaw Esme's failings.

Next Esme greeted her mom, who did the scariest thing in her repertoire, which was to cock an eyebrow. The hairs there had shed long
ago, so she'd taken to penciling them in with black liner. Every month,
the curve got more pronounced and severe. It was a sickle, an arch, and,
by now, a delta above each eye. When raised, the brow was lethal.

"Well, well," Linda said, but without the scorn Esme had been readying herself for. In fact, the A brow was a red herring. She wasn't mad anymore. Esme thought maybe she was fronting for Ida's sake, but so what? She would take it. They hugged. And the hug was nice. She had never found in her parents a source of strength since Chris went down, and it was not like one hug was going to lade her coffers with the courage of heart to right her life, but it wasn't hurting, either.

Linda said, "Ida and I were just finishing up this snowman," and, to Ida, "What's his name again?"

"Don."

Esme was not sure she'd ever heard a name spoken with greater spite. Ida jammed a stick in his eye and looked at her mom. "Your clothes are ugly," she said, and she marched back into the house.

"That went well," Esme said. "Don? Who names her snowman Don?"

"She's right, you know. If you're going wear that nonsense, at least join the army. Be for real."

Esme shrank a couple of feet. Her parents had only a vague sense of what she did, enough to know it screwed them up—New identities? Really?—but not enough to think it worth the trouble to find out more. Perhaps her father was more sympathetic, but she didn't know; they didn't talk.

She fixed the snowman's eye. Apologized for his care.

"Not to worry," Linda said. "He's cold as ice," and then she grinned, and to Esme this grin might have seemed stupid, except that nothing about her mother was ever stupid. She was too sharp and cagey to grin like that unless it was for sport or design. "Now, listen," she said. "I'm glad you're here. I've got news."

Esme followed her through the snow. Her mother was the kind of woman who always liked to speak her beef with someone hungry for it.

"Is it Ida? She looks okay to me. Or, wait, is it school? Is she failing at school?"

Linda looked on her with what had to have been contempt, though maybe it was contempt plus pity, which is kind of like cherry Pepto—not *so* bad.

"It's about your brother," she said. "Chris."

"Right, because I've actually forgotten his name."

They were on the patio under porch lights. Esme sat at the table, her mom nearby.

"We got a call from the hospital," Linda said.

The words sounded tense but happy, and since Esme still had no idea how her mother felt about Chris in a coma all these years, she assumed this meant he was dead. A twenty-four-year nap comes to an end, and her mother is released from the emotional vigil she'd been on or wanted to be on: both seemed exhausting.

Linda leaned forward, elbows on the table. She spoke the next part slow. "He said something. Out loud. A nurse just happened to be there."

The news blew Esme well back into her chair. Her brother's voice. She didn't even know its sound. "Out of the blue?" she said. "He's awake? What did he say?"

Linda picked up a bird carved out of wood, small as soap, and hopped it along the edge of the table. "The doctors said this could be prelude to waking up. But not to get excited."

Esme was surprised the doctors would presume interest let alone enthusiasm in relatives who never came, never called, but then maybe to them family was just family; you can't judge 'em all.

"Wow," she said, because what else was there? Apparently, a lot. Linda got in close to the bird, as though talking to the bird. In fact she *was* talking to the bird; it sure as hell beat talking to Esme. She said, "Of all the things. Of all the times I imagined this happening."

Now the bird was in her palm, eye to eye. "What's that? You want to know what he said?" She faced the thing at Esme. "Go on, tell her," and then, "Oh, fine, I'll tell her. He said, you ready for this? He said *Esme*. Loud and clear, too. They were amazed. Not like he'd been asleep for a quarter of a century, not like he hadn't used his lips in as long, but just like he was in the middle of a conversation. A heated one, too. They said he sounded mad."

Esme had been shaking her head for a while. Her darling brother reliving their fight day after day, the anger still on his lips, with no sense of the years that had passed, him still fourteen years old. It is 1981. Ronald Reagan has just taken the oath. The president says, "We're going to begin to act, beginning today," and the next day, her brother's life stops, and all because she let his friend ejaculate on her chest.

Linda continued to hop the bird across the table and even to chirp on its behalf, the stupid smile back on her face.

"Have you been to see him?" Esme said.

"He's been screaming for a year, what do you think?"

"What screaming? He screams? Why didn't anyone tell me?"

"Are you serious?"

Esme had begun to take issue with the bird and to concentrate anger in the bird and to make the bird proxy for all the ways she did not love her brother, daughter, parents, enough, and so, yes, she snatched it from Linda's hand and hurled it over the balustrade.

Linda stood. She seemed verged on the kind of laugh that sizes you down for life. But no, she just stood. Stood and stretched and said, "Ida and me made pineapple upside-down cake. Let's eat."

"*Now?* I want to talk to you."

"I'm hungry." And with that she slapped the table, and the laugh Esme had braced for came out. Her brother speaks for the first time in twenty-four years and her mother wants pineapple upside-down cake? Esme leaned forward and had a good look—at her mother's face and mostly her eyes. The red tracery of veins fencing her pupils. The Windex shine in each lens. The part where her lids were barely half-open, in contrast to Esme's mouth, which was hanging way open now that she realized her mother was stoned. Had been stoned this whole time.

Esme knew Linda had smoked in the sixties, was a big old hippie. But she was seventy-one, and how did someone her age even acquire marijuana? The nearest neighbor was a soldier just back from Iraq. Maybe he got high for having killed in a war without cause and maybe because he also tended chickens and harvested their eggs and brought her mother a dozen every week, he brought her a little something else, too.

Linda cleared her throat, and, with the firmness Esme had come to expect from her but which was no comfort now, she said, "I want cake."

Fine. They went inside. Her dad was at the computer in the living room, under a bearskin nailed to the wall. Not just the bear but the head too, and an old-timey rifle captioned underneath, so it was hard to know which was displayed as the better prize. Her parents had bought the place furnished, but after ten years, if you're still living with a dead bear on your wall, you're doing so for a reason. Her dad was distraught; she watched him type. Most people of his generation finger-peck and get right up to the screen, but since he only had one arm and giant googly glasses, his deportment was in a school of its own.

"His *friends*," Linda said, and snorted her way to the kitchen. "He gets one night a week. Let's go, Bill!"

His hand fell on the keyboard like Play-Doh. He looked up at Esme and the look was bleak. She touched his arm, though it did no good. You can't solace a man whose only friends are text.

Esme said, "Come on, Dad, we're having cake."

He pushed back his chair but didn't get up. His empty sleeve hung over the armrest, and the awful thing was, you barely noticed for how slack the rest of his body was. He stared at the screen like the dead stare at us.

Esme made for the fridge.

Her dad trudged to the table when it was clear Linda would not stop calling his name. Esme sat next to Ida, though she still hadn't said a word since *Don*. Her mother knifed the cake, but served only herself, a quarter wedge, huge. Her dad wasn't hungry. Ida said it tasted gross, while Linda, who had retained her good cheer throughout, opened her mouth—her mouth was full—and said, "Now, Esmeralda, daughter mine, would you like to say something about Thurlow Dan and the Helix? Because I think maybe this little lady should know more of the world than she does."

That night, Esme fought with her parents. She promised to get it right with Ida; she bought herself more time. And then she left. And now the hospital where Chris was living called three times a day. And the morgue where her parents were called three times a day. They all wanted to know what arrangements to make. If Esme didn't call back, they would dispose of the bodies and send her the bill. But it wasn't as though she didn't know what she wanted. She wanted her parents and Chris to reunite. They had died trying to make that happen; the least she could do was help. She knew she had heard this story before, about parents who died as they drove to be with an adult child who was himself dying. It turned out that when Chris spoke her name, it was the swan song he'd been trying to belt out for twenty-four years. Only in her parents' unction for a miracle, or perhaps because one was stoned and the other disabled, they pitched off I-64 on the way to the hospital. The road was narrow and ascendant one hairpin at a time, there was no guardrail, and if you went over even halfway up, you would not survive the fall. Every time Esme thought about it, she wondered whether they had any last words, too, hurled from their lips as they said good-bye. And why not? People were crying out for each other all the time.

They were stopped at a diner off the freeway. Ida had to pee. It was two in the morning, but still, this was not the most advisable conduct. Esme's face was mugged on every TV, on every channel. On the plus side, the coverage gave her a visual on the Helix House, and a sense of what people were saying.

On the downside, what people were saying was bad. For one, the feds had turned the site into a zoo. Tents, kitchen, helicopters, Bradley. Bradleys. Six tanks in a residential suburb. The team had to stump all the roadside trees just to accommodate their girth. She could tell they were M3s, though, because they had room only for five—driver, commander, gunner plus scouts—which meant this was the team's concession to context or, more likely, the government's attempt to look modulated but ready.

Ida insisted on cherry pie because she wanted an American experience, they being on the road and mingled with the people. At age nine, she was already sassy with expectation of what dreams the country would make true for her.

"Kinda late to be up!" the waitress said, and overflowed their water glasses.

"Mom," Ida said, and she probed the cherry glue stuffing for a fruit item. "Mom, you're on TV again."

Esme was wearing a black and turquoise winter hat that had a panther on the cuff—Go Panthers!—a down ski jacket, and sunglasses. She'd had the difficult task of having to look recognizable to her daughter but foreign to everyone else. She'd made a point never to wear her rig around Ida or Crystal, so this was uncharted territory. And she had navigated it poorly. Ida had asked more than once if she fell on her face last night, it looked so swollen and pink and weird, and Esme swore the waitress, while bowling pie at her kid, also had a double take at her.

"I know, tulip. But you don't have to believe what they're saying."

The menu was laminated and tacky with jam, and probably if she needed coverage in a storm, this vinyl would do, so broad was its wingspan. Every second item was waffles. Chicken and waffles. Ham and waffles. Biscuits and waffles. She ordered cheese and waffles to go.

"They're saying you and that cult guy are like friends or something."

"Tulip, just eat your pie. We have to go."

"They're *saying*"—but she said it too loud, and because Esme didn't want to silence her child with force, she did the next best thing and spilled water in her lap. Ida made a scene but at least now they were being noticed for a safer reason.

What was the government saying? That Esme had set this up; she was on her own. No one else would go down for this except maybe the few people who knew about her, though if it panned out disastrously, the buck would move up the chain of command and stop just two or three links south of the president, whose staff would say, Look, the Helix was in bed with North Korea; procurement of a reconnaissance effort had been in the hands of the same professional for years; her ties to the organization made her best suited to the work; how could we have forecast this outcome?

But only if it came to that. For now they had let slip, in case they killed anyone by accident, that secessionist activity with guns was not the joke everyone had taken it to be and that the Helix might have an arsenal that made the Chechen rebels look Care Bear.

Ida was in the bathroom. Esme could hear the electric hand dryer and imagined her trying to arch her back and high her lap in quest for the hot air. She expected it would be three more minutes before Ida showed, which meant the new guy sitting opposite her needed to hurry. He looked in no hurry. He even looked expansive—job well done; he had found Esme in less than three hours. He was DoD or CIA, FBI, whatever.

"What do you want?" Esme said. Her waffles arrived in a Styrofoam casket. The waitress looked at her replacement date and seemed to get an idea of what was going on here, which had Esme thinking about what sort of clientele this waitress called regular.

"Seems like you might be headed to the site," he said. "Just guessing, of course."

Esme rolled her eyes. This man looked about forty, too young to be for real with his noir affect but too old to find it humorous. He had frothy orange hair and tortoiseshell glasses with nose pads that were mismatched and uneven, so that the glasses sat slant on his face but not enough to be retarded. He gestured for the waitress and ordered a coffee. His suit was rumpled.

"I'm with my daughter," she said, meaning either: Be nice, I'm with my child, or: I'm with my child, we're going to the park, you must have me confused with someone else.

"I see that. She looks a lot like someone we've all come to know and love."

"Oh, for Pete's sake, what do you want?" She scanned the restaurant for a back door.

"It's like this," he said, and she noticed he had dry skin crisped along the rim of his ear. Both ears. And she thought: This is exactly the kind of thing a girlfriend or wife does not let you get away with. He's not wearing a ring, probably he has no one, and if he weren't so blowhard in the delivery of a threat I know is coming, I could pity him.

"You're wanted at the site," he said. "I'm here to make that happen."

"A driver. How nice."

"I get you there. You get him out."

Since this had been her idea all along—at least for a couple of hours—she should have been pleased with their concord. But she was not pleased, which was like when your coin turns up heads and you are let down, apprised of feelings that were secret to yourself until then. Only it wasn't feelings she had but terror.

"And after that?" Not that she didn't know the answer or the spectrum from which an answer would present itself: immunity, a presidential pardon, or just her taking it in lieu of the fifty staffers who saw the Helix proliferate and did nothing precisely to hasten a crisis that would justify trawling nationwide for the last liberal drowning.

"Just get your daughter and let's go," he said, and when she didn't get up he covered her hand with his own and squeezed until it hurt, which was when Ida erupted from the bathroom, saw this man pledged in affectionate consort with her mother, and skated down the lane for their table.

"Dad?" she said, and the glow on her face was colors a person was lucky to see once in her life.

They were in a van with a table in the back and a screen that dropped down from the roof. Ida was watching a soap opera about thirteen-year-olds that was, apparently, in vogue. Esme looked over her shoulder and said, "Hey, Jack, how many episodes you got?" Despite her negligence as a parent, or because she was well practiced in its art, she knew the value of a pacifier when she saw one. So did the escort, since he said they had enough to get them there. Still, she decided to test what was what. "Hey, Jack, what if Ida needs to be sick?" He said there was a bucket with a snap top and a deodorizing puck adhered to the underside. "Hey, Jack, what if we don't get there in time?" He said, "In this weather, time rushes for no man."

The light from Ida's entertainment console was enough to write by, but it still *felt* dark. Like flying at night when yours is the only light in the cabin, everyone else asleep, snoring. It was, Esme thought, a shit way to be.

"Hey, Jack," she said. She could see his eyes in the rearview, and they were closing. "Hey, Jack!" She poked him in the shoulder.

"It's Noah," he said. "*No-uh.*"

"Sleeping Beauty's more like it. Let me drive."

"And stuff me in the trunk. Sounds like a plan."

"We've gone ten miles in the last hour. Who can fall asleep like this?"

"I'm fine."

"I'm Sneezy, how do."

Their eyes met in the rearview. He was not amused, but at least he was awake. And talking. In almost any situation, talking is like doing squats in your tight jeans—it gives you room to breathe.

"So," she said, and by now she had made use of the swivel part of her swivel chair. She was faced forward and square with the tension of this drive—the snow, the wind. She said, "How'd you end up with this job, anyway? You work for Jim?"

"Thurlow Dan is a terrorist," he said. "A sociopath. And for once being married to you, this taints you. And your kid. So just go back to her and stop talking to me."

Esme U-turned quick, but it was okay: Ida was passed out, lips parted and chapped because she was congested. Esme could hear laughter—the audio had been leaking from Ida's headphones all night—which meant Ida couldn't know what had been said outside the soap in her ears. Esme was about to turn off the TV, except perhaps this was the noise Ida needed to sleep, and in no galaxy did she want to wake her up. Who knew what that shitbird up front would say next.

The snow had picked up. Noah had his face near pressed to the windshield. Wiping the view with his hand, as though the frost were what stood between him and Mexico. They fishtailed once. Twice. Three times a heyday, only what happened here was Ida waking up green. Esme could actually see the green overrun her cheeks as she said, "My stomach hurts." What could Esme do? She tossed her the bucket. It thumped her chest.

"Pull over!" Esme said, and it was done. He killed the engine, and what was left was a gale that rocked their luxury caravan and a child who was retching and crying into the pail. Esme unlocked her seatbelt and made for Ida's chair. Tried to rub her neck and pull back her hair, and also to hear what she was saying besides "I want to go home," because Esme could hear a word mewled among the rest, and this word was not *home* or even *Mom* but more beat-up, like a worry stone or blankie, the thing you've handled, clutched, cuddled so much it's barely what it was, except—for you—it is that much more.

Every two seconds, a big rig rolled by with almost zero clearance. But if it was frightful outside, it was worse in the car.

Esme said, "Soon, buttercup, we'll be going home really soon." And when this seemed to make Ida cry worse, and when Esme could not produce tissues and instead offered up her sleeve, which was already drizzled in tears, she said, "Honey bun, what can I do? Just say the word."

They were long past the upflue of pie, which meant this retching wasn't about a biological intolerance to cars so much as the expulsion of childhood from her daughter's life. How could you stay a child through this? Esme could barely watch. Heave, retch, weep. Face obliterated in afterdamp. "Anything you want," she said. "Just tell me."

"I want your phone"—and when it seemed like Esme was game for this, the crying rolled back, sobs were snuffles. Esme ransacked her bag and pockets.

Ida dialed fast and crammed the phone to her ear as though they were at the rodeo but she must be heard. Esme did not think who she was calling in the middle of the night; she was too spent with release from the dread that her daughter would cry this way for life.

It was ringing—no one was home—but as Esme reached for the phone, voicemail picked up and she heard her mother's voice, and in this voice Esme apprehended the word Ida had been mumbling throughout. She'd been asking for her ma. Not Esme Ma, but Linda Ma.

If Esme had seen her green, no doubt Ida could see her blanch. She had forgotten to disconnect her parents' phone? This should have come as no surprise, since she had not done anything apropos of their death except to mourn, and she had barely done that.

She did not listen to Ida's message, but when Ida was done, she clammed the phone shut. "I keep calling," Ida said. "Maybe their voice-mail's broken?"

"Try to get some sleep, tulip. I know this doesn't seem like much of a vacation, but just you wait, tomorrow is going to be fun. You'll see."

"Will you spend the day with me?"

Esme looked out the window. The snow was piling up around the car. They would be iglooed in an hour. Her guess? Noah's attempt to get her to the site was so low-fi, there couldn't be anyone else besides Jim calling the shots. If this had been on a bigger dime, someone would have pulled in for rescue and transport. A better car. A motorcade.

"Let's talk in the morning," she said. "We're going to be here for a while, and Mommy has some work to do."

Ida settled in. If her body had taken over the rendering of grief in her life, it was too tired to play on. Esme watched her close her eyes, then looked at the index cards she had written so far. Her story was almost done.

39. Lo, this is getting impossible. Our daughter scares me. What have we done to her? I guess I just didn't try very hard when I had the chance. Sure, we left New Paltz, but to understand what happened next, you'll need some sense drummed into you. For one, let's be frank: No way were we going to recruit defector POWs in North Korea. Too risky, too hard, too cruel. If our guys out there wanted to come home, we wouldn't be able to help; if they wanted to stay, we wouldn't be able to

flip them without exerting pressure of the kind no one's proud of later. I knew this—I think we all knew this—which is why they took me off Yul the second a more interesting, albeit improbable, contact came along. A guy—let's call him J.T.—who owned a cake shop in Queens. He was a baker, once ran with the mob. He wore a Brylcreem pompadour that hadn't moved in twelve years, and was connected to the feds, who leaned on him for news every now and then. But he wanted more out of life. He had issues, among them the sense that no one cared enough about U.S. POWs. And so, North Korea, which probably had some explaining to do re: our guys MIA from the war. Unlikely as it sounds, this baker had already made nice with the Vietnamese U.N. mission—he'd gotten them hooked on shortcake—so they facilitated contact, and soon enough, North Korea's ambassador to the U.N. was eating red velvet cream pies at J.T.'s place.

40. Not long after, I started going there, too. And you know how it is when you're a new mom and your husband's sleeping with other women and you feel fat because you are fat, and unwanted because you are unwanted, and all the love that child and husband have taken from your vault is so accessorized with hurt, it barely looks like love—you know how that constellates into adulterous behavior of your own? So, yes, one second you are eating vanilla sponge cake with lychee buttercream, and the next you are panty-ankled on the stove top. So, yes, I went to Corona. I met J.T. I went once, twice, many times after that. And it wasn't like you noticed, because how much were you home?

41. The bakery was by Shea Stadium, where it's all chop shops and drug fronts. It had stone-wall siding and a shingled mansard roof. A cupcake weather vane and a big old American flag twenty feet up. Inside were framed photos of J.T. with Important Asians and with the relief pitching rotation for the Mets. He had been to North Korea with various businessmen. When he got there, they'd loaded him in the rear with sodium pentothal. Years later, when I heard tell of your plans to go—I intercepted an email Isolde sent her mom: *Look, Mom, one woman's cult is another's Fulbright*—I knew they'd do the same to you if not worse.

42. You might be wondering what the Baker has to do with anything. I'll tell you. In 1996, when a submarine ran aground at Kangnung and

released almost thirty North Korean commandos whose mission might be to terrorize Seoul; when the North needed to apologize for the incident because they had been busted, though they absolutely did no want to apologize; when the Agreed Framework between the North and the U.S. to denuclearize this most volatile and strange state was under threat; the navigating of these parlous waters somehow fell to J.T., who let it be known that the North might possibly have seven American POWs they might possibly be willing to send home, provided everyone forgot about the sub/commando incident. Seven POWs? Three of whom might be my soldiers?

Not surprisingly, then, I got a call: Go heavy with the Baker. At the time, Ida was just learning to talk. Though it wasn't like she was saying either one of our names. Her first word was *Lou,* for the stuffed alligator she slept with. So the call could not have come at a better time; it gave me the chance to dwell on less hurtful things. We moved into the back room of J.T.'s shop. He knew I was Agency, but he didn't much care. He went about his life. He would sit with the ambassador, the minister, and company, and since the banquette was bugged, I'd nurse Ida and listen in, and listen harder when they spoke Korean, which they often did, since the guys liked to keep J.T. insecure about how well he was trusted. I ate a lot of pie. And because J.T. didn't really want us there—he was already seeing a woman in the kitchen who would strafe my arms with hot lard and go, *Oops!*—he put me on dish duty seven days a week. The composition of this food began to resolve in my veins. I had trouble waking up, I was tired all the time, and, for the way my breast milk started to taste, Ida deprived me of my one calorie-cutting exercise. She started to throw up my milk and then to refuse it altogether.

43. I did not have a new place to live, but only because I wasn't ready to look. I'd have to start over. Send Ida to safety. Recommit to my work and stay away from you. If I went back, I'd have told you everything and put us all at risk. And I was done hurting. Enough.

But I was also running out of time. Ida was cranky or teething or maybe she just had heartburn. Whichever the case, she wailed with a frequency that, in the abstract, was admirable for its allegiance to habit but that began to annoy the Koreans, not to mention the other customers. The

State Department had given the Korean mission a twenty-five-mile leash in any direction from Columbus Circle, but there were plenty of other bakeries to patronize, and also, my time there was not proving effective. The guys talked about hunting and baseball and sometimes about how to win respect from the West via the pluming of their nuclear capacity, but even this was more like jock talk than actionable intelligence. They never mentioned MIAs. They never mentioned my soldiers. So I had to produce something fast, which was when I came on the idea of posing as an orthopedic physician for the Mets and going with J.T. to North Korea. He'd already befriended the team's pitching coach and once taken him to the North as a companion and wingman. He'd already taken the Koreans to many games, and to the dugout for autographs. The plan was feasible. A little crazy, but feasible. And anyway, I wanted out of that shit-hole kitchen. I wanted my passions released. I wanted to reclaim the protected intimacy of being thrust into a target's life on the sly and for a limited time, and I wanted to escape the fear born of love for you and Ida—the fear that there were feelings in this world that could undo your resolve to live isolated from the trauma and wreckage that come in train of relations with other people.

44. Sure, my parents were not so keen to divorce their identities, but only on principle. And yes, they were not so keen to take Ida, but only in practice. In the end, something of their ideals and de facto needs got answered in the assumption of a new life in North Carolina.

As for me, I hired Martin. We worked up the face of a doctor any shortstop would trust. I studied tensegrity, contractile structures, capsular and noncapsular patterns of motion. The rig was up in a month; passable intelligence on the stuff of orthopedics took two, and so at the end of 1997, I took my first plunge into the most isolated, radically autonomous, and lonely community of millions on earth.

I never managed to get in touch with the defected soldiers. But I did make contacts on the inside and was able to pass on information about North Korea's weapons program that seemed credible. I was doing my job and doing it well except that my life continued to feel elsewhere. It *was* elsewhere, since even as I was working North Korea, I never stopped working you.

So naturally when Jim got wind of your rapport with the North, it made all the sense in the world to give the job to me. And when you went ahead and accepted their money—*are you insane?*—I said I'd help shut you down. So long as the government came to me, I could protect you. So now you know: all along, I've been protecting you.

They were racing down the highway. Civilian traffic had been diverted and their jeep absorbed into a caravan of the policing authority. Ida had posed no questions about what was going on and did not appear in the least riled by the sirens or fanfare, but this did not mean she wouldn't be soon enough. Esme, who had been working on what to tell her about Thurlow for ten minutes plus ten years, made a joke about them knowing how to make an entrance, and when this got no response, she said, "Ladies and gents, please welcome to Cincinnati the lovely, the talented, Ms. Ida Haas!" She ventured the play din of a crowd.

Ida said, "Stop it." And, "No wonder Dad left you."

Esme did not move; she was lock-eyed with the mongrel of feeling that had reared up in the car. The outrage (Thurlow left *her?*), the relief of seeing Ida blame Esme and not herself, the wilderness of her child's mind (What else does she think she knows?), and then just the dread of having to set her straight. Because if they were going to get a moment together, all three of them, Esme wanted Ida to know enough to try to keep it with her for life.

No traffic, no people, herewith: Cincinnati. The river blue, molared with ice, the wind patrolling the city street by street; this place was bleak like Pyongyang but without the excuse, which meant it was actually bleaker. They rolled through downtown and then doubled back, and in the way you can sense a water mass well before you see it, so it is with the ambience of a crisis in play. Sirens and floodlights might beacon the news, but it's the sublimated chaos—chaos in hand—that radiates for miles.

A tony neighborhood. Mansions. Many architectural dogmas in effect. Tudors, castles, Victorians, and there, up a hill, the stone square presidio Thurlow Dan called home.

The cordon site was like a fern whose pot was entirely too small. It had proliferated well beyond the road—a two-way lane, but barely—up neighboring lawns, and into a Tudor opposite the Helix House, whose family had been moved to the Marriot and given plane tickets to Puerto

Rico in thanks. On scene: special ops, National Guard, local police, Men in Charge. Women, too, but no matter, just people whose job was to revise, at a clip, how best to storm the castle.

The road was a gauntlet of authority vehicles. Paper cups in the gutter, caskets of four-way chili swept curbside. Two loudspeakers rigged to gaslights. A pumper truck with coffee on the grill; three ambulances up a lawn and the rest parked at a golf course nearby.

There was no way to drive through this mess, so they had to park and wend, which was no picnic. Noah had Esme's arm in a pinch. Ida refused to take her hand, so Esme tried to keep her one step ahead, which meant treading her heels and getting nasty looks for it. It was freezing, and since no one knew how to talk to one another despite the headgear and mics and direct connect, they got stopped every two feet.

At first Noah just flashed his badge and passed them through, but as they got closer, and the barring command got more imposing, the badge no longer cut it. What was needed at this point was a badge plus an extraordinarily compelling reason to bother the assistant special agent in charge—so what, exactly, was their business here?

"It's the ex-wife," Noah said. "That good enough?"

He said it loud; there was no way Ida had missed it. And so, there it was. Esme died a thousand times over. And based on the Moses part that opened up before them, the information must have struck the ops with similar intensity, likewise the news choppers overhead, which nearly clipped each other for best vantage of the freedom given this mother and child. Who were they that the way was clear?

Not that Esme had moved. To have had the work of disclosure done for her, without fuss or warning—she was exhilarated and traumatized, though both fell short of the flowered comprehension in her daughter's face, upturned and saying with unmistakable clarity: Yep, now is the moment when the tropism of my attachments could go this way or that. Now is your chance to shine on me the torch you've been carrying for my dad, and we can be a family whether we get to him or not.

Esme knelt so they were eye level. She didn't know where to begin. But Ida had it figured out; she turned away and headed straight for the Helix House.

Ran for the house, so that when a cop scooped her up, it was a tantrum like no other. She bit his arm. Drew blood. Esme did not expect her to listen, but she said, "Sweetie, stop, I'll explain everything, I swear," and like that, Ida was calm. She walked back and pressed her whole body into Esme like she was the dunce and Mom was the corner. It was Ida's first kindness in days and maybe her first ever apropos the labor of forgiving your parents, and so when she whispered, having pulled her mom in close, "Can you help Dad?" Esme didn't have it in her to say no.

The special agent in charge came out the Tactical Operations Center to greet them and share the latest: You took too long. The feds are done talking. They were done hours ago, but now they are *really* done. Thurlow's dad was back in the house against orders, Norman had cut off all communication, the hostages were probably still in the den, there were guards straggled throughout the compound, and unless Esme had a better idea, it was T minus five.

The team had set up in the living room of the Tudor house across the street. Persian rug, mahogany hutch, and, above the fireplace, a mantel of framed days in the life of the family displaced by this operation. Kid in Little League, missing teeth. Kid in hockey helmet, missing teeth. Girl plus trophy held high. And it wasn't that these photos had seized for posterity special moments in time so much as the feeling inspired by these moments: You are a marvel, you are forever.

Esme looked at Ida, who sat recessed in a loveseat, hands in a clump between her legs, chin to chest. And without warning, it happened: Esme felt the right thing at exactly the right time.

She had compulsions, hangups, fear, but she also had clarity. Her parents were dead. Her brother had died with her name behind it. She and Ida had no one left; they barely had each other. But what they did have with Thurlow was a dynamic, and in this arrangement of lives vectored to and from each other, whole universes were given home. Isn't that what people mean when they talk about family? The unspoken, unseen, but eminently felt?

She told the SAC that she did have a better idea, yes. And after she laid it out, he extended his arms as though readying for a catch. She could see his palms—the skin was thick and dense like beeswax—and understood anew the expression *The whole world in his hands.*

The math was easy. Risk Esme, who was trained and largely responsible for this situation, or risk the hostages, because, without credible intel, anyone caught with so much as a hot dog in hand would get shot. If Esme got taken or hurt, HRT was going to assault the compound anyway; if she could end this thing without bloodshed, all the better, job well done.

The SAC said: "If you're not out in ten, we won't wait." Esme understood. She asked for a second with Ida, but when they went to the other room, she didn't have to tell her much. Ida was on board—she was brave, a natural—and fleeing the house within five minutes of the bustle grown up around Esme as they fit her with a camera. Her plan? To rendezvous with Ida at Reading and McMillan, at a manhole the city opened last week. Ida would find it easily—just walk south and walk fast, and if Esme wasn't there in an hour, call Martin.

At last, Esme was in the Helix House. In the first-floor pantry, where hostages might have been but weren't. Same for the den and the other rooms. Her team of four was gone. Unclear where, though she suspected they were scattered throughout the underground of Cincinnati. No problem; she'd pick them up later. In any case, they were not here, and that was good, and Wayne agreed. She'd found him toting his wife and bird down the hall. Under the circumstances, he should have been pleased to see her, but no, the look on his face was all hate. He said no one else was left in the house but Thurlow, and then he kept walking.

Esme knew she had to get to Thurlow ASAP, but instead she dwelled on the stuff around her. The pens he'd held. The pillows he'd touched. She disconnected her headcam. So long as SWAT thought the place was rigged and manned, they had time. Ten minutes wasn't much, but it would do. That, a few cans of gas, accelerant, and a lighter.

She paused outside Thurlow's door and rested her hand on the knob. They had been happy once. Since then it had been x days, months, years, and she still missed him with a degree of agony that would have sent most people running back to him a long time ago. But not Esme. Instead, she had ignored the need, boxed it up, put it away, acquired new experiences to box and pile until her tower had grown nine thousand boxes high and there was no chance she could feel that first box on the bottom, right? Princess and the pea. Such a deranged moral to offer a child. The more sensitive you are to pain welled deep in your psyche, the more noble your spirit? It was better to be noble than happy? She pressed her ear to the wood. And the weeping she heard inside needed no interpretation. It's true that when your subject weeps and so do you, it is hard to tell your hurt from his. For a person who listens, rare are the moments you don't have to.

VI. In which: A masquerade down the coast of North Korea. The missing on our lips. Order in the House. Tedium.

THEY WERE TOGETHER. It was a party. Left, right, red, blue, let's examine this with love, and on network TV, too. In the house, the House of Representatives: the makings of a scandal, a probing of the facts.

421 Rayburn, Washington, D.C. Oak and silk and fleurs-de-lis. The chairman and his statement. Thanks to you and you and you. Today is momentous. It is about accountability and oversight and truth, but in human terms, it's about everyone we are missing. Four Department of the Interior employees. One cult leader. One ex-wife. Our key players have disappeared, and here we are, holding the bag. Among developments of equal sensation, there has been OJ in his truck, Rodney King, and Columbine, but for analogue to the hopes and dreams of the masses bound up in the fate of a few, we have on heart Baby Jessica's two-day ordeal at the bottom of her uncle's well in Midland, Texas. The organizing sentiment back then? If she is okay, *we'll* be okay. Everyone just wanting to be okay. So, okay, order in the House. Let's get this hearing under way.

First up: guys who wore their suits half assed and hair askew. One psychologist in the House—his glasses were sloped like a ray of light come down through the panes.

He was here to testify on behalf of the mind and what it does in the aftermath of trauma, for instance, what it might do to the four hostages should they ever be found. What is memory. Flashback. PTSD. Will they sue? This was what the representative from North Dakota wanted to know, though he padded the question with so much blarney, it seemed he was asking the shrink whether the emotional dissipation of a cult leader was cause enough to burn his house down. Because that's what happened, right? The feds burned his house down? No? It was burned from the inside? Whatever.

It was time for the Ph.D. He had come with case studies of kidnapees past and of renown, and miscellaneous data that summed in template how the sundering of people from their lives could pan out in the long run.

Patti Hearst, scion. Kyoko Chan, scion. Frank Sinatra Jr., Charles Lindbergh Jr., John Paul Getty III, Adolph Coors III. Shergar, champion racehorse. Shin Sang-ok, South Korean director. Johnny Gosch, sold as catamite or fate unknown. Colleen Stan, locked in a box. Victor Li Tzarkuoi, ransomed for $134 million. Muriel McKay, mistaken for Rupert Murdoch's wife and abducted from the sleepy village of Wimbledon, in which tennis legends are made but successful kidnappings are not. The Born brothers. Terry Leonhardy, Foreign Service officer, died of heart disease at age eighty-eight, kidnapped twenty years before in Mexico City. Terry Waite, hostage negotiator, who was nabbed in Beirut and kept in solitary confinement for four years. Terry Anderson, pinched by Hezbollah and jailed for six years alongside several Americans, including one Edward Tracey, everywhere referred to only as an "itinerant poet," which has struck the Ph.D. as odd. Also worth noting: first name Terry does not correlate positively to an increased chance of abduction, witness homophones Teri Garr and Terri Schiavo, whose degenerative neurological problems, now that he thinks on it, do suggest something accursed in the name, prospective parents beware. (Terry Southern, crestfallen artist steeped in drug abuse, alcoholism, and financial insecurity; Terry Gilliam—no, wait, Terry Gilliam is God.)

There is no more welcoming venue for peroration and longueur than a congressional hearing, but still the chairman exhorted the doctor to get to the point—What is your point?—as the doc drummed his fingers on the table, thinking: My point? Kidnapping is part of the national consciousness. Should I move on?

Oh please, yes, move on.

The doctor said: Among postings online about kidnappers at large and lionized by his people is one about North Korean potentate Kim Jong-il.

But he was stopped there.

Mr. Chairman, I gather the good doctor is trying to get it on record that the Helix and Kim Jong-il are in bed together, and I want it known this is balderdash.

Mr. Chairman, unless I am dotty, I don't think the doctor was claiming kin between North Korea and the Helix, but that it's actually my good friend from Massachusetts who is trying to get this absurd rumor on record, which is an affront to the comity of these proceedings and also the intelligence of the American people watching and—

Another motion on the table. Procedural squabbles. Mutual yielding for the sake of getting finished before the next ice age. Objections for the record. Objection to the objections, also for the record.

The chairman took a long drink of water and called for order. But his mind was elsewhere. He was thinking that in a different life, he might have been Helix, too. Thurlow Dan was probably a nut, but couldn't a nut still be spokesman for that anguished and desolate feeling you had every morning just for waking up alive?

It was time for a witness. Vicki swore to tell the truth, hand on the Bible, though she gave her right hand, much to the merriment of all who noticed, all but Vicki, because, what, a hooker was so lost to virtue she didn't know about God and swearing? She'd just forgotten, is all.

She took her seat. At first she'd been cowed by the pomp adhering to her part in this. A car and driver, plus a suite at the Mayflower Hotel. She'd done her best to look right. Wore a cream skirt suit in defiance of the season. Fussed with her hair, trying to tamp down a spike in the front with wax putty and clip. Traded the black enamel of her nails for sunset pink, deracinated the studs from either cheek, and plugged the holes with that face powder Thurlow had given her. For all its claim to a natural provenance, it was still going to infect the shit out of her puncture wounds—like they were ever going to heal— but she'd done this just the same because it was Capitol Hill and a big fancy hearing, plus her parents would be watching from their convalescence home, she knew it.

The questions came fast: if Thurlow knew in advance the feds were coming, if the kidnapping was premeditated, if she knew anything about his contacts in North Korea, not that he had contacts, but if he did, the stipulations of that arrangement, the whereabouts of his arms cache, if he had an arms cache, the whereabouts of his second and third in command, the whereabouts of the hostages because, my God, it had been two days and *no one knew where they were*, and then of course, Thurlow, the vanishing cult leader, and Esme, who was now in violation of the Espionage Act, the Patriot Act, the Human Decency Act—*Poof!* they were gone.

Vicki swatted down every question with ignorance, and when they pressed her and began to suggest she was lying, she recalled them laughing about the Bible and got pissy.

"I don't *know*," she said. "Why don't you ask the brains?" and she pointed at the sky because Esme was out there somewhere. "I'm just the hooker you hired, remember?"

The chairman closed his eyes. And people wondered why everyone in D.C. was having affairs and secretly gay—like his wife of nine hundred years could relieve the tension and annoyance of having to cycle through the gears of justice, the gears lubed in molasses, and he close to tears.

It was time for the butler. In every murder mystery—Murder? Who said anything about murder?—the butler either had the answers or knew how to get them.

Martin took the oath, though not even the girl deputized to hold the Bible was listening, so that when the time came for *I do,* Martin had to say it thrice before she stepped away.

Order, order. Where is Esme Haas? I don't know. Where is Thurlow Dan? I don't know. The hostages? No wait, let us guess: You don't know. Correct. Is there anything you do know? No.

Well, so be it. In some universe, this must count as progress.

The last hour of the hearing was given over to the index cards recovered at the crisis site. Could Martin decipher them? They were in code. And written in multiple inks, ballpoint and felt tip, as though the author wrote on the move. Esme's scrawl had no regard for the architecture of letters or the language to which these glyphs should bow down, assuming she wrote in her mother tongue, which was English, though possibly in the tongue of her learning, which was Korean. The latitudes of this scrawl were formidable, from left to right, and graved into the card stock with the intensity of a last chance.

The cards were bound with a thick blue rubber band. Only reason the fire investigator who collected the bundle knew it was any more important than the other ten tons of wreckage was that it had been doused in a fire retardant.

He took notes at the scene: Points of entry undisturbed. Walls strafed with bullet holes. Smoke lifting from the carnage in duffel bags. His soles weeping into the asphalt. A birdcage melting down.

Alongside the ambulances and helicopters, there was music. The

sizzle and wheeze of wood and plaster, parquet and trusses, of memories risen from the char, all consolidated in dirge for a fire well spent.

He knew exactly what everyone wanted to hear, which was that this
fire had been started inside and on purpose.

If this stack of index cards could survive a blowup like that, someone wanted them read. He put them in his bag, intending to return to the
site tomorrow.

Trouble was, he'd been taken off the case overnight. Was he a *federal investigator*? No, he was part of the Cincinnati Fire Department,
est. 1853, oldest in the country, thanks. Fine, but go home. And then
to D.C., where instead of being asked to testify, he'd produce some
killer evidence in the form of index cards that would earn him a seat
in the front row, so that on day one of this joint hearing of the House
Committee on the Judiciary and the House Committee on Oversight
and Government Reform, a fire investigator from Cincinnati took real
pride in his work.

Into record: an affidavit in code, comprising sixteen index cards, the
content of which might be germane to the unpacking of motive charged
to a hearing such as this. Perhaps if the committee knew what Esme
Haas had been thinking, they could better suss out the whereabouts of
the hostages. No doubt they were with her, or vectored out of the compound by her? If, of course, they were not dead. Please do not be dead.

Martin was put to work. Apparently, it wasn't masquerade he liked
so much as transformation. Because, in an irony that belied his life's
commitment to disguise, he laid bare the stuff of Esme and her mono-
logues issued for the wooing of Thurlow Dan out of his house.

Ensuing: debate about who should read the cards into record. Ensuing: was it prudent or even tasteful to hire an actress? If so, would
she sight-read or practice? Come time to animate someone else's beating heart, this can make all the difference.

And so, into record:

45. Lo, I want to tell you about North Korea and what actually happened when you were there. Looking back, I realize it was a flash point
for us. Or for me, anyway. So I guess, after all these years, this is my
Helix moment. This is me confessing all.

It's true I'd been to Pyongyang a few times, with J.T. or as part of a tourist consortium from Japan, but for this last trip to see you there, it seemed prudent to enter the country with greater stealth and regard for the peril attached to my plans. The dissident movement in North Korea is alive and metastasized now that cell phones and digital cameras have breached the border. You can reach people on the inside, and they can reach you. This was how I made enough contacts to get down to Pyongyang from the north, where I'd enlisted help from Christian missionaries in Yanbian. They ran an orphanage for North Korean kids whose parents were living in the woods until they died, there being small opportunity for escape to Vietnam and even less to Mongolia, where the Chinese border patrol was much less easily bribed than the North Korean.

46. I was to hide with a couple and their five-year-old son until dark. It was a big risk for them, but since I'd come with rice and cured beef, a Zippo and butane, they took me in. To their home, which was a lair they'd dug by hand from the hillside. It was five by five, tops. Sustained by a four-foot square of wood that was rotted through and a tarp that caught moisture from the ground above and had to be drained several times a day. This family had already been repatriated to North Korea once, survived a detention center, and fled the second they got out. Yet, for a sack of beef jerky, they were willing to jeopardize what they had and keep me safe.

47. This day was also trial run for my Korean countenance. The nose, flared and recessed. The uncreased single eyelid and epicanthal fold. The ebon hair I'd had cut to accommodate a ponytail and bangs. The Yoo family had not been told about me; they expected a Korean, which is what they got. I knew how to act, and I kept my mouth shut. But it was difficult. Their son was stunted; he looked about three years younger than he was, though the time lost on his body was taken up by his parents, who looked sixty-plus, though they were half as old. They spent much of the day rubbing his hands and feet, and lapping the den on all fours, frostbite being the least dangerous but most avertable consequence of this lifestyle. The boy did not know the alphabet or numbers; he had not learned how to hold a pencil; probably this couple would have to give him up; and then what? Why go on? What illusion

of value could they impose on the day-to-day once they'd parted from their child? Nightfall could not have come sooner.

48. Christmas is heretic in North Korea, but Constitution Day, at the end of December, usually means fewer guards on the border. I headed out at 3 a.m. I hiked the two miles from the hills between Liangshui and Mijiang to the Tumen River, which marks the border. In winter, it's ten below and dark as tar. You can walk for an hour and still not make it. During that hour, either you meet no one, you bribe border patrol, or you beg for your life. The land is pack ice, but the snow keeps prints all season, and for how remote and forbidding is this terrain, only despair can explain why it's so well traversed.

49. The dark was condensed in the valley between hilltops, though if I wanted to find my guide's spangle—he'd be waiting for me on the North Korean side of the river—I'd have to depart from this safety and get to high ground. I was wearing canvas sneakers swaddled in washrags; the ascent was slow going. And not much reward once you got there. Paddy fields in spring and summer, tundra in the winter months, and at night no lights, cars, industry, or people. And yet, for the pandemonium in my heart, it was as though I stood among the eight hundred thousand who had made this crossing to date. Only they went in the other direction, from the certainties of famine and death to mortifications unknown but free. Only for love does anyone willingly go back.

50. The river was frozen, and the crossing a skeleton race at half speed, chest pressed to the ice. I met no guards, just Chul-min, who'd sat behind a bush for the three-hour window in which he'd been told I would come. From there we went to a farmhouse just a mile east of the train station at Simch'ong-ni. Then: Hoeryong to Musan to Hyesan to Kanggye to Pyongyang. Three hundred eighty miles. A six-hour drive by car, six days via North Korean rail.

51. There's a reason most people never see anything of North Korea but Pyongyang. It's because the rest of the country is squalid beyond all imagining, and this to spite the homogeneity of its design: single-story homes in a grid, whitewashed timber or stucco walls, the rooftops an orange clay tile, and every plot squared in with a brindled picket fence. There is no cement to pave the roads and no shoes to walk the cement,

so mostly people are barefoot, even in the snow. The filth seems meticulous and prolific in its outreach—even the soap can't stay clean—which makes sense of the delimited color scheme of people's clothes: black, gray, black, brown. No one stands out unless you know what to look for. The border towns are crammed with smugglers and People's Security Force officers not sharp enough to serve in Pyongyang, and all are engaged in one illegal activity or another—trucking in contraband like PCs or just stealing fertilizer from a truck—and with one motive in mind: to stay alive. For this reason, strangers are unwelcome. I spent that first day in a janitor's closet at the train station. Fuel being scarce, the schedule was a joke. A train came when it came. By the tracks: people asleep on the ice, in wheelbarrows, playing cards, trading nylon for corn, which cost a lot of corn. Faces wan and tapered, and everyone's hair falling out. Amazing how hair and dust always find each other; the stuff blew across the tracks like briar.

52. You couldn't travel without a permit. Mine was forged, and so when a train finally did arrive, I boarded the caboose and sat in the back. Two boys tried to freeload but were tossed by a female guard so shrill, two other kids gave up the con before she even got there. In North Korea, arrest and gulag are redress for most any crime, but often it depends on who's watching.

The train was four cars, three of which looked Korean and one that was slightly larger, probably imported from Romania twenty years ago. I doubt it had been serviced since, and for the shrieks issued from the engine, the chassis, God knew, I didn't think we'd get far. I wore a wool hat, pulled low, and stared through the window, past the black rime cleaved to the pane and at the countryside that could probably walk itself to Pyongyang faster than us.

53. The track skirts the Yalu and cuts into the base of one mountain range after another. My viewing options were this: the relatively prosperous towns on the Chinese side—Tumen looks like Six Flags at night—or the wasted and unrelentingly depressed landscape of North Korea on the other. I passed the hours undisturbed until we stalled just outside Hoeryong, next to a fishery qua morgue because there'd been no electricity to recycle or purify the water or just no money for food. Either way, the fish were dead and suffusing the air with a vapor

so pungent it made everyone weep. My nose ran; my lungs threw up whatever came down, which became a problem since the one thing a prosthetic face cannot sustain is tears. I deboarded the train and fell in line with several women headed to a factory down a gravel road paved in snow. It was 5 a.m. Maybe they'd get an hour's worth of electricity today and make a sock. I covered my mouth with a scarf and tried not to breathe; the effluent was ammonia and methane, though no one else seemed to care.

54. I was about to sever from the group when one of the women had the same idea. She had a look I'd seen before. It said: Soon I will be dead. The others did not argue, didn't even break stride. But the one who trailed had come to a stop, pitched left, right, and, when neither direction appealed, straight down. She wore black sweats and a thin parka, a shawl round her head, and slip-on sneakers. Nothing fit; this was not clothing so much as coverage. But it was still worth money, so that when she called me over it was to ask if I'd buy it off her in bulk. She was at least seventy years old; she'd fit in my carry-on luggage.

I looked around. It was still dark, and anyone not at work would not be coming. She sat in the snow and began to undress. It was December, freezing, and her jacket seemed to unzip one tooth at a time for how slow she went. I risked speech and said, "What makes you think I have money? Get up," and since I could hear the generators kick on at the factory, I said, "There's work."

She smiled, but even the black before dawn had nothing on what opened up from inside this woman. She was dying; she was ready. And there was nothing unusual about it. Every day, millions of lives were resolved in this horrible place in the same way.

"I have a daughter," she said, and she took off her sneakers, which she held out to me. "Three thousand won." A month's salary. "Just give it to her. I know you won't steal. I can tell you have a child, too."

I wanted this dialogue to end, but I couldn't leave her in the snow. I tried to help her up. No chance. It was as though the end of her life had consolidated in her body, given her heft and presence. I took the sneakers, sat down. Probably she had roundworm. The skin of her face was almost brittle, her eyes punched deep into her skull, but I still thought she could make it.

But no. She simply lay down in the snow. And when I bent over to check her pulse, she said, "Foreigners are not liked in this country. If it's really worth it, get who you came for and run."

55. I got my new face at the inn. And another at Hyesan, which I passed through unbothered, though I might have preferred bother to the kind of fear I'd begun to experience the closer I got to Pyongyang. The kind that molests the confidence of a heart called up from the minor leagues.

Next: a few hours in Kanggye, home to Plant 26, where many of the country's nuclear aspirations are pursued underground.

Finally: Pyongyang. For the ride in, I'd upgraded my face and clothes to reflect the outsized prosperity of the city's demographic, at least compared to the north. I wore leather pumps, which cost six months' salary at the *jangmadang,* and notably false eyelashes, because augmentations of beauty meant wealth. Ah, irony: I was a Western woman wanting to look like a Korean who wanted to look Western.

56. We rolled in at noon to music pumped from loudspeakers at a square nearby. I think it was the anthem "No Motherland Without You," in which one hundred men chorus Kim Jong-il's glory to mesmerizing effect. With the trumpets, horns, voice of the people risen up as one, I left the station all in favor of the socialist state, too. The majesty of this place was undeniable—the giant courtyards, monuments, imperial architecture—and dwarfing of whatever private aspirations you woke up to. I bowed to the wind and headed south, toward the river. The music trailed off. *We cannot live without you, Kim Jong-il. Our country cannot exist without you. The people believe in you.* It was a festive time to be in Pyongyang, close to the New Year, when the city dolls up. No power for most of the night, but plenty to train footlights on Kim Il-sung, whose likeness was cloned in statues across the country. A big guy, Kim Il-sung, or so the statues would have you believe. The chest is pumped; the gut is jut.

I moved on. Most roads are too wide to traverse if there's traffic, which there never is, but still, you have to underpass your way across town. The city is almost as built underground as over. The metro is but a quarter of the action down there. Bunkers, escape routes, and residencies for when the shit hits—at 350 feet below ground, you can build most anything. I wouldn't be surprised if the architecture under Cincinnati once looked to the North for inspiration.

57. Martin was waiting for me near the Chungsong Bridge, on a park bench by the water. We were conspicuous for being outside in this weather, but inconspicuous for the same reason: No one trying to hide would present themselves thus. Martin was too tall to make like a Korean, so we'd agreed on Russian Here for Business. We couldn't talk for more than three minutes in the open, just enough time to discuss where he'd set up shop. He said I was late. He said he needed eight hours for our Glorious General Who Descended from Heaven face. I said we had six. He said Kim Jong-il was the hardest face we'd ever done. I said we had six, let's go.

58. We reconvened in a café near the hotel district where foreigners are a common sight. The proprietress showed me to the basement without comment; she might have been more surprised if we'd sat down and ordered lunch. Martin had his gear arranged on a blanket. For light we had a kerosene lamp plus dapple from a window that gave us the shoe view from above. He sat me on the floor. Glorious General Kim Jong-il has four look-alikes in his employ, probably more. Some have had plastic surgery; others were just born with it. I had Martin. Martin plus six hours plus the high handicap of having to impersonate an impersonator, *sartor resartus,* which took the pressure off. Or so you'd think.

He said, "It's Popsicles down here—how can you be sweating?" Nonplussed Martin. Swabbing my cheeks. "My fingers are numb. These conditions are terrible."

"Get some tea."

He snorted. "I don't think we paid her to serve us." Though, judging from the contraband all over the basement—like that aerial wasn't snatching broadcast news from Seoul every night—the lady of the place did business of all kinds. "Just relax," he said. "We've done this a thousand times." He applied powder. Blew on my skin.

"Seriously," he said. "Whatever it is, shut it down. I can't work like this. You need to stop sweating."

And what could I say? Was I supposed to tell him that, after all this, it seemed possible I might not be able to breathe in the shared car space of my ex-husband?

59. Eyes closed. And when they open, it is to a handheld mirror, eye level. Hello, I say. Greetings. I am sixty-three. I am five-two without the platform shoes I've never been seen without. I am rotund. My hairline has withdrawn midway up my skull; it hopes to reach the summit by 2012, Year of the Perfect Strong and Prosperous Nation. I wear girly glasses, but I am a man at heart. I like women who take off their clothes for money, and ravioli with pumpkin filling. My favorite garment is the anorak; my favorite color is brown. I am mysterious and unreachable, North Korea cannot live without me, and just now I am about to meet a gentleman from the United States who will tell me about the Helix and its plans to bring our people together. We will drive around Pyongyang. And a few hours later, when I ask about his family, he will say things about his wife and child with a subtext of longing whose content is the loneliness we're born into and cannot shake, but so what, so what, so what. It is the wife who matters now. The wife and child, nothing else. And for this information, I will begin to rethink my life.

60. So now it's on record: How dangerous is Thurlow Dan? Not so much. When he was in North Korea, all he did was tour the city with his sweetheart in disguise.

The chairman wiped his brow. It was getting on 4 p.m., the sleepiest time of day. He thought if this were Spain or Israel or any country more attuned to the circadian needs of the body, he could at least recess for a siesta. But no. They would carry on until the very Western hour of 5 p.m., the happy hour. The hour a chairman returns to his wife and her cause du jour—the weeding of our SWAT and HRT personnel for those with jiffy finger: boys who don't think, just shoot. Was there any chance the hostages got sniped and no one was telling him? Doubtful. His private theory? The four detained by Thurlow Dan were dispersed throughout the country, having escaped the Helix House hours before it blew and wanting, horribly, to escape everything else. The chairman understood. Were he not accountable to the people for answers, he might even have wished them luck. Either way, those stories would out.

VII. In which: Four short stories after Kim Jong-il's *On the Art of Cinema*. In which stories are not so much similar as empathic. A city under a city. Labia, gambling. The USS *Pueblo*. In which: Run, run, run for your lives.

Anne-Janet, the set should reflect the times.

All things considered, this wasn't so bad. A cot in the Helix House. A chance. An emotional context for events that might never transpire elsewhere, events called kissing and touch. Anne-Janet planning it out; Ned was her target. Anne-Janet taking the reins because she had survived cancer and incest and was not about to be cowed by a dark place in a dark time.

"You okay?" she whispered, and she put out her hand, which he couldn't see or did not take.

Not cowed, but maybe a little discouraged. And unhelped by the warfare in her head. Half going: Kudos for exploiting alone time with a guy you like, AJ! Half going: Um, in the hours since being kidnapped, you have done nothing but augment an attraction that was already burlesque, and some ideas any sane person would dismiss. Among them: if you were kidnapped with a guy you liked, mutual duress was supposed to hasten the intimacy between you. Forget the barter of secrets and memories in the afterglow of sex, forget the dating and twaddle and rollback of your defensive line until you either had to love this person or kill yourself. Forget the prelude, just head straight for what your heart needed, which was a place to go when you were scared and lonely and, in this case, detained in a cult leader's house in the suburbs of Cincinnati.

Right? Wrong. And Anne-Janet wasn't stupid. She had not forgone self-doubt. She could never forgo self-doubt, since amid the miscellaneous fallout of being a victim was the constant suspicion that your feelings were nuts. If you'd fallen prey to the world's incapacity to bring people together but were thinking only of how to get kissed by Ned Hammerstein, it was likely your priorities were askew. And if the task of releasing your lips from a burlap hood and clamping them around his hard-on was more pressing than escaping environs that might be your last, you were, arguably, a crackpot.

It was getting late. Three or four a.m. Their wrists were still cuffed behind their backs. They had each been assigned a bed, two on either side of an opaque screen that partitioned the room and was bolted to the walls. Presumably this was to guard against rebellion in numbers and to ensure the four could not see each other, though Anne-Janet thought the precaution redundant, since they'd already been given hoods. In any case, it didn't work. On their first night they'd tried to band together. What the hell was happening to them? There were expletives and incredulity and sentences that fell off the ledge (But— What the— Why in God's name—). They felt, in the main, duped by the arm of government known as the Department of the Interior and, worst of all, lacking the means to recompense themselves for the wrong done them. But that was as far as their shared feelings went. While the others groused, Anne-Janet had the sad thought that the kidnapping would not do for her what it would likely do for them, which was to make inconsequential, even silly, all the bewilderments and crises that had obsessed their lives to date. Quite the opposite. She had experienced such hardship that this check on her perspective only confirmed how dreadful it all had been. The others were panicked, she was calm, and in this calm managed to foreclose on just one more way to feel a part of the group.

Well, to hell with the group. She might have been paired with Olgo or Bruce, but the guards had chosen Ned and in this was a call to action. Even the layout of the cots was a call to action. That, or it was just having to sleep in a cot at all, but the arrangement invoked for her the bedtime dogma of summer camp and, in tow, feelings you tended to experience more acutely at camp, the bleating heart and onus to complete rites of passage before the summer was out. Anne-Janet was so behind on everything that the rites were as looming and fearsome as they were for girls half her age, and probably, for being so deferred, they were worse.

"Ned," she said. "You awake?"

"Like anyone could sleep in this nightmare."

"Want to talk?"

"What's there to say? This isn't happening."

"I dunno. You could ask me about me. Pass the time. Chitchat."

No sooner said than she rolled her eyes to China. Half her head going: Good one, AJ! The other yelling: Crackpot! She'd already told Ned about her mother and the hip, and, from what she could gather at work, everyone knew about her cancer because on her second day, a hospital renowned for strides in oncology but not discretion had called every extension on the floor looking for her.

The cancer had happened so fast. One second she was just bloated; the next she was having a colorectal neoplasm excised by a doctor who said she was lucky to get away without a colostomy, because there's always that chance, and what young lady wanted her colon popped out her small intestine? She was irradiated. Poisoned. The skin of her hands and feet turned horse hoof. Her cancer was on the move, her cancer was in retreat. Move, retreat. Stage three. It was hard to imagine herself into next week, and for this shortsightedness she wanted the payoff. A reconfigured mental state. To live without fear. Go out on a limb. Do drugs whose effect you cannot predict, have sex with people you do not know. Surely this was someone's idea of fun—why not hers? The months went by without a recurrence. And since she had done nothing to inch out on that limb, the rest was easy. Did she want to go to Cincinnati and share a hotel room with one Ned Hammerstein, on whom she had a crush? Absolutely. Because the refurbished mental state and drugs and edgy lifestyle were all fine and well, but what Anne-Janet really wanted before she left this life was intercourse. Intercourse with a man who liked her and might even look at her the way they did in the movies and who, if she had to say it, was not related to her in any way.

"Chitchat?" he said. "Nice weather we're having"—and he began to laugh and then to snuffle.

"Visibility is excellent," she said. "Not a cloud in sight."

"Okay, wait," he said. "I don't like this game. The weather's important to me—oh, forget it." And the snuffling got worse. She told him to stop.

"I can't. It's probably three in the morning. I have a sister now. I need to get out of here."

"You can," she said. "Cry now, and what will you do tomorrow? Or the day after that? We could be here months."

"*Months?* Don't say that."

"Well, it's possible. So all I'm suggesting is: ration."

"I don't think you can run out of misery. We've been *kidnapped;* I can be miserable for as long as we're here."

"Wrong, wrong." Sitting up. "You can dry out. Lose your ability to feel. One day you are sobbing for the beauty and horror of it all, and the next you are Stonehenge."

"These fucking hoods," he said. "I can't breathe."

Only he was breathing fine. In and out—what more did he want? He was afraid of small spaces, hated the elevator, and had earlier complained that his face was aswelter. There was no way to doff the hoods, and breathing at a clip only made the sensation worse. Anne-Janet had suggested he visualize, and to the extent she had stopped hearing the suck and wheeze of his lungs, it had worked. You are sitting on the bottom of the ocean and observing the sky. After a while, he'd asked how she'd gotten so adept in the pursuit of calm and she said, MRI. Four every year. Spend enough time in the coffin space of an MRI and you become inured to its terrors. If Ned understood that she was, with this response, vanishing the difference between arming yourself against fear and not needing the armor at all, he did not say. He did not have to. Anne-Janet knew the difference; she wore armor on her teeth.

"You're doing fine," she said. "But if the ocean thing isn't working, maybe try to think of yourself as one of those hawks who wears a hood to keep calm. And maybe, if it helps, that the falconer is your mom. Or a friend. I dunno."

She could hear him shifting in his cot, turning on his side. Maybe he was fetal. Maybe he was thinking about how to flirt, too. Equally mindful of the bad timing of it all, the inappropriateness of it all, but willing to go out on that limb just the same.

"Remember our speed date?" he said. "How I told you I'm adopted? Just found out? Remember that part? Mom's not so high on my list these days."

"Oh, right," she said. "Let's just stick with the ocean. I'm on the floor, too. It's sort of mushy."

"Lot of fish, though."

"Yeah? What kind?"

"I don't know. But they're tropical."

"What are they saying?"

"Not much. I do all the talking."

She smiled and laughed and then, for laughing, she blushed. Blushed in the dark, which bereaved the color of its biological purpose, which was to wile. So this was wiling the blind.

"Ned, do you think we're actually in danger?" and she tried to sound in earnest, a little timid but ready to blossom at the first sign of hope. Because the fact was, she didn't think they were in danger, but then she was not asking for his opinion so much as trying to undo the impression she had given him that she was bossy. After all, for the purpose of shooting up an ordeal with amorous content, wasn't panic the grail? She should grope for his lapels. Weep into his collar. Fling her arms around his neck and heave with bosom cleaved to his chest.

"Definitely," he said. "I think we're going to die here. Unless—do *you* think we're going to die?"

"I don't know," she said, and she meant it, because if the danger wasn't mortal, it was spiritual, her spirit in free fall the longer this conversation failed to twin up their fears in lust.

Back and forth. She weighed her options.

At home: a sick mom and the burden of caring for this mom, which would fall to her alone. That, plus an emotional terrain that smoldered as though after a great fire but that could yield up nothing new, and in this the paradox of trauma: the past could live on in you with an energy you could never muster for the life that was happening to you now. And just think: tomorrow, she could be returned to all that. Unharmed, unchanged.

She rolled on her back and arched her spine to accommodate her wrists. She knit her shoulder blades until they hurt. As proportions went, her arms were orangutan vis-à-vis the rest of her body, so she was able to loop them under her ass and set them on her thighs. After that, the pick was easy. Thurlow's men had frisked her but failed to consider the wire of her push-up bra, or what a girl with skill could do with it.

First thing, she took off her hood. A light shimmied under the door, dim and distant, and so the room was almost as dark when her eyes readjusted. She stood. And looked at Ned. He was on his side, legs drawn up. She tiptoed his way.

There were nice things about this man that seemed nicer for being unseen. His hair, parted down the middle, the kind you can rake through without snag—it had acquired a glow in her memory that struck out against the doom of where they were now. The same went for his hands and face—ruddy and bright, owing to joys wrought in the freeing of Anne-Janet from her darker self.

She sat cross-legged by the side of his cot. She could see the outline of his lips pressed into the burlap. His breath was warm on her face and came steadily, which meant he was asleep. She tilted her head as though they were lying next to each other and tried, just for a second, to imagine herself into the miracles she'd heard about. You wake up in the morning and someone else is there. Maybe this someone is already up and looking at you. And because you are loved, you do not think about the crust in your eyes or the eruptive skin events that have uglied your face overnight, just that this person is pressing his forehead to yours and saying hello and about to peck your lips, and because his own are so pledged in love for you, this contact seems to reprise the first kiss you ever had, because every first kiss, in its fumbling and tender way, promises the world, which means that this person who loves you has just woken you up in elegy and homage for the happiest you have ever been.

She leaned in closer. And thought: So what if he's wearing a hood? Maybe this is better. Except just then he turned away and got on his back and arced his pelvis, which probably had to do with the cuffs and not because arousal is passed by osmosis. Either way, she did not think, just clamped her two hands over his mouth and straddled his lap.

He bucked, nearly threw her off, but she got in his ear and whispered fast, "Shhh, don't wake the others," and he did not buck again.

"What are you doing?" he said. "Get off me."

"No."

"You're out of your handcuffs? Take off my hood."

"No."

"Are you crazy? What's happening?" And when she started to rub up and down his groin, he said, "Okay, stop it. You're scaring me."

"What if I did it like this?" and she reached for him with her hand. "Is that better?"

"Please, stop. I don't want to do this."

But Anne-Janet was not listening. She unsnapped his coverall and tried to kiss her way down his stomach the way she'd seen. Ned rolled onto his side; she rolled with him. Finally, he got on his stomach and clenched his body so tight there was no way to get at him.

She backed away as though smacked. "Oh my God," she said, and she started to cry.

"Can you take off my hood now?" he said. "It's okay. We're all freaking out."

"Oh my God," she said. "I have to get out of here."

"Wait," he said. Hissing almost. "Anne-Janet!" He got up and staggered in the direction of her voice.

"I am so sorry," she said. "I'm a freak."

"You are not. Just calm down."

But she was already at the rebar grille, gripping the ribs until they gave, and out she went like the Incredible Hulk or one of those animals with the opposable thumbs escaping the zoo and running for its life.

She had not cried violently in years, but now the tears were coming so fast she could barely see where she was going. The house was much bigger than it had appeared from the outside—the multiple hallways and doors and rooms—and behind each, who knew, a guard in wait for the first hostage to escape. She wiped her face and ran.

The floors were tessellated and smooth underfoot, peel-back linoleum. The walls were bare and the lighting a spine of halogen bulbs recessed into the ceiling. So many ways to go, but when she heard footsteps and voices on her tail, she booked for the nearest door, which was locked. Same for each after that. Finally she just sprinted down the hall, thinking it had to go somewhere, which it did. A giant kitchen.

She made for the island, opened the sous-cabinet doors, and prayed there'd be room enough to hide among the pots, pans, colanders, lids, and dozen candy thermometers. She prayed in vain; the lights went on.

"What the hell?" said Vicki, reaching for the nearest blunt-force-trauma object, which was a steel spatula.

"Jesus crap," said Charlotte. "You scared the Jesus crap out of me." She was pressing her heart and fanning the air in front of her lips.

Anne-Janet was holding a Calphalon stockpot overhead. Her arms were trembling with the strain, so she bucked her head at Vicki's spatula—an equine gesture, part nod, part rear—to propose détente. It worked. They laid down their arms.

Vicki sat up on the counter and brushed her feet against the drawers. She was wearing a rubber halter top latticed across the sides with chain mail that clipped up fishnet thigh-highs and matching thong. Charlotte went to a utility closet for a spool of duct tape. Anne-Janet backed into a corner and raised her fists. She'd seen enough martial arts on TV to know that if she chambered properly and kept her weight distributed, pulled back with one arm while releasing her jab, she was gonna get killed.

"What's wrong with you?" Charlotte said. "I hardly think we're the enemy." She sat on the floor and began to wrap her boot, which was split at the toe like a duck's bill.

"We're just TCs," Vicki said. "*Ex*-TCs." She reached for a roll of paper towels and tossed it at Anne-Janet.

"Traveling Companions," Charlotte said. "You'll know soon enough. We keep Thurlow company while he makes company for everyone else." And even though she was annoyed about the ransom tape, she said these words admiringly.

Anne-Janet scanned in her head the dossiers of everyone living here. She was still weeping, but the towels helped. "So you two are the prostitutes? Because I have a bunch of you on file, a Swede and some others, but nothing about you two."

"Oh fuck a duck," Charlotte said. "You're one of the spies? I thought you were the new TC."

"No way," Vicki said. "Like a TC would ever look like *that*."

Despite all, Anne-Janet was hurt.

Vicki jumped off the counter. Her ass had left a steam print on the marble. "Oh fun," she said, and pointed to her thong, which had lost purchase, so that Anne-Janet could see her mons, bald but for a cross of pubic hair. "It's supposed to be a capital *T*," Vicki said, and covered up. "But I get lazy. Funny, though, right? *T* for *Thurlow*, except it looks like Jesus on my cunt."

Anne-Janet began to make for the door. "I think I'm going to go," she said. "Except, should I be worried you guys saw me? Because I think we all know what I'm trying to do here."

"Sweetie, look at you. You been through enough." This from Charlotte, who was done with her boots and checking her watch.

"Plus," said Vicki, "the whole house is under surveillance, so it's pretty safe to assume someone besides me saw what just happened in your cell. So, you know, do what you feel."

"Oh God," Anne-Janet said, and slunk to the floor. She pressed her face into the roll of paper towels and began to wet through one sheet at a time. "Can you get me out of here? I can't breathe in this place. I can't deal."

"Not exactly," Vicki said. "But you can come with us. Charlotte's got an appointment in the Sub."

"A special procedure," Charlotte said, and she beamed like summer sun. "I've been waiting for this for six months. Get my labia fixed. Snipped and tucked."

Anne-Janet stared up at her but just could not summon the words.

"I'm happy for you," Vicki said. "But just for the record, I think big lips are nice."

Charlotte frowned. "They're gross." But then she laughed and said, "You know, at first, when I heard all the trouble outside, all I could think was that if the feds busted up the place before my vaginoplasty—! So I've been praying. And here we are."

Vicki shrugged. "With your luck, I bet they storm the OR just when your pussy's in a clamp."

"Nice," Charlotte said. And then, to Anne-Janet, "So you want to come?"

"Yes," she said. "Only, to get this straight, it's not in the house, right? We'll have to leave?"

"Of course. This isn't wire hangers in your poon or anything. It's totally state-of-the-art. At the clinic."

"The clinic."

Charlotte and Vicki exchanged a look. Vicki said, "Now, wait just a minute. I thought you were an agent. Like with the government and all that. I know Thurlow is always saying you people are incompetent and don't know anything, but come on. You're messing with us, right? You can trust me, I'm in the know."

Anne-Janet shrugged. Took a gamble. "There's lots of clinics, I can't keep track of everything the Helix does. But whatever," she said, and she hugged the roll. "Lead the way. Just get me out of here."

Charlotte said, "The Sub's not Helix. No way. It's just private enterprise down there."

"Yee-haw capitalism," Vicki said. "But I don't have an extra set of gloves." Charlotte didn't either. "I bet there's some by the hatch. If not, it's no big deal. Just try not to hold the rope too tight."

Anne-Janet followed them out of the kitchen, through a supply closet, to a mudroom staffed with hiking boots. Vicki traded her stilettos for Timberlands, and said, "Why is the black pair always out? I hate these camel ones. They don't match at all."

Anne-Janet looked her over. "I think maybe it's just a clash of styles," she ventured.

"Well, *somebody's* been reading *Glamour*," said Charlotte.

Vicki snorted. She harried the slack in her fishnets and revolved the hasp lock about her neck so that it faced front. "All set," she said. "Let's rock."

Vicki and Charlotte got on either end of an oval floor mat and pushed it aside to expose a door. There was some talk about the code, and when was the last Thurlow changed it because if you entered the wrong code more than twice, it would lock you out for good. They looked to Anne-Janet, who said Vicki had it right, and since they really wanted to believe she knew things, they gave it a go, and *presto,* the door clicked free. It was a long way down, and immediately Anne-Janet understood the wisdom of gloves as she abraded her hands on the rope ladder.

So these were the tunnels. She'd read about them. A tunnel scheme fanned out beneath the streets of Cincinnati, the plan grown from a precept that said anything can be accomplished with money. Contractors hired by the city to oversee municipal planning, and in whose yawning regard for the work little got done—these people could be bought. And so they were. Nothing blasts through limestone better than graft.

She figured they'd walk through the tunnels and come up through some manhole in Kentucky. She figured they'd be there soon. Hoped, in any case. It smelled like dead squirrel. The linoleum of the house flooring had given way to a duff-like substance that squished underfoot. Crawling was out, stooping was in. If you stood upright, you'd graze your skull against the roof, which was slimed in moisture. The TCs wore caps. It all made sense.

They had fallen in line and said little. It seemed to Anne-Janet an hour had passed. Her hands were starting to feel like pulled pork. A blister on the gunwale of her big toe had just released fluid into her sock. These were not good developments. This was not a sterile environment. They came to a fork.

"Which way?" said Charlotte.

"Oh, fuck me," said Vicki, and again they turned to Anne-Janet.

"What?" she said. "Like I memorized the blueprints? How should I know?"

They went left. They should have gone right.

Eventually, they spotted light slewing beneath a door at the far end of the tunnel. They were accustomed to the dark, so already, from this distance, they had to blink and squint. It seemed possible, for all their left turns, that they were back where they started, in which case a more circumspect fugitive might have hewn to the wall and crept up on the door for the purpose of surveillance. But no. Anne-Janet was too tired to care. She trotted up to the door and gasped for the pain in her foot.

"I wouldn't do that," Vicki said. Anne-Janet pressed on.

The door was more vault than door, and locked from the inside. In fact, there was no handle or knob to let them in, just an intercom and button.

"What's the big deal?" Anne-Janet said. "It looks like a bank."

"But it's not," Charlotte said. "Could be many things, but not a bank. Let's go, okay?"

"Why?"

"Because," Vicki drawled, "if you don't belong here, bad things happen. You need an appointment for every place in the Sub." And when Anne-Janet pushed for more, they betrayed a brochure's worth of info, highlights of the Subterrain: Below the Garfield Suites Hotel, a brothel full of Singapore girls, codified by an airline, fetishized by a nation. In the cellar of the Verdin Bell and Clock Museum, access to the operations center of a Deepnet marketplace for counterfeit money and contraband of the month. There was gambling. Ultimate fighting between inmates sprung from Queensgate jail for this purpose. A sweatshop for the sewing of official Major League baseballs, the work farmed out by Rawlings's Costa Rica factory, where the oft-suspected juicing of the ball occurred. There were maps for sale online, though you had to know where to look, and the maps were not cheap. There were passwords to be bought. Security clearance. There were in the tunnels only people who belonged, attired according to venue, which is why three women in costume (two whores and an electrician) were able to tour the spread unremarked, the consensus of any observers being that they hailed from or were headed to Flaunt, in which you impersonated who you wanted to be and were applauded for it. The Sub was decades old. It had probably started with an underground speakeasy and proliferated from there.

Anne-Janet's mouth opened, but only for a second. "Oh, come on," she said, and when the others did not flinch, she said, "You're saying that beneath the city of Cincinnati is some kind of second city? That's insane."

Vicki shrugged. "It's not. There's people doing all kinds of ugly shit in back alleys and basements all over the world."

"This is just a little more organized," Charlotte said. "A little more high-class."

Anne-Janet didn't have time for this nonsense, and so she pressed the button, which cued on the other side of the vault a wind chime followed by static on the intercom and a voice—May I help you?—which came as a relief, because, while Anne-Janet was playing it cool, it did occur to her that this door might in fact be the chthonic maw of snuff videography. Go in and you never came out.

"Fuck," Vicki said. "I don't know the entry script for this place."

"No shit," Charlotte said. Like anyone knew the script. The script was valued at ten thousand dollars street, assuming you could get it, which you could not.

Anne-Janet bent in close to the intercom and said, "Hi, can you let us in? We've been walking for a while and I need a bathroom."

Charlotte was now cursing volubly. "My 'plasty is in *twenty minutes!* Let's go!"

"You're not gonna make it," Vicki said.

Anne-Janet depressed the button again.

"Six months," Charlotte was saying. "Free because of some new technique. Like I have health insurance. Like insurance was gonna pay, anyhow. *Six months.*" She slouched to the floor. "I think Thurlow got sick of me because of my labia, okay? It's one thing to be tossed aside because your man thinks you're working for the feds, but way worse if he thinks you're gross. You got off easy."

Vicki joined her on the floor.

"Hello," Anne-Janet said. "My friend here is running late—can you just let us in already? Man, oh man, if you only knew who I was."

"What was I thinking?" Charlotte said. "Why am I even here?" She had her face in her hands. "I'm not a Helix Head. I don't even care that much if I stay alone. But Lo was just so sweet. Said we'd be like a family. All of us. I don't know. I'm an idiot."

Vicki began to rub her back. "You're not an idiot," she said. "You're not."

"Look," Anne-Janet said, and she drilled her finger into the button. "I just had the most mortifying experience a person can have with another human being, and I have never felt more self-disgusted in all my life, I might go up in flames for how bad I feel, so please just let me in"—at which point the door began to open with ceremony, inch by inch, so that the light from within came upon them like a benediction.

They sprung to their feet. "Just get a map," Charlotte said. "If you can. Then we're out of here."

There was an anteroom. Carpeting in hues graham cracker and shrimp. A row of plastic chairs bolted to the wall. It resembled a bus depot or processing foyer for the urban sanitarium of last resort. At the desk, behind a glass partition, the intercom lady, in a sports visor and white seersucker tennis dress with red and green piping down the middle and neckline. So perhaps this was a gymnasium. A super-fancy gym.

Charlotte and Vicki huddled against a wall. Outside the purlieus of the Helix House, they had grown shy. Anne-Janet asked for a map. The tennis pro qua receptionist laughed and said, "Just fill out this form and bring it back up to the desk when you're done."

"I don't want a form, I want a map."

"Most people don't come through this way. Since you people did, you have to fill out the form. Several, actually." She closed the glass. It was smudged with handprints (fingers splayed, palms flat) and the imprint of a forehead that together were like a pillory for clients to fit themselves into during a losing encounter with the tennis pro.

Anne-Janet perused the questionnaire. Her first thought: This is not a gym. Her second: Oh, man, this is *so* not a gym. They wanted to know her age, weight, and emergency contact info; okay. But they also wanted references, a waiver form, and a confidentiality agreement more draconian than your average mortgage contract, plus a brief sexual history (if applicable), an explanation of that history (if applicable), a profile of her sensitive spots and no-no's (if not submitted in advance), a blood report, and a letter from the client's referring therapist.

She thrust clipboards at Charlotte and Vicki. Vicki didn't even look, but Charlotte skimmed it over and, when she was done, seemed even more distressed than before. "We have to get out of here," she said. "I know what this place is, and we need to go."

Vicki seemed less convinced. "Yeah, but maybe they can do a 'plasty here, too."

"Earth to Vicki," Charlotte said. "The people who come here don't *need* vaginoplasty."

"What do you mean? Some people are *born* with big lips. Not every busted lip is because you fucked all the boys in Kansas."

It was slow dawning for Anne-Janet, but then her ears went cherry at the tips. "So let me get this straight, people come here to, ah—"

"Customize their first time, you got it," Charlotte said.

"*Customize?*" Anne-Janet said. "Whatever happened to flower petals and satin sheets and a real guy saying he loves you, and not just because he wants to ejaculate on your face?"

"No such thing," said Vicki. "And from what I saw in your cell, I'm guessing you know that, too."

Anne-Janet just shook her head.

Charlotte poked at her temple with her index. "And anyway, hello, since clearly neither me or Vick is new on the pony, we're gonna get mistaken for cops or something, and then we'll turn into you, all kidnapped and stuff, only we won't get treated half as nice and probably we'll get shot."

"Also," Vicki said, because Anne-Janet's incredulity was annoying, "it's no stranger than some john hiring me to do it. Only real diff is that sometimes in here you get daughters of sheiks or whatever who want a controlled experience."

"A *controlled experience*," Anne-Janet said, and the lady in her heart—her name was Pollyanna—plucked a rose and died.

The Pro took off her visor and spoke to Anne-Janet. "Okay, you're all set. If you are amenable to the day's arrangement, there's been a cancellation. We can get you in now."

Anne-Janet stammered. "Oh, no, there's been a mistake. I didn't come here for this."

"What do you mean?" the Pro said, staring at Anne-Janet. If she had a racket in hand, she might well have served out a motivational speech about the game—You don't choose it, it chooses you—though, in any case, what she did offer amounted to the same thing. She said, "I just read your questionnaire and bio. You know we do revisions, right? We can take you back, re-create the context, and change whatever you didn't like. So, about your father, not to be rude, but you are so obviously in the right place."

Anne-Janet's mouth opened. She looked at the Pro, looked at the hookers.

"Sign here?" the Pro said. And then, to Vicki: "Maybe you both want revisions, too? There's something here for everyone."

Charlotte said, "Like virtual reality? Do we get to wear helmets?"

"Okay, this isn't *Blade Runner,*" the Pro said. "You just describe everything for us, and we will re-create it down to the last detail."

"Wow," Vicki said. "My first time. Bradford King. I was fifteen."

"You remember his name?" Charlotte said. "Mine could have been any one of five guys. Maybe six—who knows who went first that night."

Anne-Janet continued to look from one face to another. A revision. How horrible. How New Age and barbaric and disclosing of her most awful moment to a set designer and stagehand.

"Yeah, I remember Bradford," Vicki said. "We all wanted to call him Brad because Bradford was just so serious, but he wouldn't have it. I remember trying to call him Brad during sex and him just not being able to cum at all and yelling at me for it."

"Nerves?"

"Beats me. He was nine. Maybe it was too soon."

Charlotte reached into her purse, as though looking for her wallet, as though in this wallet might be the 20 K it would take to get relaid by five drunken boys in plaid boxer shorts. "Can you charge this to the Helix House?" she said.

The Pro nodded. "One of our most active accounts."

"I'm in," Vicki said. "What the hell. I'll call him *Brad* as much as I want."

"Me too," Charlotte said. "We'll see who gets the roofies this time."

They turned to Anne-Janet, who was just then feeling such a mess of grief balk in her throat, she could not talk. She'd heard it said that a girl whose father wrecks her becomes a woman no man can reach, and so far her experience had borne this out with depressing accuracy. Thing was, she wasn't just unreachable; she didn't know how to reach anyone else, either. What she'd just done at the Helix House? It underscored the bottom line: She was heartbroken. All the sentiment that attached itself to the condition was in play, with the caveat that the offending party was her dad and that instead of suffering acutely and with foreknowledge that she'd get over it, she hurt with moderation and diligence. A tide erodes the coast, the glaciers will melt; hers was just a slow assailing of the big things—the heart things—whose demise would change the world. Only not today. Tomorrow either. Who could go on like this? She was lonely beyond what she could endure.

She signed on the dotted line.

"So what do you need?" the Pro asked. "Just so I can get a sense of it."

"A lock on the door," Anne-Janet said. "A twin bed, a kid's room, and a lock on the door."

"Sure thing," the Pro said, checking her computer screen. "Only it seems like some people are looking for you. You and three others."

"That's okay," Anne-Janet said. "All I need is a lock. So that when your actor tries to get in, he can't. After that, anyone who wants to find me won't have any problem at all."

Ned Hammerstein, begin on a small scale and end grandly.

Some people had wives and kids and the parents who'd given them life. Other people had a Lear jet forty-five-thousand feet up, a childhood plane, the *Bernard,* which they'd outfitted for cloud seeding and weather modification. Thus Ned, flying away or flying to, a hegira turned pilgrimage for a twin sister who more than likely would not give a shit to find out he was alive and might even fear the responsibility once she did.

"Cheer up," his mother said, as if she could know; she had not looked at him in hours. Busy, busy. Touring the cargo bay, ransacking plastic bags for utensils and napkins and cold cuts and fruit. They were just over Colorado Springs, a couple of hours to go.

She held up two canteens, "Coke? OJ?" and looked hopeful. Feed the boy, curb his wrath.

He stretched his legs but didn't get far. The bay was stuffed with kegs of acetone and silver iodide, dry ice, ammonium nitrate, urea, and some beat-up NEXRAD equipment. He'd painted the plane himself, attempting to render the original cover art of *Cat's Cradle*—hands plus string loomed over a cityscape at night—but producing a slop of color that passed for abstraction in some circles but not in most. The wings were fitted with racks and flares that looked like the tines of a comb, and under each wing, giant cigar tubes of acetone–silver iodide—smoke generators—once the standard for seeding an updraft, provided you wanted rain.

Milanos on a paper plate, arranged in a crop circle. He took one to make her happy. For the fifth time, she asked about his health, and whether English Breakfast was okay, because she had Earl Grey in her fanny pack, so if he wanted Earl Grey, just say so. She dropped a spoon, then another while bending for the first, and throughout refused help, saying, apropos of nothing, "Your father's doing well," while pointing vaguely at the cockpit. He noticed her hands. The fingers were spindly, the skin thin but loose about the knuckles, and capped with nails corned-beef pink. He noticed the rest. Her cheeks were seasoned brown—liver spots and the bronzer she used to conceal them—and, where once showed the natural crimps of skin from nose to dimples, two ruts trafficked her tears so well, it was like city planning had landed on her face.

"Allergies," she said, waving him off but accepting a tissue anyway.

"Nice outfit," he said, and pointed at the TV on which was playing a tape of her giving a press conference the night before, urging the Helix to let her boy go. His mother in California cazh, tea rose ascot and blouse, and his father by her side in a double-breasted jacket. Amazing how their son might be shelving billy clubs in his ass, jailed and terrorized in the omphalos of dissent in America, and still they looked ready to yacht. Assuming they still traveled together, which seemed unlikely, given the spite in her voice every time she said *we* or *us,* as though the real resentment here was not so much Ned's kidnapping as the assault of this crisis on their disunity.

She turned it off. "All I'm saying is: We were trying everything."

"I believe you."

"This was hardly your average kidnapping. You can't buy off a man who asks for nothing; who knew what he wanted!"

"Mom, I know."

"Oh, I was so worried," she said.

Not that they had asked, but it was the old guy of the house who'd let him out. Shoved him down a rope ladder with instructions to *keep going.* And to call the police. Except Ned wasn't going to do that. Forget the police, forget the feds; all he wanted was to wash the tunnel shit off his face and hightail it to Los Angeles. Because, for all those hours in the Helix House with nothing to listen to but his heart, after a while, he swore he'd heard a second heart. Not Anne-Janet's, who was nuts and who'd disappeared; not Olgo's or Bruce's; but from inside, as though knowledge once cataleptic was now chanting what he wanted to hear most: Your twin is in L.A. That, and news from the PI, who had finally tracked her down.

Ned was ecstatic. He knew that one way to make life winnable despite the duress of physical and spiritual decay that was its chief characteristic was to experience intimacy with and through another human being. Progeny were good for this purpose, barring the financial commitment and moral obligation and opportunities to fail them, which were abundant. Marriage was good, barring its encumbrance and foreclosure on spontaneity. But a sibling, a *twin*—you could be a part of that for free. The trouble, really, was what came next. The unknown of other people's feelings. How could you control those? Not even the Helix could make other people love you. Trust you? Maybe. But love you? No chance.

He drank down the last of his tea and stood. "It's okay, Mom," he said, and he bent down to kiss her on the cheek by habit before pulling up short. What a disaster. She looked at him, and in the glaze of those blues was a pleading that revolted whatever compassion he was trying to rally in her defense. They were not even related! He turned away, feeling pity and rage in equal measure but, in the main, resentment, because from now on he might always have to feel complicated about her and this was terrible and he was sad. He made for the cockpit. The plane had twin-engine jets, room for eight plus crew, with about three thousand miles before things got fumy.

He stared at the back of his father's head. The hair—white, cropped thick and sea urchin—was his most resilient feature, so that even as his prostate, liver, and bones were crapping out on him, the hair said: I am virile! And also, apparently, I can fly. Ned had called his parents from Kentucky and told them to come get him, but he had not meant this literally. Six years since JFK Jr., eight since John Denver. Of all the crews to enlist, they chose themselves? Max had heart trouble. He kept nitrates in his breast pocket and some in Larissa's purse. So, him at the controls—it wasn't because he was young at heart but precisely because he wasn't, the logic being that it was better to gesture against age and frailty by risking your life than to admit you were simply too old to pilot.

"Dad, you're listing," Ned said. He was standing in the doorway with one eye trained on the panel. "Stay the course."

"Aye, aye, sonny," Max said. "Chip schooling the old block," and he listed worse.

"Honey!" Larissa said, alarmed and coming up behind Ned, because the plane had banked left for no reason.

"Helpful!" Max said. "It really helps when you do that!"

Ned looked from one to the other. He decided it was grim, having to save a marriage. Tedious, too. The emotional calculus—How far can I go, how much can I say, what is retaliatory and what constitutes a new offense?—was enough to fatigue every second of being alive to think on it.

"Mom," Ned said. "Don't you even want to know? What it was like or if I got hurt?"

"We can see you're not hurt," Max said. "It was barely three days."

"So now we're quantifying trauma?" Larissa said. "Is that your latest?"

"Oh, right," Ned said. "You're going to blame each other for what happened to me but forget about me altogether."

"Not really," Max said. "We blame you entirely. Your mother warned you about the Helix, but you, being so smart and Ivy League, blew her off. Reap what you sow, kid."

"Dad, I went to Kenyon. And enough with this blue-collar bullshit. You're a millionaire."

"I came from nothing. No one silver-spooned me all the chances you've had."

"So it's my fault I got *kidnapped?* My fault everyone in this country hates each other? Look at you two! Setting a great example."

"Oh, stop it," Larissa said. "We were worried sick."

"Silver-spooned," Ned said, and he looked about his plane with disgust. He hadn't been silver-spooned so much as *bribed*. What sort of parents let their child do anything so long as it was expensive? Guilty parents.

"It's just *turbulence*," Max said as the plane capered through the sky. "Even the Red Baron had turbulence." He laughed but clutched the yoke hard.

Ned had wanted to see his sister right away, only he had wanted to impress her, too. So he revised the plan. Study the weather in Cincinnati. Maybe seed the clouds overhead and flood the city. Hone his skills, then head out West. Some bullshit excuse, bereavement leave, whatever. Until then: briefings whose details he had missed.

When the time came, he had no idea who or what he was scouting.

If that little troll who'd vetted him at speed dating was chief of a cama-rilla deputized to bust the Helix, and if this troll had drafted him into the mix—he found this out only after being kidnapped.

ETA: twenty minutes. He closed his eyes and went over what to ex-pect. The PI had not been forthcoming with data on his sister, mostly because he didn't have any. Her name was Tracy. She lived way out in the Valley. Someplace rural—farmland, mountains—with a husband, Phil, and a toddler son, Willard. Anything else? Hang on. Ned had waited thirty-five minutes while the PI took another call, only to get shut down when he returned.

"No, that's all I got."

"But what does she look like?"

"I don't know. I didn't take photos."

"What do you remember?"

"I don't know. I wasn't paid to make out with her."

"Hey, that's my sister."

"Are we done here?"

"No, wait, isn't there anything else you can tell me? Is she tall?"

"She's your height."

"Really? What about her hair?"

"She's got your hair."

"Yeah? Wow. But wait, you never even met me."

"Bingo, genius." *Click*.

How many ways could he tell his mother the same thing? He plugged his ears, but she would not drop it. "How about if I call the police for you? I don't mind. It's the right thing; people need to know you got out."

They'd been having this conversation all day. If he notified the po-lice, they'd take him in. There'd be debriefings. Press conferences or, more likely, a quarantining by the feds, lest he broadcast their incom-petence. Not that he could do much to tank the impression people al-ready had of them, but he could spotlight the impression, at least until some other disaster laid claim to the country's umbrage.

"Mom, I'll call after *Tracy*." He said her name and smiled.

"Don't be so hard," she said. "You make bad choices in life. You try your best."

"Oh please."

"Neddy, while you were at the Helix House, I prayed and swore if you got out, I'd make the best amends to you I could. So here we are. Flying you right to her door."

He felt the anger coalesce in words that thronged his lips and teeth, so he was surprised to hear a different feeling assert itself out loud. "Mom, what if she doesn't like me?"

This seemed to recoup for Larissa her equilibrium, because nothing better vanquishes your problems than your kid's. "Don't be silly," she said. "What's not to like? Now, buckle up, because who knows if your father can actually land this plane." She laughed and frowned and laughed again.

ETA: now. The landing gear engaged. And down they went.

California was rilled with faults and counterpoised tectonic fronts likely to rip the state from the mainland. Where Tracy lived was notorious for fire and debris flows, and in that order. It had been the rainiest winter in 115 years. Nine inches in the last week. Almost nine feet at Opids Camp, up in the mountains, where Ned had always begged his parents to send him, which they never did. Probably because they knew his twin lived just a few miles away. They claimed not to know, but who was believing them now? It had rained more at Opids this year than in Bangkok. It was about to rain again; the clouds gathered in a scrum overhead.

They taxied to a hangar that was five sheets of aluminum and loud as bombs when the rain came. There was no one there, as though what few people who attended the strip had run home to open their doors and let the mud pass through. A nice idea. At the foot of the mountains, for fifty miles, were debris basins meant to catch whatever came down, but these overflowed, so that it was possible, at any moment, to drown in a gruel of mud twelve feet high, come slopping through your room.

"Well, this takes it," Max said. The rain was coming off the roof in a wall and pooling by the hangar door. His shoes were wet through—suede loafers—not to mention his socks. He sat on a bench and struggled to meet his feet halfway.

"Let me help," Larissa said, and before he could protest, she'd crammed her fingers down his heels like a shoehorn.

Ned made for the door and looked out. A road meandered from the hangar; there was a single car parked outside. "How are we going to get out of here?" he said. Because he had not exactly thought ahead. Well, no, he *had* thought ahead—that they'd land in Tracy's yard and she'd come running to him with apple pie and lollipops.

"I rented a car," Max said. "It's the ugly one outside."

"And go where?" Larissa said. "Because one place I'm not going is that woman's. Not that anyone asked, but I am not going."

"That's the spirit," Ned said. "I'm glad you're open to this."

"Your father and I talked about it. We're at a point in our lives where we just want some peace and quiet. We've earned it. So, while we're happy to get you to her, we're not going."

Ned looked at his father to see whether there was actual agreement there or whether she'd just bullied him down. But no, there was no bullying. If Tracy's life was garbage, they simply did not want the guilt of knowing they could have done better for her.

"But she's my sister," he said, though it sounded pathetic even to him. He tried again. "If you're interested in me, you're supposed to be interested in her."

"Let's just get to the car," Max said.

They drove around Sunland. A main drag with all the amenities, and to the north, the mountains, scalloped into the afternoon sky, which was a baby's face swelled with the tantrum gathering force in her lungs.

"We need a map," Ned said. "I just have the address."

"We're not going," Larissa said. "I understand no one in this family listens to me, but all the same, we're not going."

"Fine, whatever, you can just wait in the car."

"Oh, that'll go over well."

"We can drop you off," Max said. "We'll make sure she's home and then come back for you later."

Ned pummeled his knee with his fist. "You're making this ridiculous," he said. "It's not like dropping me off for kindergarten. Why do you have to make this ridiculous? This *means* something to me."

They pulled into a gas station. Larissa fussed with her purse, look-ing for her wallet. Ned shoved her a five. "A local map, okay?"

She turned around. He was lying down in the backseat. "Neddy, I've been thinking. Maybe you should call first? Because what if she really isn't home? Or what if she doesn't believe you? What if she doesn't know she was adopted, either? Have you thought about any of that?"

He was blinking slowly, because on the lee side of his eyelids was the way this afternoon was supposed to go, and it gave him courage to check in with the footage every three seconds.

"I don't think there's another family in the universe that wouldn't tell their adopted child she's adopted," he said. "Just FYI."

"But is this really the best way?" Max said. "I'm not saying don't find your sister, but what is the hurry? A little planning, a little foresight— these could save you some trouble down the road."

He was getting a headache. "Just get the map," he said. "Please."

It was almost five. It was getting dark.

"It's a ways up the canyon," Larissa said when she got back into the car. "The man inside showed me."

"Good, that settles it," Max said. "We'll do this tomorrow. If we hustle, we can still get to the lodge for a steak dinner. I've got friends that way."

Ned reached for the map. "What do you mean? It's just up the road!"

Larissa sneezed. "Your father will catch pneumonia out in this weather. You already saw his shoes."

"Then I'll walk," he said, and he made to get out of the car, unsure whether he was bluffing or not.

"Neddy," she said. "You haven't lived out here for a while. Things are different. This area's not safe."

"What are you talking about?"

"Tell him," Larissa said, looking at Max.

"Your mother's right. There's methamphetamine labs all over the place. Have you noticed how half the people running around have no teeth?" He put the car in gear.

"It's true," Larissa said. "Even the man behind the counter was miss-ing a front tooth."

"And that means he's a meth head?" Ned said. "I need something from the store"—and he ran out. He needed air. Space. These people were unbearable, and thank God he was not biologically mandated to turn into them when he reached that age when you stop resisting your worst self. Course, it was possible his biological parents had been unbearable, too, but there was no point going down that road.

A bell rang as he walked into the convenience store. He kept his eyes on the floor and matted his hair against his forehead. The guy behind the desk was not a guy but a kid, and he was missing teeth because he was ten.

"Need something?" the kid said.

"Just looking."

"Lemme get my dad for you."

"No, no, I'm just leaving."

But it was too late; the kid was hollering for his dad, who came lumbering in from a back room. "Didn't I say not to bother me?" But then, seeing a customer, he said, "Well, well! Out in this weather? Brave man. What can I do you for?"

But Ned was backing out of the store, mumbling thanks and trying not to hear the radio, which was live from a Cincinnati hospital treating some of the people from around the Helix House. The place had gone up in flames, but the fallout was minor. Smoke inhalation. First-degree burns.

The guy whistled. "Sorriest thing I ever heard. You been following this mess? House blows up and all four of those hostages are gone. Even the Grand Poobah. Something's not right."

Ned looked up for the first time. "All four of them gone?"

"Maybe taken to a new place. What do I know. Radio's telling me nothing."

"Is anyone looking for them?"

"You just come out of a coma? *Everyone* is looking for them."

Ned felt the blood recede from his skin, roll back through his veins, and log his heart, so that it grew tenfold. *Everyone?* He fled the store and, back in the car, told his dad to gun it.

What is tolerable in a person you love? Or want to love so much you will tolerate most anything? If his sister was a meth head running a lab, and if her husband, Phil, and son, Willard, partook of the results—one enjoying them and the other sustaining brain damage no one would notice for months—if they sold meth to local teenagers who marked it up and sold it to kids in Westwood, and if their franchise rivaled for quality what was coming in from Mexico, so that if they weren't meth heads they might have been rich and put their son in a day care that served arrowroot animal crackers, if his sister's face was all bone, and the skin was loose and pocked with gore, would he still see in her proof that his life had meaning? Would she still outfit his unconscious with the fabric of their bond so that he could go out and find someone to love romantically? And if she could do this for him, would he be able to prove he was worth it? The car splashed down the road, but the rain was on break.

"Do you at least have a plan for now?" Max said. "Do you know what you're going to say?"

Ned was looking out the window for street signs. The closer to the mountains they got, the more sporadic the housing and signage, so that even though they were within a mile of her place, it took forty-five minutes to get there. Every time he thought they were close, it was as though a giant hand snaked down his throat, grabbed his lungs, and squeezed. Then when they were lost again, he tried to breathe double-quick. Get it in there, fill the sacs. He was not hyperventilating, but still he felt sick. One more U-turn and he'd lose every meal he'd ever had.

"Neddy, are you all right?" Larissa said. Amazing how well she could dial into his anxiety. A good mom. "How about we go up the road and park above the house so we can just see what's what?" Giving him a face-saving way out. He said, "If you insist," though he was relieved and grateful for this woman above all.

The road did not have a shoulder, so Max pulled onto the dirt. Fog was rolling in, dusk too, but they could still see Tracy's house, which was actually a barn, and the yard, more like nature in a fence. There were tufts of buckwheat and sage and bitter brush laid out across the ground. Cockleburs up to your neck. Ned squinted but could make out nothing of relevance from this distance except a tricycle on its side and two cars in the driveway—a pickup and a town car much like the one whose engine Max was now gunning with impatience.

Larissa reached into her bag. "Here," she said, and she thrust binoculars in Ned's hand. "I got them at that philharmonic fund-raiser. They're opera glasses, really."

"You always carry around opera glasses?"

She blushed. Ned said, "Oh," and then started to laugh and then to tear up.

"I was just going to watch for a second," she said. "Just to see if she looks like you." She cupped his face. "My sweet boy."

He swiped at the tears. He was afraid to look through the binoculars, but he looked all the same and instantly regretted it. He hurled them down the slope.

"What?" Larissa said. "What is it?"

He threw his hands in the air and again his mom said, "What?" She looked at the binoculars, some twenty feet below, and calculated the wisdom in retrieving them. She was wearing clogs and had probably not exerted herself in this regard in years.

He sat on the ground. It was wet and shrill with needle grass. "Goddamn it," he said. "If you hadn't taken so long at the gas station we could have *beat them*."

"Beat who?"

"The cops. The feds. I don't know. I saw a woman in the door, maybe it's *her,* but I couldn't get a good look because she was half-inside the house, talking to some jackass."

Larissa stared down at the car in the driveway but could make nothing of it. "What makes you think it's the police?"

"Mom, he was in a suit and tie. Look where we are. Everyone's after me—of course they were going to check in on Tracy."

"But—"

"Mom, they're the government. They know everything. And now so does she. I can't believe it."

He felt so cheated, he almost could not move. Thanks to the feds, now he'd never know how she had felt in the instant she learned she wasn't alone in this world, either. Not without blood family. Did the news come as a relief? Would it moor her to the universe and save her life? In receipt of major news for the first time, a face cannot lie.

"Maybe it's for the best," Larissa said, and she began to finesse her way down the hill.

Ned had his back to her. "Goddamn it," he said. "This was idiotic. She's probably a meth head. Maybe they were coming to arrest her. Let's get out of here. I'll call in to work tomorrow and that will be that." He waited for his mom to hallelujah the plan but heard, instead, a small cry followed by the circus of a body tumbling downhill.

"Ah, Christ," he said, and he plunged headlong after her, grabbing for balance what he could.

"I'm here," she said, and she jutted her arm from a bed of sage that, in its congestion, had hidden her whole. "I think I twisted my ankle. Go get your father? He's waiting."

"Clearly," Ned said. The car horn had been blaring through the night for three minutes. If the feds had any sense, they'd hear in the urgency of this horn a sennet for their catch.

"Mom, can you get up?" He took her by the forearms and was shocked at their girth. They were bamboo; she was so frail. She tried to put pressure on her foot but buckled at the knee. "I can't walk," she said. "How stupid."

Ned looked up the hill. The night was livid now, but he could still see in the angle of the hill's incline no way to get back up together. Unclear, even, if they could get down. He told her to stay put while he went for Max.

"Neddy," she said, and she grabbed for the hem of his pants. "I'm so sorry. This is all my fault."

He waved her off and began uphill. The sky crackled, and you could hear the dry ravel and a sound like horse hoofs on cobblestone, which was actually rocks and pebbles and earth caroming down the mountainside.

The only light for miles was a halogen nested in the gable of Tracy's barn. It guided their way as they picked through the brush.

"We can act like we're someone else," Larissa said. She was pendant between the men in her life, and, though the throbbing in her ankle was getting worse, the pendant thing was nice.

"You could help us here," Max said. "You do have one foot that still works."

"Or maybe we could just be hikers who lost track of time," she said.

"Some hikers," Max said. "The one thing we had to make that story work, and sonny boy throws them down the hill."

"I got them back," Larissa said. And it was true; the binoculars were slung around her neck.

Ned kept his eyes on the halogen. What might his sister not like in all this? How about a creepy brother come to her door with the horrible parents who rejected her.

They made it to the outlays of the house, where management started: a gate, a path.

"What now?" Max said, though he got no answer.

There were bighorn in the mountains; they lowed and baaed, and the sound traveled for miles.

They neared the barn. Ned was the first to stop. He cocked his ear. They were twenty feet from a window open a crack. He was about to press on when a child's voice sniped at the air and decked his parents. They were on their bellies fast. He just stood there.

"Ned," Max whispered, and he reached for his son's calf.

"Neddy," Larissa said, and she reached for the other.

He looked down at them. Max had served in Korea and been awarded a silver star. Larissa had served as a nurse at the Eighty-Fifth Evacuation Hospital in Qui Nhon. They knew how to take cover. A man's face in the window, and Ned got on his stomach, too. Listened hard. The voice, after all, was his nephew's. His nephew, Willard. He tried to memorize its timbre. The high notes. The jazz. He'd been told the boy was just over two. He heard running through the house and a man saying, "I'm gonna get you!" and the child shrieking and laughing and yelling, "No no, Dada," and collapsing on the floor while his mother nibbled his arms and neck, threatening to eat her boy for dinner because he was soooooo tasty.

Ned rolled on his back. So did Max. Larissa, too. They were soaked and filthy and staring at the nimbus overhead. For everything he'd been through, it was hard to imagine it was clouds up there and not a larder of tears.

He went back to listening. This family inside was a miracle. The boy romping through the house, saying: "Willard's bear. Willard's shoes." The parents keeping an eye on him but retreating to the kitchen to talk it over. The man who'd come to see them before? He was a representative from L.A. County's flood control division saying that if it rained big again, tonight or soon, probably there'd be a debris slide headed right for their barn. The fire season being what it was, the basin uphill was just not basin enough. Tracy saying, "You believe that? I don't believe that," and Phil saying, "Me neither," but both of them watching their son and believing it wholeheartedly.

"He said if there's rain, we'll have just twenty minutes before the mountain comes down," she said.

"I know."

"He said in 'seventy-eight, there was such a bad flow, all the graves at Verdugo went loose and there were dead bodies upright in people's living rooms when it was over."

"I know."

"Maybe let's make an emergency bag if we have to leave in a hurry? Sort of like how when I was pregnant, we had that bag ready?"

"Okay, but what should we pack? There's nothing important in this house but the memory of us in it." He touched her cheek.

"I'll grab the pictures of Mom and Dad in the living room," she said.

"You'd better. Your parents will have a fit if they find out you didn't save their pictures."

"Oh, stop."

They reconvened on the couch, him with the albums and her with a box of miscellany. Will's first rattle. A corsage from their wedding.

They went through everything, and the hours went by. Finally, they put the pictures and mementos, title to the house, and some insurance papers in a duffel and put it by the front door. Only then did they turn on the radio. A severe storm alert was in effect. Rain imminent.

"I'm scared," she said. "This house is all we have."

"I know."

"I love you?" she said.

"Check."

Their son came waddling into the living room and mounted the couch. He sat between them.

"Willard's book!" he yelled. "Oooooh, airplane! Flap, flap!"

"No way," Tracy said. "Who could fly in this weather? Come on, baby, let's get your boots. We're going on a trip!" She picked up her son, who flapped in her arms.

"Flap, flap!" he said.

Tracy smiled. "Silly boy," she said, though she was wrong. Because not two hours ago, a twin brother had talked his parents into reboarding his Lear jet and racing for the cloud decks off the California coast. The plan? Seed the clouds to make it rain well afield of a ranch on Alpine Way, so that when his sister was spared, Ned would know himself equal in love to whatever the universe could do for her. He set their course, he kissed the sky. And their lives were bound up for good.

Olgo Panjabi, a man sees, hears, feels, and absorbs as much as he can understand.

Say you had this cult whose impetus to knit people together had turned terrorist—did that mean you forwent the instruments of community the second things got rough? That you divested your cult compound of a way to reach the outside world? If no, then what the hell, the Helix House was a nightmare; it had no cell-phone reception, *no bars,* which was colossal in the extent of its horror for Olgo Panjabi because if he could just get his voicemail, his life would start over. He had a rash, he was scared, but still, this kidnapping in its grandeur was like the Christ birth, a demarcation of time. Whatever had happened before belonged to a different epoch, and what tragedies it sustained were receded into it, among them adulteries committed by his wife. In this new era ushered in by High Event, his wife would come back, she was on her way, he just needed it confirmed by the message on his voicemail.

He had heard the others leave—Anne-Janet brawning her way out, Ned following suit—and he had wanted to go, too, only he was frantic and when frantic, paralyzed. If not for the expected message from his wife, he might not have left at all. As it was, he'd crawled his way across the floor and poked his head through the exit Anne-Janet had made for them. Looked left, right. The rash meant he'd been released from his hood ages ago; likewise the handcuffs, because he had to scratch, and so he was versatile with the actions required for this escape. He'd crawl all the way home if he had to.

Phone in his pocket. Checking for bars every few feet. Meeting no one. Meeting someone, a tree of a woman with an accent from the heartland telling him to make for a closet, find the hatch, something something tunnel, which did not appeal to the logic of finding high ground for best reception but which did mean a way out of this dead zone.

It was dark in the tunnel; he had no idea where he was going. He worried he'd deplete the battery for checking the phone every three seconds. Couldn't remember the directions but kept walking. The plan?

Go home posthaste. Wait for his wife unless, oh-ho, she was waiting for him. Debrief in bed with kefir smoothies. The tunnel went on and on, but he could hear the rumble of cars overhead, and soon: a manhole. Ladder, life. A cover that could not be moved without a crowbar. Several such, and so he got filthier and angrier and more exhausted until, at last—a temp cover, resin grate, he could easily remove.

He ran to the sidewalk. Ran with no regard for the spectacle of himself sprouted from the nethers, waving his phone. Not that anyone cared and probably not that anyone even noticed. He waved his cell for the interminable seconds it took this device to realize it was aboveground. One bar, two. He called his number and listened to the outgoing, dialed his password, got it wrong, fingers like egg rolls, got it right, thank God. Many messages, jumping for joy. The first from Erin—Dad, where are you?—and another—Oh my God, Dad, are you okay?—and finally just her crying, saying everyone was so scared, she knew he wasn't going to get this message, but she loved him, they all did. *All?* A call from the fraud department of his bank, because there'd been so much activity on his debit card—had it been stolen?—and then a reporter from ABC news, just in case.

Ah, choices. In every negotiation, there were plenty. Be the guy who reneges on what small powers of deduction separate man from ape, or the guy who accepts what's what and acts accordingly and in everyone's best interest. Trouble was, if you recognized these options as a choice, it wasn't yours to make: You were the latter guy, the reasoning guy, the unhappy, paid-to-arbitrate guy whose wife had not called on purpose. He rang his daughter. Did so outside an electronics store with TVs in the window showing a photomontage of the Helix hostages: Anne-Janet before the cancer, in pastel tank top; Ned at some dress-up convention, brandishing an action figure statuette like an Oscar; Bruce with tripod braced over his shoulder. And Olgo? Olgo smiling hugely into the camera with Kay by his side, the red-eye spangles of the shot doing little to vandalize the joy coming off them in torrents. Didn't the others have family? Couldn't the news upturn a single candid of Olgo without Kay? Of course not. Not if they wanted to reproduce his likeness in good faith.

Erin shouted into the phone. "Dad? *Dad?*" She was incredulous and then she was sobbing, and he could hear Tennessee in the background, screaming in empathy, and then Erin calling out for someone, saying, "It's my dad! On the phone! He's okay!"

Her enthusiasm was nice but also highlighting of the enthusiasm he would have liked to hear from someone else.

"Erin, I'm fine. I'm fine, sweetheart"—and while he meant to say that he was coming home and that he loved her and that the whole time he was kept hostage he thought only of her and Tenn, of family and love, he popped out something different. He said, "But let me just ask you this: Who is that person you're talking to in my house?" Because he suspected it wasn't a woman, and if it was Erin's asshole husband, Jim, he'd lose it.

"Dad," she said. "Where are you? Are you okay? Oh, thank God," and she started to cry anew.

He was afraid to squander battery life on her sobbing and was about to press on when closed captioning from the storefront began to ticker news of interest: *The hostage Olgo Panjabi has a wife; this wife has joined the Helix.*

He took a deep breath. The cold seemed to nip his lungs like frost starred to a windowpane. "Has your mother called?" he said.

Crying stopped. A long pause. Erin scouring her mind for the right way to put it. Olgo gawking at the TV.

"No," she said. "I think she's gone."

"Don't be silly," he said.

"She's with the *Helix*, Dad. Jim told me. She's in Virginia."

The last of the ticker onscreen: *Living at whats thought to be a helix commune in richmon by the riber, sources close to teh case say,* which wasn't a case so much as Olgo's hell spelled out in third grade.

"Dad, just tell me where you are. There's nothing on the news saying the hostages were released, and Jim says no one knows anything, though I know he's full of shit. Is it a secret?"

"Yes," Olgo said, though it had not been a secret until now. He watched onscreen as one of Kay's friends from yoga—she did yoga?—said how kind and vibrant Kay was, as though Kay were the tragedy here, the one taken. Though maybe—and here Olgo's spirits rose like mercury in the thermometer—she really had been forcibly severed from her life by the brainwashing fury of the Helix, in which case she could be forced back.

He stomped at a snowbank and nearly fell in. He had not once been hysterical at the Helix House, not until the moment he realized he could get out. He clamped down on his voice with success.

"Listen. Don't tell anyone you heard from me. Everything's going to be fine, but I have to go."

"Dad, you're scaring me. Wait, oh my God, are you—is someone making you say these things? Are you, how do you put it, are you under *duress?* Just say *I love you* if I'm right."

"Duress?" he said, sneering. "I thought you were a big fan of the Helix! You and your mother both. Their biggest fans ever!"

"Dad, I didn't know they were *armed* or whatever. I didn't know you were going out there. I didn't know they were like that! I'm getting a divorce; I just wanted some friends. If you're upset about what happened, that's natural. But don't take it out on me. What were you even *doing* in Cincinnati? All this time pretending to be a nobody when really you are CIA? At first I thought you went after Mom, but then when you were gone for so long without calling and then suddenly the news everywhere and the press and Jim feeding me ten different stories every ten minutes—I guess you are CIA. I know you can't tell me, so all I'm saying is: I know."

Olgo rapped the phone against his head and hunkered down. It was freezing. Kentucky in winter. No one around except a guy down the street smoking outside a garage, and in the driveway, a car with a For Sale sign in the window.

"I have never pretended to be a nobody," he said, and then he lost his breath for the agony those words drowned him in.

"I didn't mean it like that. When are you coming home? I'm just here with a girlfriend."

"I need a few days." In the meantime, he had started for the garage. The smoking guy was in coveralls and rolling a second cigarette before his first one was out.

"One good thing?" Erin said. "I think Jim has to leave town. Maybe even the country. So me and Tenn are home free."

"Great," he said. "Now listen: when your mother calls, tell her I'm fine."

"Okay, but, Dad? She might not be coming back. Like, ever. His name is Jonathan. Just so you know."

Olgo stopped midstride. He'd almost forgotten. So enamored had he become with the idea of his wife absorbed into a cult, he'd lost sight of the recruiting lothario at the start of it all. *Jonathan?* What could be more homogenous and totemic of the white man and his intolerance than a name like Jonathan?

"I have to go," he said. "Give Tenn a kiss for me." And before she could respond, he flipped his phone shut.

By now, he was within voice of the mechanic, who took one look at him and said, "You like this car? 'Cause I got a better one in the back. Cheaper, too. Want to see?" He flicked his cigarette into the gutter and plucked shreds of tobacco from his tongue.

Olgo nodded. Buy a car, hit the road. He struggled to keep pace with the mechanic. It wasn't his way to move this fast, but it was refreshing so long as he could establish in their shared stride and silence the preconditions for talk. He needed to talk. More now than ever. If it's true that stress makes you sick, there were polyps massed on the wall of his gut like barnacles. His bones were punchboard. He had coronary heart disease. Was getting a clot. Morbidity gorged on his despair.

He took three steps for the mechanic's every one, but they were on pace. "So, how's it going?" he said.

The mechanic glanced at him. "Car's over there," he said, and he gestured at a pea-green sedan. A Ford, maybe. He reached in his pocket for the keys. "You seem like a good guy, so let's just call it an even three K." He stopped several feet from the car, and when Olgo moved ahead, he called him back, saying, "Better yet, two K."

"Fine," Olgo said. "Just give me the keys so I can make sure it works."

"I'm not out to get you," the mechanic said. "But I do have to get back to work." He held out his hand but still would not approach the car.

"The keys?" Olgo said. "I have to get to a bank anyway. It's not like I'm carrying." He was in a hurry, but he was not stupid. The car had New York plates. Probably the car was stolen, though he couldn't imagine who'd want to steal a pea-green sedan.

"Done deal," the mechanic said, and he tossed him the keys.

Olgo got inside and immediately felt something like oatmeal wet his pants. Then came the smell. Cloying and rancid. He flew out of the car, shut the door. His eyes watered. "What *is* that?" he said, and pressed his face to the window. The glass was hazy and the lighting dim, but still, he could see inside. An army of fungal spores was encamped in his new car.

"You can't be serious," he said, and turned around. But the mechanic was gone.

Olgo circled the car and began to stack reasons for why this wasn't so bad against a feeling that this was terrible. As if he could show up at Jonathan's like the Swamp Thing.

He opened the trunk. Luckily: towels and aerosol. He was on the road shortly. The car smelled as though many drag queens had passed through it. Nine hours to go. He was headed to Helix Pack 7, Richmond, Virginia.

According to the radio—which worked, thank God—P7 convened at the Fulton Gas Works factory off Williamsburg Avenue. It was only two hours south of D.C., which meant Kay might have been commuting for months. Months! He could have hurled with the thought, though now, driving down the highway, windows up, then down— the cold was unbearable, but the smell was immortal—he thought he might hurl anyway. Olgo had never known himself to be an angry man or even a man with the stamina to anger for more than a few minutes, so the imprecations launched from his mouth at every car that passed and every one that didn't; the slamming of his horn, plus coda, "Ching-chong, CHING-CHONG!" because half these drivers were Asian and no Asian could drive; the tailgating of family vehicles signed Baby on Board—none of these behaviors, nor the presence of mind to deal with them, was part of his repertoire. It was not long, then, before he veered into the emergency lane and blew a tire. The asphalt was serrous, littered with glass.

He punched the ceiling. His knuckles came back wet. Good thing he could not call AAA. Good thing he'd insisted the expense was lavish when Kay pressed for it; good thing she'd called him a miser cheapskate and turned her back to him in bed that night and for a few nights thereafter. Good thing in the year since, he'd refused to go on vacation, buy a new fridge, pay for Kay's landscape portraiture classes at Wash U, or even contribute to Tennessee's college fund. He wasn't a cheapskate, Kay's shrieking opinion notwithstanding, but just planning for the long haul. Sixty was the new forty; he'd have to make their savings and income last for another half century of life together. Together! Even now, stalled and shivery and strewn with hives, he smiled. And warmed up from the inside. He would just have to hitchhike.

Five minutes passed before the anxiety of his circumstances returned. He hoisted his thumb, then jammed it in his pocket. There were some evil people on the road. People who might be the last you saw on earth if you got in their car. Oh, this was absurd. He thrust his thumb back in the air.

Success was immediate; a car pulled over. Olgo bent down to look inside. "East," he said. "Virginia," and he probed the man's eyes for murderous intent. He was old. His face was like granite, and the lattice of declensions in his skin was chiselwork. The car was a station wagon. Mutts in the back—a Weimaraner and a medieval-looking dog with no hair—and in the front, where once was a radio and AC console, the dash had been gutted to accommodate a humidifier that plugged into the smoke socket. When Olgo opened the door, a plume of dew came at his face.

The man told him to hop in. "You're in luck. I'm pointed exactly that way."

His voice was phlegmy, as if the walls of his nose and throat were slopped in roux. He was missing fingers that mattered for making a good impression.

"The name's Jerry. You?"

"Jonathan." Olgo said it deliberately, testing the consonants for what pleasure they gave his tongue in bringing them to life.

"Well then. Hope you don't mind the dogs. The bald one, you can put one of them pups on your arthritis and the skin is so hot it cures you. Folklore, but I done it. And I got arthritis in places no one but a pup's gonna go without complaint."

Olgo looked away. If he had wanted to talk, he also had standards. He thought about retreating to the backseat, claiming fatigue, only between it and the tailgate was a trellis for keeping the dogs put that did not seem so reliable. The bald one already had his snout wedged through.

Olgo said, "Is that okay? Your dog like that? I think he's stuck."

"Not really. But just see what happens you go find out." Jerry laughed, like whatever mauling had befallen him in the past was good times.

Olgo thought he even flourished his knuckle stumps, though maybe he was just swatting the air.

"I'm going to see my wife," Olgo said. "She doesn't know I'm coming, though."

"Yeah? I had a wife once. But we don't talk. When I came back from the services broke, she didn't like it. Now my son and his family live near, but it still feels like I got nothing."

"What do you do these days?"

"This and that." He rolled up his sleeve and began to savage his bicep. When he was done, the patch of skin was candent and striking against the livid ink sealed into his arm.

"Oh Christ," Olgo said, and he reached for the door handle.

Jerry grinned. "At eighty miles an hour, I'd say you're not gonna make it."

The tattoo was bigger than any Olgo had seen on file. It stretched from elbow to shoulder, and the rungs of the double helix were pearled—this version more science, less metaphor.

"Are you taking me back to them?" Olgo said. "How did you even know where I was?"

Jerry pointed at a CB radio bolted to the underside of the steering column. The radio was waterproofed in plastic. "Looks like it'd be in the way, but it doesn't bother me none."

Olgo said, "I don't understand."

"It's like this. There's an APB out for that car you were driving, for one. Ugly business with that car. Someone spotted your plates, said there was some jackass cursing all up and down the highway. Also, the feds put out the word. Found out maybe you wasn't there when they came a-knockin'."

"So everyone knows I'm out?"

"Everyone with a CB. Whole world is listening. All that fancy equipment, and some idiot is still using the CB."

"Are you taking me to the Helix people or not? Because I'm pretty sure it's not *me* they want, just anyone. To make a point. I do this for a living, conflict resolution, so, ah, talk to me. There's no need to be confused about what we each stand to gain."

"Sure there is. We're all confused. Let's call it the human experience."

Olgo frowned. A preacher man.

"Don't look at me like that," Jerry said. "I'm seventy-nine next week. God willing."

Olgo pressed his head to the glass—how was he even having this conversation?—and began to regret in earnest having left the Helix House. Why couldn't he have waited for Hostage Rescue? Wherever Jerry was taking him, security would be tighter and the turncoats fewer.

"So let me get this right: You're a bounty hunter for the Helix? At age seventy-nine?" Sixty might well be the new forty, but seventy-nine was eighty and eighty was nine hundred.

"Seventy-eight, thanks."

"I have money. I could *get* money."

"Oh, don't talk stupit. I don't like that kind of talk. I'm principled."

"You're above money?" Olgo cowered with the thought. In all his years negotiating, it was always the principled who stood their ground with the least remorse.

Jerry shook his head, said, "I'll tell you all about it later," and pushed Play on a cassette deck sized like a hardback novel.

And so it went: Show tunes. *Oklahoma!* and *Cats* and *Seven Brides for Seven Brothers,* and Jerry singing in tandem but not in key. He had several five-gallon jugs of gas in the back, which meant they could go for hours without having to see anyone, which they did. Olgo was so clammy by the time they rolled into Blackstone, his skin was made of eel.

He did not know the area well, but he gathered they were close to Richmond, having drifted into Virginia a while ago and been headed east the whole time. Eventually, they pulled off the highway, and when they saw signs for Fort Pickett, Jerry said, "USS *Pueblo,* I was on that ship, you know."

Olgo said nothing. So Jerry was a Helix-touting ex–navy man. Bad news. Also, the *Pueblo?* God knows what the North Koreans had done to the sailors off that boat; Manchurian candidate might be a step up. How'd Jerry lose his fingers, anyway?

"That should mean something to you," Jerry said. "You're almost my age, I bet. You lived through the war."

Olgo's mouth blew open. He flipped down the visor and evaluated what he could in the mirror. The skin about his lips was pinched. The whites of his eyes were not so white. He seemed to have grown lappets overnight. In general, the impression was of a man who'd lived in the sun and slept on sandpaper.

Jerry went on. "You and me have something in common now. Both kidnapped. I didn't *have* to pick you up, you know."

Olgo gathered his wits. Another way to hatch accord between parties was to get on record their differences and then to look for shared ground. He said, "Okay, I see you think you're doing me a favor, whereas I think the opposite. Maybe we can come to terms. Because, frankly, taking me prisoner is not going to avenge whatever it is you want avenging. The Helix is finished. The place was surrounded when I left. The government is probably arresting Thurlow Dan as we speak"— though here he paused and smiled bitterly. Thurlow Dan, that wife-stealing shitfuck.

"Prisoner!" Jerry laughed. "I'm not taking you prisoner. You already been through that, and besides, it's *un-American.*"

"What?"

"Un-American," Jerry said. And then, looking at Olgo with an appraiser's eye, "Or aren't you one of us? Whole country's full of people who don't look the part, so I never know who's who anymore."

"What?"

They pulled into a gravel driveway that ramped up to a single-car garage addition on a converted trailer home. Prongs of ice hung low from the gutters, and from sky to foot was a gray so ambient, it could blanch your heart in minutes. Olgo winced and waited and summoned the courage to run.

Jerry let the dogs out. He was gripping a carnation of fabric so that his sweatpants wouldn't fall and wrestling with the rear door, which would not close. Hard to say which problem had him worse.

"Shit car," Jerry said.

Olgo's breath purled from his lips. A man across the street was shoveling snow, wearing orange camouflage gloves and a trapper hat. There was music in the air, guitar licks, and Olgo thought he saw a woman fat as a yak vacuuming inside. He surveilled their lawn and wished he hadn't: hanging from a tree turned gibbet was a deer carcass with skin rolled down from the neck, over a brick that gave purchase to a rope, and at the end of this rope, two boys, seven or eight, heave-hoeing amid the steam still lifting from the animal's flesh.

The man waved. "Eight o'clock," he yelled, and Jerry nodded before plunging a key into the front door of his house.

Run, Olgo thought, and walked inside. The man was a twig. Did not seem to carry a firearm or have an incarcerating posse in the living room. *Run,* Olgo thought, and undid his scarf, noting that Jerry's furniture was sealed in plastic. The place was overrun with cats and, in the bathroom, a litter of kittens not one week old.

"I rescue 'em," Jerry said. "Else they just howl all winter long, and the sound is like people bawling for everything that's unfixed."

There were fifteen bags of cat food pushed up against the wall. Jerry toed a rubber ball that skidded across the floor. Four cats tore after it; the others couldn't be bothered. Jerry said he'd be right back, and when he returned, he wore a terry-cloth bathrobe that exposed his skinny legs and gym socks tubed loosely around each calf. He popped a cube of gum in his mouth. "Hubba Bubba. Want one? I'm 'bout to shower."

Olgo shook his head. He'd heard of abducted children who could escape at any time but never did. Whose minds had exiled the very idea of escape, so that when asked about it later, they regarded the concept the way a toddler might consider a new word—with wary enthusiasm because haven't I heard this someplace before? Olgo had been here only five minutes and already he was stuck.

Jerry settled into an armchair. Olgo said, "So, do you want to tell me what's going to happen to me now? That family across the street, are they Helix, too?"

"They was," he said. "That's how they met. My son never went to a dance in all his life, what's it called, a RYLS, and next thing he's married this woman—there wasn't so much of her back then—and joined up." He blew a bubble and went cross-eyed to watch it grow.

"That's your son?" Olgo cursed under his breath. So Jerry did have people. Backup.

"And his wife. And them kids. I left the Helix easy enough, but for Buzzy, I got one of them exit counselors. Took us a year of planning. All nicey-nice, and for what? He's all spaced out. Dissociation, they call it, from all them hours just telling on himself in a room."

Olgo thought of Kay, her beautiful mind seized and plundered by these nuts. Why hadn't he noticed the crossroads-of-life events that prep a person for cult induction? Had she been depressed? Menopausal? Restless? Bored?

"You're *ex*-Helix?" he said.

"Yep. An' I still can barely make a decision on my own. We have this joke now: only thing scarier than Loch Ness is Together Ness, though maybe it's not so funny."

"Are we far from Richmond?" Olgo said. Though, really, what was he going to do? Pluck Kay from their midst? He couldn't know how lost to them she was, but he'd heard stories. The power of group doctrine and how the person deputized to speak for the group was more worried about winning its approval than dealing with the enemy. Assuming he was the enemy—though how was this possible? His wife of thirty-five years would choose a cult over him, thanks to the five minutes she'd been among them?

Jerry produced a knife from his bathrobe pocket. He examined his hand and began to scrape at the dirt plastered to the underside of the thumbnail he had left. Kittens mewling. A car engine that would not catch.

" 'Bout an hour," he said. "Give or take. But not to worry. I know all the back roads."

Olgo was about to ask what this meant when there was a knock at the door, then a pounding, and the sound of many people barreling into Jerry's place.

Buzz had dundrearies like it was 1975. He was dragging a grill on wheels into the kitchen, except the wheels were missing and the legs grated the floor.

Olgo sat up as Sissy thrust a pail of charcoal briquettes at his chest, because him sitting around was not going to get this dinner on the table any faster. Her hair was buff, feathered to the chin. She was chopping sausage. Said, "You know, I was just sick at my stomach when I heard about you and the others. But when Dad said he was gonna help, well, we all gladdened up a little. He's been on the road two days. Wouldn't take a cooler, neither. You like a little blood in your meat? Barbecue's almost heated up."

Buzz had cracked the transom above the back door in the kitchen, but this did little to exhaust the room of smoke. Sissy said, "You know, my family was raised similar to the type of Amish with no electricity. But all of us girls has turned out to be terrific girls. We are six, except until the Helix caught hold, and now we're two dead. So you see—" But then her boys tornadoed through the room and Sissy was up after them with a dishrag. The effort took her breath away, and she was back on the couch before long. "Buzz don't know apples about rearing kids," she said. "He ever had a thought in his head about them, it a-died of loneliness." She peeled a potato. "He left me once. Right after we got out of the Helix. Then thought better of it."

Olgo blinked at her slowly. He'd been confused and afraid and then confused all over again, but now he was something different. Bigger. His heart grew ten feet. He did not think it was an accident, him being shepherded from the Helix House and into the arms of—well, he didn't know what these people were except that maybe they were God-gifted to tell him something.

"Anyway," Sissy said, "my sisters took up with Thurlow, and one suicided for him not liking her enough, and the other got an abortion, which was afoul of God, so she died. We had such ideas, too. Just yearning to be a part of something. Stupid in backsight. But the thing is, you never knowed what you was signing up for. It all happened so subtle-like. Me, I'm not fancy-educated, okay, but half the people who talked me in were Harvard."

"Amen to that," Jerry said. He was sitting on the couch with two kittens in each hand. "So little," he said. "Helpless."

"Yep," Sissy said, and she looked on her boys. They were slamming each other against the wall to see who could do it harder and to more lasting effect. George had a cut down the side of his neck but would not cede the game.

"They was born Helix," she said. "We been out a year, but I still give 'em lots of rope. They's still learning how to be just boys. Most horrible mistake of my life. They daddy could be anyone, though probably it's Buzzy."

Olgo sat forward. His voice came out low. Reverent. He was stuck eight thoughts back. "Thought better of it?" he said. "Left you and came back?"

"Yessiree. Wasn't gone too long, neither. Sometimes, though, you can't wait. So don't you worry none."

Olgo leaned way over the table like he might clutch the billows of skin come down her shoulders and said, "When he left, did you feel like he'd taken all the colors of your life with him? All the water, the light, the air? Like he'd left you for dead except being dead would have been better? Did that happen to you?"

She laughed. "That's hokey talk. I grew up on a farm. I know how to fend for myself. Plus the Helix made me confused about Buzzy, like I weren't married to him but just to the group." And when Olgo did not return to the couch but just hung there as though waiting to be slapped, she said, "You oughtta see your face. You look like you left yer guts in the john."

"Oh, leave him be," Jerry said. "I've seen that face. I've *worn* that face. All hopeless and ruined. Eleven months in a shit-hole jail in North Korea, you bet I seen that face."

"Umm-hmm," Sissy said, and Olgo sat down. He got the feeling that though she'd heard this story a thousand times, today it was actually germane to something transpiring in their lives.

"Eleven months," Jerry said. "You know the slits wouldn't even let you sing in your room? I was never much for singing before, but just for being denied"—and he blew out another show tune that sent the cats tumbling from his chest.

"Terrible," Sissy said. "Man's just gone afoul of God."

"Our captain near got beat to death. Others too. And whenever there was free time, which was pretty much never, but when there was: no football, 'cause the huddle meant plotting. Like we was plotting to escape. Stupid slits. I still have nightmares."

"And they still got the *Pueblo*," said Buzz.

"Correct," said Jerry. "Like some trophy. Not that we tried too hard to get it back. Day we was released, a hospital in Seoul gave us each an ashtray souvenir. You believe it? Eleven months of turnip soup—and eyeball was a treat, mind you—and they give us ashtrays. I mean, this was in 'sixty-eight, so we was no one's favorite army. But still. I hate this country, I really do."

Olgo could not fathom where this was going, but he was decided to go along with it. *Left and came back* were the only words that mattered now. He glanced up at Sissy, waiting for more.

Jerry sank into his chair. "I know it's an awful thing to say."

Sissy patted his hand. "We all of us been disappointed."

Jerry spat into a napkin. "Second I heard Thurlow was in with those same who took the *Pueblo*—man. What was I thinking? Sissy'd done lost her sisters and there I was still going to meetings and saying my heart's broke 'cause of my wife and kin. Well, I had my eyes opened. And got my son out. But it didn't feel like enough, so I been biding my time, jus' hopin' I'd get the chance to do more. And along comes you four. And along comes you." He laughed and just as suddenly coughed up something with such force, it might have come from his colon. His face was twice its color, and his eyes were clear in tears. "It's stupid, I know, but even at my age, I'm still looking for a hero. So maybe that hero is me."

Olgo heard him—a hero, yes—though he kept his eyes on Sissy.

"Anyway," Jerry said, recovering himself. "Here we are. You gotta figure everyone finds his own kind eventually. We'll eat and then get a move on. We got a long night ahead of us. I best put my jeans on."

Sissy lifted her paring knife and said, "It's not like I'm okay with this, Dad goin' back in and all. But he's strong. He knows his up from down."

Jerry smiled and looked at Olgo. "Plan is for you to show up like you been invited, like you're interested. You'll have 'em all over you, so while that's doin', I'll swing round back. Best way is to isolate and ambush. Guy who used to do this in the seventies was called Black Lightning. I kinda like that. Even m' jeans are black."

Olgo nodded. He still had no idea what they were talking about.

"Try to look a little more excited," Jerry said. "Who came for me in North Korea? Who came for you? You seen the news? Hostage Rescue blew up the place whether you was there or not. So fine. No one came for us. But you know what? We're sure as hell gonna come for your wife."

And like that, the energy that was clotted in Olgo's body dispersed while something like old age moved in—fatigue, apathy, or maybe just a set of revised priorities. Suddenly, this all seemed very hard.

An hour later: Olgo and Jerry were in the station wagon en route to an abandoned factory, a box on stilts at the mouth of a floodplain that burbled with sewage now and then, where Olgo's wife would sooner spend her time than with him.

"And the RYLS?" Olgo said.

"A front group. Dating Service snatches you in, you think it's gonna be something nice, and next thing you're saying your life before was shit, you were so lonely you wanted to die, but this, this talking and sharing and crying, is a whole lot better."

"How do they get you to do it?"

"Dunno, really, but the exit counselor said it was thought control and just wanting to fit in, and maybe just 'cause the most of us is kinda sad and lonely anyway, they was workin' that for gain."

Olgo shook his head. "My wife isn't lonely. She hasn't been lonely since the day we met."

Jerry laughed. Said, "Ooowee," and mopped the windshield with his palm.

"What?"

"Nuthin'."

"What?"

"Well, I weren't sitting on yer bedpost, but with your attitude like that, I'm not surprised she left."

"My *attitude?* I thought you were ex-Helix."

"I am. But I ain't stupid about life, neither."

Olgo pressed his eyes closed with his fingertips.

Jerry nudged him in the arm. "Don't let the bear getcha. It's gonna be all right."

They pulled into the grounds, and when Olgo stepped from the car, the condemnation of landscape into which he'd been cast was staggering. The trees were bald and black and immobile despite the wind galloping down the riverbank. The snow was two feet deep. In the distance: a trestle for the freight that rolled through every day and the skeletal remains of a holding tank that looked, for its imposition on the sky, like a gallows befitting the evil of mankind. He breathed in deep, coughed it out. The snow was colored urine and coal, smelled it, too, and everywhere you looked: garbage, like someone had leaked the bag from one end of the grounds to the other.

The only building alive was the boiler room. It was up on cement risers, maybe fifteen feet above the ground where Olgo and Jerry hid. Light blazed through the windows, which were two banners of glass come down the facade. It was behemoth, imposing. Olgo did not want to go in there at all.

Jerry said, "You go up the front; I'll circle round back. I seen your wife on TV. I'll try to separate her from the others."

"Why can't I talk to her and you distract?"

" 'Cause you're a threat now. A floe."

"A what?"

"An outsider. Now come on."

"So you're just going to talk to her? How are you going to talk her out of there in two minutes if it's really as bad as you say?"

"Can't. I'll need about three days."

"We don't have three days."

But then even in the dark, Olgo could see the denture whites of this man's smile and something of the Black Lightning sobriquet flash in it. "Leave that to me. You just keep the others busy, act like you ready to join."

"How?"

"Just tell 'em your story. You don't even have to lie—it's Prereq enough. That's what they in there call a past you want to leave behind. *Good Prereq.*"

Jerry tiptoed off, under the building, into the dark. Olgo looked at the twenty steps he'd have to mount to get to the entrance and sat on the bottom one. He might not be able to endure the experience of Jerry talking to Kay, reasoning, and exposing the manipulation to which she'd been subject. If *reason* could turn his wife, love had no role to play in her decision. And if love had no role to play, maybe she had never loved him at all.

Olgo took the stairs like an old man. His knees cracked. The space between his toes was crammed with ice. But for feeling this dreary, would being eighteen again make any difference? He reached the front door, and because he was exhausted and cold and defeated even by the prospect of having to steal his wife back, he forgot to knock, just walked in.

"Hello?" Because while there were fluorescent work lights clamped to the lintels overhead, there was no one around to make use of them. "Hello?"

He looked around. Brick walls, peeling paint. The floors inches thick in debris, which crackled and skittered underfoot. A toilet moored in junk; machinery whose purpose he'd never know, rusty, limed, a tetanus party. It was like the industrial revolution had come to this place to blossom and die. He slipped, fell, and the plaster dust came over the sides of his legs like waves into a boat.

Laughter from the other end of the floor. He picked his way across. A wall, half-crumbled, hid his approach. He scanned for a breach, eye to the hole. And, wow, what a difference a wall makes. On his side was the collapse of industriousness in America; on the other was an IKEA showroom. Navy-blue couches with white trim, Chinese lanterns chandeliered from the pipes overhead, twenty people arranged around a table, cast in haloes of light, sipping tea. The floor, overspread with quilts; and in a corner, a wood-burning stove going full blast. Everyone shoeless, in bright wool socks that bunched at the toe, symbol of Christmas comfort the world round. Olgo could smell the tea, an herbal blend, sleepy and sweet, and felt his tongue unstick from his palate. He scoped the room for his wife and, not finding her, began to pay attention to the scene, which was the group listening to a speech by Thurlow Dan. Listening rapt, listening whole. Faces angled at the CD player as though it were the man himself.

Olgo tuned in. "It's like this," Dan said—assured but tender—"every person on earth is always, every second of his life, and in one way or another despite his good deeds, shackled to himself and suffering for it. We default to egotism and isolation. We default to the loneliest place a heart can go. But you know what else? Every one of us, consciously or not, also lives the lives of his generation and his peers—friends and family, the people we love—and so the task here is simple but huge: to rise above ourselves and see each other."

The track ended there. No one said a word, but all eyes shifted at what seemed to Olgo to be Olgo. Stares funneled and condensed in his peephole. He had not known he would show himself until this moment, when he was to be their star. His feet were asleep. Threads of wool cleaved to his neck as sweat watered his armpits and inner thighs, and it seemed from one second to the next that the blood was either draining from his limbs or storming through them. He was about to stand when a voice belonging to a man pressed against the other side of the wall began to address the group.

Oh, how stupid, these people weren't seeing him at all. His heart lunged at the speaker through the brick. It was Jonathan, of course, which meant that when Olgo rounded the wall, he seemed to be looking at not just Jonathan, but at Jonathan with Olgo's heart flopping around his feet like the day's catch.

No one was startled to see him. Jonathan put out his hand and said, "Ah, great, you're a little early, we weren't expecting the pledges for another hour, but welcome! We're so glad you came."

Olgo, who had sunk his fists into his coat pockets, removed one for a quick shake hello. He didn't want to blow his cover, though it was hard. Jonathan was depressing. Not especially young or handsome—he wore jeans and a hooded sweatshirt; his hair was thin and straight and piebald; no feature stood out for its beauty or size—which meant he had less tenable and thus more winning qualities to offer Kay Panjabi.

Jonathan said, "Come meet the others," and introduced them one by one. A mixed group of men and women, midthirties, forties, fifties, with nothing shared in their lives but the joy of their comportment. One gave him her seat on the couch. Her name was Teru. Used to be an accountant. Came into the Helix three years ago. Was thirty-five but looked eighteen. "Here," she said, and she passed him a mug of tea. "You look exhausted. Let me take your coat—my God, it's freezing!" He did as told—the coat really was cold and wet—and when she gestured at his boots and then at a corner where everyone else's were gathered, he let her have them, too.

"Fresh socks," she said, and she held up a pair—thick, woolly, ecru with blue heel and toe. He said thanks. The socks had been beached on the stove; they were warm to the touch. Teru vanished with his old pair like a nurse with the offending bullet.

A woman bearing a tray of peanut butter cups and caramel popcorn drizzled in chocolate and coconut shavings walked by. Olgo noticed a dish of oatmeal cookies on the table. This new woman, whose name was Myla, sat next to him. Tucked one foot under her thigh, put the dish between them, and said, "Whatever it is, don't worry. You're in the right place."

Her eyes were gray and swimmy, as if filmed in a clear lubricant that gave them the appearance of water. "Cookie?" she said, and she broke one in half.

He shook his head. He was getting tired. He flexed his toes, sipped his tea. Noted an aroma float into the room and waft around his face like a turban.

"Pie," she said. "Mixed berry. Fresh cream, too. I made the crust myself"—and here she smiled. "Pie makes pretty much everyone feel better. And if you're here, chances are it's 'cause you want to feel better."

Olgo looked past her. He said, "Is this it? Is this all of you?" He'd lost all hope that his wife was elsewhere, but then where was she if not here?

"There's more in the back. One's making tandoori chicken. Her specialty, apparently. Oh, no," she said, seeing his face, "how rude of me. I mean, there's vegetarian options, too."

"It's not that," Olgo said, and he upturned his nose, trying to detect something of his wife's favorite dish in the smell of mixed-berry pie. But it was no use—the pie overwhelmed. There's no fighting pie; there never was.

"You want to talk about it?" she said. "I'm all ears. When I came in, my husband had just died, and even though my friends and kids came by and took me out, it just wasn't any good. But I get what I need here. You will, too."

The irony was not lost on Olgo, who'd been trying to talk to pretty much anyone for three weeks, and here was this woman offering him the gold standard. Well, what harm in talking? Retain your pretense, betray no facts, but still: get it off your chest. But when he opened his mouth, he wasn't so sure or in control.

"I don't know," he said. "It's hard."

"That's okay," and she squeezed his arm. "There's no other world besides this one. No TV or radio, no clue what horrible things are happening out there. So just talk if you want. Otherwise we can sit and drink our tea, and that's not so bad, either."

"It's just—" But then he felt the hurt rush his mouth as though to secure a home there and never move out.

"For me," she said, "I didn't even know what I felt or why, just that I felt awful. And scared. Like maybe things were just never going to be right again. But look at me now." And Olgo looked; she looked calm and together and happy to be alive, which was the exact opposite of how he looked, he knew it.

The room was filling up with people from the outside, but still no

Kay. Jonathan made the rounds, extended his largesse without caveat, greeted everyone with the same smile and warmth and appeared to mean it equally. The discrepancy between the pledges and the members was overt and telling of the same story fifty times over. The pledges gathered in a circle: Jin, who oversaw cleanup at a Korean spa in D.C.; Mark, in town for his youngest daughter's wedding; Ruby, with newborn strapped to her chest, the child knocked out—but just wait.

Olgo, when asked to speak of his life, took a pass and blushed and felt a hand take his—it was Myla—and another take his right, Mark with the daughter-bride. Once around the circle, then twice. The more you told, the more the group applauded your candor, Jin winning kudos for confessing to a hand job or two at the spa—she needed the extra cash but also the gratitude; no one ever looked on her with that kind of gratitude at home—and Ruby for sharing the isolation of motherhood, the late nights and death-row thinking.

There were canapés on the table—goat cheese, wasabi crackers—more tea, and when the circle broke for dinner and Kay still had not appeared, with or without Jerry, Olgo returned to the couch and stared at the wall.

The pledges who'd spoken were thronged, he was alone, and it seemed like the Chinese lanterns had recast their glow from where he sat to where the confessants were. A member walked by; Olgo caught her sleeve and said, "So how does this work?"

She smiled. Sat opposite him on a canvas ottoman. Leaned forward with her hands clasped between her legs. "You share and belong and find what you need."

He winced and quivered at the lip. "But does it help?" he said.

"You tell me."

He took a deep breath, so deep that maybe it solicited his wife from the dark, because all of a sudden, there she was. Across the room. Seeing him but making no move in his direction.

"We are all kinds," the woman said. And Olgo smiled, but grimly. *We.* One of his favorite words. Who knew that it could turn on him, that something as steadfast as *we*—even the letters were bonded tight—could cede its joys to context.

Kay's hair was in a ponytail. Her sweater was pastel green. Behind her stood Jerry, who just shook his head and held the side of his face like he'd been slapped.

"I feel broken," Olgo said. "Totally confused. Like I don't understand anything."

And he took the long view. As a professional, he'd been reared in the ways of empathy and the seminal texts that gave it name. He knew all about having to activate something in yourself so that you could apprehend the thing or person before you. But he also knew about the urge to apprehend nothing, at least nothing coherent, and to be redeemed from the anguish of trying. What did he really know of other people? How had he spent his life divining intent and motive and need without having the vaguest idea of what went on in anyone's life but his own? And not even his own, for which failing he now had ample evidence? He took the long view and floated right up and out of his body. This woman had offered him help. His wife was on her way.

Bruce Bollinger, the director must not force the audience to cry because the hero cries.

A documentarian will follow his subject into hell and not come back. Not if the action is award winning. Bruce could hardly believe his luck. Kidnapping was bad, but six whores and a cult leader? This cult leader's double-crossing dad? The most engaging threat to the Union in more than a century grown from the rigmarole of people convened in mansions across America? How many filmmakers would kill for inside access to a story like that? This was God doing for Bruce what he could not do for himself.

Problem was, with every hour he was trotted around the Helix House, presumably to star in the ransom video, the place seemed to empty. People were vanishing. His options were vanishing! It was like scrambling for the last few seats in musical chairs. At first he'd wanted the dad, Wainscott, because, my God, the man had raised a cult leader, *lived* with this cult leader, and then betrayed him, though raising and living with the cult leader would have been story enough. Thurlow Dan was no Hitler, but didn't you wonder about Hitler's parents? Stalin's? Charles Manson's mom tried to sell him for a pitcher of beer, but there was only so much you could get on record. So, Wayne was the plan. The Early Years.

Problem was, Wayne had a seizure. What the hell. A phony seizure to get him out of the compound but also out of Bruce's reach. A second choice was the hooker, because those spikes pronged from her cheeks were just balls-out weird. And since he'd seen their simulacra on a girl at Crystal's place, he figured here was a trend worth noting. So, free of his hood and left in the charge of guards not remotely interested in guarding him, Bruce was able to wander off and hunt his story down. Hunt and fail and return to the cell, if you could call it a cell, only to find the bars had straggled and everyone was gone.

No small wonder. He too heard the helicopters. The sirens and bull-horn. He was aware HRT intended to storm the place, and he'd seen enough on Waco to know what this meant for him if he did not get out.

But he also knew he would not get another chance this good. Who'd want to buy video footage of his wife's hinky bladder? Decisions, decisions. To stay in the house was suicide, and so, what, the documentarian is suicidal? That was what he was saying? He was rapacious and hypersensitive and bearing out the artist's paradigm whenever he screwed someone over in the pursuit of his work, but suicidal? Bruce decided to make one more tour of the house, and if he came up short, he'd march right out the front door. Look, he'd settle for a guard. View from the bottom rung up. He'd settle for that! Please bring me a guard.

Down one hall and another, through the kitchen, back to the pantry, living room, office, another office, five more offices, and about to give up, when, apropos of a voice outside counting down—oh my God, they were counting down—his stomach sent up word it was time to find a bathroom. He began to run, opening doors, and nearly whacked in the head a guy crouched on the floor, sobbing. Bruce said in a commanding voice he didn't know he had, "Stay here," and got to the bathroom just in time.

For all that, it was slow going. The guy in the hall—his last best subject!—could leave. He rocked back and forth. Finally he ran out of the bathroom feeling vaguely nauseated for his efforts and looked at the spot where the man had been. Goddamn it. Only, the man had not actually left but retreated to a corner where he now sat upright, crying into his arms, which were folded across his legs, bent at the knee.

Bruce had worked with subjects in the field for years. He was not shy or awkward around strangers, even in the weirdest of circumstances. But this guy? He seemed unstoppable in the effluence of his grief, so that Bruce did not know what to say and was even a little afraid to say anything.

He tapped him on the shoulder. Nudged him in the leg. Said, "We need to get out of here, okay?"

Norman covered his ears. "Go away. Leave me alone. I want to die."

Bruce took a step back. "Okay, buddy. Let's get you out of here and then you can die. Sound good?" He wanted to stand him up so he could glean something of the man's role. A guard? The janitor? Bruce reached for his elbow.

Norman shook him off and looked up. His face was all bloat and jowl. "I was *crying*," he said.

"I can see that. But we're on a bit of a deadline. Know what I'm saying? You can cry after."

There was literature on the subject of how to deprogram a cult member, and much lore about a desperado named Black Lightning who went around kidnapping cultists for the purpose of deprogramming them, and about how this Black Lightning collapsed moral boundaries and made nominal the difference between free and captive thought, all of which material might have served Bruce well if he'd read any of it and not just printed a bibliography, which he barely skimmed, anyway.

Norman put on his glasses. "What's the point?" he said. "They're going to put me away for the rest of my life."

The fireworks in Bruce's heart were so boisterous, he could not believe this guy was not running for cover. The rest of his life! He must be important.

"I wasn't suggesting we waltz out the front door," Bruce said, all casual, not wanting to betray the lusty and viselike grip he was prepared to exert on this man if he didn't play along.

Norman seemed to perk up a little. "There's the tunnels," he said.

Good, good. The tunnels. They'd be found, of course, but not before Bruce was able to eke from their time together a little trust and the golden promise of exclusive rights and access.

"After you," Bruce said. And then, "I'm Bruce, by the way. And if you're wondering why I don't just walk out of here without you, it's because—" Though here he stopped. Norman was not listening, and this was fine. At least he'd gotten his name. Norman Sugg, chief of staff for Thurlow Dan, VP, second in command—jackpot.

They went to the basement, and as Norman was keying in a pass code, he said, "I guess I could live down here indefinitely. That wouldn't be so bad." He leaned his forehead into the metal of the door, which was more slab than door, and started to cry again, only without the purposed and cleansing intensity of before.

Bruce was beginning to see something of his wife in this man and was determined not to make the same mistakes. And so: whatever instinct tells you to say, say the opposite.

"Why don't we just take a break here for a second. It might help if you talked about it."

"Don't make fun of me. I've been through enough."

"I'm not making fun of you. What do you mean?"

Norman finished with the pass code—it was an incredibly long sequence; who could remember a sequence that long?—and waited for the door to open with obvious impatience because, where five seconds ago he was ready to languish and die, now he was energized with disdain for Bruce Bollinger.

"Here," Norman said, and he gave Bruce a hard hat with a light and reflector strips. "I need for you to stay safe."

Bruce nodded. Their dynamic seemed to redefine itself at a clip. It was hard to keep up. Maybe Norman thought he'd win points for good governance of the kidnapped? Bruce was running out of time. He imagined SWAT fanned out in the tunnels and waiting for them at every turn. He imagined Norman giving him the slip. He certainly seemed to know the tunnels well, never stopping at the forks or Ts. If only Bruce were half as confident. There were so many inroads into a man's trust. Be innocent, friendly, unafraid, curious. Ask about his family. His history with the Helix. Keep it local: So, what are your dinner plans? Ask questions that imply faith in the subject's good heart. He was still debating the right way in when they heard footsteps, or at least the suck-squish of feet in the mulch that passed for flooring in this place.

Bruce spun around to rake his light across the walls, looking for where to hide. Norman was unbothered. Bruce nipped his sleeve and tried to pull him from the center of the gangway. The suck-squish got closer, and with it the sound of two men who were, whatever they were, not SWAT. Bruce let out a whistle that died in fear because there were actually worse people to encounter in a tunnel than SWAT. The men were discussing oil revenue stymied by the Iraq war and laughing at this nonsense. They'd never been so rich.

Oh, right, naturally: The tunnels were witness to oil magnates in bathrobes and flip-flops.

Bruce could hear them chuckling well past seeing their lights retire. "Do I even want to know?" he said.

"You'll catch on," Norman said. And with that, they reached a door. A door back to the world where everyone wanted what Bruce had.

"No, wait," he said, and he slapped Norman's hand away from the intercom button and, for good measure, put himself in the way of the button, which had assumed for him the ruinous potential of the Red Button.

"Oh good," Norman said, "I deserve this," and he upturned his face and closed his eyes, waiting, it seemed, to be struck. So there it was. Strike a man and you own that man.

"Maybe I can level with you," Bruce said. "Maybe that's the best way to go here."

Norman narrowed his eyes and pushed Bruce out of the way with a single have-at-him. This man was incredible. Good-bye sheep, hello wolf. The door swung open just long enough for Bruce to pick himself off the floor and dive in. He nearly lost a foot in the jamb as it shut behind him with what sounded like the wheeze of an air lock. If he had been suddenly launched into space, he would not have been surprised. Already he felt the atmosphere of his grip on the world becoming less dense. He could hear Norman's feet slapping the tile floor, which suggested they'd moved from the public arteries to something financed.

"Wait up," he yelled, and he plunged down the hallway. At the other end were two doors, they looked like barn doors, and through the slits of their mismatch flared a light that was, even in slits, radiant. Seen from the back, Norman looked like a boxer headed into the ring. Bruce caught up with him, the doors parted, and only then did he realize he'd been subject to white noise that had grown into a din that was now the symphony of a casino packed with joy.

Oh God, he loved a casino. He'd sworn off the casinos and replaced their void with drink, but the swap had always felt short term. Unwise, too. Drink was less costly but also less lucrative, which was why, incidentally, the bank loan for *Trial by Liar* had failed him and why if he'd just done the prudent thing and continued to bet his way to freedom, etc.

He took a deep breath. An underground casino. Amazing. These days, to get to a decent casino you had to travel far, and often onto the Indian reservations, which were dry counties and annoying for it. Who wanted to poker through the night with Sprite and maraschino cherries?

The place-name was spelled out in vanity bulbs underscored with red tube lights. The Resistance Casino and Sports Lounge. By the entrance was a cherub statuette that doubled as a scanner, or so it appeared as Norman swiped a card across the cherub's face, once for himself and once for Bruce. They stepped inside and immediately Bruce teetered on the edge of hope. Really? Hope? Yes. On his left: the world's greatest subject for a documentary; on his right: the money to finance it just in case no one else agreed. He was excited but also relieved. As though he'd just loosened his belt after a large dinner. It had been six months since he'd dropped money in this way. And his paychecks from Interior went straight to the bank, though no amount of savings would get him and Rita out of the hole. Between them, they had eight thousand dollars and the house. And the car. Though the car was leased and the house was double-mortgaged. So they had eight thousand dollars. His credit card spending limit was a quarter of that. He couldn't even get an advance. He felt in his pocket for his Visa.

The books he'd read on addiction said that a need passes whether you give in to it or not. So you might as well hang tough. Because it would pass. And pass again. And again and again, and what book talked about that? He'd always want to be doing something great. Why was that an illness? The advice was retarded. In fact, trying to impose a rubric of thought on something as unwieldy as need simply made him feel all the more needy.

The gaming floor was arranged by square and corridor, so that each room bled into the next. It was huge. It was so huge, an area had been cordoned off for throwback, so that if you missed the good old days, here was a slot machine for you. The levers grimed in sweat. The jangle of coins in the hopper.

"I've only been here once or twice before," Norman said, "but in case you missed it, everything I believe in just collapsed upstairs, so what the hell, right? You get your betting card at that booth across the floor."

Bruce did not even hesitate; he flew at the booth and returned in seconds. So much was alive in this place for him. The black pile carpet snarled with orange and cyan, magenta and wheat. The colors dizzied by chandeliers and fluent across the walls, which were marble and bright. He'd put $500 on the card and took his place on a swivel stool at a bank of dollar slots. The touch-screen instructions told him what to do, not that he needed their guidance. He hit the Spin button. Lost $100, made $1.25. "Whoo!" he said. "Just getting started." He clapped his hands and rubbed them together.

Norman looked bored. He watched the others up and down the aisle. He sighed.

"You realize you're not helping," Bruce said. Four hundred dollars was three hundred. Wham.

"No one even recognizes me," Norman said. "I don't know any of these people."

"Casinos aren't for friends," Bruce said, and, by way of adduction, a man next to him caught his wrist in a tube attached to the respirator hitched to his wheelchair.

"This was a bad idea," Norman said.

Bruce waved him off.

"You're already out three hundred? You go down fast."

"Hey, you can be positive or you can take that doomsday shit elsewhere."

"Okay."

Bruce took a long breath. Muttered, "Don't go far," but never turned around to see which way Norman went. Two people were waiting for his chair. He could feel their eyes on the screen, watching his credit dwindle. He was hemorrhaging by the minute, and then by the second, unable to hit the button faster than he was losing money for it. So maybe Norman was more talisman than not. He pressed the button again, lost again, and heard as though for the first time the quiet at his back. Norman? He spun around. Ah, Christ, Norman was gone.

He popped off his chair, which actually felt like a popping, a freeing, because he'd nearly lost his mind for a second. Priorities, Bruce. Jesus. He scanned the room. Cruised the aisles. What the hell? The casino was not *pied*, it was just white, so how was this roly-poly black man able to blend in? He began to run. A woman in marching-band jacket and matching skirt was stopped at the end of a row, manning a cart of drinks. He bought two cups of whatever she was serving—*Ahhhhhhhhhhhhh*— smacking his lips, exactly the Scotch and soda he'd been praying for. He asked if she'd seen a black man. She said, "Once or twice."

He made for the bathroom. There were no pay phones anywhere, nor the usual spotting of people on their cell phones, either. He was not ready to call his wife, but it would have been nice to know he *could* when the time was right. Because the longer he waited, the harder it would be to pretend the delay was anything but vindictive. Rita wanted to name their kid after Thurlow Dan? Yeah? Maybe while she was waiting by the phone for Bruce to call, she could explain his absence to her swollen belly thus: Your namesake stole your dad. He'd call her the second he locked down Norman and secured enough money to back the film.

In the bathroom, the toilet seat was veiled in a cellophane doily that moved on its own. At the sink, the faucets were automated. The paper towel dispenser reacted to the motion of his hands. This was no place to be when probably the one thing that could stop your headlong plunge into financial destitution was the voice, the reason, the care of another human being, or even just a reminder that such humans existed and were worth being good for, which was precisely the kind of reminder dispatched by the robotic amenities on duty in the Resistance bathroom.

How could he have let Norman go? No, no, how could he have sent him away? Was nothing sacred next to gambling? Next to his work? Would he sell his wife for a buck, especially if the buyers trafficked in slave labor and prostitutes and had never told their story on camera before? The vampirism of art was pathetic—he knew it was pathetic— and yet there he was, teeth bared.

He was being methodical now, touring the rows of slot machines from left to right and stopping at ATMs as he went. Stopping and taking out the max from each. Shredding the receipts and leaving a paper trail. Pausing at a slot—just one—lose $100, make $1.25. Norman? He thought he saw the black hand of fate larking about the poker tables, and he headed that way.

An irony that frequents gamblers who are and are not addicted to gambling? They are and are not very good. Bruce took a seat at a table. High stakes, no dealer, just a friendly game among five. Four guys and, who knew, the queen of England; she was at least eighty and wore a Day-Glo pink suit and, pinned to her lapel, a diamond brooch shaped like the Commonwealth. She, more than the others, looked on him like fish food. The others were sizing up his affect for clues to his talent, while she plumbed his heart and knew he was doomed. Everybody in? Yes.

He hardly paid attention. He was in free fall, which was the madness he liked best. It was like adulterous sex when you knew your wife was due back any second; like sharing needles with someone you knew had AIDS; like driving through the desert with a tank on empty.

It was not about risk but ruin, not about chance but certainty, and though you didn't want your wife to find out, or yourself to end up with AIDS (there were easier ways to devastate or die), you'd still suffer this fate just for the thrill of its prelude.

Bruce tossed his chips as if feeding the birds and finally offered up his tower and watched as this tower was assimilated into a cityscape across the table.

He maxed out his credit card and bet his wedding ring. The queen of England said there was a special phone for guys like him and gestured at a console Bruce had not seen before. It looked like one of those car-rental kiosks in the airport. Call 123 for Visa, 456 for AmEx.

"Representative," he said. He pressed one, then two. Three for stolen cards. "Representative." Because if he got one on the phone, he'd say: My card was stolen, and I need a new one right now.

He watched the game wind down and started to press all the buttons at once. Goddamn it. "REPRESENTATIVE."

He returned to the table. Everyone in play seemed to have at his disposal many chips, silos of chips, so that it was just insulting to see his wedding ring back up for grabs. The man who'd won it had a braided ponytail, which he stroked lewdly every time he anted up, and more so when saying, "It didn't fit, not even my pinky."

My God. His wedding ring was going to pass from one asshole to the next. It wasn't even real gold. The man with the ponytail clamped Bruce's wrist midair. "The ring's in play. Leave it alone."

"I'll buy it off you."

Laughter.

Bruce reached for it again. This time, a hand clamped his neck from behind. Security. He tried to wriggle free, but the clamp was tight and siphoning off air he probably needed to live if this kept up. It didn't. The hand shrank from him like a bat from light, and when he spun around, the guard was gone; here was Norman.

"What the hell?" Bruce said.

"How about *thanks?*"

"Thanks. But what the hell?"

"The Helix has friends."

"The Helix is over."

"Correct. But news travels slower down here than you'd think."

"I'm sorry about before. This is not a good place for me. I have a—a *history*. Can we go somewhere and talk for a second? I want to talk to you."

"I don't feel like it," Norman said, and he sank his hands into his pockets.

"I don't think you understand. You have to talk to me. You're my only way out at this point. Don't you see the wreckage of my life piling up all over this casino?"

Norman shrugged. "When Thurlow and I were kids, one Halloween we were the Hamburger Helper hand. We spent months sewing pillow cases and making the hand big enough for two, but then when it was time to trick-or-treat, we realized we forgot to make eyeholes for us both. Only he could see. Even then I thought it was a metaphor."

Bruce heard a siren go off two banks down—someone had won a jackpot. He tried to focus. He said, "I just don't get it, really. My wife got all excited about the Helix, but I couldn't understand what she was excited about. When I pressed, she'd just get angry and say I was badgering her, and God forbid I said maybe it was the hormones—she's pregnant—well, that made it even worse."

"You told your pregnant wife she's hormonal?"

Bruce laughed. "I know, I know." And something in him dislodged, because when was the last time he was met with compassion on any topic, especially the thousand missteps he'd made with his wife? When was the last he indulged the camaraderie of a guy who, just for being a guy, a straight guy anyway, understood what traumas inhered in the pleasing of your wife? He said, "It's rough out there, lemme tell you. My son's due in a little less than four months."

"You got a name for him?" Norman said.

"No"—and he shrank into himself and vowed not to say another word.

"The thing about the Helix," Norman said, "people used to say Christianity was a cult, too. Anything that's a threat to convention is a cult, which is the saddest part of all, because when did this horrible loneliness get to be the norm, so that whatever tries to break it down is threatening? None of us expected Thurlow was going to kidnap anyone."

"Fair enough," Bruce said, swearing not to talk, not another word, "except for the part where you're urging people to civil war or whatever and still thinking the man is Mother Teresa? Isn't half your manifesto about leaving the Union and governing yourselves? What's that got to do with bringing people together? In fact, now that we're talking about it, the stupid fucking Helix is ruining my marriage. It's not the money or even that I'm irresponsible or that my priorities are screwed; it's the fucking Helix. Tearing my *union* apart. So, yeah, big success over there. Huge. *Congrats.*"

Norman's face went dead, and what light had crawled into his eyes went dead, too. He said, "There's someplace I have to go. You are on your own."

Was Bruce the worst documentarian ever? He was. "No, please, wait. I'm sorry. It's been a long day. I was kidnapped? Look, I'm sorry. Let me go with you. We can talk some more."

"Thanks, but no. I paid my dues cocounseling. I was thirteen and doing RC in New York. Thirteen! I *discharged*. I've cried and yawned and laughed my guts out. I've been looking for a place to fit in all my life, and all my life has brought me to is this. Can't you just leave me alone?"

"How about I come with you without talking?"

"It's a free country," Norman said, and he walked away.

They left the casino. By now Bruce had gotten the idea there was a second life here below Cincinnati. Clubs and bars. Spas and brothels. Whatever could not be conducted aboveground was encouraged below. They walked the tunnels as before, and this time when they passed three guys toting gunnysacks, and one stumbled, so that a hundred official Major League baseballs rolled out and crowded their feet, Bruce said nothing, just bent down to help. It did occur to him to filch a ball and whistleblow—See? They're juiced! Right here in Ohio!—but only for the second it took the bearers to read his mind and threaten his life. At least, such was conveyed in the hairy eyeball coming off each one.

Finally, they came to another door. Bruce looked for the card scanner—he was going to be helpful from now on—but there was none. They broached the front desk, where a woman flipped through a binder of names, looking for Norman's. She wore a headset, which freed her hands to fly about her face as she yelled into the mouthpiece because the system had been down for *hours*, and it was Neanderthal having to thumb through a binder looking for guest names and IDs. "Think it's good business when one of the Supreme Court justices stands here while I'm trying to figure out which one he is, and he's like, Name rhymes with *urea*—which isn't helping me any—but what am I supposed to do, let him in? He could be, what's those two, Woodward and Bernstein, so look, my point is, when's the system going to be fixed? Ugh, hold on"—and she found Norman on the list and asked for his ID, and when that cleared she let in Bruce, too, because Norman was high Helix, enough said.

She buzzed them through frosted glass doors.

Bruce did not ask where they were headed—*No talking*—and then they were there, in a theater that sat three hundred inside soundproofed, padded walls. The energy of the room was condensed in two guys who were beating the crap out of each other in a wire-framed cage. The fighters looked like soccer dads nabbed from home in the middle of Sunday sports. Like Fight Club for fatsos. One wore a football jersey and cargo shorts. The other was in a green henley and chinos. The audience was three-sixtied around the action; the bleachers were wood, the ceiling a rig of spotlights and flood; and because the space was not much bigger than the concentric arrangement of show and crowd, steam appeared to rise off everyone without prejudice.

Bruce said, "What the—"

Norman skirted the ring and had words with a referee, who wrote something down on a clipboard. The ref made room for them in the front row. Their neighbors were cased in garbage bags, which made sense to Bruce only when the sweat rained down on him two seconds later.

"I don't believe this," he said. "What is this?"

Norman flagged down a vendor and bought a hot dog. "It's amazing, right? You ever see *Ultimate Fighter* on TV?"

"Yeah, but those are real fighters. Athletes. These guys are—I don't know what they are."

"Sure you do. They're just normal guys."

"That one's got an inhaler."

Norman made short work of his dog. "Once you get a feel for it," he said, "what does any of that matter? This serves a purpose. I signed up."

Blood and cracklings oozed from one of the guy's kneecaps. Bruce visored his face as flings of skin came at him.

"Signed up to do what?" he yelled. As the sound of the crowd was in ebb and flow, Norman's words were more or less audible. He looked at the audience. On many legs were thousand-dollar jeans perfectly aged and smelted at the knees. Designer T-shirts and jewelry soldered to taste. These people were rich—that much was clear. He needed a camera; he asked Norman's advice.

"Oh, you're just not very smart," Norman said. "God knows why the feds sent you."

Since Bruce had no idea, either, this did not mean much. He pressed. Norman said, "You think you'd be getting out of here alive with a camera? You think being held at the Helix House was scary?"

"Yeah, but it can't be long before the feds come down here looking for me. Or *us.* I'm a little surprised they haven't shown up yet."

Norman laughed and wiped spit from his cheekbone. "They aren't coming here. If they come down here, they'd have to *explain* here. And how good's that going to make them look?"

"Oh," Bruce said, feeling shoots of panic rise up from the mulch his brain had become over the last few months. Norman was right. Probably when deals were brokered between overtly hostile nations, it happened here. Diplomats fondling twelve-year-old girls? Down the hall. No one was coming for Bruce. No one at all.

When the fight was over, an MC stepped into the cage, followed by ring girls who upheld news of the docket. Next up: the walk-ins.

Bruce began to get a bad feeling. He said, "Maybe it's time to go, huh?"

"Sure," Norman said. "You go on without me. I'm up." He gave Bruce his wallet and keys and in so doing seemed to forsake more than the miscellany of his pockets. He mounted the three stairs to the ring and the gate swung open. On the other side was his opponent, who wore a black catsuit, a cape, and Oreo face paint that might have seemed doggerel if only. His hands were pork loins. He could probably clock Norman from the other side of the pen, such was the length of his reach. He weighed three hundred pounds at least.

Norman did not even hesitate, just looked up at the ceiling, maybe at God, and stepped in. The gate shut behind him. *Click* went the lock.

From his pocket the referee pulled a laminated card that was encomium for all things barbaric and unfair. In gist: Poke each other's eyes out, anything goes. Agreed? If so, let's get it on.

The Orca—because that was what he was called—backpedaled around Norman, who seemed to have committed to a spot in the middle of the ring. He didn't follow the Orca with his eyes or even flinch when the thing came up behind him to speak his intent just in case Norman thought this was going to end well.

The crowd began to jeer. "Put 'em up, black boy!"

Norman, who'd been lock-eyed with the floor, upturned his cow face and smiled. The Orca knocked him down with one hand, and the crack of his head against the floor—and the floor was vinyl foam, which discouraged this sound 99 percent of the time—roused from the audience a gasp that turned to laughter when Norman smiled anew, got up, and returned to the spot of his choosing. The Orca's face paint was dusted in glitter, and his catsuit was made of rubber, and though the costume had none of the pathos that halos your average clown, it still should have beat out for pity Norman's carriage in the moment. But no. Norman was, in the outpouring of his body and the soul inside, effigy for the Bozo punching bag Bruce once whaled on as a kid. Weighted at the bottom, always coming back for more. People celebrate resilience, and mostly Bruce did, too. How else to scrape himself off the floor every day he woke up unsuccessful and broke? But still, every now and then, looking at himself in the mirror, he'd catch sight of Bozo and his stupid optimism and think: Just for today, don't bounce back.

The Orca, who'd probably grown up bullying kids at school, was undeterred by the ease with which Norman went down. Only it was not so entertaining, and the audience was getting mad. The Orca tried to spice things up, reverted to choreographies that had made his career in the WWF. Except it was hard when only one of you knew the moves and the other just wanted to die.

Bruce started to yell. "Get up, Norman! Fight back!" He came off his bench and pressed his face to the grille, and the chain link grooved his skin, but so what? He rattled the cage and, unbelievably, started to cry. He knew about this kind of thing, okay? As a kid, he'd been classed among the weak and advised by teachers schooled in permutations of self-disgust to give himself a break. As an adult, he dismissed this advice and hated himself thoroughly. Norman, fight back! But no, he was in a heap and not getting up.

Bruce plunged his arm through a diamond hole in the cage and groped for Norman's hand; he just wanted to hold his hand. Was everyone template for someone else's feelings? Norman had to bounce back because, who knew? one more bounce and the Orca might go out with a heart attack, because life couldn't beat you down every second of every day; there had to be some successes here and there. Get up, Norman! He strained to reach into the ring, and finally he managed to tap Norman on the arm.

The Orca went wild. "Tag team!" The grin on his face was so big, his gold fang implants caught the light from the overheads.

"Tag team!" went the crowd, and like that Bruce was borne up on the needs of three hundred. He tried to resist but was pushed through the cage door so fast, it locked shut before he could reestablish contact with the workings of his inner ear and stand upright. The Orca, meantime, had straddled the top rail and was brandishing his arm as though he held a lasso. Bruce scrambled for Norman, who was attempting to pull himself up by the cage wire and fishing words from the blood welled in his mouth, words like, "Get out of here," and "I don't want your help."

The Orca came off the rail. Bruce looked into his eyes and was horrified to see in them the weary acquittal of a guy who just can't afford to retire. He must have been at least sixty.

Bruce backed up into a post and then, like a rodeo clown himself, tried to draw off the Orca from Norman, who was still scaling the fence with the intent to escape—or so Bruce told himself.

He put up his hands, palms out, and when this failed to stall the Orca, and when the Orca was, essentially, on top of him, he counted it down. One: Even if there were a phone anywhere in this nightmare, he couldn't call his wife, not anymore. In fact, he couldn't even go home. Not without a wedding ring. Not having exhausted their savings. Two: He'd had the greater share of moral authority between them for a whole day, and he'd blown it, and for what he'd done in the casino, he would never get it back and would probably have to yield the raising of their son to her, because he couldn't think of a single quality that suited him to the privilege. Three: He drew back his fist and let it rip.

Probably, though, he should have looked. His bones glanced off the Orca's elbow. Only Bruce was hurt. He stuffed his hand under his armpit, then sucked on his knuckles and winced like it was sour candy.

The Orca was scandalized. The crowd was festive. Go get him, Orca!

Bruce lay down, recalling advice he'd once gotten from a trail guide in the Adirondacks—Just play dead—which he and Rita had done in their tent as a bear pawed through their cooler, and which he did for the rest of that night because she was ovulating and he was terrified. Why hadn't he been more supportive? Tried harder? Maybe if he hadn't been so afraid, she'd have gotten pregnant sooner and not needed IVF or bed rest. Maybe, in the clarity imposed by news of a child on deck, he'd have honed his talents or gone to therapy. Why he'd been clutched with self-loathing every day of the forty-two years it had taken to get him spread-eagled on the cage floor, he did not know, except that self-loathing was the problem, self-loathing was the devil. He saw Norman get up and lurch his way, wanting, it seemed, to supplant him on the mat. And then he saw the Orca balanced on the top rail as sweat poured down his cheeks and streaked his face paint, and, as the Orca vaulted off the rail and scissored his thighs in the classic wrestling finisher, the guillotine leg drop, intending to land one on Bruce's neck, he saw all of this and thought: When I wake up, my life will start over.

Bruce woke up. He vomited down his chest. If his pancreas came tumbling out his mouth in the next heave, he wouldn't mind; he'd never felt worse in his life. The most profound hangover he'd ever had—twenty-two grasshoppers plus a fifth of tequila the night Rita said she was pregnant—was Disney compared with the variety of afflictions at work in his body. The guillotine leg drop strikes again. He'd been head-traumaed, which did not even come with the benefit of amnesia. His thoughts perseverated. Where was Norman? Was he okay? He tried to sit up. Rolled back his eyelids just enough to case the room. Empty but for the bed he was on. A woman at the door in a nurse's uniform. She peered at a chart and whispered, "You're going to be fine. Let me help you change out of that mess." Where was Norman? Was he okay? He slurred out the words as best he could—Christ, he was slurring. She said, "I'll be back to check on you in a little bit," and left the room. There were flowers in a corner. He eased himself off the bed to read the card. Who'd send him flowers with a card? It said, *I'm sorry. Best wishes, Fred Spitalowitz, a.k.a. the Orca.* It was hard to make out in the dark, but the O appeared to double as a smiley face, which brought to mind the Orca's real face coming right at him, so that he threw up all over again. It seemed to Bruce he threw up more than anyone he knew. He crawled back to bed and had nightmares.

Someone was tapping his shoulder. Norman? It was not Norman. Not the nurse, either. He thought for a second it was Rita, but only because whenever he saw a beautiful woman, it put him in mind of Rita.

The woman, satisfied that Bruce was awake, took a seat opposite his cot, which seemed to have turned into a queen. He was sure there'd been no chair there before and now, suddenly, a La-Z-Boy? Also, the bedding seemed to have improved. She offered him a box of tissues, which had also materialized out of nowhere. Maybe he should ask for a Porsche, because, quite obviously, he was dead, and here was the genie to prove it.

"How are you feeling?" she said.

"Who are you?" He sat up and swung his feet off the mattress, only they didn't reach the floor, which was so infantilizing, he drew the blanket to his chest and scurried for the headboard. In brighter news: the pain behind his ears had subsided, and he even felt interested in food. How long had he been knocked out?

"If you're hungry, I can have something prepared for you in no time."

A mind reader. Wonderful.

"Anything in particular? The doctor says you are cleared to eat whatever you want."

He patted himself down. Was there surgery? What had the Orca done to him?

"No surgery," the woman said. "Just a concussion. And I know how you feel. I just had one myself."

Bruce looked at her warily. She really was reading his mind. She picked up a phone and said, "Roast beef on rye. Muenster, bacon, avocado, honey mustard."

"What's going on?" Bruce said. "Only my wife knows I like that sandwich."

"Maybe I'm your wife."

"That's not funny." Unless—wait, did he have amnesia? He looked at his body. Mole on his knee he'd had removed twice—once for vanity, once for prudence—to no avail. Rubble heels, because he would not put cream on them at night, and the one time Rita had persuaded him to sleep in socks filled with Lubriderm, he'd had a wet dream that embarrassed them both. Pale swath of skin on his ring finger because he was the world's biggest loser. Nope, he remembered everything.

The woman smiled. "I'm just saying I can be anyone. We've met before."

Bruce did not have enough ex-girlfriends from which to pool the one crazy whose likeness he'd blotted out. A colleague? Maybe one of the homeless from *Trial by Liar*? He shook his head and said, "I'm sorry, I don't remember. I just want to go home. I miss my wife. Probably she's going to leave me, but I still want to see her before it happens."

Someone came in with a trolley bearing a giant sandwich under a stainless steel dome. A can of Dr Pepper, a basket of hard pretzels, and possibly the greatest and most counterintuitive pleasure on earth, carrot cake. He wanted to ask more—Where am I?—but the food was Svengali in its hold on him. He felt ligatures of beef fat wedge between his teeth and rejoiced.

"I'm sorry," she said. "Fred got a little overzealous with my instructions."

He shook his head. He preferred not to dignify the man with a name. He was the Orca. Now and forever, the Orca.

"I don't understand. Are you saying you run that show? Is that it?" He'd finished his sandwich and pretzels and was scraping the frosting from the carrot cake to save it for last. If this woman had come to silence him, fine. Unless she wanted to *buy* his silence, which was even better. "I was with a guy in there, a short black guy—any idea what happened to him?"

She crossed her legs. And only now did Bruce notice she wore some kind of military uniform.

"Norman, yes. He's fine. I got him on a plane to someplace nice. I've always liked him. He's had a rough life, but he'll be all right now."

Bruce had the first coherent thought he'd had in a while. The feds. Good grief, he was a moron. *Someplace nice.* Like Guantánamo. Why the feds and the Mob were always talking in this arcane patois everyone understood anyway was beyond him. Still, the feds had hired the Orca? To do what?

"Apprehend you," she said. "But the feds didn't hire him, just me. I've got people all over the Sub. But no one was supposed to hurt you."

"Can you stop with the mind reading?"

"Maybe if your thoughts weren't so primitive, I wouldn't keep guessing right."

"So now you're going to insult me? You'll have to do better than that. My wife calls me a caveman ten times a day."

"Oh, right," she said. "I almost forgot," and she retrieved from her pocket Bruce's wedding ring.

He snatched it and shoved it back on his finger and felt greedy and fearful and gnomish.

"Are we on better terms now?" she said. "I did you a favor; now you do me a favor?"

He made for the door. It wasn't locked, but on the other side was a guard with his arms folded across his chest. He made for the curtains, and though he expected they were trick curtains behind which was a concrete slab, he was still shocked to see the concrete slab.

He didn't know what to say, and anyway, she'd say it for him: We're just a few miles from the Helix House. Outskirts of town. But no one's going to find us.

He was exhausted. He pressed his forehead to the slab.

"What do you want?" he said, and then aired every question he had: "Is it that you need me to go along with some story for the press? Whatever you tell me to say is fine. It's not like I have any answers of my own. Why send me and the others to the Helix House to begin with? The four of *us*? Why send a psychotic to play hero and break my neck? Why give me the most amazing and tragic documentary story ever and then take it away?" He closed his eyes and pictured Norman's face in the instant he'd lost the Orca's punishing rage to Bruce—the disappointment and resignation writ into his every pore—and said, "Just leave me alone."

She joined him by the curtains. "I can fix at least one of these things. That's why you're here."

He laughed. "Unless you want to dump eight thousand dollars in my bank account in the next three seconds, I doubt there's much you can do for me."

"How's a hundred thousand?" she said.

"Funny."

She snorted and produced a bank statement, *his* bank statement, dated today, or at least one day after he last knew what day it was.

"Now do I have your attention?"

Martin drove him all the way back to Rockville. It took nine hours with stops for gas. Bruce lived just off the highway, half an hour from D.C., in a Cape Cod that looked regal, as far as he was concerned, he was so happy to be home. It was the middle of the night. They circled the house three times to make sure no reporters were there.

Martin killed the engine. "I'll wait out here," he said.

"I don't know. I have to talk to my wife. I'm not doing this unless she's okay with it, and I'm not going to rush her just because you're waiting." He said these words and swelled with pride. His priorities were like the stars—aligned in patterns no one could see from Earth, and all the more beautiful for it.

"I'll wait here," Martin said.

Bruce ran into the house and made straight for the bedroom. He was ready to grovel. He'd get on his knees and take Rita's hand and grind her knuckles into his eye sockets like a pestle to nut, if that's what she wanted. Had she been alone this whole time? He was supposed to have been gone only for two days and had not made plans for anyone to come help Rita beyond that. She'd have called a friend, right? If something felt wrong with the baby and it was 4 a.m., she'd have called a friend? He opened the door and yelled her name, but when he got to their bedroom, Rita still didn't seem to realize he was back. She was sitting up in bed, above the blankets. She wore sweat shorts and a sweatshirt. Her legs were parted, she slouched, but the moon of her belly was rising.

"Rita?" he said. His voice was gentle. He stood in the doorway and watched. Either this was his wife so furious she could not talk, or his wife kicked into a whole new register of feeling that was too refined for the language she had to express it.

"You missed the reporters," she said. "They've been here every day, only what's to see? I haven't left this bed."

She had yet to look at him—she did not appear to be looking anywhere—and he could tell from the musk coming off the sheets that she was in earnest. She had not moved since the second he'd been announced missing. No longer kidnapped, just missing.

"Baby, are you okay?" He did as planned and knelt by the bed.

"I answered the phone once, thinking maybe it was you, but it was just the press."

"I know, I'm sorry. But there was no way—" He paused, because even in pain, when her feelers were down, she always knew when he was lying. "I made the wrong choice," he said. "But would it mean anything to you if I promised things were going to be different? Starting tomorrow, I will look for work. Anything I can get."

Rita took his hands and slipped them under her sweatshirt. Her belly was warm and frosted in cocoa butter. "He kicked a lot while you were gone. Missed his dad, I guess."

He sank deeper onto his knees. It was true there were people out there worse than him, but that hardly mattered now.

"Go," she said. "I want you to go."

But he could not get up. He willed himself to get up—he owed his wife no argument—but he couldn't. It was what he deserved, to be cast out and abandoned and, in the bearing of this punishment, to be reminded of its cause. Only he could not bear it.

Rita touched his cheek. "I got another call, too," she said. And she told him all about it. A call from the woman on TV. The woman named Esme. Asking for Rita's permission, because there was a family outing she needed on film and only one person she wanted to film it, the documentarian who swears to see love where others cannot.

"Go," Rita said. "We'll still be here when you're done."

His body believed it before the rest of him. He stood up tall. And felt reconciled to the goodness in himself that had been, at last, ready to prevail. He kissed his wife and unborn. Made for the front door with no need to look back. In his mind's eye, a documentarian sees love where it is abundant.

In sum: one must learn to love one's people ardently.

They were together. As a family. Two fugitives and a child in a camper van, hurtling through the woods. Dad in the passenger seat, his wife at the wheel. His wife? Yes, his wife, driving like nuts, as their child in the back looked from one parent to the next, going: Wow. Just: Wow. How little they knew of each other. How little time they had left. She held a videotape to her chest. A gift from her dad. For after, he'd said, which turned out to mean: For after I am gone.

Bruce sat in the back with camera aloft. He'd arranged the lights and from this arrangement had developed a mood. Tender and elegiac, while the snows fell from Ohio to North Carolina. He felt, in the making of this film, like a balladeer, for theirs was the action of tragedy that's often told in song. But only from his vantage, which was not shared. The three were happy; they were on the road. In action: a country station yodeling its best, and a child whose parents were tributary to her needs. A child whose thoughts skewed from the brake that might pitch her through the windshield—she was rooted between the front seats, had refused the belt—to the man, the *dad,* in the passenger seat, whose presence did not reconstruct the geometry of her universe so much as animate the triangle she'd long imagined herself a part of anyway. My dad is famous. My dad is God. My dad is right here, with me.

Bruce did not say a word for the rest of the day; he just trailed the family as it went.

The van was registered to a woman who had died a few months back; Martin set it up. There were provisions for a week, though a day was probably the most they could expect. They drove in silence but always turning to look at one another. By nighttime, all Thurlow had managed to say to Ida was that he'd missed her. He was afraid to say anything else—he did not know her at all—but he marveled at the joy dawned in his heart just to have her near. He waited for her to sleep—maybe he could talk to her in sleep—but she fought to stay awake. Her eyelids rolled back with terror every time she nodded off; she did not want to miss anything. Thurlow felt this wide-eyed girl could see right through him. Finally, she went down. Neck angled like it might snap for the weight and bounce of her head against her shoulder, but holding fast.

He was not a strong man, but he could lift his daughter and tote her to a cot in the back. The rest was in his head. Dread of letting her fall. Dread of waking her up. Dread when she groped for his arm after he swaddled her in a blanket—for swaddling was all he knew of how to care for her—and then the retreat, like the end of an endless night, of every sorrow of every year intervening, as she said, half-asleep, "Dad. Don't go."

He and Esme spoke in the front. The future was bleak; they left it at that.

She told him about their meeting in North Korea. The DoI employees, her plan.

He told her about the ransom tape. His demands for wife and child. To have them back, to live as old.

Esme drove on without a word, though to everyone who saw this on film later, she seemed to glow, irradiated with feelings that, for their light and color, were as an aura that repelled the gloom of every day she'd spent without him.

"But why didn't you come six months ago?" he said. "Or six years? Why didn't you tell me what you wanted? Everything could have been different."

She gripped the wheel. It was fleeced and hot. She said, "I didn't know how. Please leave it at that. We have what we have."

They wended through the woods until the way was impassable by camper van. The roads were icy, the angles acute.

Esme pulled over. It was a Sunday dawn in the Pisgah National Forest; no one would be coming this way for hours. Only someone did come. He passed them, then stopped, because the van was not so much pulled over as whaled on the margin of a road that had no margin for this. Of the two, Thurlow was the more recognizable, so Esme took her chances. A stranger just trying to help. Were they okay? Yes, just camping. Did she know there was a turnoff just up the road? She did now, thanks, and with that, the man left without a hint of recognition;

he was old and hermited to the woods, and probably did not know the cold war had ended, either.

But Esme knew better. "Quick," she said, packing a bag and giving Thurlow one. "We don't have much time."

He did as told, but without vigor. Couldn't they stay in the van? Drive around? Just be with each other? He looked back on the camper with a heavy heart. It was not as if he didn't know where this would finish for him, all hours but one till the end of his days in a ten-by-twelve cell in the most isolating penal institution on earth. Where the government sent its evil, the evil and his beloved, who'd simply waited too long to know herself.

The astronomical center was close enough, and Ida, for having come here every summer for years, knew the way. She said, "Are we meeting Pop?" and from the lift in her voice Esme knew this was the apotheosis of joy for her child, to have parents *and* grandparents together at last. The right time to break the news had come and gone. Esme nudged her on.

For February, the weather was clement, and they were able to trek through the snow with ease. Flecks of light breached the canopy of leaves overhead, so it was not until they came to a clearing that the morning sun made its brilliance known. The trees were slick and pitched in tar, the ground painted new, and everywhere a glaze that refreshed the land as though no one had ever come this way before.

Thurlow looked up. A cloud drifted across the sky. "My God," he said, squinting. "What is this place?"

Ida skid across a patch of ice. "Come on, Dad, I'll show you."

His heart near broke for the sound of it. *Dad, Dad, Dad.*

Esme nodded. She was right behind them.

They reached the foot of a steel lattice that sprung 120 feet in the air. A radio telescope.

Ida said, "It's for listening to stuff from outer space. So we know who's trying to reach us."

Esme smiled. "That's right, tulip. Because the world's got ears, they're always open. Now come on. I've got a surprise."

There were landings all up the side of the scope, and stairs between each, and though Ida was scared, she didn't look down. In ten minutes they were in the dish, which was like sitting in some giant's breakfast bowl.

Gaps had let out the snow, so mostly it was dry. Esme opened her knapsack. She had powdered donuts and hot apple cider in a thermos.

"A picnic," she said. "How 'bout it?"

Ida wanted to know if they were allowed to be up here.

Thurlow laughed and grabbed his daughter and held her tight until he was red and wet in the face.

They got on their backs and stared at the sky.

"Hear anything?" Esme said.

"You're not supposed to *hear* them," Ida said, though she knew her mom was kidding.

Thing was, they all heard it—faintly but not for long—sirens closing in, wailing the news. Ida could have wormed up the side of the bowl and peered over the rim, but why risk it? The hours ticked by. They got twelve. *A Day in the Life of Family* was what Bruce would call it later. Look at the clouds, what do you see? My favorite food is grape jelly. I like skating and candy and coconut soap. My worst fear has been that this day would come and it wouldn't be enough, but it's plenty. I have been shadowing you for nine years. The mistakes we made. The child we had.

The film showed on PBS and was released on DVD. It made the evening news alongside the Intelligence Commission's report slamming the government for its failed assessment of WMDs in Iraq. After that, the pope died. News anchor Peter Jennings got lung cancer. Prince Charles and his paramour got hitched. And waiter Dave Franklin, who had just gotten off work at TGIF, had a first date with the Bakelite salesgirl of his dreams. Problem was, the date ended in the chagrin of sex. Nice girls didn't put out so freely, at least not with Dave Franklin, whose experience of women ranged from the close-but-no-cigar to the haha, no. In bed, he was cavalier. Assumed positions he had seen only on video. But after, he was mortified about his socks, black dress, which he had forgotten to take off. He turned on the TV and stared madly at the screen and hoped she would just go away. It was 4 a.m., and here was a documentary about that cult leader and his family of three, sipping cider in a radio telescope 120 feet in the air. The mother saying she'd hired the documentarian to film the daughter every month and to send her the tapes when possible; the father saying he wanted copies, too.

Meantime, the salesgirl had wrapped a sheet around her body because she really liked Dave but had maybe been frugal in the expression of her feelings, and so, she, too, stared madly at the screen. The film rolled credits. An epilogue said that three of the Helix House hostages had gotten home safely but that one died with his parents in a plane crash off the California coast. A few government officials were headed to jail. Most were not. The salesgirl fumbled for the right words, not *I like you,* but maybe, *Can we talk about it?* And as she thought it through and the screen went black, Dave took off his socks, and grew his heart just enough to fathom her own. He reached for her hand. Didn't let go.

Acknowledgments

Big thanks to the following people and organizations for helping me write this novel:

Bard College, the Corporation of Yaddo, Casa Libre, the MacDowell Colony, the Pisgah Astronomical Research Institute, Michael Bronner, Mary Caponegro, Martha Cooley, Steven Ehrenberg, Bill Geerhart, Myla Goldberg, Claudia Gonson, Michael Hearst, Brigid Hughes, Bill Karins, Patrick Keefe, Robert Kelly, Bradford Morrow, Nelly Reifler, Helga Siegel, Lydia Wills, John Woo.

Leigh Newman and Peter Trachtenberg, both of whom saved this novel from the trash.

Stacia Decker, a tremendous reader and agent, both.

Fiona McCrae, for her incredible guidance and unflagging engagement with this novel from the moment it fell into her hands. Also: team Graywolf, which got behind me and pushed.

Jim Shepard—again and again, with boundless gratitude, Jim Shepard—who shows me how it's done.

And finally: My family, in particular my brother (whose work on nuclear nonproliferation was invaluable to me), my stepdad, and my mom, whose response to *Woke Up Lonely* in draft—draft after draft after draft—spurred me on to greater extremities. I could not have written this novel without her.

A Graywolf Press Reading Group Guide

Woke Up Lonely

A Novel

Fiona Maazel

Discussion Questions

1. While Esme believes abstractly in Thurlow's ideas, she has a hard time buying the healing powers of the Helix: "Loneliness *was* a pandemic. . . . Thurlow had that right. It was the rest Esme couldn't get behind. Fellowship among strangers as antidote to a life's worth of estrangement?" (page 29). Do you agree or disagree with Esme? Do you think that Thurlow's philosophy is good and it's his practice that's flawed?

2. Ned posts to an online forum that "the thing about Luke is that he's able to do what no other Jedi has so far: he can feel love without turning evil" (page 55). Replace the word "Jedi" with "human being" and think about it. How many characters in *Woke Up Lonely* do terrible and selfish things for someone they claim to love? Do you think self-interest is ultimately the pandemic, not loneliness?

3. When talking to Lynne, who is actually Esme in disguise, Bruce reveals that, "I'm terrified [my job at the Department] marks the end of a period in my life when I tried to do something that mattered. I don't know who I am anymore. I am estranged from myself. Isn't that ridiculous?" (page 88). How are Bruce's thoughts ironic given his feelings towards the Helix?

4. In the midst of his attempts to make a ransom tape, Thurlow Dan says, "I would like . . . the chance to humanize this story so that among those for whom the expiry of my life will come as good news, there are two who might someday know of the sorrow wrought in my heart for them" (page 111). Do you think Thurlow's story humanizes his character? Do you feel sorry for him once you know the truth?

5. During his first speech, delivered at a college lecture hall while Esme is giving birth, Thurlow says: "Everywhere and all the time people are crying out for each other. Your name. Mine. And when you look back on your life, you'll see it's true: woke up lonely, and the missing were on your lips" (page 155). How does this statement thematically represent the book as a whole? Why do you think Maazel chose *Woke Up Lonely* for the title?

6. When Esme passes Ida off to Crystal for an ice skating trip, she realizes that "with love comes expectation" (page 135). What is this realization significant for Esme? Do you think her character changes throughout the novel? If so, how?

7. Though the Helix is a fictional movement, many therapeutic and even religious groups like it exist. Do you think communities of like-minded people can bring relief or do they further estrange us from reality? What aspects of the Helix appeal to you, if any?

8. On one of her notecards Esme writes: "I wanted to escape the fear born of love for you and Ida—the fear that there were feelings in this world that could undo your resolve to live isolated from the trauma and wreckage that come in train of relations with other people" (page 222). Why do you think love breeds fear, especially for Esme? Is it love that causes our self-interest or can love actually cure us?

An Interview with Fiona Maazel by John J. Kelly

First things first. Why did you choose Cincinnati to create the underground city of vice, complete with its brothels, gambling joints, and other devilish temptations for the full-fledged armed standoff that takes place in *Woke Up Lonely*?

I chose it primarily because who would suspect such things are transpiring just below the bedrock of Cincinnati? Who would notice a cult compound in one of the more tony neighborhoods of Cincinnati? That and I'd been reading about the Underground Railroad and about the actual tunnel system under Pyongyang and saw a connection there I could exploit.

From early on Esme believes that, as you write, "people who were dead inside would do most anything." Do you believe that is the root of most cults?

No, I think cults tend to attract people who are very much alive inside. Alive with feeling that has no outlet, no image of itself in the world, and no way to understand itself. So if you are confounded by your inner life and searching for help, a cult can seem more than palatable. I'm sure I'd be vulnerable to a cult insofar as cults are insidious and crafty and very good at finding your weaknesses and using their cure as bait. If someone invited me to a Super Smart Writers Club and said all the Super Smart Writers were in it and *only* the Super Smart Writers, well, I can see myself walking that plank.

What kind of research into cults and cultish activity did you do while writing this novel?

Oh, I read a ton. About Waco and Ruby Ridge for the stand-off stuff, and then mostly about political cults and therapeutic communities like est. I think I've said this elsewhere, but orthodoxy—religious fanaticism, et al—is very hard to write about because it is always and only one thing. It's one dimensional and just can't provide that much of interest for a writer to sustain over the long haul. This is why the Helix is so flexible; it's many things to many people. This is also why it falls apart—because it's *too* many things.

Much of the plot revolves around this hostage crisis, but it seems like this novel is even more about the problems of loneliness, isolation, and divisiveness in America today. What was it that inspired you to write about these topics and what were some of your most surprising discoveries as the book took shape?

I've long been preoccupied with loneliness. It seems central not just to the human experience but to any discussion of our empathic facility—as individuals, a group, a country. Loneliness feels epidemic to me sometimes, though really not because of social media, as so many people like to ask me. Social media cuts both ways in that it can help people who are already isolated and harm people who use it to replace more traditional forms of camaraderie like, for instance, Capture the Flag. Regardless, I wanted to think about what loneliness looks like for people who are actually not solitary creatures. Who have families and friends and employment. What does loneliness feel like for them? How does it manifest? What will they do to fix it? As for surprises, that's a tough question. I'm not sure. I guess I am always somewhat surprised by how my plots unfold. I knew I'd be writing about a cult leader, his ex, and four hostages, but I had no idea what would become of the hostages once they got out. Those sections are, to my mind, the best in the novel, but I hadn't planned them.

So many of the characters seem to be at odds with their true identities and feelings. Doesn't it seem paradoxical that while we can have all sorts of real friends who we communicate with at our jobs or on the Internet, we feel even more alone than ever?

Not to me, no. Your question is based on the idea that friendship can correct loneliness, when, in fact, friendship can correct solitude. Loneliness is all about being unreachable and unknowable *despite* having friends. Often, friends just make things worse because of the very premise you've offered up here, which most people embrace. Why am I so lonely when I have so many friends? It'd be nice to let that question go. To me, it sounds like: why do I have brown hair when I have so many friends? Two totally unrelated things. Sure, there are degrees of loneliness that can be assuaged by friendship or even a chat room, assuming your brand of loneliness actually proceeds from a deficit of friends. That exists; I'm not saying it doesn't. I'm just interested in a more chronic, deep-seated feeling that we are all walking through life utterly alone in body and soul.

The main protagonist, Thurlow Dan, is such an unrelenting enigma. He's literally uncomfortable in his own skin; a fat man in a thin body constantly counting calories. You portray him like such a kind and loving soul, but regardless of his tens of thousands of acolytes and followers, his one true love, Esme, eludes him throughout the novel. His level of self-loathing is phenomenal. Did you originally intend for him to be so completely screwed up?

Yes! That was an easy call for me. You know the old saw about dentists having ugly teeth and therapists being crazy—in this spirit, it made sense to me that a man spearheading a cult that wants to cure loneliness should, himself, be shot through with grief for his errant wife and child, utterly estranged from the world, and, okay, fat in a skinny body.

One of the interesting plot lines is Thurlow Dan's and the Helix's interactions with North Korea and Dear Leader Kim Jong Il, which gets the rapt attention of the CIA and other US investigators. Other than the obvious bizarre and disturbing news flashes regarding North Korea, was there anything else that prompted you to link the Helix and that country?

So many things, really. North Korea is the last black spot on the map. The Hermit Country. A place whose ethos seemed to dovetail nicely with the Helix's mandate. North Korea is itself a cult—it governs like one—while also celebrating the individual and his pioneering spirit, even as it's a communist state. I imagined my cult leader would find many things of interest there. Also, after seeing a spot on *60 Minutes* in 2007, I think, about four American GIs who crossed the DMZ to live in North Korea, I got fixated on these guys and wanted to include them in the novel. I couldn't believe four soldiers were living there unknown to the rest of the world, but very much a presence in Pyongyang. They all became movie stars in propaganda films. I could have written an entire novel just about them.

Obviously, so many people are drawn to this novel because they experience the same contradictory emotions as so many of the characters you've created. Has it ever struck you that simply by writing this novel you are also helping people recognize that they are not alone in their loneliness, just as Thurlow Dan tries to provide hope?

I hadn't thought of the novel as a therapeutic offering beyond knowing that any novel—if done well—can relieve people of the anxiety of feeling alone with themselves. So if that's the case with mine, I am very pleased.

The novel features a lot of spying and surveillance and you've said that the film *The Lives of Others*, which is all about people whose entire existence is closely monitored because of perceived potential political threats, was an early inspiration for this novel. Americans have put up with a slow, but steady increase in the way their privacy is invaded. Do you believe we've allowed this to happen in exchange for a better sense of security?

Ah, now we're getting into it. I think we've relinquished our civil rights in the *name* of better security, but I have no idea if we are actually more secure than we were before the government began its illegal dragnet of our phone conversations and emails. But even so, I guess the real question is: Is it worth it? Would I rather give up certain freedoms if it means staying safe? Well, you can see where that kind of bartering might lead us. So for me, the answer is no. Democracy can never be taken for granted; it has to be kept up like anything else. Give a little here, a little there, and before you know it, we're living in a police state. So I'd rather keep my right to privacy and worry more about Al-Qaeda than less, though I realize I say this from the comfortable position of assuming Al-Qaeda won't be bombing my house.

It seems like most of your characters in *Woke Up Lonely* are fighting or afraid of being empty inside or out of touch with their feelings. Have you experienced this in your life and what kinds of things do you do be as alive and in the moment as possible?

I'm sure everyone has experienced this in his/her life and that I'm no exception. A version of this question I got on tour a lot was: Are *you* lonely? And my answer varied from night to night. Sometimes yes, sometimes no, it really depends on how I'm thinking about loneliness in the moment. As for being alive, this is not hard for me. I listen, I look, I pay attention to what's happening around me. Done.

This book has received such enormous praise and a number of reviewers have praised your ability to mix pathos with comedy, when appropriate. When you are in the process of writing are you making a conscious effort to incorporate humor and if so why is it important?

Actually, most of the time, I often feel like a bouncer at the door who rejects humor nine out of the ten times she shows up pleading to get in. Humor is a default for me, and can be really destructive. Humor can deflect feeling, resist feeling, guard against feeling in ways that deny your work the very pathos you've tried so hard to generate. Humor can also provide some relief from gravitas that's verged on the sentimental or melodramatic. So it's a great tool, but something I need to use sparingly. I think I did better with it in this novel than in my first. I think my first novel was a little too antic, though some people said they laughed out loud. But I don't know how many people are doing that as they read *Woke Up Lonely*.

Without giving away the ending, there is a bit of redemption at the end of *Woke Up Lonely*. Did you want to be sure that readers finished with a "reason to believe"?

Yes! Some readers have said the book is unremittingly bleak, which upset me. *I* thought the novel was shot through with hope, especially by the end. It's bittersweet, but still, I wanted people walking away with a sense that most of us are good and that good things are possible, even likely, if you just stick around.

I'm interested in your process as a writer. Do you ever do any outlining or do you just let the plot and characters take you where they may go? Also, what do you concentrate more on developing, plot or character?

Depends on the project. I didn't outline my first novel, but I planned rather carefully for *Woke Up Lonely,* though I kept having to revise the plans because they weren't working. I couldn't get the book off the ground when it opened with the four hostages. And I couldn't make Thurlow's sections work when his video narration was delivered as just one block instead of being stippled throughout an account of what was happening to him as the siege progressed. So I had to do a lot of revising and rethinking over multiple drafts until I got it where I wanted. But still, I had an outline. As for plot or character—I don't think you can really treat them separately. "Character is fate"—good old Novalis—and I agree. So there're really no point trying to develop plot without thinking about character or vice versa. I do them in tandem.

You've been compared with such great novelists and short story writers as Kurt Vonnegut and George Saunders. What other writers' work do you enjoy or have been influenced by? In particular, are there any writers who make you laugh?

Dorothy Parker makes me laugh. James Thurber. George Saunders absolutely cracks me up. The list is long. As for influence, I really struggle with that question because I just don't know. I've read only one Vonnegut novel, and only because so many people kept saying our fiction is similar. I guess I just don't understand influence or how to gauge it. I'm sure everything I've ever read has influenced me in some way. I know that sounds like a cop-out, but it's really not; it's just that I don't know. All I know is what I like. For instance, I'm not sure *Crime and Punishment* makes a showing in my aesthetic, though I'd be delighted if it did.

I know (from a video on YouTube) that you work with a card hanging above your typewriter that gives you inspiration to write great prose. Can you tell the story of what's written on that index card?

I've actually had many cards above my desk over the years, but the one that's there now says: *Jim thinks I can,* which dates back to an email correspondence I had with Jim Shepard—who's a great writer and who was my first fiction professor in college. I was really despairing about *Woke Up Lonely,* about being able to revise it well, about being able to turn it into anything other than the mess it was. And I think Jim probably wrote back something like: I think you can do it, just remember that. So I decided to remember it quite literally, and wrote it on a card and put it where I'd need to see it. Incidentally, I love that you think I use a typewriter. But no, just a boring old computer for me.

I can't finish without asking you what you're working on now. Can you give us a preview?

I can! I'm working on a new novel called *What Kind of a Man.* It's about emotional incoherence. About being unknown to yourself. Coming to a bookstore near you in, oh, five years or so.

Portions of this interview first appeared in City Beat Weekly *(Cincinnati).*

Book Notes: A Playlist for *Woke Up Lonely*

Fiona Maazel

I can't listen to music when I write. If I listen to music, I end up listening, and since I can't even drive a manual vehicle, this requiring of me too many actions at once, imagine me trying to listen and write at the same time. I can, however, listen to music before I work, which is what I generally do. I can put words on paper whenever I want, but if I want them to be any good, I need to be able to lay bare my inner life and to be as vulnerable about it as possible. And since I'm generally a guarded person—someone once told me my defenses were gothic in terms of their rigor and intricacy—finding ways to shed the armor often includes listening to music. Okay, sometimes I just think of whatever painful things have happened to me until I get just upset enough. Sometimes I'll read some short fiction I find especially moving. But mostly I'll listen to music because music is penetrating and immutable insofar as I can't dilute its power of effect.

"Lonelier Than This," Steve Earle

In the way of research for *Woke Up Lonely,* I read a lot of books on the topic of loneliness and solitude. But I also listened to a lot of music on the subject, which turns out to comprise ninety percent of the music out there. While writing the novel, I listened to this song compulsively and was struck dumb by Earle's notion of people calling out to each other in vain: "Maybe this is as good as it's gonna get and I'll always be this way. I'll just wander this world callin' out your name." Seemed like a great way to describe what *loneliness* feels like—the hopelessness of it all. The pathos. So it's no coincidence that throughout the novel, references to calling out for each other abound.

"Darker with the Day," Nick Cave and the Bad Seeds

I'm wild about Nick Cave. His nasty phase, his ballad phase, his acutely religious phase—whatever he does, I'm interested. There was a time when I listened to *No More Shall We Part* obsessively. It's moody and even a little ridiculous, but also so committed to its own affectation that it wins me over every time. In my mind, Nick Cave and Thomas Hardy, who is one of my favorite authors, belong together—both engaged in contrivance and histrionics that still manage to stir me to a contemplation of bigger things.

"Candy Says," Antony and the Johnsons cover

Not sure there's a better rendering of self-loathing out there—self-loathing and dread—as "Candy Says," and when Antony applies his tremolo, his flutter and transgendering aesthetic, he manages to alchemize shame into a kind of aura that lingers in the air well after the song's over. This was useful for me to think about when trying to write about people who are estranged from themselves and how the shame of that estrangement can become pandemic.

"Always Already Gone," The Magnetic Fields

I have a close friend in this band, so it's always a little embarrassing to write about them, but I'm a huge fan! "It seems you were always already gone"— what a way to characterize the pathology of loneliness, of the person who is always already not there, and thus always apart from. We tend to think of loneliness afflicting the person who's been left behind, but I like to think about the person who leaves compulsively. I am reminded of what Leonard Cohen once told an interviewer in the nineties about his failed romances: "I was unable to reply to their love. Because I was obsessed with some fictional sense of separation, I couldn't touch the thing that was offered me, and it was offered me everywhere." When trying to write up one of the characters in my novel—the cult leader, Thurlow Dan—I had this idea in mind, that he be unreachable *both* by choice and birth.

"I Felt Your Shape," The Microphones

I went through a big Microphones phase in the summer of 2008—which should give you a depressing sense of how long it took me to write this novel. I drove down to North Carolina to visit the astronomical research center featured at the end of the book. I stayed in a lovely cabin and spent a lot of time watching the hummingbirds and listening to this song.

"Woke Up New," The Mountain Goats

None of this novel is autobiographical, but since it took me five years to write it, I was able to channel various traumas into its pages, among them having to part from someone important to me. I listened to this song during that time, impressed by what seems so fundamental about loss—the sense that even the little things seem unmanageable now that you are alone with them.

"The Bleeding Heart Show," The New Pornographers
I wrote a chunk of this novel in Tucson, Arizona. One of the happiest months of my life. I'd get up at four or five in the morning and do some work, go running through the canyons around eight, then back to work until dinner. It was intense, but at the end of every day, I'd jump on my bike and ride around the city listening to the New Pornographers. In terms of unmediated experience, nothing rivals the high of bicycling around a beautiful place listening to "The Bleeding Heart Show," and telegraphing that joy into the next day's work. Because it's not all gloom and doom on the page. Sometimes, exuberance is required. Exuberance has its place.

"All the World Is Green," Tom Waits
If I could see anyone in concert, it'd be Tom Waits. I'm just waiting for the chance. In the meantime, his music has basically soundtracked multiple years of my life and these last few are no exception. "Pretend that you owe me nothing and all the world is green"—I weep almost every time I hear that line. Pretend all things are equal. Pretend there's moral equity in the world. Pretend there are no discrepancies between people to resolve. Pretend the world is Edenic. You have only to think about where we are these days—politically, culturally, ethically—to find in these lyrics a much bigger indictment than Waits likely intended.

"Marry Me," Syd Straw
I probably first heard this song at Fez, in NYC, which has since closed down. And I remember being just devastated by its lyric—its insistence on love as the thing that actually prevails. I happen to believe this, too, despite all evidence to the contrary, which often makes me feel embattled and terrified—of being alone with my faith, of being wrong. Much of *Woke Up Lonely* gathered strength from these twin anxieties. Incidentally, Syd Straw sang this song at a friend's wedding. Their marriage has since broken up.

"Which Will," Lucinda Williams cover
This is actually a Nick Drake song, but I like Lucinda Williams's version better. Blasphemy, I know. But it's a little more raw. A little more dire. If you won't love me, who will you love?—again assuming that love is a given; only its object changes.

"Long Gone Lonesome Blues," Hank Williams Jr.

I cannot stand country music, though you'll notice a couple of country singers on this list. I nearly named my novel after this song, except I didn't want to undermine the book's project by making it too sing-songy, or, you know, yodely. But I think there is an implicit rapport in American culture between the rugged male out there on his own tilling the land and notions of solitude and loneliness.

"True Love Will Find You in the End," Beck

It will? Beck sounds so haggard on this track, it's hard to believe him. Though I think that's the point. I think he's got a will to believe (via Daniel Johnston) that's so hard-won—so hard to maintain—that it cost him his voice. Plus the song manages to iterate one of my favorite philosophical arguments on the topic of faith as put forth by the great William James in his lecture "The Will to Believe," in which he contends (in essence) that it's not just okay but even a good idea to believe in something without evidence of its existence. For him, belief is a kind of self-fulfilling gesture (something like: build it and they will come) and also a precondition for getting the thing you believe in. By his logic, God will not reveal himself to you unless you have faith. Similarly, romance will not materialize in your life unless you believe in it first, and seek it out first. In short: Go, Beck. Or, more properly, go Daniel Johnston. Which is sad when you think about his life and its troubles, but I digress.

"Get Me," Everything But The Girl

Tracey Thorn's got an amazing voice. She's probably best known for her more electro-pop stuff with Everything But The Girl, but I like their early stuff, too. It's a little maudlin, but that's okay. One of the central questions of *Woke Up Lonely* gets reprised in this song: Do you ever get me? Does anyone? Can anyone?

"Fall in Love with Me," Iggy Pop

Remember that famous scene in *Moonstruck* when Nicholas Cage insists Cher just get in his bed? Wow, I bet no one's ever grouped Cage, Cher, and Iggy Pop in the same thought, but never mind. When all else fails, when you're done with the polemics and yawning, prolix deliberations on the topic of loneliness, just get adamant. Fall in love with me! Right now! Do it!

This playlist originally appeared at largeheartedboy.com. Reprinted with permission.

FIONA MAAZEL is the author of *Last Last Chance*. She is winner of the Bard Prize for Fiction and a National Book Foundation "5 Under 35" honoree. She teaches at Brooklyn College, Columbia, New York University, and Princeton, and was appointed the Picador Guest Professor at the University of Leipzig, Germany. She lives in Brooklyn, New York.

The text of *Woke Up Lonely* is set in Sabon, an old-style serif typeface based on the types of Claude Garamond and designed by the German-born typographer and designer Jan Tschichold (1902–1974) in 1964. Composition by BookMobile Design and Digital Publisher Services, Minneapolis, Minnesota. Manufactured by Versa Press on acid-free 30 percent postconsumer wastepaper.

Also Available from Graywolf Press

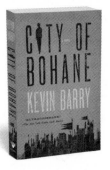

Many Graywolf authors are available to chat with your book club or classroom via phone and Skype. Email us at **wolves@graywolfpress.org** for further details.

Visit **graywolfpress.org** to sign up for our monthly newsletter and to check out our many regularly updated features, including our On Craft series, Pub Talk series, Poem of the Week, author interviews, special sales, book giveaways, tour listings, catalogs, and much more.

GRAYWOLF
PRESS

Graywolf Press is a leading independent publisher committed to the discovery and energetic publication of contemporary American and international literature. We champion outstanding writers at all stages of their careers to ensure that diverse voices can be heard in a crowded marketplace.

We believe books that nourish the individual spirit and enrich the broader culture must be supported by attentive editing, superior design, and creative promotion.